Under the Twisted Cross

Under the Twisted Cross

Margaret M. Barnhart

Library of Congress Control Number:		2010913270
ISBN:	Hardcover	978-1-4535-7243-6
	Softcover	978-1-4535-7242-9
	Ebook	978-1-4535-7244-3

To order additional copies of this book, contact:
Xlibris Corporation
1-888-795-4274
www.Xlibris.com
Orders@Xlibris.com
85382

CONTENTS

PART ONE: NOVEMBER-DECEMBER 1943

I   Sounds of Capture 9
II   Hats Off for Soup 21
III   Native Sons 33
IV   Somewhere in Between 45
V   Riding the Rails 52
VI   Across the Wire 64
VII   Kid Russki 78
VIII   Northern Light 86

PART TWO: STALAG IIB 1944

IX   Lucky Strike 97
X   Fritz 110
XI   Goon Baiting 117
XII   Food for the Soul 131
XIII   On the Town 143
XIV   Backlash 154
XV   Gospel According to Luke 166
XVI   The Weight of Darkness 176

PART THREE: TO THE WESTERN FRONT: JANUARY-MAY 1945

XVII   Out of the Box 191
XVIII   Foot Soldiers 202
XIX   Luck of the Spoon 209
XX   Notes 220
XXI   Waiting Out the Night 224

Part One

November-December 1943

I

Sounds of Capture

Click. That's the sound that woke him—not even a loud noise—certainly nothing compared to the artillery barrages and machine-gun fire he'd finally learned to sleep through. An exploding grenade or mine couldn't have startled him awake more sharply than that sinister click—almost a whisper of metal parts. Nick knew what it meant even before coming fully awake: the enemy was upon them.

The moment between hearing the click and opening his eyes unraveled slowly as in a dream; he remembered other sounds and wondered if, like a drowning man who supposedly sees his life replay in the seconds before death, his last moments would be a replay of the sounds in his life. Every clank and slap and clatter and bang that had ever startled him from sleep resonated in his mind during that first moment of capture. He wished for any one of those to replace the ominous sound that pulled him from sleep this misty morning near Naples, Italy, November 10, 1943.

A heavy clatter of skillet and stove lids woke him the last morning at home. The noise, more insistent than usual, indicated his mother's frustration. He guessed that she had not slept well during the night, that she had emotionally wrestled against the reality of his being drafted into service.

"I'm awake, Ma!" He threw back the quilt and sat up, rubbing the sleep from his eyes. The morning light filtering through the narrow curtained window showed a gray sky. Nick sighed, knowing the weather would just compound the gloom already surrounding his departure. He glanced around the small, sparsely furnished guest bedroom that had never been his personal domain. None of Nick's siblings lived here with their parents. Five years earlier, Marcus took over the farm when the folks retired; soon after, he married and now raised two young daughters as well as grain and cattle. Jacob, the youngest, had enlisted in the Navy after the attack on Pearl Harbor and currently served in the Pacific. Elsie taught school, and Agnes married before age nineteen. Nick, the oldest, left the farm for a factory job in Cleveland, Ohio, seven years earlier before the threat of global conflict. Then he had anticipated returning home for a family visit once or twice a year, but that infamous December morning nearly two years ago changed a great many intentions.

Now seven years worth of belongings had been boxed up and stored in his parents' attic. Two medium-sized bags near the wardrobe bulged with freshly laundered clothes and bundled personal items, all he would need or be allowed at training camp and wherever else he might go in the coming months. Even that might be too much baggage.

Nick had enjoyed living in Cleveland. The city offered so much more excitement than he'd ever known in North Dakota. He'd made several friends, including a particular woman friend, and he'd found a good job as finisher at Cowles Tool Company. However, when the notice from the draft board came, it had seemed best to temporarily move his things back home. After the tour of duty, he would consider all his options. Then, too, he wanted to make his farewell to his folks in person before reporting to Camp Wheeler in Georgia. After all, he couldn't know how long before he might see them again.

"Good morning, Ma." Nick stepped into the kitchen after he'd washed and dressed. His mother harrumphed her greeting. Smiling, he brushed a kiss against her cheek.

"*Ja!—Was machst du?*" She blushed.

"Thought I'd kiss a pretty woman before I go off to be a soldier!"

"*Du—du—!*" She tried to scold, but her eyes clouded and instead of remonstrating, she embraced him and sighed, "*Ach, du!*"

"Ma, this is so unlike you." Nick returned her hug.

"That shows what you know," she groused, and turning back to the stove, she cracked eggs into the large skillet. One of the yolks broke, bleeding yellow in the pan.

"*Ach, Gott!*" she muttered. Nick, placing his hands on Ma's shoulders, drew an appreciative breath.

"I wish I could pack up these delicious smells to take with me," he said. "Home-cured bacon! Coffee! Fresh biscuits! I bet heaven smells like this."

"I hope you don't too soon find out," Ma said under her breath, and Nick pretended not to hear the note of bitterness. He didn't want an argument to spoil his last morning at home, but his mother had not yet finished her fight.

"Why should you, almost twenty-eight years old, have to go off to the war now? Soon you'll be old enough—they shouldn't be able to draft you!"

"Ma—"

"I already have a son I worry sick over. Must I send another?"

"Emma"—Pa, just returning from his traditional morning walk, had heard—"let's not go over this again. This is a difficult time, and we must all do our part. Nick too." Then clapping his hand on Nick's shoulder, he added, "We're proud of you and Jacob both. You do what you must. But," he warned, "don't let the army make you hate your own people!"

Nick thought of the relatives he'd never met—faceless, in some cases nameless aunts and uncles and cousins who, many years before, chose not to follow his father to America. However, Nick figured that he most likely would end up fighting in the Pacific rather than in Europe—perhaps even somewhere near Jacob.

"Besides"—Nick turned back to his mother—"we all know the situation is growing more serious on all fronts. If we hope to stop the Germans and Japanese anytime soon, more men are needed. They'll be calling up every man under forty who is not needed more at home. Here I am, without wife or children or land obligation. I might as well do my job now—"

"But your job in America is important. You're helping the war effort—"

"Believe it or not, Ma, women are being hired to do the work I've been doing. I'm not irreplaceable at Cowles."

"Don't say that!" Ma barked just as Pa quelled the growing disagreement with a firm "Let's all sit down for a nice breakfast together!"

Their meal took on an uncomfortable formality as each suppressed emotions that agitated to be expressed. They remarked at great length on the weather—gray, with a light mist falling—and how the dampness seemed gloomy, but probably was a good thing for the farmers. Finally breakfast ended and Pa rose.

"Well"—he pulled out a pocket watch—"I suppose we should head for the station. We'll just load up the bags, Mother, and then we're ready to go."

"I'm not going," Ma announced. "I'll say my good-by from here. I'll not watch you get on that train."

"Ma."

"No. I've decided. You have your duty there. Mine is here. We each do what we have to do."

"Okay, Ma. I understand."

After a long embrace that said more than words, Nick picked up his bags and headed for the door. He heard the clatter of dishes and pans as Ma began to clean up the breakfast things. The sound felt comforting, like something to come home to.

Click. Nick opened his eyes.

"*Steht auf! Hände an die Köpfe!*"

For just a second Nick thought about reaching for the weapon at his side. Maybe he could grab it and fire several rounds before the young German soldier had time to react. Then he remembered: he, as well as the rest of the squad with him, was out of ammunition. Gradually other noises increased around him. A company of German soldiers aimed their weapons at the squadron, greatly outnumbering the ten American machine gunners.

"*Alle steht auf!*" they shouted.

"Jesus Christ!" cried the American nearest Nick.

"*Sei' still!*"

"You motherfu—!" A boot to the soldier's kidneys reinforced the German's order for silence. Nick saw that resistance now would not be heroic or even wise. It would get them all killed. Slowly he raised himself, lifting his hands to his head.

"*Ich komme*," he assured, and the soldier's eyebrows lifted slightly. The German looked quite young, though Nick couldn't pinpoint his age. Slight whisker stubble and the dirt of trench fighting grimed the soldier's face. He could be anywhere from his late teens to midtwenties. Struggling to his feet, Nick locked eyes with his captor. His heart pounded, and he hoped fear didn't show in his own eyes as blatantly as it did in the young German's face. It was an enemy's fear he had to watch out for.

"*Ihr seid Kriegsgefangener!*" another voice barked over the rest. *Prisoners of war.* This had seemed such a distant possibility when he'd boarded the train back in North Dakota only eight months earlier. Even now, the whole scene had a dreamlike quality—not quite real, yet all too terrifying. Emotions collided within him. He couldn't deny the fear of the unknown, yet he also felt a strange sense of relief, then immediate shame. The fact that he could understand and speak the language of the enemy reassured him only a little.

Nick swallowed hard, throat aching with thirst. The squadron had been cut off from communication and supplies by enemy artillery fire two days before and spent the last day and a half without food or water. Until now it had been bearable because they anticipated reinforcements to reach them soon. Unfortunately, the Germans—in a surprise attack from the rear—reached them first. Even now, rifle fire resumed but that caused a new concern. Soon the squad would be a target for fire from their own forces.

A command came for the captives to drop down. Nick obeyed and with the others belly crawled out of the line of rifle fire on ground muddied by the drizzle. Then, behind enemy lines, the commanding officer ordered them to their feet again. With hands against the backs of their heads, and under an order of silence, they began to advance farther into enemy territory. Their steps took on a rhythmic sound—not quite marching, not exactly shuffling. It reminded Nick of something.

Chuff . . . chuff . . . chuff. Nick stood next to his father as the train chugged into the station. With a shrill screech of metal against metal and the plosive hiss of steam, the locomotive slowed past them, then stopped. The train seemed an odd jumble of cars, some for freight, some for passengers. On the depot platform stood a pallet filled with cream cans, ready for shipment to the nearest dairy processing plant. Nick appeared to be the only passenger waiting to board.

"Thought maybe it would be one of those newer diesel engines doing the pulling," Nick remarked, silently wondering why he found it so difficult to talk to his father when no one else was around to take part in the conversation.

"No," Pa observed. "No, hasn't been one through here in a while now. The war, you know."

"Yeah, I guess diesel fuel is needed more elsewhere, isn't it?"

The silence between them grew as they both watched the cream cans being loaded onto the nearest freight car. Nick shot sidelong glances at his father now and then, suddenly surprised at how much his father had aged in the last few years. Pa's once dark, thick hair had thinned considerably and now grew almost white, as did the distinct mustache with its jauntily curled tips. Pa's shoulders that had been broad and strong enough to carry one-hundred-pound sacks of feed—the old neighbors still told tales of Nick Sr.'s remarkable strength—sloped more now, looking as if they had borne too much during the years.

"Well," Pa began weakly, "I suppose—"

"Yeah. I guess." Nick resisted the urge to embrace his father. Pa had never freely displayed affection for his children, and Nick, more like his old man than he'd ever thought he'd be, didn't quite know how to break the stubborn reserve that existed between them.

"Looks like the cream's on board," Nick observed at last.

"I guess you're next." Awkward, Pa extended his hand and Nick grasped it in his own, their handshake abrupt but strong. Then Nick picked up his two bags and stepped toward the passenger car.

"Oh, wait a minute!" Pa called out. "I almost forgot to give you this." He reached into the oversized pocket of his overcoat and pulled out a small bundle wrapped in brown paper and tied with twine. "Ma made these for you. Honey cookies. She used up the last of the honey."

Nick smiled as he took the package.

"Be sure to tell her thanks, Pa."

"And she said to tell you to write home as often as you can."

"I'll keep in touch."

"And to stay warm. And wear clean socks."

Once more, Nick turned toward the train. This time he reached the boarding step before Pa called to him again.

"Wait!" Pa huffed as he hurried closer. "If you see Jacob—"

"I don't know if I will, Pa. The chances are pretty slim."

"If you do, you just look out for each other, you hear?"

For the first time in Nick's memory, his father's eyes seemed watery as he spoke. The steely blue softened as something deep and genuinely caring replaced the familiar coolness. Nick found his own eyes stinging, but he blinked away an emotional display.

"We will, Pa," he said, his throat tight. "We will."

Nick took a seat near a window where he could see his father standing on the station platform. A whistle signaled departure time, and the train jerked into motion with a slow huffing sound. Outside, Pa lifted his arm but did not wave his hand. His gesture, almost like a salute, seemed frozen in place. As the train picked up speed, Pa appeared to grow smaller, less distinct, until he blended into the background of the diminishing depot. Nick watched familiar buildings shrink as the train moved steadily away, first the depot, then, where Main Street paralleled the railroad tracks, the butcher shop, grocery store, barbershop, and finally the grain elevator, and a hardware-and-feed store. When the tranquil little community at last disappeared into the distance, almost as if swallowed up by the prairie, Nick leaned back in his seat and closed his eyes. Before long, the rhythmic *chuff-chuff* of the engine and clack of wheels on track lulled him into a morning nap.

Their footsteps didn't hold a steady rhythm, but became more and more ragged as the men wearied. The now-heavy rain mucked the rough slopes of Mount Rotondo, making every step a struggle against the pull of thick Italian mud. In spite of their slow progress, the sounds of battle decreased behind them. Every step took them farther into enemy territory, lessening whatever hope they might have of heroic Allied rescue.

Nick lost track of time, having surrendered his watch to the Germans, along with his weapon. Pangs of hunger warred with dread in his stomach, leaving a leaden pain. His shoulders ached, the muscles twitching and burning from holding a position of surrender for too long. He wondered why they couldn't just put their arms down? Weaponless and heavily guarded, they presented no danger walking with their arms at their sides. But he didn't want to be the first one to try.

At last the squadron rounded a bend, where the course met with another, more traveled road. There, a sizable company of Nazi soldiers herded yet another unit of captives. Nick counted eleven men. The two groups met and halted.

Sharp orders rang out. Nudging and shoving, the Germans forced their prisoners into a group, indicating they should all sit.

"*Hände*—!" An officer shouted, gesturing them to lower their hands. Collective sighs and groans accompanied this release. Nick hunched over, rubbing the ache in his shoulders. He shivered. Maybe they'd be better off if they continued to march. The November air had a definite bite to it, and their wet, muddy clothes gave little protection from the penetrating cold.

"Goddamned krauts!" A lieutenant from the second group of captives muttered. He sat down not too far from Nick, a thickset, angry man who glowered at his captors, then spat contemptuously toward the boot of the German soldier nearest him. Nick drew in his breath, waiting for the inevitable repercussion, but the soldier seemed not to have noticed the insult. Wishing there was a little more distance between himself and the lieutenant, Nick listened carefully to the Germans around him. They appeared to be discussing a wounded compatriot. The young Nazi who'd first disarmed him that morning gestured toward Nick, and then three German officers approached and stood before him.

"*Verstehen Sie Deutsch?*" The commander asked.

"*Ja,*" Nick answered, then rose to his feet as ordered.

"You will come with us," the officer continued in German. "You—and that one." He gestured toward the defiant lieutenant, who glared first at the Germans, then at Nick.

"You will carry one of our wounded."

"What the hell is he saying?" Lieutenant Stocks demanded.

"They want us to carry a wounded soldier."

"Oh they do, do they?" Stocks spat again. "They want me to give aid and comfort to the enemy? They can just go to hell."

"*Kommt Ihr mit!*" One of the officers pulled Nick and the lieutenant away from the group of prisoners toward the ruins of a stone house built against the hillside.

"Wait!" Stocks resisted. "I ain't going to carry no goddamned wounded kraut! And you can tell them that!"

Nick looked from Stocks to the German officer, uncertain whose order he should obey. As a private, he owed obedience to anyone who outranked him. Here he stood in the presence of two officers—one from a squadron other than his own, the other an enemy.

"*Was sagt er?*" The German demanded.

In German, Nick answered, "The lieutenant suggests that one of the other privates help carry your wounded."

"The lieutenant suggests?" At this, the officer stood directly in front of Stocks, glowering. "Tell your lieutenant that it would be best if he made no more *suggestions.*"

Tension grew. Nick wished he had not been singled out to participate in this particular dialogue; he especially wished the German hadn't chosen Stocks. He wasn't used to intentionally altering someone's order, but he knew he had to *mis*translate some of the conversation to keep an ugly situation from turning worse.

"What'd he say?" Stocks asked, his eyes locked with those of his captor.

"He said—"

"*Lieutenant!*"

"What?"

"I outrank you, private. You'll address me as 'Lieutenant' or 'Sir' as is fitting my station."

Nick wanted to punch the self-important little bastard who seemed to have no comprehension of their dangerous situation. With some difficulty, he controlled the urge.

"*Lieutenant,*" he amended, not without a note of sarcasm, "the officer said it would be best if you didn't make any more suggestions. If you ask me, under the circumstances, we'd be smart to do what he tells us."

"Well, soldier, I'm not asking you," Stocks said quietly, still leveling his gaze on the German officer. "Here's what you can tell him. Tell this *dog* to take his orders and go *fuck* himself!"

"Lieutenant—" Nick attempted.

"I said *tell* him!"

"*Was sagt—?*" the German asked at the same moment.

Nick swallowed hard. Two-day thirst compounded by the perilous situation made his voice raspy.

"The lieutenant," Nick translated, "refuses, respectfully refuses, to carry out your order."

"Does he."

Before Nick could answer, Stocks roared and lunged at the German officer, grabbing for his throat. The German tried to reach for his sidearm, but Stocks' grip tightened around his throat and the German desperately tried to loosen the hold. One man howling, the other gurgling, the two struggled with each other, knocking Nick to the ground. He turned, scrambling in the sticky mud to get away from the action, while around him voices clamored in both German and English. Rapidly repeating gunfire erupted from somewhere, warning shots to control and silence the roused band of prisoners. Still on the ground, Nick turned and once again looked into the barrel of a machine gun. He eased his glance toward the combatants. The German's face was nearly purple both from rage and from Stocks' strangling hold. Just then, one of the other German soldiers, handgun extended, approached the two. He calmly fired the weapon directly into Stocks' left temple, and the lieutenant dropped heavily.

A momentary silence followed, then gunfire again. This time, the enraged Nazi officer, his face still contorted, fired his own weapon repeatedly into Stocks' already dead body. Disgusted by the sight, yet not able to look away, Nick saw Stocks' body pocked by gunfire, each new wound erupting in a spurt of bloody matter that pooled, then blended into the muddy ground. In the eerie stillness after the execution, the officer turned his gaze toward Nick.

The German's boots made a sloshing and sucking sound in the mud as he stepped closer. Nick closed his eyes, hoping for a clean and merciful shot. But no shot came. Opening his eyes again, Nick looked up into the face of the officer who towered over him, weapon still at the ready.

"*Steh' auf*," he ordered once more, and Nick picked himself up. His heart had never pounded so hard. He could hear it; he thought the whole company could hear it.

"Ordinarily I shoot any soldier who doesn't obey a higher-ranking officer," the German now spoke in perfect English. "But your lieutenant seems to be—rather ineffectual—at his command. Come with me. And *you*"—he gestured toward one of the other prisoners, a young private who looked no more than seventeen or eighteen—"you will come too."

Nick and the kid followed their captor into the stone shelter. On a makeshift stretcher lay a badly burned German soldier. Rough and stained bandages swathed most of his face and one hand.

"We leave now. You will carry this man."

The way had already been rough. Exhausted, cold, and hungry, Nick wasn't sure he could muster enough strength to bear this load. If he could just have a drink to get rid of the feeling of sand and grit in his mouth. Stocks' riddled body remained sharp in Nick's mind, but he took a chance.

"*Bitte—wir haben Durst. Wir brauchen Wasser.*"

The officer narrowed his eyes momentarily, then nodded. Stepping outside the shelter, he barked an order. In a few minutes, a soldier moved among the prisoners carrying a battered old pail and a broken dipper. The water was murky, swirled with an oily sheen. Small twigs and other ground matter floated in the liquid. Nick lifted the dipper to his mouth. He closed his eyes and tried to ignore the dank, sour smell that emanated from the bucket. The water was wet. That's all that mattered.

So much water—thousands and thousands of miles of water. Nick's first experience of the ocean came upon embarkation from New York. On the deck of the *Susan B. Anthony*, he watched the undulating surface of the sea—finally with only minimal queasiness. The first day had been hell; he'd actually *felt* green, as if he were moldering from the inside out. Nothing would stay down, not even clear, tepid water.

On the third day at sea, the *Susan B. Anthony* joined a convoy heading for Africa. Nick counted eighteen ships. For a length of time they sailed steadily in one direction, then abruptly altered course. The ships he had seen ahead off starboard appeared portside as they completed formation. It was a defensive move. Nearing the war zone, the convoy zigzagged its course, giving the ships a better chance of evading enemy attack from above or from below the surface of the water.

So far, Nick rather enjoyed being in the army. Training camp had been tough of course, but the sense of urgency behind it had made the time pass quickly. He'd met many remarkable people, and many people he hoped never to see again. On American ground, to him the war still seemed surreal, evident on the home front mainly by ration books and patriotism posters and, more recently, the changes in the labor force. An occasional gold-star emblem in a window gave proof of the deeper sacrifices of the war.

The first time Nick felt dangerously close to the war came on the troop ship with a sudden call to battle stations. Enemy aircraft headed their way. All the guns on the entire convoy went into action adding to a deafening combination of sounds: the ship's alarms, strafing from the air, and ack-ack from the convoy. The air lit up, then became hazy in the smoke. Only after the planes were driven back did Nick realize how heavily his heart pounded in his chest, his throat, even his ears. He wondered if eventually he would be able to face battle without fear.

The rest of the voyage was quiet; even the ocean remained calm. Near noon on a mild day, the ship landed in Algiers. From there, Nick joined a transport by stock train, then by boat first to Sicily, then to Salerno, Italy. Seeing some of the aftermath of battles, he hoped it wouldn't be long before the next boat ride home.

For a while he tried paying attention to the time, estimating hours by the number of steps he took in what seemed like a minute. With every step, however, the stretcher and its burden seemed to grow heavier and more unwieldy. They slowed over difficult rises and slipped down muddied slopes. Sometime toward nightfall, the daylong rain finally ceased, but the air carried a bitter chill, and the weary men shivered.

"I . . . I don't think . . . I . . . can go . . . much . . . farther," panted Ross, the kid holding up the rear of the stretcher. Nick had thought the same sometime

before and would have said something if he'd had the energy. He swallowed hard
again; water had become his primary concern. The sip of vapid liquid earlier had
not gone far in quenching thirst. Even the emptiness in his belly seemed mild
compared to Nick's want of water. Several times during the trek, he had lifted his
face into the rain, attempting to catch on his tongue a substantial drink. That, too,
had been unsatisfactory, only increasing his desire for more. He thought of the
bitter irony of water. He'd seen so much of it on the ocean, none of it drinkable;
here he struggled through a climate heavy with rain or mist, yet a day in the midst
of it did not give even enough to sip when what he truly needed was to drink deep,
to gulp.

At last, when Nick felt he couldn't take another step, the command came to halt.
They'd arrived in a small village, which Nick first thought to be deserted because of
the empty and dark streets. No light emanated from the buildings until a single door
opened at the side of the nearest structure. Only then did Nick note the blackout
curtains.

"Put the stretcher down here." Nick couldn't see who had given the order.
Wordlessly, he and Ross lowered the stretcher near the door of the building. Almost
immediately two nurses emerged and, without a word or glance at the prisoners, took
the wounded soldier inside, slamming the door behind them.

"*Mach schnell!*" Again, the order came to get in line and march. Nick followed, with
Ross close behind. They had not gone far when the second order came. "*Halt!*" Again
the group stopped, ringed by soldiers with weapons at the ready. For a while no one
spoke, but then a murmur rose as the Americans cautiously started to communicate
with each other.

Ross nudged closer to Nick.

"Are you scared?" he asked, his voice high and trembling. Nick did not respond.
After a moment, Ross continued, "Back there? Back when they shot the lieutenant?
I . . . I think . . . I think I soiled myself."

"It's okay," Nick answered, keeping his voice low. "I'm sure you're not the only
one."

"Do you think they buried him?"

"I don't know," Nick answered; then another soldier from Stocks' company
remarked, "Lieutenant Stocks was an asshole!"

"Still," Ross mumbled, "somebody should have buried him. I wonder if he had any
family. They'll be wondering—"

"Kid, *all* our families will be wondering!"

Nick had not thought about his family until that moment. How long would it
be before they received the telegram from the War Department? *Missing in action*,
it would say without giving too much detail about where. Then, days of torturous
waiting before they might hear from him. Would he even be allowed to contact them?
What if—? But Nick didn't want to finish the thought. Just then the German officer
who'd first spoken to Nick approached.

"You will translate," he commanded, though Nick wondered why the Nazi didn't just order the men directly. He did, after all, have command of the language. However, he knew this was not the time to argue and so simply nodded.

"Tonight you will all be in here," the officer opened the door of a small stone outbuilding that had previously been used for storage. It had no windows. "Tomorrow, we move once more. Soon someone will come to you with food and water. If you do as you are told, there will be no trouble."

Nick translated, then entered the dark building with the others. Crowding close to keep warm, the men sat on the dirty, straw-covered floor, leaning against the walls or against each other. Ross squeezed between Nick and another.

"Do you believe them?" The kid's voice still trembled. "You don't think they'll just take us out tomorrow and shoot us, do you?"

"If they intended to shoot us," Nick answered, "they had plenty of chances to do it earlier."

"Yeah. Yeah, that's true." Again a brief silence, then, "Oh God, I'm scared. I never wanted to fight. I'm supposed to be a cook, not a combat soldier."

"You?" Someone derided, then announced, "Whattaya know, troops? We don't know where we are, and we don't know where we're going, and we don't know what's going to happen to us tomorrow—but at least we got us a *chef* to keep us company!"

"Oh yeah? Well, we could all use some mess right now. Tell him to snap to!"

"I—don't," Ross stammered. "I don't have any—"

Nick put his hand on the kid's shoulder, shaking him lightly. "They're just having a little fun with you, kid. Look. Try not to worry. Think of it this way—at least now you won't have to fight for a while, huh?"

It seemed a long time before the door opened again. Three people entered; one held a lantern while the other two brought in buckets of water and several loaves of bread. Neither spoke as they passed among the men, dispensing first the bread, then one dipper of water per soldier. Nick welcomed his crust of bread, but it was coarse, dry, and almost tasteless, doing little to ease the pangs in his gut. He choked it down. When the Nazi held a full dipper toward him, Nick grasped it in both hands and gulped the cool water, this time free of sediment or oil. Delicious.

"Wait," Nick ventured, just as the soldier took the dipper away. "One more? *Bitte?*"

For a second the German soldier hesitated, then dipped a small amount from the bucket. Nick took it and sipped more slowly this time, relishing the feel of the water as it trickled through his dry throat.

"*Danke,*" he said, gesturing with the dipper to the others. The soldier nodded and made another round through the ranks to offer each prisoner a second drink. Soon, the soldier with the lantern called, "*Genug!*" and the three left. The prisoners, exhausted from both the strenuous march and the anguish of not knowing their future, settled as comfortably as they could. When they spoke, their voices were low.

"Think escape's an option?" one offered.

"Are you nuts? Surrounded by Germans? Which way would we go if we got out of this building?"

"Not everybody, you asshole. But a couple or three might make it through."

"Leaving the rest to get shot as a result!"

"I don't like just rolling over and giving in. It's—"

"Survival. That's what it is."

Nick closed his eyes. *Survival,* he agreed, then directed his thoughts homeward. *I'm surviving, folks. I'm okay for now. Think of me.* He imagined his parents at home, comfortable in the warm house. It would be early afternoon there, just after dinner. Ma probably had cooked one of her tasty soups or stews, and they'd enjoyed that with soft, fresh bread and jam and glasses of delicious, cold milk. Maybe right at this moment they were listening to the radio in the front room and watching snow begin to fall outside. Ma would pick up a piece of crocheting or embroidery while Pa would lean back and soon begin to snore.

Thoughts of home came with a pleasant kind of ache, but Nick couldn't ignore the cold darkness around him. He squirmed, adjusting to find even the slightest comfort on the floor that seemed to grow harder with each passing minute. A sound from outside the building caught the prisoners' attention. Alert again, they listened to the clank and rattle of a chain against the door, followed at once by the distinct *click* of a padlock. The air inside the sealed building grew close with the smell of unwashed bodies—and another scent vaguely familiar: the smell of fear.

II

Hats Off for Soup

"Nikolaus!" a voice growled, bearlike. "Come, come now, name the seven deadly sins!"

Nick shivered, staring. The priest's bald head glistened in the light; Nick could almost see his reflection in the old man's forehead—the reflection of a very frightened boy.

"Um—envy?" Nick remembered, and an unseen chorus cheered his response with "*Sieg heil!*"

"That's only one!"

"And—um—gluttony?"

"*Sieg heil!*"

"Two!"

"Um. I think—hunger?"

The priest roared. Eyes flashing, his dark, bristled mustache twitched when his lip curled into a sneer. He picked up a wooden measuring stick and whacked Nick across the shoulder blades. Large rosary beads cinched around the priest's waist rattled.

"Ow!" Nick bawled.

"One stroke for every wrong answer! Continue naming the seven deadly sins!"

Nick searched his memory for the elusive answers. He was sure he had them right, but every word he offered brought about the same result.

"Thirst?" *Whack!*

"Ow! I mean—fear?" *Whack!*

By now his back and shoulders burned. Yet he tried again with "Please, Father. I'm sure it's deadly to be hungry."

"But it isn't a *sin*, you louse!" *Whack!* "Niko*louse*—!"

"*Alles raus!*" Another voice broke through the dream. Nick blinked awake, blinded by the glare from the doorway where a German officer stood silhouetted.

The burning pain in his limbs and joints had not been a dream. Cramped and cold, he rolled his shoulders, then lifted and flexed his arms to loosen the stiffness. Moans from others in the room let him know that the rest of the men also woke uncomfortably. Nick scrutinized his disheveled fellow prisoners. He couldn't decide which was worse—the dream he'd wrestled or the reality he woke to.

Standing up proved to be an effort too. His feet ached from yesterday's march, the cold dampness penetrating through his shoes. He shivered, remembering words his mother used to say when he was young. *If you keep your head and feet warm, you will not feel the cold.* How he longed for a pair of thick, warm socks.

"Oh shit," someone said, just waking, "I thought it might have been a dream."

"Not a dream," another responded, "just a damn nightmare."

"God I'm hungry!" This brought silence again as each man recognized the emptiness in his belly and wondered how long before that ache diminished.

The soldier who'd awakened them was a sergeant, a *Feldwebel.* He ordered the men to exit the building in single file. As each man passed, the feldwebel called out a number. Just outside the door stood another soldier, holding misshapen loaves of bread.

"*Eins,*" Feldwebel counted the first prisoner, who then received a portion of the bread. Nick fell into line with the others, followed immediately by Ross.

"*Neunzehn,*" the feldwebel announced when Nick reached him.

"*Wohin gehen wir?*" Nick dared to ask where they would be going. The officer paused in his counting to give Nick a sharp look, then gestured with his head.

"*Nord,*" was all he said.

"What does that mean?" Ross asked, and Nick replied, "North. We're going to be moved north."

"Into Germany?"

"That would be my guess."

"Oh God," Ross moaned, looking even more like a lost little boy than he had the day before. Glancing at the other captives, he whispered, "I hope we can all stay together. At least—I hope we'll all go where you go." Like a shadow, Ross hung close behind Nick.

Outside the door, Nick held the bread in his hands and stared at it. The piece was no bigger than his fist. He nibbled at it, hoping to make it last longer, but the small bites crumbled like dust in his mouth. Another bite, bigger this time, and Nick tried to savor the taste awhile. The texture seemed unusually coarse, and the bread tasted like no other he'd ever eaten. He took another bite, then a fourth, and the bread was gone.

"This stuff tastes like sawdust!" one of the captives muttered. "What the hell is in it anyway?"

"I don't even want to know," another responded. "I just want a bigger piece next time."

Nick studied the scene around him. High clouds diffused the sunlight in a gray-white wash that made the buildings of the village seem without dimension, as if they consisted only of false fronts. A few of the Italian civilians moved through the streets, some on bicycle, but most on foot. One very round little man carried a large, covered basket. Nick imagined it contained food items and hoped the basket would be delivered to the kommandant guarding the prisoners, but the man disappeared around the corner of a stone church. None of the civilians glanced at the group of prisoners in the village square.

"Think we're invisible?" someone voiced Nick's observation.

"I wish we were," Nick answered. "Then we could just walk away from here." He stretched his hand to the man who had spoken. "The name's Bremer. Nick Bremer."

"Robert Ambrose. You're the German."

"No, I'm an American," Nick clarified.

"I don't suppose you're too worried about what they'll do to you."

"I don't know what to expect any more than you do," Nick countered, then turned away. Two German soldiers approached the prisoners, each holding one handle of a large urn. They placed it on the bottom of an upturned wagon, then ordered the prisoners to line up once more.

"*Kaffee*," one guard announced, filling a tin cup with the steaming brown liquid. He handed this cup to the first prisoner in line, and the second cup to the next. After the first two prisoners had drunk their share, the two cups were refilled and handed to the next two waiting. The line moved slowly. Once more Ross nudged in behind Nick.

"What is it?" he asked.

"Coffee. Or what passes for coffee. You know—ersatz."

"But I don't like coffee."

"Kid," Nick sighed, "it doesn't matter whether you like it or dislike it. Just drink it. It'll help warm you."

By the time Nick received his cup, the coffee had cooled to lukewarm. Still, he gulped the liquid, ignoring its bitterness. Ross drank his without complaint. "Now what?" he asked when all the prisoners finished.

His question was answered by the arrival of a German officer—the same lieutenant whose orders Nick had interpreted the day before. This officer eyed his prisoners sharply, then once more gestured for Nick to be brought to him.

"*Wie heissen Sie?*" the kommandant asked.

"Nicholas—Nick—Bremer," Nick hesitated, watchful. The German's expression remained stony.

"Bremer," he repeated. "It is a name with which I am familiar. You have family in Germany?"

"None that I know."

"Your people have lived long in America?"

"A number of years." Nick's personal background did not qualify as classified information, yet he felt hesitant about telling too much. The officer continued.

"I was in America once. Pittsburgh. Do you know it?"

"I know *of* it. I've never been there myself."

"A stinking city," the German sneered. "A *cesspool* compared to our own beautiful cities. I cannot help but wonder why any German would leave a glorious place like our Berlin for one of America's dirty cities."

Nick didn't answer.

"Can you?" the officer challenged. "Can you think why?"

"I suppose—," Nick hesitated, then asserted, "There are things besides beautiful buildings that make people look elsewhere—for opportunity."

"And now *you* will have opportunity to look elsewhere," the officer gloated. "What a pity you won't be seeing our finer places—those that have not been destroyed by your bombs. But you will see Germany. Please tell the other prisoners to prepare for the transportation north."

Nick almost laughed. *Prepare?* What preparation could they make other than tighten their bootlaces and stand in line? Still, he repeated the order to the men. In a short time they heard the sound of a train pulling into the nearby station. Once more, the prisoners lined up, then marched. The streets had cleared of civilian pedestrians, but Nick spied a woman standing in a shadowed doorway, gripping the hands of two small boys. As the prisoners passed, Nick saw one of the boys point and heard him call "Americano" before being hushed. The woman and both children quickly disappeared into the building.

"You know what we are?" Nick heard someone murmur behind him. "We're animals, and this is a damn zoo!"

"*Halt!*"

The soldiers stopped. A locomotive pulling only four cars waited for them on the tracks. A Nazi guard strode toward the second car behind the engine, opened a latch, and slid the door open. Nick turned to the soldiers behind him. "You're right about the zoo," he said dourly. "Looks like we're about to be caged."

Their transportation was a stock car, its slatted wooden walls reinforced with metal bars, giving no protection from the wind and cold. Silently the men climbed into the stock car. When all twenty were aboard, the guard closed the door, securing it firmly with a padlock.

"Christ!" Ambrose swore, "We're going to freeze to death!"

"My kingdom for a horse blanket!" another joked, but no one laughed.

The men gathered close, arranging themselves on the floor where a little straw had been scattered. The only other item in the stock car was a three-gallon pail in one corner—their toilet. After a quick shout and signal from the Nazi guard outside, the train began to move.

At first no one spoke. Huddled close for warmth, the men wrapped themselves in the silence of their own thoughts. Nick couldn't help remembering the comfort of previous train rides: soft seats that allowed him to stretch out, a dining car that offered real coffee and plenty of food, sleeping berths with blankets. Right now, he'd be satisfied with just the blanket. Nick shivered; though the train maintained an almost excruciatingly slow rate, the cold felt more severe as the train moved. Outside, a light rain began once again.

"Maybe if we get up and move around," someone offered, "we'll be warmer."

With that, the group shifted; some men rose, the motion of the train rocking them unsteadily on their feet. They began to pace from one end of the car to the other, swinging their arms, lifting their knees, sometimes losing their balance as the train rocked. Those who remained seated huddled even closer, watching. At last one of them shouted, "Y'all look like a bunch of goose-stepping Nazis!"

"I'll tell you one thing!" came the rejoinder. "Goose-stepping Nazis are a hell of a lot warmer than we are! So just shut the hell up!"

"He's right," Nick mumbled, and rising to his feet, he joined in the awkward calisthenics. It did help. As long as he exerted his limbs, the cold subsided, though not quite enough to feel comfortable. One by one, the remaining prisoners joined in.

"Hold your breath when you get to this side," Ambrose warned, "That piss bucket reeks!"

"No more than we do," another answered.

"What I wouldn't give to be in a nice warm featherbed right now."

"Hell, I'd be happy if I could just take a hot bath and change my clothes."

"A good coat and a swig of brandy would be enough for me."

"Give me a swallow of cheap whisky and that old horse blanket Bandy wanted and I'd count my blessings."

One after another, the men topped in, each claiming satisfaction with just a little less than the one before. It became a kind of game, sardonic, but in a way helpful. Finally, one of the men stopped marching. Caught in their momentum, those behind him bumped into each other and the parade came to an awkward halt.

"I'm tired of this," the weary soldier said, then kicking the loose straw into a pile, he dropped heavily to the floor. Again the men responded en masse, sitting close together in the straw, knowing it wouldn't take long for the cold to creep back into their bones. They huddled, silently for a time, until Robert Ambrose spoke.

"It appears that we're going to be sharing accommodations for a while. Maybe we should get to know each other. We know the guys in our own company, but we don't know the others. Just say a name, you know, and maybe something about—"

"Name's enough," one of Nick's fellow machine gunners muttered. "It'll be a lot easier if we don't get too close. Just in case."

"In case what?" This from young Ross.

"Jesus, kid, you gotta have it spelled out for you? We're prisoners of war here! We got no rights! We're riding in a railcar God knows where. Don't you know what a prime bombing target railroads are?"

"But . . . we wouldn't . . . I mean they wouldn't . . . not their own guys."

"They don't know we're here, do they?"

"Oh G-God—," Ross stammered, but Ambrose cut in.

"Robert Ambrose, that's me. Infantry. I come from Omaha." No one responded to his introduction so he continued, "How about you, German? What's your story?"

Nick didn't much like the way Ambrose referred to him, but he chose to ignore any misgivings for the time being. Wearily he answered, "Nick Bremer. PFC. Machine-gun squad. I carry—carried—the ammunition. I lived in Cleveland, Ohio, for seven years, but my home state is North Dakota."

"And you know German."

"Yes," Nick acknowledged. "I understand the German language."

"I'm glad one of us does," said the next soldier to introduce himself. "I'm Joseph Bandershoot. Guys call me Bandy. I used to teach. Shakespeare mostly." This pronouncement received a few derisive hoots, but Bandy ignored them. "Your turn, Chef."

"Ross Logan," the kid responded. "I like to cook. It's what I'm supposed to be."

One by one, the men identified themselves by name, adding occupation or place of birth or some other seemingly trivial bit of information. At first, Nick thought the exercise purposeless, but gradually he found himself growing more interested in the men whose fate he shared.

"Al Jenkins," grumbled one of Nick's company. "Montana. And that's all anybody needs to know."

"Amen," a gregarious youth stood up and doffed his helmet, revealing fiery red hair. "The less said, the better. Loose lips sink ships. Name, rank, and serial number—"

"Oh put a sock in it!"

"And stick that helmet back on your head. You're flamin' hair's hurtin' my eyes!"

"Hey, how come you still got your helmet? They took mine away."

"The name's Mark R. Murphy," the young soldier resumed. "People call me 'Red.' Never have figured out why."

"Maybe it's your nose," offered a poker-faced Jerry Smithson.

"Huh?"

"You know—looks kinda like you been inhaling too much Irish whisky!"

It felt good to laugh. In spite of the physical discomfort and the uncertainty of their situation, Nick began to feel a little more at ease. He enjoyed the camaraderie developing between the twenty men. Not just anonymous prisoners of war, they all had names and families and histories. In Nick's own company of machine gunners were men like Chuck Bradley, who professed a distant kinship to the general—a relationship all the others good-naturedly dismissed; David Erickson claimed frequently to have been mistaken for the film star, Leslie Howard; John Drummond and Johnny Ames, from opposite ends of the United States, found they shared more than just first names. Both stood over six feet tall, and both played musical instruments, sometimes performing for audiences. Donald Cooper preferred being called "Coop," and Joe Stone had once shaken hands with Babe Ruth. Nick chuckled hearing Mike Summers tell about being dumped by three lovely cousins with whom he'd had liaisons—"but not all at the same time!" Finally, Frank Tellman showed off his bruise received from the boot of his captor the previous morning. "What a rude awakening that was!" he added.

From the second company, Jefferson D. Spencer, a very gracious Southern gentleman, introduced Phillip "Foul-Mouth" Matthews. Then Pete Masterson waxed nostalgic over southern California, a place he'd visited only once, and Freddy Hobeck showed a snapshot of his pretty, young wife and infant son. Finally the last man in the group made his introduction.

"I'm Lt. William Severts," he intoned. "I guess that makes me the commander of this outfit. And I'm scared to death."

This brought silence again, as each man recognized his own fear in the lieutenant's eyes. The respite of good humor ended, replaced once more with the sharp awareness of discomfort and danger. The train wheels clacked against the iron rails. The sun at last broke through the clouds but didn't seem to have much power over the icy wind that sometimes whistled and sometimes moaned through the stock-car slats. The train kept its steady speed through the countryside, not even needing to slow down when it passed through a village. Mile after mile clacked by.

Nick pulled his knees up, resting his head and arms against them. He tried to ignore the twinge in his stomach, tried not to think of food. At first, he closed his eyes, hoping to force himself to sleep, but whenever he did that, images of platters heaped with food cruelly teased him. He wondered if the other men were haunted by hunger, or if he alone felt this insatiable need. From somewhere within the group, a soldier stirred, then rose.

"I can't wait any longer," Coop moaned. "I gotta go."

He moved unsteadily toward the bucket, then paused, turning to face the group. With a cynical smile, he asked, "I don't suppose anybody here has anything like a Sears and Roebuck Catalog?" The others didn't even look up.

"No, I thought not," Coop continued, then bent to scoop up a handful of straw. "Guess that's what this straw is for. Shucks. Here we thought the Nazis were thinking of our warmth and comfort."

The prisoners all averted their eyes, granting Coop the only privacy possible. Just then, a quick sob burst from the midst of the group. Nick looked up, not at all surprised to see Ross's shoulders heaving. No one made a move to show the kid some compassion, yet not one of the soldiers derided him. They all felt the same hopelessness, wondering how far this train would take them, what awaited them at the end of the line. Inwardly, Nick welcomed Ross's crying. It gave voice to their unspoken dread.

The kid reminded Nick a little of his own younger brother, about the same age as Ross. He breathed a silent prayer, hoping that Jacob remained uninjured. It had been several weeks since he'd heard word from home, and the news the folks wrote was weeks older than that. For all he knew, Jacob might also have been captured. The thought raised an additional concern, and Nick suddenly wished Jacob were here with him rather than off fighting the Japanese—a people neither of them knew nor understood.

Just then the train whistle shrilled two sharp blasts. Nick pulled himself to his feet. He pressed his face against the slatted wall of the stock car, trying to see what lay ahead. In a moment, the train began to slow down.

"What is it?" Smithson asked.

"Coming into a station," Nick answered. "I think we're going to stop."

"Aw *crap*!" Foul-Mouth Matthews had just sat on the bucket, his trousers bunched around his ankles. "Goddamned son of a bitch, *shit*! It has to be now?"

The others ignored him, scrambling to their feet.

"We're taking a sidetrack," Ambrose announced. "Maybe there'll be food here. They can't starve us, you know. It's against the Geneva Convention."

"Yeah," Al Jenkins spat. "Like that matters."

Gradually a teeming village came into view. The train crawled to a stop on sidetracks just past a station house.

"Oh my god," murmured Bandy. "Look at all of them."

A crowd of Nazi soldiers lined the tracks and even more groups of them assembled in the streets or moved in and out of buildings.

"Are we in Germany?"

"Can't be."

"What are they all doing here?"

"Maybe they're all waiting for us?" Ross groaned. "Maybe they're just going to shoot us right here—like cattle."

"Will somebody shut the Chef up!" Foul-Mouth demanded, straining to complete his duty. "*Damn* it! They're not gonna shoot me with my pants down!"

"*Every*body, just shut up," Nick demanded. "I'm trying to hear what's going on."

The men quieted, their eyes darting between Nick and the activity outside the railcar. Guards, who had been riding more comfortably in the cars ahead of and behind theirs, disembarked. Nick watched the German lieutenant approach another officer. He tried to overhear their conversation but couldn't distinguish the words through surrounding noises. The only information Nick gleaned came from snatches of conversations by those who happened to pass close by the stock car.

"Anything?" John Drummond asked. Nick faced him and shrugged.

"Not far from Rome, I think. Sounds like they're waiting for a troop train. I guess that's why we're sidetracked. Once that leaves, we're probably going to roll again too."

Drummond nodded, peering at the scene through the slats. He made a low whistling sound, then murmured, "This'd be a prime place for a bombing mission." Noticing a now-familiar face, he stepped backward and head gestured toward the station platform. "There's your friend. I think he's sending someone this way."

The German officer stood with a group of soldiers, pointing toward the prisoners. The men with him nodded, then called to yet another group. Again, Nick struggled to hear. Finally he faced his fellow POWs and announced, "They're bringing food and water. I expect it's more of the same."

"I hope it's *a lot* more," uttered Ambrose. "That crust of bread this morning was hardly more than a mouthful."

Alert now to the possibility of food, the Americans lined the wall of their temporary prison. It seemed to take forever for the assignment to be carried out, but finally they saw five German soldiers approach the car. One carried a couple of bread loaves; another held a water pail. The amounts of both looked pitifully small.

"I suppose we should count our blessings," Jenkins sneered, as one of the enemy soldiers unlocked the prison car. The last two Nazis in the group stood with their rifles at the ready.

"They think we're stupid?" Foul-Mouth wondered. "Do they think we'd try to make a break for it *here*?"

"*Brot und wasser*," the Nazi with the keys announced, and the lean feeding began again—a fist-sized hunk of bread and a few quick gulps from a tin cup.

"Got any jam?" Coop asked the soldier doling out the bread. When no answer came, he tried again. "Okay. How about just a bit of lard?"

"*Sei still!*" The soldier at the gate ordered, scrutinizing the prisoners. "*Wer ist Bremer?*"

Nick stepped forward. "*Ich heisse Nick Bremer.*"

"*Kommen Sie mit.*"

"*Warum?*" Nick dared to ask why he should follow the soldier. The German merely pointed toward the station and remarked, "*Suppe.*"

"What does he want?" Ross queried.

"He said they have soup," Nick reported. "Finally something to fill our bellies!"

All the men responded to this call. As one the group surged toward the door of the railcar. This created a commotion among their guards, who stepped in close to point their weapons directly at the prisoners.

"*Nein! Nein!*" They shouted, and the soldier who had asked for Nick called, "*Nur eins! Nur Bremer!*"

Only one would be allowed to join the line for soup. Nick didn't have to translate this message. He could tell by the faces of his fellow prisoners that they fully understood he had been selected for special treatment. For a moment, Nick warred with his hunger. Soup would be just the thing right now. But if he followed the soldiers and filled his own need, the men would despise him. Perhaps they would even accuse him of collaboration. Incarceration with them would be hell.

"*Danke, nein,*" with regret, he refused the offer, feeling his stomach rumble in protest. Some of the prisoners around him also protested.

"Are you nuts?"

"If it were me, I'd go eat my fill."

"Every man for himself—especially if you're German."

The last remark stung. Nick spoke sharply to the captors, pleading that all the men have a share in the meal.

"Only you may get in line," the German soldier insisted.

"But all the men are hungry! We'll be no trouble—we'll go one at a time—whatever it takes. Just give them some food."

A discussion erupted between the guards standing outside the railcar. Soon the soldier who had brought the bread left the group, heading for the station. Nick watched him approach the commanding officer, gesture, and point. The officer glared at the prisoners, made some remark Nick couldn't hear, then shrugged and turned away. In a minute, the soldier returned.

"You may bring some soup back to the others," he announced, and Nick flashed a grin to the other Americans, translating the news. He started to climb out of the stock car but was stopped once more by the soldier, "*Bringen Sie etwas.*"

"What?"

"Something to carry the soup in," the soldier continued.

"*Wir haben nichts,*" Nick protested, looking about madly for some container that might be useful. The German only shrugged.

"What? What is it now?"

"We have to find something to carry the soup in or we won't get any."

"Christ!"

"We'll find something!" Spencer insisted and the men began pawing through the straw on the floor and patting their own pockets for something, anything, that would hold liquid.

"All I got is a spoon," Ross commiserated, holding up a slightly bent steel spoon. Somewhat abashed, he added, "It's my good luck charm."

"Goddamit! There's nothing here," the men groaned, then fell silent. A few turned their glances toward one corner of the car. Soon all the men eyed the pail.

"You don't suppose—," Bandy offered.

"No!"

"If we empty it and wash it out—!"

"It would take more than a measly cup of water to clean that thing out. I'd rather starve!"

"You just might do that, Bradley."

"*Mach' schnell, mach' schnell!*" The guard grew impatient.

Jenkins spun once, his eyes lighting on Red. He strode toward him and, in one swift motion, swiped the helmet from the redhead.

"Ow!"

Jenkins grabbed a fist full of straw to wipe out the inside of the helmet. He handed it to Nick, growling, "Here. Bring the damn soup." Then turning to Ross, he added, "And, Chef, keep that spoon handy. We're all going to need it."

Nick grabbed the helmet. The German eyed the makeshift soup pot with a smirk, then stood aside so that Nick might precede him toward the station. They shouldered their way through the building and out a rear door. A line of soldiers and civilians led to another door, this into a metal-sided outbuilding. Nick took his place in line, holding on to Red's helmet as if it were some kind of treasure.

The line moved at a moderate pace. Excited by the possibility of further relieving hunger, Nick breathed deep, wrinkling his nose at a pungent odor that hung in the air. At first he thought it might be fumes from several vehicles idling in the street. As the odor grew stronger, he dismissed that idea—unless the German forces had taken to burning their filthy socks for fuel.

Only when he reached the doorway did he realize that the smell came from two portable boilers inside. Steam spiraled from the boilers, dampening the hair of the women who stood behind them. One by one, the men in line held out cups or bowls, into which the women ladled foul-smelling, grayish liquid. Nick could not imagine what ingredient gave the slightly thickened broth its aroma, but as he edged closer, he heard one of the soup ladies identify powdered turnips as the base.

Both women poured soup into proffered containers without looking at or speaking to those in line. One after another passed through. Some said thanks, but most sniffed critically and swore under their breaths. When it was Nick's turn, he held out his helmet. The woman started to pour liquid into it, then stopped, noticing the unusual container for the first time.

"*Was willst?*" she sniffed, now recognizing his uniform.

"*Bitte,*" Nick answered. "*Suppe.*"

"Hah!" the woman guffawed, causing both her chins to shake. She brushed aside a strand of hair that had steam curled over her eyes. With a guttural tone, she continued, this time in broken English, "From *that* you will soup eat?"

"It's a perfectly fine bowl," Nick defended. Seeing a glint of humor in the woman's eyes, he teased, "It works real good. I just used it to wash my feet."

"*Ach—phew!*" the woman roared, holding her nose. She repeated Nick's remark to her soup partner, and both women chuckled. The first one filled her ladle with the hot, off-color soup and dumped it into the helmet.

"To cut the stink of your feet," she badgered. The second woman elbowed her, holding out her own filled ladle. This, too, she dumped into the helmet, adding, "To cut the stink of her soup!" Grumbling from those in line behind Nick ended the brief moment of levity. Nick, holding the helmet carefully so not one drop of the soup would spill, followed the Nazi guard through the station and once more to the train.

Impatient, the men started shouting for Nick to hurry the minute they saw him emerge from the station house. When he reached the car, several arms reached out to relieve him of his burden, then another pair to help him up. Almost immediately, the guard slid shut the door of the stock car, locking it securely once more. Nick faced his compatriots. Without discussing a plan of action, the men formed yet another line. One of them hustled the spoon from Chef's grip and passed it to the first soldier, who held the helmet. Almost reverently, he looked at the soup. Reaching into the helmet with his fingers, he pulled out a single strand of red hair.

"A little extra flavoring," he remarked, then dipped out a spoonful of soup and sipped.

"Christ, this is awful!" He grimaced after swallowing it, then passed the helmet and spoon to the next man in line. Some of the prisoners sipped from the spoon; others slurped. Each man rationed himself to one spoon full. When the helmet of soup reached Chef, he took one sniff and shook his head.

"No. This is too awful."

"Just eat," Bandy shoved the helmet back toward him. "You never know. Someday you might dream of having a treat like this."

Ross swallowed hard and nodded. He closed his eyes, drew a deep breath, and held it until he had swallowed the distasteful brew. Gagging, he handed the helmet to the next man. After all the men had tasted, there remained enough soup in the helmet for each soldier to have a second, though more sparing spoonful. As if part of some sacred ritual, the men stood silent while the helmet passed from soldier to soldier. Johnny was the last to receive his share. As soon as he sipped the last drop, he handed the helmet back to Red.

"Kind of a small helmet," he observed. "Sure don't hold much. I thought Red had a much bigger head than this." For a time, no one spoke. A few men plopped down in the straw once more. All wondered how long their internment would last, how hungry they would ultimately be.

"Maybe it just takes some getting used to," Nick offered doubtfully. "Maybe if we just had a little salt and pepper—"

"That was some vile-tasting soup," Bandy admitted. "Nothing could make it taste any better. But I sure wish there had been more of it."

"Ya couldn'a made it taste any worse," Jenkins grumbled, "but I'm still starving."

"Yeah," from Ambrose, "guess we shoulda used the shit bucket."

The others looked at him, appalled at first, but recognizing at last the baiting tone of his voice, they smiled, chuckled, and finally relieved their tension with zesty laughter. Outside the railcar, Nazi soldiers heard and paused their own discussions. Curious but wary, they stared at the caged prisoners. Some of them lifted their weapons; others just shook their heads and turned away.

III

Native Sons

"I used to dream of visiting Italy," Bandy mused, breaking the stillness. When no one responded, he continued, "Sandy beaches, fine wine, architectural wonders—"

"Pasta," Ross sighed, and Bandy nodded.

"Babes with big bazooms," Foul-Mouth dreamed aloud. A few of the men snickered.

"But look what ya got instead," this from Jenkins. "Boches instead of babes, with bazookas instead of bazooms."

"The Germans don't have bazookas. That's *ours*."

"They have us. What's ours is theirs. One of the basic rules of conflict, Chef: what one side gots, the other side gits. Might have a different name, different shape, but pretty much the same bang."

"But," Ross puzzled, "we're all machine gunners. All they got is our machine guns."

"Wake up, kid!" Jenkins sniped. "You don't see much past your own nose, do you. In all the fronts of this damn war, you don't really think we're the only saps unlucky enough to fall into enemy hands?"

"Leave the kid alone!" Lieutenant Severts had not spoken much in the last two days, and his sudden order surprised the men. Recognizing this, Severts cleared his throat and attempted to return the conversation to its original track.

"My mother," he said, "used to dream of visiting Rome, particularly the Vatican. She thought that having an audience with the pope would be like being in the presence of Jesus himself."

"Right," Jenkins scoffed. "Jesus himself probably hightailed it outa this country when the devil krauts moved in. As for your pope—"

"Don't you be sayin' nothing against—"

A train whistle ended the brewing argument. All twenty prisoners watched the awaited troop train pull into the station on the main tracks. Though this blocked their view of the station, a buzz of voices outside indicated that a sizable number of soldiers were gathering to board.

"Wonder what offensive they're planning," Drummond whispered, then added, "*Goddamn!* I wish there were a way to stop them."

The others fell silent as similar thoughts crossed their minds. Somewhere in the next few days, these soldiers would be attacking Allied forces, killing men just like the twenty who watched here, numb and helpless to prevent it.

"Damn the whole damn German race!" Ambrose swore, then locking eyes with Nick, he added, "Sorry, German. Didn't mean you. I know, I know—you're *American.*"

Nick gave no response but met Ambrose's glare with his own until Ambrose finally looked away. Nick leaned his head back against the slatted wall and closed his eyes. He knew he shouldn't feel so defensive. After all, millions of Allied forces played parts in this war, and many of them were of German descent, had been raised with German as their native tongue, or learned it later for any number of reasons. That alone didn't make them sympathetic to the Nazi ideal. But here, with this small group of men, Nick was the only one who could effectively communicate with the enemy. First-generation American, his connection with "the old country" probably seemed pretty fresh. What would he have to do to convince his fellow POWs that he was 100 percent loyal American? Ambrose's words played again and again in his mind like a scratchy recording: *You're American. You're American. You're American.* Those words unleashed a memory from long ago.

Six years old, Nick sat in the front row of the brand-new schoolhouse. On the shiny wooden desktop lay a lined tablet and two pencils that Pa had sharpened with a pocketknife that morning. Nick's lunch pail, containing a bread-and-jelly sandwich and a few carrots from Ma's garden, waited under his desk. He felt excited. Ma had spoken of this school for many weeks, thankful that it was less than two miles from the home place rather than the five-and-a-half to the old schoolhouse.

Eleven other children sat in the three rows of desks; two appeared to be about Nick's age and the other students ranged in age upward to thirteen or so. Nick recognized all of them, having seen them in church every Sunday, or at occasional social events. They all lived on farms within three or four miles of each other.

On a small platform at the front of the one-room building stood the teacher's desk, which held a shiny blue globe and a large book—a dictionary, Nick later learned. Behind the desk, a slate chalkboard lined the wall. A banner bearing the English alphabet spanned the length of the board. Above that hung two portraits of somber-looking men. The one with white hair looked very severe, like Pa often did after Nick had done something naughty. The other portrait showed a dark, bearded man with sharply chiseled features. His eyes didn't look stern, but sad.

A large, encased pendulum clock hung on the wall at the back of the room, where the students couldn't see it but the teacher could. When the clock began toning the hour of eight, the students hushed their excited first-day-of-school whispers and stood as their teacher strode to the front of the class. Reaching her desk, she turned to face the students. With a stiff smile, she began to speak.

Nick couldn't understand a word she said. Ma and Pa had told him that he would be learning to talk in English once he got to school—like a true American. This was only the second place where he'd heard English spoken. At home they always spoke German, and most of the families he knew spoke German, and even at the little country church, what the priest didn't intone in Latin, he admonished in German. The only other place Nick had heard someone speak English was in the stores in town, but even there, people seemed to fall into a mixture of the two languages.

The older students responded to the teacher's words by turning toward one corner of the room. A little confused, Nick and the other two beginners did likewise. Out of the corner of his eye, Nick watched for further signs. When he saw the bigger kids lay their right hands across their chests he did the same, but when they began to chant something in one voice—he felt at a complete loss. Afraid to do otherwise, he moved his lips, staring at the flag in the corner.

The children then resumed their seats and the teacher picked up a red wire-bound book from her desk. Tapping a pencil on the desk, she called for attention, then looked at the younger students. To the little girl at Nick's left, she addressed what sounded like a question. The little girl looked wide-eyed back at the teacher, her lips trembling. From somewhere in the back, one of the older children whispered, "*Wie heisst du?*"

Their names. The teacher wanted to know their names. Nick felt relieved. The little girl murmured her name, then Teacher stepped in front of Nick's desk, posing the same question. As Ma had told him to do, Nick stood up beside his desk and responded eagerly, "*Ich heisse Nicholas Karl Bremer!*"

At this, the teacher rapped her pencil sharply against the top of Nick's head; he winced with the sting. Bending low, she brought her face level with his. Her eyes seemed cold as she delivered the first English sentences Nick understood—not by her words, but by her tone. "You are American! No German here!"

Putting her hands on his shoulders, Teacher spun him to face the rest of the class. She spoke above him. "My name is Mrs. Kidder. As long as I am your teacher, I will not tolerate your speaking German in the school. I know that many of you come from German families, but you are in America now and must speak like Americans. So"—she wheeled Nick to face her again—"do not let me hear you speak a word of German in this school!"

Though Mrs. Kidder's words still sounded meaningless, Nick clearly understood that he'd done something very wrong. His face flushed with shame. He hoped Ma and Pa would never hear of his misbehavior. For the remainder of his first day of school, he bit his tongue rather than speak a word of German and, in his mind, rehearsed over and over again the day's lesson: *I am an American. My name is Nicholas Bremer.*

That evening, Nick shared some of his day's experience with the family, proudly repeating his first English sentences. Ma and Pa beamed.

"Mrs. Kidder won't let us talk German at all," Nick informed them, this time in the language familiar to him. "Not even during recess."

"Well, after all, we are in America. We should talk like Americans do. In fact, that's what we'll all do—right here at home! You'll remind us, Nick."

"I don't think Mrs. Kidder likes German people, Pa," Nick confided.

"That's probably because of the war," Ma interjected. "Her husband was gassed in the Great War and is almost helpless now. That's why Mrs. Kidder had to go back to teaching school. Her husband can't work." At Pa's scolding glance, Ma exclaimed, "Well, it's true. Everyone knows that. The ladies at church told me."

"But"—Nick needed to know more—"are German people bad?"

"*Nein*—no!" Pa snapped. "Germans are good people, they work hard, serve God, do their duties. It isn't the people that are bad. Sometimes they just have bad leaders."

"Oh." Nick was relieved.

"Remember that, Nick," Pa instructed. "Never hold a whole group of people responsible for the bad deeds of a few. Germans are good folk."

"I'm glad."

"But watch out for them Roosians. Them you can't trust."

"Yes, Pa."

In spite of his eagerness, the first few months of school were somewhat difficult for Nick; his struggle to understand Mrs. Kidder resulted in her perceiving him as a slow learner. At home, Ma and Pa helped as much as they could, attempting to converse in English around the children, but the best they managed at home was to slowly blend English words into German sentences. Gradually, however, the process became easier.

One morning in late spring, shortly after the last day of school, Nick awoke from a dream. Remembering it, he shrieked, waking everyone else in the house.

"*Lieber Gott!*" Ma hurried into his room, followed closely by Pa who demanded, "*Was ist los?*" Instead of a frightened, trembling Nick, they found their son bouncing excitedly on his bed, ignoring the protests of his younger brother Marcus.

"I am American!" Nick clamored. "I had a dream in English! At last, I am a real American!"

"Hey, Bremer!" A man's voice brought Nick back to the present. He turned to Jenkins, who gestured with his thumb toward Ambrose. "Don't let him get to you. He's full of it—just likes the sound of his own voice, I guess. He don't really mean nothing."

"I for one think we're lucky to have a German speaker in our midst," Bandy volunteered. Then, nudging Nick with his elbow, he added, "I just hope that if you get preferential treatment, it will carry over to the rest of us."

Nick accepted the conciliatory offer with a nod. Whatever their backgrounds, these men all shared a similar fate. Divisiveness would not be in anyone's best interest, and Nick felt certain that he himself was not important enough to receive preferential treatment. In fact, he feared he could be in for just the opposite. What if they pressured him into becoming some kind of stool pigeon? What if his own fellow captives wouldn't trust him?

Apparently Nick was not alone in his uncertainty. Shortly after the troop train began to pull out of the station, Ross sat down next to him. The banter between the POWs had ceased, and all the men sat or stood lost in their own thoughts. Nick didn't encourage conversation with Ross, but the kid seemed to find it necessary to talk.

"Do you think we'll be interrogated?"

"I'm pretty sure we will."

"Oh man. I don't know what to say. I don't know what they'll do to me if I don't tell them what they want to hear."

"What can you tell them, Chef?" Nick asked. "What information can you possibly have that they don't already know?"

"I dunno. That's what scares me. I've heard guys say they can make you say things without your ever knowing you've said them."

"Just remember the rules," Nick advised. "Name, rank and serial number. Most of us here are just regular grunts—no rank, no special knowledge other than how to fire machine guns. No matter what you tell them, you're giving them information they already have."

"Think so?" Chef sounded hopeful.

"Yeah. I think so." This seemed to ease Ross's mind for the time being. Once more Nick leaned back and closed his eyes. The hum of voices outside had subsided, replaced by the hiss and squeal of a train beginning to move. Hundreds of German soldiers headed to the front where Nick had been only two days earlier. He wondered if the Allies there had held ground or if they'd been turned back. Morale among the troops had been high of late, especially after the victories in Sicily and Naples. The slow but fairly steady drive northward gave them hope that they would eventually take all of Italy. Of course, it was still a long way to Berlin, Nick realized, but with the Russians making a strong stance on the eastern front, maybe they would soon squeeze the Nazis out of power.

You can't trust a Russki. Pa's voice suddenly replayed in Nick's mind, and he had to smile as the memory of another event unfolded.

"*Unglaublich!*" Pa ranted as he paced. "*Gottverdamtes Russki!*"

The whole family had been seated at the dinner table when Agnes broke the news. Frank Helzmer had proposed to her, and she'd said yes. No one was surprised by Pa's outburst.

"What for do you want to marry a Roosian?" he demanded. "Do you know what you're doing?"

"I love him, Pa. And he loves me." Agnes' eyes flashed her defiance. "And nothing you say will make us change our minds."

"Love!" Pa scorned. "In my day, love was something that *grew* between a man and wife. Not something that *made* a man and wife."

"Well now it's my day, Pa," Agnes asserted. "Frank and I want to marry with your blessing—and his father's blessing too. But if we have to, we'll marry without it."

"His father?" Pa now challenged. "His father has objections to you?"

"Just like you, Pa. He thinks that Russians should marry Russians and Germans should marry Germans."

"And so it should be!"

"Come on, Pa. That's just foolish." Nick chose that moment to join the argument. He never could understand the distrust that existed between his relatives—immigrants from the Banat region of Hungary—and families who had come to America from territories in Russia. These people shared a common German ancestry, yet they retained some kind of nationalistic feud. They were civil to one another, attended the same church, and lived in the same communities, often working together or playing together. Yet for some reason, intermarriage between them remained taboo. To Nick's generation, it seemed ridiculous, particularly in this country where people from many nations came together to form one.

"You call your father a fool?" Pa's face flushed an angry purplish red; Nick could actually see one of the veins pulsing under Pa's skin. Ma must have noticed it, too, for she began to scold.

"That's enough, Nikolaus! You'll make yourself a stroke!"

"Besides," Nick rejoined, "Frank's a great guy. He's a hard worker, goes to church, doesn't drink too much, and from what I've seen"—this directed to Agnes—"he's respectful, and one hell of a dancer."

"That is not the point!"

"Well then, what is the point, Pa?" Agnes demanded.

"That he's a nice boy, a good worker is just fine. He should find a nice, hardworking, Roosian wife—that is the point!"

"You're not in the old country now," Ma insisted. "Things are different here. It's modern age."

The argument continued for some time, with Ma and the kids united against Pa. Though they didn't quite manage to change his way of thinking, they did eventually elicit a grudging resignation and, eventually, Pa's blessing on the union. The night before the wedding, the Bremers and Helzmers sat for a meal together. The two patriarchs remained cool until Frank, with a mischievous twinkle, broke the ice.

"You know, this could have been much worse." He covered Agnes' hand with his own. "One of us could have been *Lutheran!*"

The vividness of his memories surprised Nick. Long-forgotten details—the quirky way Frank Helzmer lifted one eyebrow when he was about to tell a joke, Pa's spittle-spewing temper tantrums, the determined squaring of Agnes's shoulders—all played clearly in his mind as if he were watching scenes of his life on a film screen. Closing his eyes and concentrating hard, Nick recalled the timbres of individual voices; when he breathed deep and slow, he could almost bring to mind particular smells—lilacs that decorated the church for Agnes's wedding, the upholstery of his first car, the one he drove to Ohio, even the industrial city smells that at first seemed offensive but later became exciting.

Nick opened his eyes again when he felt the train lurch into motion. Outside it was now almost dark.

"We're off," Bradley said.

The train resumed its steady, slow rate. Stock car rocking and wheels clacking, the monotonous pattern of sound and movement eventually had a lulling effect on the twenty tired men. They shared body heat in close grouping, but nothing else—no scornful remarks, speculations, or apprehensions. Some slept fitfully; more simply stared off into the darkness, while others closed their eyes and let the reels of memories unwind. For an hour and a half longer, they rode in silence. At length the train slowed again, but not to take a sidetrack.

In the blackness outside, Nick could see no station, nor any structure that resembled a town. It appeared that the train had stopped at some kind of temporary siding in the middle of seemingly vacant country. The guards in the other cars disembarked. Some carried lanterns or flashlights; all had their weapons ready. For a long time nothing happened. What they waited for, Nick couldn't imagine. Finally, after some murmuring among the guards, one Nazi soldier opened the stock car gate. He said nothing, but merely gestured to the men inside. None of the POWs spoke, but their sudden apprehension became palpable.

What are we walking into? Nick wondered, knowing that the other men shared in this dread. Under the cover of night, in an unidentifiable location of a strange land—would all of them simply disappear here? How easy it would be for the German soldiers to gun them all down and walk away. Their status would remain MIA forever, leaving unanswered questions and no hope of retribution.

With hesitating steps, the men followed orders to move. Ten steps—then twenty and on. Nick felt a surge of hope with every step taken. Perhaps they did have a destination other than an unmarked mass grave. After several minutes of hiking, the men stumbled onto a deeply rutted road that veered slightly off to the left. The soupy muck slowed their progress; even the Nazis began cursing the "goddamned Italian mud."

Then, around a sharp curve in the road, they saw their destination below them—a prison compound at the base of the hill, evident by its searchlight tower and double border of coiled barbed wire. Nick heard the low-gear rumble of trucks. On the road in front of them, a steep grade leading to the compound, three trucks headed toward them, the beams from their headlights bouncing as the wheels churned through heavy mud.

"*Halt!*" An order rang out. "*Aus der Weg!*"

As quickly as they could, the Nazis and their prisoners moved off the road, out of the way of the approaching trucks. Nick heard their captors grumbling something about the trucks being late. As had become their practice, the Americans bunched together.

"Did you hear what they said?"

"Do you know what's happening?"

Nick shushed the whispered questions while he listened to irritated voices from their guards. Slowly the trucks rumbled past. Canvas tarps covered the backs of the trucks so no one could see what might be inside.

"I might be wrong, but I think they're carrying prisoners. Probably heading for the train to be shipped somewhere else. This must be a temporary camp."

Once the trucks had rumbled off into the darkness, the Nazis barked orders for their prisoners to march into the compound. Mud-covered, damp, and cold, the weary band at last reached an open area near one of the long brick buildings of the compound. There they stood, silent for now, waiting further orders. At last, the kommandant—or *oberstleutnant*—emerged from his dimly lit personal quarters. He paced in front of the group, eyeing the prisoners each in turn, as if evaluating them. Finally he stopped and asked one of the guards, "*Jemand hier für Sonderbehändlung?*"

Nick could feel the curiosity of the men around him, but he didn't dare speak just now. Besides, he wasn't entirely sure what the kommandant meant in asking if anyone needed "special handling." It could mean preferential treatment—or severe treatment.

"*Nein*," the officer who had been in charge of the men until now responded. "*Nur ein Offizier.*" Only one officer—Lieutenant Severts. Out of the corner of his eye, Nick glanced toward the lieutenant. The man remained stone-faced.

"*Fünf Tage*," the oberstleutnant ordered for the lieutenant, then Nick heard "*drei Tage*" for the enlisted men. It could mean only one thing: solitary confinement. By nature of his rank, Severts would spend the next five days in solitary; the others, only three days. *This is it*, Nick thought, surprised that reality of capture seemed to hit him only now. *Now it begins.*

Apparently they wouldn't all be placed in solitary, however. After a moment, the kommandant ordered only five of the group to follow a guard, while the remaining fifteen still waited. Nick, Lieutenant Severts, Red, J. D. Spencer, and Jenkins numbered the first five. Accompanied by three guards, they headed toward another low brick building, with a narrow windowed door in the middle. This appeared to be the only window in the building at all. Inside, they found themselves in a long, dim hallway; its only illumination came from a bare, low-wattage bulb at one end. In the wall opposite the main entry were several dark heavy doors, some of them closed. Nick noted that five remained open—their own private cells.

The guards neither pushed nor shouted. One of the Nazis approached an open door, then pointed to Severts, gesturing with his weapon. Wordlessly, Severts entered. The door closed with a solid bang. The guard placed a padlock on the door and snapped it in place. One by one the men entered their cells, Nick stepping into the last one. Just before the door closed, he saw in the dim light that the room was a windowless, brick cell, perhaps six feet square, with a concrete floor. A dented and chipped enamel chamber pot appeared to be the only object within. Then the door clanged shut, leaving Nick in utter darkness, alone with his own thoughts.

Three days. If he had only three days to live, it wouldn't be much time at all, but three days isolated in complete darkness seemed interminable. He groped the wall, sitting down in the corner farthest from the chamber pot. Thank goodness for the power of memory, he thought. In here he had nothing to do but remember. He didn't even have to close his eyes to make the images replay in his mind.

Pa managed to get through the period of wedding preparation without causing a stir. In public, he made no further references to the "damn Roosians." At home, however, his grumbling increased. Ma tried to be sympathetic, but even her patience wore thin when Pa wouldn't look at or talk to Agnes at supper two nights before the wedding.

"Please pass the jelly, Pa," Agnes requested.

"Elsie, give your sister the jelly," Pa barked, then murmured, "Never thought I would live to see the day. Like a knife in the back of the whole family. If my folks were alive today, this would be the death of them. Marrying a Roosian."

"Pa—," Agnes began her protest.

"And what about your aunts? What about them? Did you give them even a thought?"

It was hard for the Bremer sons and daughters to think of aunts they'd never met, but they understood Pa's concern. His own immediate family—parents and two sisters—had remained in the old country when Pa immigrated to America. His parents had passed away within two years of each other shortly after Pa married Ma. The two sisters, both nuns, lived with an order that did missionary work somewhere in Russia. For a time, they kept in touch through letters. Then had come the Revolution of 1917. Pa had heard nothing from his sisters since. For a while he hoped they would contact him again, but after many years passed without any sign that the nuns had ever existed, he became convinced that they'd met premature deaths at the hands of the Russians. For their sake, Pa retained a deep distrust of anyone of Russian descent.

"It's like Agnes is betraying them, that's what this is."

"Oh for heaven's sake," Ma finally cut in. "Frank Helzmer's folks have been living in America longer than you have! They had nothing to do with whatever has gone on over there. It is high time you stopped dwelling on the past and acted like the proud father of the bride. Besides," Ma added, "Agnes couldn't have chosen a more decent man."

"She could have—"

"Whssssht!" Ma shushed, and even Pa appeared startled by the fire in her eyes.

The wedding itself, a simple affair, took place on a mild Saturday in January. The times didn't allow extravagant celebrations. Family and guests witnessed the wedding mass, then gathered for a modest meal in the church basement. Frank appeared very dignified, and Agnes radiant. A potentially tense moment occurred when the priest asked who gave the bride in marriage. Pa hesitated just slightly, then answered in a humble voice, "*Ja.* I suppose—her mother and I do."

All went smoothly after that—the supper, the dancing—until Pa and Mr. Helzmer had each sampled just a few too many glasses of homemade wine and beer. Their voices slurred; they began by calling each other names, at first in a good-natured manner. As the liquor took hold, the pseudo-friendliness became surly, then threatening. At last, the verbal feud held the attention of the entire assemblage. At Ma's pleading look, Nick attempted to step in.

"Come on, Pa," he said. "It's time we went home." Pa shrugged Nick's arm off his shoulders, growling, "G'dam Russki's *nicht gut* enough f'r Anges—Ang—Ag-*nes!*" At that Mr. Helzmer roared, "*Du gottverdamtes Boche! Du—*"

Afterward no one remembered who had thrown the first punch. In a flurry of screams and pleas from the women and orders from the men, the two patriarchs flew at each other like animals challenging each other's territory. Nick and Marcus grabbed Pa's flailing arms while Frank attempted to restrain his own father. When they managed to keep the rivals secure, Ma strode to Pa. Her eyes grew watery in her reddened face. She glared at Pa for a moment, then with an intense whisper, she accused, "Nikolaus Bremer. For *shame!*"

He'd looked at her, then at his sons, and finally recognized the crowd around him. Shrugging himself away from the hold Nick and Marcus had on him, he brushed the sleeves of his coat, as if they had dirtied him.

"Hmmph," he grumbled. Turning, he faltered up the steps to the main doors, then disappeared into the darkness outside. Looking equally sheepish, Mr. Helzmer followed soon after.

As weddings go, Nick remembered, Agnes and Frank's had been pretty exciting, one they'd undoubtedly tell their children and grandchildren about for years to come. He shivered. Accustomed now to the dark, Nick could make out the faintest line of light just below the door. About halfway up the door, another faint line showed. Nick assumed it was a pass-through. That meant he'd at least get bread and water while in solitary.

Solitary, he thought, remembering the card game for one that Ma had taught him to play. He wondered if he could put a game together in his mind and pass the time more easily. Nick had no idea how much time had passed. Even with the faint line of light bleeding into the cell, he had no way of knowing if it were daylight or dark outside. He assumed that the dim hallway outside his cell remained half-lit at all times. At one point he tried communicating with whomever might be in an adjacent cell, first tapping, then hammering on the walls with his fist. He got no response. Never had he felt so alone in the world.

Just then the pass-through clanged open. Nick squinted at the guard who peered in at him.

"*Etwas zu essen,*" the guard stated, then offered a cup and a heel of bread. Nick scrambled to his knees to grab them.

"*Wie lange*—?" he started to ask, but the pass-through clinked shut, cutting off any reply. Nick first downed the *sauerbrot*, then gulped the water, very little of both. He had no idea how long it had been since his last meal, and certainly no clue how much time might pass before the next. The nearest challenge right now was not to let his isolation get to him. He had to keep calm and alert. Nick created a regimen of calisthenics to keep his body in shape, and alternately sang songs or recited poems he'd learned in school to help keep his mind alert. Sometimes he just counted until a new thought distracted him and he lost his place. He replayed the assembly-line work that had become so automatic to him at Cowles, and recreated the faces of his landlady in Cleveland, the waitress at a diner not far from where he lived, his boot camp buddy, and others whose names he either never knew or had forgotten.

When he didn't use his own voice, Nick listened to the silence and remembered sounds. At first he remembered them singly, then one rapidly turned into another: thunder on a summer day became combat explosives; the delighted squeal of his nieces and nephew when he teased them turned into frightened screams; even the unrelenting *ticktock* of the old schoolhouse clock transformed into the *ba-bump, ba-bump* of his own heartbeat. Soon he came to hate the subtle hiss of silence.

What is that? he wondered. *The sound of my own blood?*

When food came the second time, Nick assumed he'd finally made it through the night. This must be a morning ration of the second day. Or would this be considered the first of his three-day sentence?

"Maybe I should count nights instead of days?" he wondered aloud.

Sleep helped. Because he had no reference to day or night, Nick could never tell how long he slept. His naps might have lasted hours or just moments. Sometimes he even fell asleep without closing his eyes. The wakeful hours, however, dragged by. Nick tried to remember incidents from every year of his life—trivial as well as monumental. The first three years seemed blank, but he managed to relive something from every year after that, from receiving a tin horse for his fourth birthday, to falling in the rain-swollen creek and nearly drowning when he was nine, to the school picnic after eighth grade. Then there was his first semiserious relationship at age eighteen. He could see her face clearly, and he would never forget her name; he'd always thought it sounded just like a waltz: Sylvia Katharine Josephson. Finally an image came to him from his twenty-third year. It had been his first visit home after moving to Ohio.

Pa, Nick, and Marcus planned a deer-hunting trip into Montana. Nick hoped this would give them all a chance to become close, as a parent with adult sons should be. They would be gone four days, staying in a somewhat dilapidated cabin owned by the cousin of a neighbor. Days they would hunt, but during the evenings, huddled next to a rusted, pot-bellied stove, they would talk to each other, play cards, drink beer, and generally just be close.

Then, the morning before departure, Pa announced, "I've decided to ask Frank to come with us."

Frank? Nick sent Marcus a quizzical look. *Frank Helzmer?*

"I thought he hated Frank's guts," Nick whispered.

"Nah—not anymore," Marcus responded. "Not since Frank and Agnes had the boy."

Not only did Pa *not* hate Frank, he actually seemed to prefer Frank's company to that of his own sons. During the trip Pa laughed loudest at Frank's jokes, admired most Frank's shot, and rated Frank's pancakes even above his own.

"Doesn't this bother you?" Nick finally managed to ask his brother.

"Nah. Believe me, life's a lot easier now that those two get along."

"But Pa seems to get along better with Frank than with either you or me."

"Yeah, well—you know—he's Pa," Marcus replied, as if that were explanation enough.

Not until they had returned to North Dakota, and Frank had gone home to Agnes did Nick mention anything to Pa. While listening to the radio after supper that evening, he casually broached the subject.

"You know, Pa, that Frank's a pretty good guy."

"Uh-huh. Real good to Agnes and the boy."

"I remember how you hated the sight of him only a couple years ago. Him being Russian and all."

Pa's face reddened just a little; then he cleared his throat, leaned forward in his chair, and delivered one of his own bits of wisdom.

"Well, you know, Nick. You can't hold one man responsible for the wickedness of a whole nation."

Just then, the cell door burst open. Though the light in the corridor had not changed in intensity, the suddenness of its appearance blinded Nick. His eyes watered. He raised his arm to shield the glare. A Nazi soldier stood in the doorway, backlit so that Nick saw only a shadow for a face. The soldier spoke in clipped English.

"You are Bremer? The American German? The *oberstleutnant* has for you some questions."

Uncertain, Nick rose to his feet. Could three days have passed already? Or had his time been reduced for some reason? He squared his shoulders, then stepped toward the Nazi.

"I am Nicholas Bremer, private, United States Army. One-hundred percent American."

The German smirked and stepped back, gesturing for Nick to precede him. As Nick stepped past, still blinking in the light, the soldier gave him a mock salute.

"*Heil Hitler,* American. *Und willkommen*—to the *Dulag.*"

IV

Somewhere in Between

Fresh, cold air hit him with an almost intoxicating intensity. Nick filled his lungs and held his breath until a wave of dizziness forced its release. Until then, he had not realized how good it could feel just to breathe. He almost smiled at the armed guard waiting for him to collect himself.

"Where are we going—*wohin gehen wir?*" Nick asked. The guard gestured toward a small, sturdy brick building, then shoved Nick with the barrel of his rifle. Together they headed toward what Nick assumed would be his interrogation. He glanced uneasily around. German soldiers moved between several long wooden buildings, and one soldier manned a wooden block tower near the compound's entrance. The barracks looked ramshackle in the glare of outdoor lights, the strongest coming from the tower. Squinting, Nick could barely see the natural half light of dawn on the horizon—or was it dusk? Nick realized that his senses of time and direction had left him. He glanced toward the wooden barracks but saw no sign of his fellow prisoners.

"The others. Where are—?" Nick started to ask, but the German silenced him with a sharp prod to the shoulder.

"It is not for you to ask questions."

Nick couldn't help himself. After a few more steps, he tried again.

"What time—what day is this?" When his guard chuckled, Nick turned to face him. The guard's eyebrows twitched; one corner of his mouth lifted in a crooked, cynical smile.

"You have been eleven days a guest of the Reich."

"Eleven! But—"

"*Nicht* eleven," the guard nudged him again. "*Nur sieben.* Seven-eleven. In English they sound too much the same."

"Your commander said three—"

"*Ja, ja.* Three. Three days it is. Eleven days, seven days, three. Maybe only one day, huh?" Again, the man's eyebrows twitched. He smiled wider, enjoying his little game. By then they had reached the door to headquarters. The guard knocked, then opened the door, shoving Nick inside.

"*Heil Hitler,*" he saluted hastily to the officer sitting behind a makeshift desk just inside the door. "*Hier ist Kriegsgefangener Bremer.*"

The kommandant waved a return salute without lifting his gaze from a stack of maps on the desktop. He sniffed, wrinkling his nose. Nick waited silently, fully aware of the unpleasant smell emanating from his own body. After several minutes, the kommandant gestured toward a wooden chair against the far wall. The guard hastened to bring it closer.

"Sit down, please." The kommandant spoke smooth English.

Nick sat. For a long time, he and his captors remained wordless. The kommandant tapped a pen against the table as he studied his maps. A slight sputtering sound caught Nick's attention, and he darted his eyes until he found the source: one of a pair of light bulbs in wall sconces behind the commander hissed and glowed just a bit brighter than the other. A flick of the switch or just a slightly jarring move would burn it out. Just as Nick thought it, a muffled pop sounded and the room dimmed even more. The kommandant sighed, then slowly rolled up the maps. He stared at Nick for a long moment; Nick lowered his own gaze to the tabletop, concentrating on the scratches and stains in the wood. Finally the kommandant rose, replaced the maps in a metal filing cabinet in one corner, and picked up a small package from the top of the cabinet. He returned to the desk and sat.

"Perhaps you would like a cigarette?" The kommandant pushed the pack across the table toward Nick. The label read *Lucky Strike*. Nick looked at the kommandant.

"Yes, yes. American cigarettes." The German nudged a cylinder from the pack and handed it to Nick, then took another for himself. "Your country produces not so impressive a military, but the tobacco is quite good, yes? One more thing we can look forward to after the final victory." Smiling, he reached into his pocket to bring out an elegant-looking, silver-plated lighter. He lit his own cigarette, then offered the flame to Nick, holding the lighter so that Nick could see the exquisite engraving of an eagle.

"You like this?" The kommandant responded to the question Nick didn't ask. "A fine piece of workmanship. No doubt crafted by some very skilled—and wealthy—jeweler." He flicked the lighter once more before replacing it in his pocket. "It was a gift—shall we say, a souvenir?"

A breathy snicker sounded from the guard near the door. Nick felt the muscles in his face tighten, but he remained silent.

"Wait outside, please," the kommandant ordered. "And check supplies for more light bulbs." This time, with a brisk *Heil Hitler!* the guard left the room.

"He is a good soldier," the officer remarked with a smile after the door had shut. "Not an agreeable man, but a good soldier."

Once more, the two men sat in silence, smoking. Nick felt the German's steady gaze on him. It unnerved him, but he willed himself to show no signs of discomfort. Finally, the questioning began.

"So you are not an officer?"

"What? No, I'm not."

"There seems to have been some misunderstanding. You were named by others as an officer, disguising yourself as an enlisted man—"

"What!" Nick couldn't help but think of Ambrose. "No! I never—who? Who said that?" His sudden impatience elicited yet another smile from his interrogator.

"It does not matter. It has all been straightened out. You seem no worse for your time alone, hmm?" When Nick didn't answer, the kommandant changed tone.

"I don't think there is anything you can tell me that I don't already know, do you? I know you and your comrades surrendered to the supreme forces of the Reich at a location near—what was the name—Mount Rotondo?"

"Nicholas Bremer," Nick responded automatically. "Private. United States Army. Serial—"

"Yes, yes, I know." Kommandant dismissed Nick's protocol and then changed the subject entirely.

"I understand that you are from German family?" Again, silence. "Oh, come now, *Herr Bremer*. We are just making conversation. There is so little of military interest we learn from enlisted men. You are here because now I have time to talk, and, at present, no officers to question."

Nick wondered about Lieutenant Severts but did not ask.

"So—from where in Germany did your family emigrate?"

"Nowhere in Germany," Nick answered. "At least—it wasn't Germany then."

"Ah. I see."

"My father left for America after completing his military service—before the world war," Nick offered, adding, "The last one, I mean. The one you lost."

The kommandant laughed aloud.

"I see we are in agreement," he said. "A second one we will not lose!"

"That's not what I meant."

At this the kommandant slapped his hand sharply on the desktop. He stopped smiling, and his eyes darkened with intensity as he leaned forward.

"You think you will take Italy from us, don't you? You think you can set your sights on Berlin? You are mistaken. The Allied powers will never reach Rome. They have no discipline, no leadership. While we sit here now, they are being turned back, retreating with their tails between their legs, like dogs. Your bombers and your—what do you call them—bazookas? They have little effect on Germany's superior military machine. Did you not know that we possess, even now, a weapon that is capable of defeating the empires of both Britain and the United States? Both countries in almost one sweep! It is only our sense of humanity that has kept us from using it—so far."

Nick did not know. He doubted the kommandant's fiery claims, but he could not know with any certainty that the Allied advances made since Sicily and Salerno had held. As for secret weapons . . .

"If there were a secret weapon," he challenged at last, "why would you tell me about it?"

Here the kommandant relaxed once more, leaned back in his chair, a satisfied smile crossing his face.

"Because," he said, "you are a lucky man, Bremer. For you, the war is over."

Just then, as if on cue, the door opened and the guard reentered.

"Ah, Reinart," the kommandant acknowledged him. "I have finished with this prisoner. Take him to the barracks. No—wait. Take him to the showers."

Nick rose, relieved that his interrogation had concluded so quickly, that it really hadn't been so bad. He felt even more relieved at the thought of a shower, wondering how long it had been. He hesitated at the door, then turned back to face the kommandant.

"Yes?" Kommandant asked.

"I just wonder—what day is this?"

"It is night," the kommandant answered. "The night of the fifteenth of November. Have you any more questions?"

Nick had many questions in mind, but he posed only one more.

"When—how do I notify my family that I am alive?"

"In time. You will fill out your capture card when you have been placed in a permanent facility. Until then, it is wise not to make any foolish moves. Prisoners in transit, you see—" He left the rest of his threat unspoken.

Nick followed the guard through the door. They had not taken more than a few steps outside before the kommandant's voice called out again. "Reinart! Next time, the showers first, before they come to me. I am so sick of the stink of these *Allies.*"

The door slammed.

November fifteenth. Let's see, Nick calculated as Reinart led him away from headquarters. *Captured on the tenth. Cut off since the eighth. Over a week in these clothes.* He looked forward to standing under a spray, even a trickle of hot water, scouring the grime of combat and captivity from his body.

"In here," Reinart ordered, opening the door in one end of the barracks. Nick stepped into a cold, dimly lit room that smelled of mildew and damp stone. Straight ahead, a brick-and-plank shelf held a few piles of folded towels. Against the wall at Nick's left were a urinal and a deep sink, each crusted with rusty stains; from the wall opposite these, two shower taps protruded. A bent metal shelf between the taps held two meager, misshapen blocks of lye soap.

"Five minutes," Reinart ordered. "No more."

For the first time in many days, Nick stripped out of his uniform.

"Give it to me," the guard demanded. Nick started to hand over the filthy bundle of clothes, then stopped and pulled it close against his chest. A few moments before he couldn't wait to remove the garments. Now, he didn't want to surrender them.

"No. I have to keep this. I have to have something to wear—"

"We provide you with clothing. Dry—maybe even clean, *ja?*" Reinart sneered.

"*Mach schnell.* You now have four minutes."

Nick hesitated, then reluctantly surrendered his uniform. The moment it left his hands, his breath quickened and he felt that too-familiar fear return. Without his uniform, he was essentially without his identity as an American soldier. He became a nobody, a nonentity caught somewhere between attackers, perhaps the most dangerous place to be.

POW in transit. He suddenly realized the implication of the kommandant's words: his position was another kind of no-man's land, unprotected even by the civilized decrees of the Geneva Convention. To his army, he was an enlisted man missing in action—lost, vanished, as if he might never have existed. To his enemy, he was a nonessential, an expendable piece of cargo.

"I must have my uniform back," his voice quavered, and he was almost surprised when Reinart replied, "All your personal items will be returned to you in time. Now, three minutes and a half."

The shower felt anything but soothing. Icy water trickled from the tap, enough just to dampen his body. The soap, harsh and smelling rancid, left him feeling coated in a different kind of grime. When Reinart suddenly shouted, "*Genug!* That is long enough!" Nick was actually relieved.

Reinart pulled two cloths from the shelf and tossed them to Nick, who caught them before they fell to the floor. The cloths were not towels as he had surmised, but articles of clothing: trousers and a loose pullover shirt, both items made of coarse burlap. Reinart kicked Nick's boots across the floor.

"We have not enough shoes," he claimed. "You may keep these—for now."

Nick picked up the boots, trying not to show his relief.

"*Danke,*" he murmured and pulled the cracked and muddied boots on to his bare feet.

The two men then left the washroom and walked silently around the outside of the building to a door in the opposite end. Reinart opened it and gestured with his head for Nick to enter. Lit by a low-wattage bulb, the long narrow room seemed mostly shadow. Triple tiers of bunks lined the walls, many appearing to be empty. In the center of the room, just below the low-hanging bulb, a small iron stove emanated a little warmth for the men who gathered around it. Nick recognized his companions among them. Their low murmurs stopped as Nick stepped further into the circle of dim light.

"Well, what do you know," a familiar, jovial voice murmured. "Bremer's back from the dead!"

"Hey, Red," Nick answered, feeling lighter than he had in many days. He clasped the man's hand in a firm shake. "When did you get out of solitary?"

"Aw, hell. I was only in a little while. Same as Spence there, and Jenkins. Guess they suddenly remembered they ain't s'posed to keep us alone in the dark. It's against the rules."

"Really," Nick speculated. "Somebody must've forgot that little rule for some of us." He tried not to look at Robert Ambrose, whose voice had joined the others in welcoming Nick into the circle. At that moment Chef hopped off his middle-tier bunk and flung an arm across Nick's shoulder, shaking him and almost knocking him over. Nick found Chef's enthusiasm to be somewhat embarrassing. He shrugged out of the kid's embrace.

"Boy am I glad to see you!" Chef crowed, undaunted. "We thought—well, we didn't know what to think."

"Yeah," this from Jenkins. "Them assholes don't like to tell us nothin' what's happening."

"We find out things, though," Ambrose added. "Especially from the newest arrivals." He gestured toward several bunks in the shadows. Nick nodded a silent greeting.

"Guys," Chef addressed the nearest strangers. "This is the soldier I told you about. He's the one can understand what—"

"It ain't hard work to understand these jokers," one of the newcomers dryly observed. "They sprecken-sie English better'n I do.

"Yeah, but—" Chef tried again, but Nick interrupted him.

"What about Lieutenant Severts? I don't see him."

Here the men looked at one another in silence a moment. Finally Jenkins said, "We ain't seen him either."

"He's been shipped out," Ambrose offered. "I keep telling these guys this. An officer does not stay with enlisted men. There are different procedures for officers 'cause chances are they know a lot more than we grunts do."

"But we don't know for sure," Chef argued. "We didn't know about Bremer here, did we?" Turning to Nick he confided, "We thought maybe you and the lieutenant was shot."

"*Chef* thought that. None of the rest of us did. Some of us were hoping maybe you and the lieutenant snuck away."

Nick sat down on the nearest vacant bottom bunk. Its flimsy, excelsior mattress rustled under his weight. Folded at the foot of the mattress was one coarse, thin, gray blanket. Nick unfolded it and pulled it around his shoulders. For the first time in many days, he began to feel a little warmth course through him.

"So," he mumbled, "this is home for us then?"

"Not quite," Foul-Mouth Matthews spat. "This is just purgatory! We ain't even seen hell yet!"

"We're not even in Germany, we don't think," Spence added. "This is our first transit camp. We'll be shipped out of here when they get enough guys to make a transport worth the time. We number forty-seven now."

"Forty-eight with Bremer!" Chef corrected. "If the Germans would just get a few more—"

"Right—forty-eight." Spencer scowled at the kid, then faced Nick again. "They won't transfer us out till they got at least ninety of us poor suckers."

"How do you know all this?" Nick wondered.

"I asked," Spence smiled.

Nick leaned back in his bunk, grateful for the little comfort it gave him. He sighed, then murmured, "This sure beats hard floors or muddy ground. All I need now is one good meal and—"

"Well, don't expect anything like that," another of the newcomers warned. "The food here is lousy, and there isn't much to go around."

"What about Red Cross?"

"Because we're still *in transit*," Matthews echoed the kommandant's tone, "we haven't filled out the Red Cross cards yet. So the Red Cross don't know where the hell we are—"

"Or even if we are," Ambrose interjected. "Ergo, no parcels, no extra food, no warm socks, nothing. So if you came out of the cooler hungry, Bremer, you're just going to stay hungry. Like all of us."

"But we got it better'n some," Red offered. "Wait till you see the ones on the other side of the compound. They're not Americans. We aren't sure what they are. We aren't allowed to try communicating with any of 'em but it's sure easy to see that the Germans don't like 'em at all. I never seen such ragged, hollow people before. Compared to them, we got it good."

"Gee," Jenkins sneered, "words to live by. No matter how hard it gits, there's always some sucker that gits it worse. I'd sure hate to be the poor bastard at the bottom of that line of *crap*!"

After this, the group had little more to say to each other. Some huddled around the stove awhile longer; others crept to their tiers, wrapping the blankets close around them. Chef sat down on one of the vacant bunks next to Nick, who chose to lie still, his eyes closed. Chef cleared his throat once, then whispered, "Nick? You awake?" Nick grumbled his response.

"It's not that I want bad things to happen to the good guys," Chef's voice trembled. "But I'm so gut scared we're not gonna make it outa here. If only there were more of us so we'd get shipped—I mean—I don't want—"

"I know, kid." Nick sighed. "Just 'cause you're the only one to *almost* say it doesn't mean the rest of us don't think it. But"—and here he turned away from Chef, tugging his blanket still closer around his shoulders, almost covering his head—"I don't want to think about anything right now, okay?"

"Okay, sure. I just wanted you to know that. Anyway, I'm real glad you're back. I'm real glad you're not dead—that *we're* not dead."

So am I, kid. Nick did not speak his thoughts. *If nothing else, at least we are still alive.*

V

Riding the Rails

"*Schnell, schnell!*" Reinart barked as he burst through the barracks door. Stamping his boot heels sharply against the floor, he hissed through a sinister smile, then shouted, "*Kriegsgefangener raus!* Prisoners rise—out! *Raus—Alles raus!*"

"Ah geez," one of the prisoners groaned, "it's the Snake again." Throughout the barracks, men stirred from various stages of sleep, jumped into their boots, and wrapped their thin blankets around themselves before scrambling toward the door. They elbowed each other, shoved, or pulled, each trying not to be the last one in line. Beside the door, Reinart smirked, gleefully tapping a frayed leather riding crop against the palm of his left hand.

"Damn it!" Foul-Mouth Matthews growled as Jenkins pressed past him, forcing him to the end. Matthews hustled past Reinart, trying to evade the inevitable penalty for being last. The hated German guard relished this part of his sport. With a triumphant laugh, he raised the crop and struck Matthews twice, once across his back and once against the backs of his thighs.

"Goddamned-son-of-a-bitch!" Matthews stumbled out into the prison yard, barely controlling his rage. "I'm gonna get that bastard. I'm gonna get my hands around his scrawny neck and choke that sneer right off his ugly face!"

"Sshhh, keep still." Nick helped Matthews back to his feet. "Sometimes it's best if you don't say anything. Reinart's just waiting for any reason to attack. The guy's itching to shoot somebody."

"And I'm itchin' to fight back," Matthews spat. "And so would you if you had any balls!"

"Shut up, you idiot." Nick answered under his breath. "Use your brains."

In the cold predawn darkness, the men lined up in groups of five for their daily count. Nick and Matthews stepped into the formation, joining Chef and two of the more recently interred prisoners. They stood in silence, shivering, while Nazis counted heads.

"Fünf! Zehn! . . . zwanzig . . . dreissig . . . sechzig . . ." and on until finally the call came, "Ein hundert vier und zwanzig! Alles gut!"

"One hundred twenty-four prisoners." Nick whispered to his companions as they broke formation. "So much for shipping us out when we reach ninety."

As on previous mornings, after the head count, the prisoners milled only briefly before heading back to the barracks. In a way, it surprised Nick how quickly he and all the other men adapted to the routine of captivity. Mornings held the obligatory roll call, followed by the day's first meal. Typically, this consisted of a slab of dry black bread and the bitter ersatz brew the Germans dared to call coffee. Insipid as this meal was, the men looked forward to it, for it would be all they'd get until evening.

The remaining hours of the day seemed to drag by. Bored by inactivity, the men spent the time catching up on any war news from new inmates, or telling jokes or stories of home. The second roll call of the day came after an evening meal of watery cabbage or turnip soup and yet another crust of bread. Then when all the prisoners were accounted for, they remained in formation out in the cold while the kommandant treated them to a daily update of Allied battle losses.

This morning, however, before the prisoners had moved very far, a single shot rang out.

"Halt!" A voice—not Reinart's—brayed, followed at once by another burst of rifle fire. All around, men dove to the ground, folding their bodies into the smallest targets possible.

"Oh geez, oh geez," Chef whimpered next to Nick. "I don't wanna die!"

When no further shots rang out, Nick dared to raise his head, dreading what he might see. He wondered who might have been foolish enough to try to escape, especially from such an open and closely watched area. Around him, the other prisoners began to pick themselves up, murmuring.

"What in the heck?"

"Who'd they get?"

"Next time you will pay attention, ja?" This came from the Snake, Reinart. "You have not been dismissed. Today you stand where you are until ordered otherwise!" He snapped orders to the battery of guards, who moved in closer with weapons ready. Reinart turned and marched to the kommandant's headquarters. Just before entering, he faced the prisoners in the compound.

"Anyone who takes one step," he bellowed, "will be shot!"

For several minutes the men stood silent and motionless. When Reinart didn't immediately return, they began to shift slightly, murmuring among themselves.

"Why are they doing this? What's going on?"

"Hey, Bremer!" An intense whisper came from Ambrose, who stood only two rows behind Nick. "What did that Nazi pig tell those guards?"

"Nothing you don't already know," Nick answered. "He told them to shoot anybody who moves."

"What for?" Chef's voice trembled. "What did we do? I mean, we didn't do nothin'!"

Just then the kommandant himself emerged. He scrutinized the group before him for several minutes before stepping toward them. From somewhere outside the camp, a low rumbling sound captured his attention briefly, and he gestured to one company of guards. They headed for the gated entrance.

The rumbling soon grew to a roar; all the men turned to watch a convoy of covered trucks approach the compound.

"Must be another bunch of prisoners," Ambrose guessed. "Cripes! I thought Italy already surrendered. How come we're still—?" His voice dropped as Jenkins shushed him.

"Them trucks is empty." Jenkins spat into the dirt. "Boys, I think our bus is in."

Once inside the compound, the trucks stopped, their engines idling. Two soldiers emerged from each cab, and two more jumped from the back of each truck. These soldiers surrounded the prisoners, shouting and poking at them with bayonets.

"Knock it off, you Nazi bastard!"

"What the hell—?"

Confusion followed as the prisoners moved first one way, then another to dodge their tormentors. Some of the men tripped over others, sprawling on the ground only to be kicked, then yanked to their feet.

"Just move toward the trucks," someone finally shouted, and as they did so, the chaos settled. In front of headquarters, the kommandant stood, hands on hips, and shook his head. He signaled to the grinning Reinart, who then blew a shrill whistle. German soldiers and Allied prisoners stopped their commotion.

"Why do you make everything so difficult?" Kommandant interrogated. "Have you forgotten how to maintain order, hmmm?" Again he gestured to the guards, then spun on his heels and returned to headquarters, slamming the door behind him. Reinart immediately took charge, ordering the prisoners into the backs of the trucks. This time the men climbed aboard without incident, one after another until the driver called enough. Reinart then motioned two guards into the back of each truck.

Among the first to climb into the third truck, Nick leaned into a corner, then lowered himself to sit, pulling his legs in close to allow more room for the other men. In the dark, confined space, the air reeked of diesel fumes. Nick edged the German-issue blanket across his nose, hoping it might filter the smell. He watched as more men filed in. Surprisingly, Chef was not among them. For the first time since his temporary solitary confinement, Nick was without his shadow. With that realization came a brief sense of freedom, but that did little to ease the blunt throbbing that started at the base of his skull. Lowering his head to his knees, Nick closed his eyes and swallowed.

You can't be sick, he told himself, groaning. *Not here. Not now. Don't be sick.*

"You sick?" A voice whispered. Nick recognized the voice of one of the last prisoners to arrive at the compound, a young chaplain. After swallowing a few more times, Nick looked up. The chaplain's smile made his already boyish face look even younger, in spite of the fact that he was completely bald.

"I'm okay," Nick finally reported. "Guess I just have to get used to the fumes."

"Maybe we won't have to ride for very long."

"Maybe." Nick didn't share the chaplain's optimism. It seemed very likely that they were on their way to their permanent internment, somewhere inside Germany and far from the battlefronts.

"Anyway," the chaplain assured, "if you're feeling sick, you won't miss the rations we're apparently not getting this morning."

Almost immediately, one of the guards assigned to ride with the prisoners hopped aboard, carrying a bundle wrapped in burlap. While the truck idled, he unfolded the burlap to reveal several loaves of the now-familiar black bread. Scanning the band of prisoners, he selected a few of the loaves and tossed them carelessly into the group.

"One loaf—five men," he explained. "And do not be greedy. It is all you will have for some time."

A few grumbles indicated the prisoners' dissatisfaction with the apportionment. A brief argument rose about who should be in charge of the loaves, and which five men belonged to what group, but it was quickly settled when they discovered that the guard had miscalculated. They had enough bread so that only four men had to share a loaf.

"Well, what do you know?" Red crowed. "Hey, Klaus! I guess you can't count, eh? It seems—"

"Shut up, you moron!" Another warned. "Just divvy it up before this guy takes it back."

"Sorry."

Further discussion ended when the guards unrolled a tarp, covering the opening at the back of the truck. Now in darkness, the men rode in silence. They could only guess at the direction they headed, knowing uphill and down by the forward and backward motions of their bodies. While they rode, a few men nibbled at their bread ration. Like most, however, Nick tucked his portion inside his shirt. That way, if he happened to fall asleep, no one could take the bread without his knowing it.

In his mind, Nick tried to retrace the roads they had marched to arrive at the transit camp. The first sharp curve he remembered from that earlier trek, but after several more swerves that caused the men to sway to the left or to the right, he couldn't be certain that they were headed back to the railroad.

Because they could not see outside the truck, the prisoners had no view of the countryside they passed through; nor could they determine by changing daylight the passage of time. After what seemed a long time riding, one of the prisoners nudged Nick and whispered, "Hey, think they allowed us anything to drink? I'm so thirsty I feel like I've been suckin' the Sahara."

Thirst bothered Nick too, as it must have tormented all the men. Otherwise they would have devoured their first portions of bread by now.

"*Entshuldigen Sie mir,*" he attempted to get the guard's attention. "Excuse me. *Haben Sie Wasser mit? Wir haben Durst.*"

One of the guards turned to the other and raised his eyebrows. The second guard only shrugged, then shook his head.

"*Später*," he announced; then Nick clarified for all the men, "Later we'll get what we need. When we reach the station."

"Great," Red grumbled. "Now how are we going to enjoy this delicious hard, dry bread?"

Again time passed without conversation, as the men wrapped themselves in their own thoughts. After what might have been one hour, or even as many as three, the truck began to slow down, then eased to a stop, though the engine still idled. One of the guards pulled the tarp curtain aside a bit, then nodded to his partner. "*Sie kommen.*"

Before he closed it again, Robert Ambrose, who crouched close to the tailgate, caught sight of another convoy of trucks trailing down a steep, rough road about a quarter of a mile away.

"Whew," he whistled low. "More POWs is my guess. I gotta wonder if—"

"Don't wonder," another shushed him. "This is a world war. There's lots of men fighting it. We're just a few."

"We few," came a third voice, "we lucky few—"

"Shut up, Bandy. Keep your quotin' to yourself!"

Nick had no idea what Bandershoot might have been starting to quote, but based on Bandy's annoying habit, he had to assume it was something from Shakespeare. He'd never read anything by that author and wasn't sure that he ever would. If he remained in Bandershoot's company for a great length of time, he wouldn't have to.

In a few minutes, the sound of truck engines increased as the second convoy caught up with the first. Once more, the vehicle lurched forward, and transport continued. This time, Nick guessed, it was less than an hour before the vehicle stopped completely, its engine falling silent. The sudden stop in vibration created an odd sensation in Nick's body, as if his skin had stretched tight, creating an unreachable itch. He clenched and opened his hands, then shook them and moved his shoulders, arms and legs as well as he could in the confinement. Others around him did the same.

The guards pulled the tarp aside and hopped off the truck. Lowering the gate, one gestured to the men.

"Now you will step out. Line up with the others."

Some groaning accompanied the group's exodus as the men stretched their stiffened limbs. Almost the last to emerge, Nick squinted in the harsh sunlight and filled his lungs with the considerably fresher air. Around him, other prisoners emerged from the trucks. Ordered or prodded by their German guards, the captives formed several lines heading toward a railway siding just down the slope from where they stood. Nick stepped into a queue that slowly progressed toward the train of livestock cars. In a few minutes, he felt someone nudge him from behind. Turning, he looked into Chef's relieved face.

"I'm gonna stick with you," the young prisoner announced, "okay?"

"Fine," Nick answered. "Whatever you want."

When the men reached the tracks, just before each one hoisted himself aboard, he was given a drink of water from a barrel that stood near the tracks. A dour-faced woman in uniform supervised the rationing. As each man thanked her for the drink, she attempted a smile and said something sweetly in response.

When Nick's turn came, he drank deeply, relishing every drop of the cold, fresh water. Handing the mug back to the woman, he nodded his greeting and added, "*Vielen dank*. Many thanks." She arched one eyebrow in a comical manner and repeated the sweet-toned line she'd spoken to all the other prisoners.

In response, Nick tensed and stepped back, coming down hard on Chef's toes. "Ow!"

"Sorry. It's just—sorry." Nick looked back at the woman who continued to smile. Without further word, he climbed aboard the railcar, where the men jostled each other to claim their own space while making room for others.

"She seemed nice," Chef chatted when he rejoined Nick a few minutes later. "What did she say?"

"Does it matter?" Nick didn't feel like translating the woman's words. Besides, they might not be true, just a little harmless defensiveness for the *Vaterland*. Still, the words seemed so much more venomous spoken as they had been in such a sweet tone: *I spit on American prisoners—and in their drinks!*

Soldiers continued to herd prisoners into the railroad cars, halting the process only when they felt they couldn't squeeze another body in. The men arranged themselves as well as they could, claiming cramped seating space on the cold, metal floor, where a thin layer of straw provided little insulation. Those who lined the outer area of the car, leaning their backs against the slatted walls, felt the cutting November temperatures even before the train started to move. Though he might have been more comfortable with a wall to lean against, Nick felt grateful for the body heat generated in the closer interior of the car.

It surprised no one that the German guards did not ride with their captives in the open cattle cars. After they slammed the doors, barred, and padlocked them, they boarded one of the closed cars, either right behind the locomotive or at the very end of the train. In a few minutes, the train moved forward.

Nick took out his portion of bread and bit into it. What a difference it would make if only he had a dab of jelly to spread on it. He closed his eyes as he chewed, trying to imagine the flavor of his mother's homemade chokecherry jelly or strawberry preserves.

"Mmmmm," he sighed. Nearby, the chaplain echoed him.

"I was thinking croissant," he murmured.

"I don't even know what that is," Nick confessed. "But it sounds a lot better than what we have here." He offered his hand and continued, "We haven't met. I'm Nick Bremer."

"Cy Popp," the chaplain appeared eager to talk. "Of course, if I were home in a parish, I'd be known as Father Popp, but that sounds kind of silly, doesn't it?"

"You're a priest?"

"Yes. Not Catholic, though. Episcopalian."

Some of the other men took an interest in the conversation.

"You were in a combat unit?"

"Yes, I was. Where would I be more needed?" Cy smiled. "At least that's what I told my bishop—over and over, until I finally drove him past his patience and he gave me permission to enlist."

"I'll bet you're sorry now, aren't you?"

"Well," the priest hesitated, "of course I'm not especially happy about the situation right now. On the other hand, I'm alive, I'm not wounded, and so far, it's been several days since anyone has fired a gun at me—well, *directly* at me."

"Wait a minute," Ambrose observed, "you're a chaplain? That means you're an officer. What are you doing with us enlisted men? Why aren't you on your way to an officers' prison camp?"

"I honestly don't know how that came about," Cy answered, "but I can say that I'm glad of it. Lucky again."

"No offense, Padre," a reedy voice interjected. "But some of us counted our blessings a long time ago. There weren't very many then, and it seems like there's even fewer now. So don't bother with that 'we're lucky' stuff."

Cy smiled but said no more. Conversation stopped as the train picked up speed, whipping the icy wind through the cars. The men shivered and huddled close. With little else to do, some of them closed their eyes and tried to lose themselves in sleep. The train moved on, chuffing hard up steep grades in the rugged country, seeming to speed up only a little more going down the slopes.

After several hours, the train stopped, and guards herded the men into a nearby barn. There, several fires contained in rusted barrels offered a little warmth, and the prisoners gratefully gathered close to the flames to enjoy the meager provisions given them: a tasteless, thin gruel and weak tea. Then, the men slept until dawn.

On the next leg of their journey, the prisoners rode in the backs of trucks; some miles later, they disembarked the trucks and marched for several miles until they came to yet another rail line, where they boarded yet another familiar-looking train.

"Oh, thank God!" Red moaned, collapsing on the floor. "I never thought I'd be so glad to see a cattle car. I don't think I can take another step."

Around him, others echoed similar sentiments. Nick, followed as usual by Chef, found himself once again near the middle of the car. He and the prisoners closest to him, arranged themselves in such a way, that they could lean against each other's backs, providing some comfort to their aching bones. Nick flexed his toes inside his boots, wishing more than anything to soak his sore feet in warm water and then to towel them off properly. The constant dampness, he knew, was dangerous; he wanted to avoid even a mild case of trench foot.

"Any idea where we are?" someone asked.

"Huh-uh." Nick felt too tired even to guess. He didn't feel like talking at all, but the man leaning against him apparently did. "Maybe Austria? Could we be in Austria?" When Nick didn't respond, the prisoner continued, "My wife's parents came from Austria. They were just kids when their parents settled in Indiana. Must've had other family there waiting. Anyway, my father-in-law likes to talk about what a beautiful country Austria is. I bet he never got a view of it from a livestock train." Many minutes passed before he talked again, this time, almost to himself. "God, I miss my wife."

Wife. Nick played the word over in his mind, finding it to his liking. He could have had a wife to miss. Back in Ohio, Helen had wanted to get married—almost did the proposing herself just before Nick enlisted. But he'd hedged, claiming that neither of them should have to be put in a position of waiting, wondering, worrying. He had thought there'd be time after the war ended for them to make a commitment. He remembered Helen's response.

"If you don't want to make a commitment now," she'd announced, "don't expect me to wait for you. I'm not a nun. Don't expect me to be."

"I don't," Nick had answered. "But we have no way of knowing what might happen—how long, or even if—"

"People who need absolute assurance of the future will never decide on anything!" Helen admonished. "But I guess you really have decided, haven't you? You've decided not to marry me."

"Only for the time being," he'd reasoned. "Later—"

"There is no later. There is only now. If not now, then never. God what a disheartening word."

They had ultimately resolved their argument, in a way. Helen agreed to think of him and worry about him, and drop a line now and then. Nick agreed that he would not expect her to wait. Then he'd left Ohio to visit the folks in North Dakota. After that came Basic, then transport overseas, battle, capture, and now internment. All in all it had been about nine months since he'd last seen Helen. He kept his part of the bargain, though it wasn't easy; he could only assume that she kept most of hers. There had been no letters.

Hours and miles rolled past. For a short time during the height of day, bright sunlight warmed the air enough so that the prisoners no longer shivered. Twice before dark, the train pulled on to a siding and waited. During these pauses, everyone disembarked, but they received no rations. By now, of course, every crumb of the bread loaves distributed the day before had been eaten. As twilight settled, the captives boarded the train one more time, encouraged only slightly by overheard remarks of "soon there."

Later, Nick had no idea how long he'd slept. A sudden screech and whoosh of steam startled him awake. The train slowed and ultimately came to a stop. Soon came shouts, and the sound of running footsteps.

"What is it?" Nick asked, and next to him, Chef shrugged.

"Hey, Bremer," someone called. "Squirm your way over here, will ya? We wanna know what's going on."

Nick stood up, nudging and jostling his way around the men until he reached the gate of the railcar. Outside, several soldiers hurried past them, one of them laughing. Nick pressed his ear close to the slats of the car and listened. He caught only fragments of conversation as more soldiers dashed by.

"Well? What's going on?"

"I don't quite—" Nick listened again. "The train hit something. I think. I don't know what it is." He strained to hear the conversation outside the car over the questions from the men inside.

"Ask 'em, why don't you?" Someone insisted.

Nick turned to the man who had spoken close into his left ear. Eyes flashing, he snapped, "Why don't you ask! I don't have any pull with these guys. Just wait and see. I'm pretty sure we'll find out soon enough."

They waited, those nearest the side of the cars watching whatever activity unfolded. Several soldiers ran off, disappearing into the dark. When they returned, they dropped bundles of something onto the ground.

"Wood," a voice called out from the railcar next to the one Nick rode in. "They're collecting firewood."

"Maybe we're stopping here for the night." A flurry of activity followed. A small flame began to lick at the pile of wood; soon it grew into several flames, and finally into a blaze that lit up the night. Soldiers just outside the circle of light appeared as macabre shadows, just a degree darker than the darkness around them. Some of them appeared to be carrying something. Several others simply stood around the fire, laughing and shouting orders.

"I don't like this," Bandershoot murmured. "We're too far away from anything. I got a feeling that something real bad is—oh man, we're in for it." His suspicion soon spread among the men, and they grew still with dread. With the quiet behind him, Nick found it easier to hear the discussion taking place beside the track.

"Oh man," Nick said, understanding at last. "Lucky bastards."

"What?"

"Either this train hit a cow, or an earlier one did," he reported. "These guys are having themselves a barbecue."

"Yuck," Chef observed. "That can't be very—"

"Shaddup!"

All the prisoners fell silent as they watched the performance just outside. Through the skinning of the animal, the discarding of parts too severely damaged, the rigging over the fire, they remained still, dreaming of succulent steaks or ribs or roasts. Later, when the scent of roasting beef reached them, they began to moan and sigh.

"This is hell," one griped. "It's so close I can almost taste it!"

"And so far away, you never will."

"I'd damn near sell my soul for just one bite."

They had no choice later but to watch the Germans enjoy their feast. Several times, the men inhaled deeply and desperately, almost as if they might draw shards of the precious meat through the air and into their mouths and bellies.

"Even a bone," Chef almost pleaded, his original doubts now put aside. "I'd be real satisfied just to gnaw on a bone."

German soldiers continued to slice pieces of beef from the smoking carcass. They chewed and swallowed, emitting appreciative sighs and belches. Every now and then, bits of fat dropped into the flames. The crackling and sizzling added to the torment of the famished prisoners.

After sating themselves, many of the guards gathered in small groups around the fire, engaging in casual conversation as if they had just stepped away from their own dining tables. Soon one of them began to sing. One by one, others joined in until a full men's chorus serenaded the poor prisoners in their railcar cages.

Had he not been so very hungry, Nick might have enjoyed the impromptu concert. He couldn't help but admire the precise harmony and soulful feeling the soldiers gave to the lyrics, but the delightful sounds came in too great a contrast to the prisoners' desperate hunger. He didn't blame his companions at all when they muttered, grumbled, and cursed. Then the German chorus intoned a new melody, one that almost every Allied prisoner also recognized, though the words were strange to most of them.

Vor der Kaserne vor dem grossen Tor
Stand eine Laterne, und steht noch davor
So woll'n wir uns da wieder seh'n . . .

As the chorus continued, a bellow rose from the railcar next to Nick's.

"Goddamn you, boshe bastards!" Foul-Mouth Matthews had evidently reached the end of his patience. "That's *our* song!" The singing trailed off, and an ominous silence followed. One guard made a low comment to his comrades, causing them all to erupt in laughter.

"*Wollen sie essen?*" He brayed before his men. "*Dann müssen sie singen!*" The soldiers stepped away from the now-dwindling fire and formed a crooked line in front of the railcars. Their taunting became unintelligible until one officer ordered silence.

"*Wir müssen ein Lied hören!*" he shouted at the prisoners.

"What's he saying?" Chef asked, and the men in Nick's car nudged in closer, almost crushing him against the wall.

"They want to hear a song," he interpreted.

"No way! We're already in a cage! Now they want to make monkeys of us?"

"For our supper!" Nick added louder. "They want us to sing for our supper."

For several minutes, pride warred with hunger. When it seemed the former would win, one of the guards picked up a remnant of beef and held it out in front of him. Still steaming, its smoky, meaty aroma was intoxicating.

"Mmmmm," someone breathed, and soon that murmur became a sustained note, picked up by others. "Hmmmmm." It didn't take long before one uncertain tenor voice began to sing. Nick turned and, in the dim glow from the fire, recognized Cy Popp. Others turned to face the chaplain. Cy grinned and patted his belly, continuing to sing with a less tentative sound. A few others joined him, and before long, the prisoners united in song. Those who didn't know the words hummed along.

> *Underneath the lamplight by the barrack gate,*
> *Darling I remember the way you used to wait,*
> *'Twas there that you whispered tenderly,*
> *That you loved me, You'd always be,*
> *My Lili of the lamplight, my own Lili Marlene.*

After one verse, the prisoners stopped singing. The German officer who had ordered the music shook his head, then gestured to three guards. They strode back toward the fire, returning after a time with fragments of beef. While they handed this through the slats of one railcar, the officer ordered the prisoners to sing again.

"*Noch einmal,*" he called, "Again!" Lifting his arms, he directed his soldiers to join in as well. While the guards distributed portions of the carcass to every car, German lyrics blended with English in the popular song. Voices grew lustier with every line as each chorus tried to outdo the other.

> *. . . So woll'n wir uns da wieder seh'n . . .*
> *. . . That you loved me, You'd always be . . .*
> *. . . Wie einst Lili Marlene . . .*
> *. . . My own Lili Marlene.*

Inside their cages, the prisoners grabbed whatever sliver of meat they could, intent that every man would receive some. For the most part, they weren't fussy. Some gnawed on bones while others chewed gristle; fatty pieces or bloody, rare slices, or even crusty, charred portions made them smack their lips as they relished every morsel. Afterward, the men licked the grease from their fingers.

Later, as the train continued on its way into Germany, some of the prisoners tried to sleep as they huddled against the cold. Nick, wedged close between Chef and the Rev, as he now called Cy, pondered that moment of camaraderie the prisoners had shared with their captors. It had grown out of hunger and a song, and had ended abruptly when both were done. In returning to their assigned posts, the guards had once more become cold, sarcastic, and belligerent; likewise, the prisoners resumed their bitterness, resenting their inability to change their course.

Maybe, Nick wondered, *it will be less exhausting if we just hate each other. At least then we know where we stand at all times.*

Beside him, the Rev stirred in his sleep, then awoke with a start. He looked around, as if uncertain where he was, and sighed.

"I dreamt I was at home, carving a goose."

"Tough to wake up," Nick murmured.

"Hmm. Well. That was a pretty welcome feed we had back there, wasn't it?"

"Yeah. Pretty welcome."

"And fitting, don't you think? Considering what day this is."

Nick frowned. What day? He had no idea what day it was; most of the days had become so much like the ones before and carried no identifying characteristics.

"I don't know," Nick answered. "What is it? Sunday?"

"Maybe it's nothing special here," the Rev replied, "but if we were home right now, we'd be looking forward to our Thanksgiving dinner."

Nick didn't respond at first. *Thanksgiving,* he mused, *a day to give thanks for all our blessings.* He could think of only two.

"Thank God we've made it—so far," he finally said. The Rev smiled and, as if reading Nick's mind, added, "And thank God for dead meat!"

VI

Across the Wire

" *Willkommen!*" A paunchy officer addressed the newly arrived prisoners of war, his voice amplified through a megaphone. "Welcome to the stalag, now your home!"

The formation of new, disheveled GIs in the stalag numbered more than two hundred. Standing at the end of one of the rows, Nick couldn't help but notice the large contingent of guards at the perimeter. Just as threatening as their drawn weapons were the several dogs that strained at leashes, snapping and snarling. Nick recognized some of the dogs as German shepherds. He couldn't identify the other breed, but their stiff, pointed ears and bared teeth left little doubt that these animals had been trained not only to guard, but also to kill.

"Soon will you all be processed," the kommandant spoke in clipped English. "But first—" He snapped his fingers, and a non-com hurriedly unrolled a printed poster and held it up high. Too far away to read it, Nick assumed that it contained much of the message the kommandant continued to deliver.

"As prisoners of war, you should know that escape from the stalag is not a sport! Always *das Vaterland* has observed the Hague Convention and punished recaptured prisoners *mit* minor discipline. It has been our way. *Aber* England"—here his voice grew more passionate—"opened gangster war *mit* terror commandos and sabotage *hier in Deutschland!* Now it has become necessary that we have forbidden zones, shall we say, 'death zones?' in which all unauthorized personnel will be shot on sight! Soon you will recognize these zones. Only inside camp will you remain safe!"

Kommandant handed the megaphone to the soldier at his right, then waved his order for the guards to proceed with formalities. Shouting and shoving, soldiers managed to herd prisoners away from the kommandant's headquarters toward a long, low building, where they once again formed lines.

Few prisoners spoke as they shuffled toward the building. Like many of the others, Nick observed the camp where they would very likely remain for the duration of the war. The stalag covered many acres and looked to be divided into at least two compounds separated by barbed wire. On each side of the wire barrier stood several long brick barracks. Other POWs leaned in barracks doors or drifted just outside the buildings to watch the procession of new inmates.

"It's like a whole city," someone murmured.

Nick studied some of the prisoners wandering in the compound across the barrier. *My God*, he thought, *will we look like that?* Men stared back, their faces so gaunt, it seemed their eyes had sunk into their heads. Several layers of tattered clothes or blankets hung on their thin bodies. He knew that he and the men with him had lost weight in the weeks since capture, had become grizzled and unkempt, but they didn't appear nearly as haggard as the prisoners across the wire.

"Move it," the man behind Nick hissed, nudging him. Nick faced forward once more and closed the gap in line. *One minute at a time*, he cautioned himself and did not look again toward the other compound.

Not until he'd reached the building's doorway did Nick realize just how cold he'd become standing in line. Waves of warm air from a coal stove inside thawed his numb body just enough to make him feel again, and he shivered uncontrollably. Four uniformed Germans sat at a long table at the far end of the large room. Behind them, four more soldiers stood, collecting pieces of paper after each prisoner's interview and handing parcels to the POWs at the head of each line. Every five to ten minutes, Nick moved forward a step. The acrid scent of coal smoke grew sharper, throwing him into recollection of another cold day and a different coal fire.

That morning in March when he was nine years old, he'd played along the creek near the house, a place he'd been warned to stay away from, especially during high-water season. The night before had been cold, and a thin sheet of ice covered the surface of the water, tempting Nick to shatter it. After breaking the ice in several spots, he'd tried tossing a stone too large and lost his footing. Tumbling down the embankment, he'd splashed into the frigid creek. He had gasped for air as he struggled to find footing and pull himself out of the water. It had taken all his strength, but he'd finally made it to the top just in time to see his father scowling down at him.

"You're not drowned then?" Pa had asked, his voice almost as cold as Nick's body.

"N-no, s-sir."

"Your ma told you not to play by the creek?"

"I g-guess s-so."

"Go on then! Get inside and out of those wet clothes before you freeze to death!" Pa had shouted, then added under his breath, "No point whupping you till you're warmed up enough to feel it!"

Later, huddled in a quilt in front of the coal stove, Nick sipped the chamomile tea Ma had brewed for him. He could hardly control the shivering but felt almost grateful for the chill. He hoped he'd never be warm enough for Pa's whupping.

Not until he stood only three men from the front of the line did Nick begin to feel some warmth. He shook his head, dismissing the memory of an easier time, and concentrated on the business unfolding at the table. The soldier seated behind the table didn't even look up as he asked his questions.

"Name and number?"

"Jon—Jonathan Steiner," the prisoner at the head of the line answered, then rattled his serial number.

"Nationality?"

"American."

Questions and answers continued in slow monotone, until the German asked, "Religion?"

The prisoner hesitated, turned to look behind him, and then replied. "Jewish."

Still the German soldier didn't look up. Writing on the capture card, he announced, "*Evangelisch.*"

"No, I'm not Christian," Steiner corrected, "I said—"

"I know what you said. We all know that American Jews are not fighting on the front. They are safe at home in the US of A, making money. Or running your government, *nicht wahr?*"

"That's not true!"

"I say it again: Protestant." This time the soldier did look up at the prisoner before him and, lowering his voice, warned, "Don't be a fool. Next." Thus dismissed, the man called Steiner stepped to the side and the line moved forward once more.

When Nick's turn came, he provided the information for his capture card, then grasped the brown cardboard suitcase handed to him, and followed those ahead of him out a side door. A small group of GIs stood apart from the crowd. One of them spotted Nick, lifted his hand, and waved him over. Nick joined Chef, Cy, and several others he'd come to know in the past few weeks: Bandershoot, John Drummond, Red, Johnny Ames, and an unusually quiet Foul-Mouth Matthews. They waited awhile longer, hoping to recognize more of their original group, until one of the soldiers leading a dog shouted at them to move on toward the barracks.

Nick estimated the barracks' size at roughly sixty yards long and fifteen yards wide. A central washroom divided the interior. On either side of the washroom, triple-tiered bunks lined the walls. Nick's group was ushered to the rear unit, where two coal stoves furnished a little heat. A square, crooked table surrounded by four wooden chairs stood in the center aisle at one end of the barracks; another with only three chairs stood next to one of the stoves at the other end. On the narrow wall at the rear of the barracks was a urinal, with a tattered sign posted near it: *Night Use Only.*

Nick followed the others to locate and claim a bunk. He chose a lower bunk; Chef claimed the one above him, while a soldier neither of them yet knew, hoisted himself to the top and lay down with one arm covering his eyes. The Rev landed a lower bunk across the aisle from Nick. Next to Cy, John and Johnny dropped their parcels on the flimsy mattresses. On each bunk lay one worn wool blanket.

"Might as well see what we got here," Matthews grumbled as he tore open his parcel. The others followed suit, each finding a pair of heavy socks, two handkerchiefs, soap, comb, razor, and cigarettes. Without a word, the men lifted their loot to examine each item. Nick squeezed the pair of coarse, hand-knit socks in his hand. Several threads on one of the heels had broken, but that didn't bother Nick. He chuckled, "Wow. I feel like I just got the best present in the world!"

"And it ain't even Christmas," Matthews quipped, eyeing his razor as he rubbed his stubbly beard. "Hot damn! I got something to look forward to: a hot shower, a shave, dry socks, and"—here he glanced at the packet of European cigarettes—"a bad smoke!"

"No hot shower," an unfamiliar voice broke through. The newcomers turned to the approaching veteran prisoner, whose smile flashed gold. His oily dirt-blond hair had grown into long spikes that stood straight up from his head. He laughed aloud.

"Yeah, I know. I'm a sight for sore eyes. My name's Greg. The fellas call me Grease." He held out his hand in greeting, adding, "Can't imagine why. Anyway, you should know—hot showers only once a week, and it ain't our turn today."

By now others had gathered around the group of new prisoners. Some introduced themselves, while others leaned against the bunk posts, watching and listening. After the obligatory greetings, they inquired about the latest war news.

"Where d'yall get captured?"

"You think we might be getting any closer to victory?"

"What's happening on the home front?"

For a long time, the men discussed the war, hungry for any indication of Allied advances. After the war updates, they reminisced about home, wives, and girlfriends. Some grumbled while reporting details of their capture and subsequent treatment, while others gloated about their strength and survival. Veteran POWs offered American cigarettes to the newcomers, and before long, a comforting haze of smoke surrounded them. Nick lay back on his bunk, listening and watching, and for the first time in many days, he felt some of the tension leave his body. He didn't even know he'd begun to doze off until he was startled awake by a bang and clatter near the barracks entrance. Three German soldiers entered and hoisted a tub onto one of the tables. It smelled all too familiar.

"Oh boy," someone gibed, "it's time for chow." Then, nudging Nick, the POW directed in mocking rhyme, "Grab your goods and get some foods!"

"My goods?" Nick wondered.

"Yeah, you know—something to hold the soup *du jour*. Over there."

Following his comrade's direction, Nick turned his glance toward the smaller coal stove. There, a roughly made wooden crate held a rather limited variety of small containers, mostly dented mugs and flattened food tins.

"Use one of those till you get something of your own," the soldier pulled an odd-shaped bowl from a box beneath his bunk. "I made this here one myself. Used to be a gourd. Must've got thrown in with a bunch of spoiled squashes brought in a few months back."

Newcomers grabbed containers from the crate. Nick pulled out an oblong tin, recognizing it immediately.

"Spam?" he pined. "Man, could I use a bite of that!"

"God bless the International Red Cross," someone answered, adding, "We're all supposed to get one food package per week, but it's more like every ten days or so. Unfortunately, the latest allotment has already been distributed. You guys probably won't get your first Red Cross package until next time."

"Ah shit," Matthews grumbled next to Nick. "I was already tastin' it."

Disappointed, Nick stepped into the line that formed near the table. Within a few minutes, he received his portion of the detestable concoction and a chunk of *sauerbrot*. In spite of the unpleasant taste, Nick ate greedily. Several of the prisoners who had been in camp awhile offered to share some of their hoarded Red Cross goods. For the first time in weeks, Nick drank his bitter coffee sweetened, topped off his meal with a palmful of raisins, and temporarily curbed his persistent hunger with a stick of chewing gum.

Much later, when the men had bunked down for the night, Nick lay with his hands behind his head, listening to the softened sounds in the barracks. A few men spoke in low tones; across the aisle, Cy Popp whispered a prayer, and from the bunk just above Nick, sniffles conveyed Chef's yearning for freedom or home. Long, plaintive notes from a harmonica sounded from somewhere, wrapping the night with a sense of nostalgia. Nick sighed. No longer a prisoner in transit, he felt a kind of security in his new surroundings. It allowed him a night of unbroken sleep.

The days that followed established the prisoners' routine: mornings began with the obligatory prisoner count, during which the men sometimes stood for an hour or more if the count was inaccurate. After the second day in the stalag, Nick realized that many of the POWs intentionally fouled up the count, sometimes by ducking low in formation so they couldn't be seen, other times by sneaking into another line to be counted twice. Roll call, or *appell*, as the Germans called it, was followed by an insubstantial breakfast, followed in turn by long hours of boredom. The men filled those hours as best they could. Baseball, football, or group calisthenics took place in the compound; some stayed in the barracks to play cards or read, while others practiced on small musical instruments that had been provided by Red Cross and YMCA organizations. In one of the barracks, several former teachers and businessmen invited soldiers to join them for informal lectures on history, economics, and literature.

Nick and several of his nearest bunkmates fell into the pattern of walking perimeter every afternoon. Keeping several feet away from the proscribed free-fire areas or "death zones," they explored the stalag, their interest always drawn to the compound on the other side of the wire. Several times they made eye contact with prisoners there, and nodded a greeting, but received only cold stares in return.

"Who are they?" Cy Popp wondered. "And why are they so much worse off than the rest of us?"

"Those guys are Russians," Grease answered. "Slavs, too, maybe. The Germans hate them."

Again Nick remembered his father's words about "the Rooskies." What was it about Russians, he wondered, that made people, especially German people, mistrust and despise them? His glance fell upon one Russian prisoner in particular, a very slight, unbearded young man huddled against the leeward side of one of the buildings. Cy apparently noticed him at almost the same time.

"My Lord," he exclaimed. "Look at him. He can't be more than—what? Fifteen or sixteen? They're sending *children* into battle?"

"He's almost nothing but skin and bones," Nick observed "Poor kid."

Just then, the object of their conversation looked up and met their glances. He stared back for just a moment before rising; a half-smile appeared on his face, and he raised his left hand in a hesitant wave.

"America," he called to them, then pointing toward some of the activity on the American side, added, "Base-bole, *da?*"

Before the American prisoners had a chance to respond, another Russian prisoner stepped in front of the kid, shoving him roughly back toward their barracks. Turning his hostile glare toward the Americans, he muttered something, then followed the kid into the building. Nick, Cy, and Grease resumed their unofficial patrol.

"We should do something," Cy said after a lengthy silence.

"Sure," Grease answered. "Want to play some cards? Throw a ball around?"

"No. I mean we should do something about that kid back there."

Grease laughed. "What're you gonna do?" He asked. "Invite him over for tea?"

"I wish—" Cy hesitated. "I'd like at least to give him something to eat. Something from the Red Cross supplies. That poor kid looks like he's about to starve to death."

"Yeah, Rev," Grease concurred. "But it don't do any good to wish. Ain't no way the krauts are gonna let anybody help a Russian soldier, no matter how young he is. Besides, how would it look, feeding just one when all those guys are in the same predicament?"

"Sometimes one is all you can do."

Nick felt sorry for the kid too, but he couldn't see how they could help him. Anyone moving closer than three feet from the barrier, on either side, was very likely to be shot, with or without warning. Nick couldn't imagine trying to reach the kid unnoticed. After several days of walking around the prison and observing the general layout, he had not noticed a lapse in the guard.

"If we could just throw some food over that barrier—," Cy offered, but Grease cut him off.

"That whole Russian contingent over there would scrabble like dogs for a bone! They're all starving! Then they'd get shot, and probably so would you! Just drop the idea, okay?"

Cy nodded reluctantly and said no more, but Nick could tell by the furrows in the Rev's forehead that his friend would not stop thinking about the kid. Days later, when the American prisoners, or "kriegies" as they'd come to call themselves, received their food parcels from America, Nick couldn't help but think about the kid as well. For him and his fellow GIs, the Red Cross parcels were a godsend, providing small portions of raisins or prunes, real coffee, sugar, powdered milk, some kind of tinned meat or fish, crackers, even cheese and chocolate bars. The Russians received no such supplements to their starvation diet. Though the Red Cross operated internationally, apparently the Germans would not allow its beneficence to reach the Russians.

Back at the barracks, Nick eagerly broke open a tin of salmon and an eight-ounce packet of crackers. He dipped a cracker into the salmon, then popped the combination into his mouth.

"Mmm," he murmured, his eyes closed. "I think I've just tasted a piece of heaven." He polished off the crackers and salmon, then examined the parcel for more.

Meanwhile, the Rev also savored tidbits from his parcel. His smile widened after every bite until he grinned like a child at Christmas. Then, after he'd finished eating the portion he'd allotted himself, his smile faded. Again Nick noticed the deepening furrows in Rev's brow.

"Something wrong?" he ventured.

Cy looked up. "I feel guilty," he confessed.

"Why?"

"I've got—I'm not—" He hesitated, then asserted, "I have to help that boy! It's my job. You know? 'Feed my sheep' and all."

"What boy?" Chef queried, just joining them, and Nick described the Russian youth they'd seen in the adjacent compound. Chef's eyes widened.

"How are you going to feed him?" he asked. "You can't get across the wire."

"I don't know," Cy admitted. "But, hey, we're Americans! We're ingenious, aren't we? We'll figure out something! Meanwhile, I'm going to save a few things for him." Looking up at others around him, he invited, "You're welcome to do the same. Then all we have to do is figure out a way to get the goods to the boy, or the boy to the goods."

This proposal met with silence. Having just received real food, many men seemed reluctant to part with even a bit of it. Others felt no particular drive to risk their lives for one insignificant Russian youth, especially if it meant smuggling him into their side of the compound.

"Well?" Cy prodded.

Nick hesitated, then nodded. "Okay," he said, "I'm in—even though I don't have a clue how we're going to pull this off."

"What the hell," Foul-Mouth Matthews announced. "I'm pretty damned bored. I could use a little project to work on. Count me in. I'll help you save Kid Russki!"

The prisoners' ambition brought a refreshing sense of purpose to their long days as they gathered in groups to discuss options and assign responsibilities. Because Nick had already established walking the perimeter as a regimen of exercise, his new duties were to observe the movement and watch habits of the guards, to locate the weakest area in the barrier between compounds, and to attempt communication with the young Russian. Chef and Bandershoot announced that they would work with Nick.

Other volunteers offered to devise strategies. The primary goal was to get Kid Russki across the barrier into the American compound; if that proved impossible, a second proposal was to find a way to get food through the barrier to him.

"Huh-uh. No second." John Drummond vetoed the alternative. "Look here. If all we aim to do is get that kid more food, we'd have to find a way to do it over and over again. Even if we achieve that, how could we make sure that he's the one who gets it? Hell, there's hundreds of guys starving over there, and we're going to try to save one? We'd be starting another Russian Revolution! We've got only one option: get the kid over here. That way, we do it once and it's done."

"Except then we have to hide him." Grease protested. "That won't exactly be a walk in the park what with the krauts' surprise roll calls and barracks inspections."

"It'll be easier to slip one more soldier into our ranks than to storm the barricade every day for the next—how long you think this war is gonna last?"

Drummond's argument made sense, and ultimately the men decided upon one mission. There would be no second choice, and there would be no second attempt if the first failed.

"We're gonna need a diversion of some kind," Matthews said. "I think I'd like to be in on that. I'm just itchin'—"

Cy silenced him with a stern look, then nodded, adding, "We need to know exactly what you have in mind, and you need to know exactly when we're ready. No surprises."

"Absolutely," Matthews grinned. "Hell, I can hardly wait."

For several days after deciding to rescue the Russian kid, none of the GI prisoners saw him. Nick and his crew began to wonder if they'd declared their intentions a little too late. Of course, it would be easy for one skinny Russian kid-soldier to become lost in the growing population of disheveled prisoners.

Maybe, Nick thought of another possibility, *the other Russian prisoners are keeping Kid Russki away from the fence.*

Meanwhile, the other crews worked on a rescue plan, determining that a simple plan would be less likely to get screwed up. While they waited to hear if there actually would be a mission, they worked on perfecting the details and the timing of their simple plan.

"So what's the deal?" Grease asked Nick one night after the German guard called lights out. "Does this kid still exist or what?"

"You know what I think?" Cy posed. "I think we've got to plan a little bigger."

"Are you nuts?" Someone argued. "The bigger the plan, the more likely it is to fail."

Cy ignored the protest. "Football *and* baseball. We should have both going on. Remember the first time we saw the kid? He knew something about baseball. That was the only English he seemed to know. If we get a baseball game going—two teams of the very best players—you know, a real game with all the excitement and cheering and everything, we'll attract a lot of attention."

"You can say that again," Red warned. "Attention from the Germans as well as the Russians."

"Hell, the Germans like watching games as much as anybody," Grease interjected. "They love seeing us kriegies compete against each other. Let the Padre have his say."

"The kid will be there. I'm sure of it. Imagine an exciting play—maybe somebody stealing home or something—all the commotion between the players and the spectators. There would have to be some opportunity in that to see and communicate with the kid."

"But we still go ahead as planned with the football game?" Drummond asked. "The overthrown pass to create diversion in the Russian compound? If we stick with that plan, why do we need to add a different game?"

"Just to make sure there is plenty of action to keep the Germans busy—and their attention distracted."

Discussion continued well into the night, sometimes erupting into arguments over who should be in charge of what, or who wanted to be left out of the entire scenario. Intense whispers rose to low murmurs, then to rumblings just short of argument. Finally two voices were heard exclaiming simultaneously.

"What the hell are you doing?"

"Hey! I think we've got something here."

An eerie silence followed before Johnny Ames reported, "I lost a button. It rolled under my bunk, and I was just feeling around for it when I feel this—this—*lip* in the wood. Wait a minute." He grunted as he tried to squeeze himself under his bunk. "Hot damn, the floor moves! Get off the bunks you guys! I think we got ourselves a tunnel down here!"

"That ain't no tunnel," one of the long-term prisoners drawled.

"Oh yeah?" Johnny pounded his fist against the floor, and it made a hollow sound. "That isn't dirt under here, it's space!"

By now several soldiers gathered around. A few of them worked together to shove the triple bunk unit further to one side. Someone else lit a lamp—the tiny, primitive kind the soldiers had learned to fashion out of food tins, grease, and string—and brought it over to give the area a little more light.

Nick watched as Ames and Drummond pried at the floorboards. The excited whispers hushed when the two lifted a portion of the floor away.

"Oh man oh man, isn't this something?" Chef whispered next to Nick. "Wouldn't it be great if we found a tunnel out of here?"

"Give us that light," Ames ordered after removing the piece of floor, revealing only a rectangle of darkness. "I wanna see where this goes."

The thrill of discovery dwindled as the dim candlelight revealed no tunnel, but only a coffin-sized dugout under Johnny's bunk. Two soldiers pawed at the ground a little, hoping to unearth a trap door or at least evidence of a tunnel, but the earth was rocky and very firm.

"Well shit!" Matthews grumbled as he returned to his bunk. "What the hell's the point?"

For a time the prisoners forgot their earlier debate over the Kid Russki Rescue plans. Silently they returned to their bunks. Nick lay in the dark, wrapping the blanket around his body, cocoonlike. Only five minutes before, he had been a prisoner and knew he was a prisoner. Five minutes of excitement, of the merest glimmer of release, followed by that one second of disappointed realization suddenly made him feel more confined than ever. He agreed with Matthews. What had been the point?

"Told you there wasn't nothing there," gloated the long-timer. "It's just a place to keep Red Cross goods from the Nazis." No one responded for a long time. Finally, Cy Popp sat up in his bunk and cleared his throat.

"We found more than that," he declared. "We found a place to hide the kid."

Shortly after noon the next day, Chef nudged Nick as they jogged past the border between compounds.

"Over there," he said, gesturing. "Is that him?"

Nick and Chef stopped jogging and waited for Bandershoot, who had stopped to remove a pebble from his boot. Beyond the wire, slouched against the Russian latrine, Kid Russki looked at them and lifted his hand just a little.

"Maybe it's wishful thinking," Bandershoot said, "but I think that kid wants to communicate with us as much as we do with him." He returned the kid's wave, then gestured for him to come closer to the wire. Kid Russki looked furtively at his fellow prisoners, waited until it seemed no one paid any attention, then strolled casually to a spot within three feet of the barrier. He sat in the dirt, profile to the Americans, and waited, humming. Chef started to call out, but Nick hushed him.

"Wait a minute. Let's not make it quite so obvious. The kid's got the idea. We should look like we're minding our own business. Bandy, get down and do some pushups—like you're trying to prove something."

With a little argument, Bandershoot dropped to the ground and began to do pushups. Chef counted each one aloud, while Nick, focusing on his two companions as if he'd wagered his rations on the outcome, attempted to talk to the kid.

"One!"

"You speak English?"

"Two!"

The kid only grinned.

"Three!"

"*Sprichst du Deutsch?*"

"Four!"

This time the kid shrugged and said something in Russian. The GIs couldn't understand him. Nick tried again, this time accompanying his English words with subtle gestures. He pointed to the kid, waved his hand as if inviting him across the barrier, patted his stomach and pantomimed eating. Kid Russki turned, facing the American compound. He pointed first to himself, then to the barbed wire, and finally spread his hands outward, and shrugged.

"We're working on that," Nick said, tapping his temple with his index finger. He head gestured toward the far end of the barrier, then mimed throwing a ball into the air, the only definitive action he knew about football. The kid looked in the direction indicated, shook his head, and gestured in the opposite direction.

"Thirty-three!" Chef continued calling out loud, and Bandershoot added breathlessly, "How . . . much . . . longer . . . am . . . I . . . going? I'm . . . not . . . in . . . shape—"

"That's enough," Nick decided, and Bandershoot dropped prone in the dust.

"I think the kid has an idea too," Nick announced. Across the wire, Kid Russki began to stroll down the fence line. Nick and his crew ambled in the same direction on their side. Sometimes they stopped to share a word with other men in the area, but they kept an eye on the kid. Finally, near the rear border of the stalag, he stopped and pointed.

They had reached the point where Nick always turned away from the barrier on his walks. Not quite at the end of the fence-line between camps, this was as far as he dared to go. Nick glanced at Kid Russki, who nodded and pointed again.

"No way," Chef said, following the implication. "No way he can get through down there!"

A riotous barking began in the area where Kid Russki had pointed. This was where the guard dogs were kept when they weren't on duty. A long, low kennel building, enclosed by a link-fence, stood perpendicular to the border between compounds, half on the American side and half on the Russian side. The barbed wire fence ended at the link-fence, but there didn't seem to be any open area between them where a person could squeeze through. In addition, a guard tower stood on each side of the kennel. Nick glanced up, noticing that two soldiers manned each tower. He glanced again at Kid Russki and shook his head, but the kid only pointed surreptitiously once more and nodded before he backed away and disappeared into the mingle of other prisoners.

"What the hell is he thinking?" Nick asked when the trio of GIs headed back toward their barracks. "He expects to fight his way past four guards and a dozen or more killer dogs?"

"I saw it," Chef responded. "I mean—what he was really pointing at. Didn't you see?"

"See what?"

"The dogs. You know, they like to dig. There was a depression under the fence on our side. Maybe there's one on the Russian side, too. Maybe he thinks he can get over here through the dog kennel."

"Know what I think?" Bandershoot posed. "I think that Russian kid is crazier than we are. Those dogs would tear him to pieces."

"I guess that means we have to figure out a way to distract the dogs too," Nick concluded.

That night, a revised plan took shape involving everyone in the building—more than two hundred men—and as many prisoners from the other barracks as they could recruit. Some would take active roles in the rescue plans; others would be informed spectators, ready to fill in wherever needed. Still others intended to help create several areas of mass confusion. Most of the prisoners agreed to go along with the Kid Russki Rescue more out of boredom than any sense of altruism. It gave them something to work for.

A few days before the target day, the plan changed considerably. Instead of relying upon a single game of football between teams from different barracks, the men organized several games. The major focus would be on baseball because that seemed more likely to captivate the interest of Germans as well as Americans. In other areas of the compound, less intensely competitive games would be underway: a little pass football, some wrestling, and group calisthenics. The entire compound would be a flurry of activity.

To prevent the possibility of the Germans disallowing a sort of in-camp Olympics, veteran POWs boasted of the American sports skill in front of the guards. When the Germans themselves showed signs of interest, prisoners offered cigarettes and food parcels as wagers. The plan unfolded smoothly, especially after the camp kommandant himself stepped in, offering what he called "parole jackets" to baseball outfielders. These thin bright yellow outer vests would allow the wearers to scramble into restricted areas to retrieve any wayward-hit balls.

On the day of the game, light snow began to fall early in the morning. Prisoners watched the flakes drift slowly down and dust the ground. Cy stroked his brow, worrying. Snow cover meant the core rescue moves could be tracked and they would have to call off the plan. Some of the men wanted to call off the games immediately because of the snow, but others urged that they wait and see. By midmorning the snow stopped and the sky cleared, allowing the sun to melt the slight trace of snow. Just after noon, Cy's worried expression turned to a triumphant grin. As if in answer to his prayers, clouds moved in again and the temperature plunged. Many of the men, especially the players, worried that the cold air and freezing ground might affect their control of the game. The entire baseball game had been planned between the teams. They knew exactly who should hit the ball, and when. They had devised plans for close plays, daring steals, and even a few errors just in case the plays didn't occur exactly as intended.

"It's today or very likely never," one of the prisoners claimed. "Everything's in place today: the kid, the Germans, the games, just the attitude. We drop it now, we're not gonna get most of that back." Argument came from several quarters, but ultimately most of the men agreed.

"Let's play ball!"

Nick couldn't help but admire the precision of the operation as it unfolded in several areas of the large compound. He belonged to the crowd who watched and cheered a wrestling match near the back of the stalag, close to the dog kennel. Though he couldn't even see the baseball game from where he stood, he knew that several signal men spaced at appropriate intervals would get the go-ahead or cease-operation signs from one end of the compound to the other in a matter of seconds.

In every arena of play, the games intensified just as the baseball game did. Wrestlers scrambled more aggressively; somewhere else on the compound, Cy Popp's team threw a football farther and farther with each pass, scrabbling fiercely with their opponents for yardage and possession. The baseball game continued through the eighth inning with a three-to-two score.

At the bottom of the ninth inning, the underdog team had two men out, a tying run on base, and a batter with a full count. The next pitch signaled the moment for everything to happen at once.

Crack! A long fly ball soared over the centerfielder's head and he sprinted into the restricted zone after it. At the same moment, a volatile argument erupted among the wrestlers, resulting in competitors and spectators setting upon each other in a tumultuous fistfight. At the football game, near the end zone, the quarterback overthrew the pass, hurling what looked like a football well over the barbed wire between the American and Russian compounds. When the "ball" fell on the other side, it broke open, revealing packets of chocolate candy, real coffee, and American cigarettes, some of the best barter material available to prisoners. Immediately scores of Russians fell upon the trove in a melee. All over both camps, men fought, cheered, jeered, or scurried from one upheaval to the next. While guards at the kennel towers were distracted by the fracas, Nick and his cohorts sidled to the link fence, squeezing partially opened tins of meat into the kennel. Growling and gnashing, the dogs battled each other to rip at the tins, cutting their tongues and muzzles on the sharp edges, further maddening themselves with the taste of blood. Gunshots rang out from every corner of camp. A skinny kid slipped unnoticed from a crowd of Russian prisoners, squeezed under the kennel fence on the Russian side, scurried to another depression on the American side and burrowed under that. Just before he cleared the fence, one of the dogs broke from the frenzied pack, snarled, and snapped at the kid's foot. Murphy and Grease helped to pull the kid clear. In the process, Kid Russki lost his right shoe and scraped his leg against the bottom of the fence.

Machine gun fire soon put an end to the riot. Hundreds of prisoners threw themselves on the ground or dashed for cover around buildings. Guards shoved, kicked, or hit to restore order. When at last an eerie silence fell, Nick dared to lift his own head. Not far from him, Chef hugged himself. A tiny rivulet of blood ran from his mouth where he'd bitten his lips. At a discreet distance from the kennel and almost buried under a protective huddle of GIs, Kid Russki stirred. He shrugged himself free, grimaced at the sight of the gash in his leg, then lay back in the dirt. Meeting Nick's questioning glance, he nodded.

"*Spasiba,*" he grunted. Though Nick understood no Russian, he didn't need a translator for the look on Kid Russki's face.

"You're welcome."

Afterward Nick would remember that gratifying moment when he didn't yet know that nineteen Russian prisoners lay dead across the wire, some of them clutching chocolate bars in their fists. He would remember that temporary feeling of victory before he learned about the three American prisoners staining their yellow parole jackets crimson, before he found out that one of the bloodied bodies eventually carried out of the stalag was Cy Popp, the Rev, who had only wanted to feed his sheep.

VII

Kid Russki

*D*_{*ear Folks,*} Nick began his first letter home for the fourth time. In his first three attempts, too-frequent erasures ruined a sheet of the official POW stationery. With only one piece left him for now, he needed to choose his words very carefully. There was so much he wanted to tell, so much that would not make it past either the German or the American censors. He wanted to write about his late friend, the Rev. He longed to explain the nobility of the plan that had resulted in such a tragedy, to mention the young Russian soldier who had made himself right at home among the American POWs. He ached to unburden himself of the responsibility he himself felt for the recent deaths and the resulting murmurs of unrest among his fellow prisoners. He wanted to write away his guilt for taking a sudden dislike to the young Russian, blaming him for the tragedy.

Nick tapped the smooth-tipped pencil against the table, staring at the empty lines on the prisoner stationery. He counted twenty lines on the five-by-seven-inch paper. Without cramping his writing too much, he might squeeze six or seven words on to each line if the words weren't too long. That would amount to a maximum of one hundred and forty words in the letter. But which words? He couldn't tell about trying to remain standing in formation, exhausted, cold, and hungry, for seven hours after the rescue while Germans counted and recounted the able, the injured, and the dead. He couldn't mention a word of whatever chance miscalculation it was that allowed a prisoner to disappear from the Russian compound as if he had never existed. He dared not write anything about the rations withheld for two days. Five days after the rescue, though still shaky, Nick and his fellow POWs resumed the patterns of their incarceration. It was all they could do.

I am safe, he wrote, then paused before carefully erasing the last word. "Safe" didn't seem to be the right term. He thought of replacing it with "well," but considering the weight he had already lost and the dysentery, that, too, was an inaccurate description. Finally he completed the first sentence, *I am a prisoner of war and no longer in the fighting.* That might relieve the folks' worries some. Nick continued: *I just want you to know that I am thinking of all of you and would like to hear from you. Other prisoners say that letters from home are the best cures for what ails us. I can hardly wait to find that out for myself. If you want, you could send a package too, but be sure that you don't send more than one per month because that is all we are allowed to receive. We are fed well by our captors.* Nick smiled a little as he wrote the lie. He knew his parents would recognize what he meant when they read his next line: *In fact, I will soon be almost as fat as Banker Braun.* Scrawny old Johannes Braun had been the folks' banker for decades, as well as the butt of many jokes about the money in his pockets anchoring him against the prairie winds. *How are my nephew and nieces doing? I hope they won't forget their favorite uncle. Have you had word from Jacob? I pray that he is well and that the war will soon be over.*

Nick scrawled the last word at the very edge of the last line. He barely had space to scribble his signature beneath it. It would have to do. He knew that when his parents received the letter, they would share it with relatives and friends. Maybe in a few weeks' time, he would have several letters from home. Perhaps packages would arrive, filled with some of the foods he'd come to miss so much.

He thought briefly about writing a letter to Helen back in Ohio. Maybe he'd been wrong in not wanting to get married before shipping out. Maybe his days and nights now would be a little better if he knew he had a loving wife longing for him to come home. Unfortunately, prisoners were allowed only two sheets of writing paper per month, and he'd ruined one of his. He would have to wait until next month.

A nudge at his shoulder interrupted Nick's reverie. He looked up into Kid Russki's grin. The boy held a tattered piece of cloth in his left hand, a remnant of the ragged shirt he'd worn in the Russian section. He waved it in front of Nick's face and asked, "Want I make shine the boots?"

"No." Nick motioned him away. "No I don't want you make shine the boots. Go make somebody else's boots shine, okay? And stay away from the windows!"

"Oh-kay," Kid responded, still smiling, and ambled away to make himself useful to another prisoner. It was what he did best. Kid Russki polished shoes or mended tears in clothing and bedding—anything that would keep him in the good graces and subsequent good care of the American GIs. He also worked hard at improving his rudimentary English and entertained the troops with his flawed attempts at conversation. In the days after his rescue, Kid Russki became something of a camp mascot for many of the Americans. They bandaged the gash in his leg, burned most of his own clothes and scrounged among their own belongings for items of more American-looking clothing. They showed him how to swagger when he walked and taught him to deliver a few popular American phrases without too much of an accent. Kid Russki liked his new vocabulary and pronounced the phrases often: *H'lo Joe! What d'you know?* and *What's buzzin' cousin?* His favorite word seemed to be that drawn out *oh-kay.*

For the most part, Kid Russki stayed in the barracks where Nick resided. During morning and evening delivery of meals and through the odd inspections, he hid in the dugout beneath Johnny Ames' bunk. Once in a while he ventured outside for exercise, but only in the company of small crowds of GIs, who made it a point to steer clear of both the dog kennel and the barrier between the American and the Russian compounds. At night, Kid slept on the floor of the barracks. Because of the rescue casualties, a few bunks became available, including the one that had belonged to Cy Popp. No one offered to let the kid sleep there, and since he seemed perfectly content to wrap himself in a blanket and lie on the floor near one of the stoves, no one offered any of the other bunks either.

The POWs readily shared their daily rations with Kid Russki, and he seemed to relish the vapid soups and *sauerbrot*, or the small wilted potatoes boiled in their jackets that made up a meal. The GIs also shared, though a little less readily, extra portions from Red Cross parcels.

Nick read through his letter one more time. Each sheet of stationery acted as its own envelope, with lines for recipient's address on the back. Nick folded the sheet in thirds, then filled in his parents' names and address. He couldn't seal the letter; someone else would do that after censors had examined his words. Nick felt confident that nothing in his letter would have to be blacked out.

"All finish letter?" Kid Russki came back, this time holding a deck of playing cards instead of a shoe rag. "Time pig knuckle?"

"That's *pinochle*," Nick corrected, then shook his head. "I don't want to play cards right now."

"Ah, c'mon, Bremer," Grease stepped in behind Kid Russki. "Time for us to get back some points. How about a little six-handed, huh? Maybe we'll get us a little *pig knuckle* tournament going." He winked at the kid, then asked Nick, "You got anything better to do?"

"Nothing better than a few trips to the latrine," Nick snapped. Easing his tone, he added, "You guys get a game going. I'll just hang back and watch—between trips."

"Okay," Grease replied. "But no kibitzing from the ranks."

Twenty minutes later, Nick returned, shivering, with flakes of snow glistening in his hair and along his shoulders. The air in the barracks smelled strongly of smoke, a blend of wood, low-grade coal, and cigarettes. In spite of the cold draft that leaked through windowpanes and floorboards, a thick haze hung in the air, softening the already dim light even more than usual. Cold wintry weather kept most of the men indoors for now, engaged in various activities: drawing, writing or reading, whittling figures from soap, debating, and playing card games or dominoes. Nick joined the small crowd around the pinochle players at the table nearest his bunk. The game had already grown boisterous.

"Damn it, Murphy! You're supposed to play a count card on my trump!"

"Sorry. Sheesh. I thought Drummond was gonna out-trump your trump."

"You don't have much of a memory for cards, do you? Hey! Russki, your play."

"Oh-kay," the kid drawled, and then took a two-count trick with a nine of trump. He laughed aloud when his opponents booed. At that moment, Chef, who had been watching the game from his bunk, stood up and nudged himself next to Nick. He stared at the young Russian. Elbowing Nick, he murmured, "I don't think we should call this boy Russki anymore. Hasn't anyone ever asked him his name?"

Drummond, overhearing, answered for Nick. "Sure. His name's Anton Something. It's unpronounceable. Lots of sounds, no sense. Listen. Hey, Kid! Russki! Name? What's your name?" He asked the last question in a louder voice, as if the lad were hard of hearing. Kid Russki looked up, puzzled.

"Already say much times Anton Zhynitskov."

"See? 'Russki' is much easier to say."

"Yeah, but—," Chef spoke in a very low voice. "But we might get so used to calling him that and then say it sometime when a German guard will hear. Or even one of our guys who doesn't like Russians."

"C'mon, Chef—," someone started to deride, but stopped when Foul-mouth Matthews interjected. "He's goddamned right. We're getting too damn comfortable and easy since we got this kid across the wire. We gotta be careful not to let one success go to our heads."

"Success?" Nick could hardly keep a bitter tone out of his voice. "If that was a success, I'd sure hate to see us fail at something."

With that, John Drummond reached his arm across the table and lay his hand on Kid Russki's shoulder, shaking him gently. "We give you new name," he over-enunciated, again as if he were talking to a deaf person. "Your name—Tony."

"Anton Zhynitskov," Kid Russki insisted, but a chorus of voices corrected him. "Tony!"

"Tony Zee. That's who you are. Good old American Tony Zee!"

During the next week, the men learned all they could about their adopted compatriot. Even Nick found his personal resentment beginning to fade as Tony Zee related his own experiences. In halting English, he told of bitter hatred of anything German and of German atrocities committed against Russian men and women. He claimed that the Russian prisoners in the compound rarely received their International Red Cross rations, that the Germans kept them for themselves except when a Red Cross inspection was due.

One evening, Tony told a little about his family. He was the only surviving child, initially claiming to be eighteen years old, but ultimately admitting to being only fifteen. His mother had died in childbirth when he was six. His baby sister had lived only a few days. He, his father, and a severe aunt, both factory workers, shared a two-room apartment for several years until the war changed their lives. He had joined the fighting after his own father disappeared in battle, presumably captured by German forces. As many boys do, Tony carried a proud fantasy of somehow finding his father and erasing the shame of his capture.

"Shame?" the American captives challenged. "Why is his being taken prisoner a shame?"

Shifting from his broken English to Russian and back again, Tony led the Americans to understand that a good Soviet soldier fought to the death. To be taken prisoner was an indication of some personal flaw or traitorous tendency. Tony believed that soldiers who might return from captivity would be re-incarcerated in their own country until their supposed crime against the state might be atoned.

"That can't be right," Chef said.

Tony answered, "Is maybe so. I think it is so." For a moment, his eyes took on a distant look. Then he shook his head, as if dismissing a memory.

"After this war if I not find my father," he added, "I no go back. Tony Zee go to America, oh-kay!"

"Sure," Chef answered, ignoring the dubious looks from others around him. "No problem. You're one of us now."

Just then, the far door of the barracks flew open with a bang and a shrill whistle blasted.

"*Raus! Alles raus!*" The too-familiar call came as two guards entered the building. Before the Germans reached the mid-building washroom, Nick and his buddies scrambled out of bunks and chairs in their rear unit, making their stand to attention disorderly enough to screen John and Johnny who hustled the young Russian to his hiding place. They took their places at attention just as the guards entered the rear unit.

"Oh God, what is this?" Chef whispered next to Nick. "What's going on?"

Once more the guards barked orders for the soldiers to leave the barracks. Hearts pounding, they stumbled outside. By force of habit, they gathered in roll call formation on the grounds in an area lit harshly by spotlights. Nick couldn't help but notice that only one barracks had been selected for this sudden inspection. The windows in the other barracks appeared dark. He wondered if anyone watched from behind those windows.

Sounds from outside the circle of light indicated that other guards were in the compound. A short time later, the kommandant himself stepped into the light. He looked at the men standing before him, then shook his head. Lifting his right hand, he waved another component of soldiers into the barracks. Almost immediately, the prisoners heard sounds of heavy objects hitting the floor, glass breaking, and metal clanging. They knew this was no ordinary inspection.

For a long time the soldiers stood in the night, waiting. Before them, the kommandant paced back and forth. In his gloved hand, he held some kind of object that he casually tossed in the air and caught again. Sometimes he paused to look at it closely, then he looked toward the prisoners, an unfriendly smile crossing his face. Every once in a while he stepped close to one of the prisoners, his face within inches of the other.

"It is a cold night, *nicht wahr?*" He taunted, sometimes adding, "I wonder what is taking them so long." He paced again, then stopped once more, this time facing Red. "Don't you wonder," he asked, "what it is that my men are looking for?"

"No, sir. I don't wonder," Red dared to answer.

"Is that because you know what they are looking for?"

"No, sir. I don't know what they are looking for."

"Hmm." The kommandant smiled and resumed his pacing.

After what seemed much too long a time, the guards began to emerge from the barracks. Among the Americans, a silent tension made them hardly dare to breathe as they watched for Kid Russki to be led outside. When he didn't appear, the men started to breathe a little easier.

"*Was finden Sie?*" Kommandant asked one of the guards.

"*Nichts,*" was the answer Nick heard, but "nothing" hardly explained the number of items the guards now carried out of the barracks with them: one had a coat under his arm; another carried tins of meat products, while many brought out cartons of cigarettes.

The kommandant didn't seem to be very impressed with the result of the inspection. He sighed, then turned to face the prisoners once more. He tossed the curious object in the air a few more times, then held it high between his thumb and index finger.

"Do you know what this is?" he shouted. "Can you see what this is?"

No one answered. Kommandant moved forward, standing right in front of Foul Mouth Matthews. He held the object in the palm of his hand, placing it just under Matthews' nose.

"Now can you see what this is?"

Matthews looked, then shrugging, answered, "I don't know what it is."

"It is part of a shoe," Kommandant said, and repeated louder, "It is part of a shoe found in the kennel. I wonder how a part of a shoe got into the dog kennel. Does anyone know?"

Beside Nick, Chef began to tremble. His breathing came fast and ragged. Nick slowly eased closer to Chef until their shoulders were touching. In a barely audible whisper he urged, "Control yourself. Don't say anything—no matter what." Chef nodded, swallowing hard.

Before them, the kommandant continued, seeming to enjoy his performance. "Perhaps one of you has only part of a foot, hmm?" When no one responded, Kommandant suddenly lost his smile. Instead he shouted for the guards to bring the dogs. Two more soldiers emerged from the darkness, each leading a German shepherd. The kommandant held the bit of shoe near the dogs' noses, then nodded at the guards. They led the snarling and sniffing dogs into the barracks.

Nick closed his eyes. The next few minutes seemed to last a long time before a frenzied barking sound came from inside the barracks, followed by unintelligible shouts of human voices. Finally the guards emerged, dragging Kid Russki between them. Two other soldiers hurried forward to pull the dogs away from where they had been snapping at the kid's legs. The kid struggled to keep his eyes open as the glare of the spotlight hit him. In that wash of light, the kid looked ashen and even younger than his fifteen years.

"Take him away," Kommandant ordered, then facing the prisoners again, demanded, "And let's find out who is responsible. The next few days might be a little easier for those who cooperate."

When no one responded, the kommandant moved from one man to another, barking questions. Waiting, Nick again felt the panic in Chef. Through pinched lips he cautioned, "It's best if you don't say anything. Just—not anything."

The prisoners either ignored the kommandant's questions, or responded with "I don't know anything about this." Some claimed never to have seen the kid before. Nick, too, only shrugged and shook his head when the questions were asked of him. He tried to keep his position close to Chef, as if his nearness might shore up the kid's courage. The kommandant, however, yanked at Chef's collar, pulling him forward.

"And what about this fancy boy?" Kommandant derided. "What can you tell me? You are not afraid of me, are you?"

Chef could not answer. Nick wasn't sure the kid would stay conscious much longer, pallid as his face had become.

"Come come come!" Kommandant ordered. "Tell me what you know."

You know nothing, Nick silently urged, wishing his thoughts could implant themselves into Chef's mind. *You know nothing—nothing!* For a while he thought Chef might have heard him because he almost choked on the words, "I don't know any—"

As the kommandant's grip moved to Chef's throat, the young prisoner shouted, "*Ick weiss nikt von Russki!*"

Kommandant stared at Chef, a triumphant smile widening his face. He released his grip on Chef, steadying the kid on his feet. He even smoothed the boy's shirt collar.

"Good. That's good," he soothed. "And you even told me in my own language—of sorts. I wonder who taught you so well." He shifted his focus to Nick, then back again to Chef. "Now, don't you feel better?" His artificial soothing tone lulled Chef just long enough to be caught off guard when the punch came. Clutching his belly, he dropped hard to the ground. Nick and Murphy started to lean in to help Chef back to his feet, but Kommandant stopped them.

"These three," he instructed the guards as he pointed to Nick, Chef, and Murphy. "Take these three away. As for the others"—he stepped away from the lineup of prisoners—"perhaps they wouldn't mind standing out here for the rest of the night, thinking about what they know and don't know."

Before he was led away, Nick heard the kommandant give one more order. "Any one who falls out of formation—shoot him."

"I'm sorry. I'm sorry," Chef sobbed, his eyes pleading with Nick as the guards shoved him past.

This is it, Nick thought much later, shivering in the utter darkness of the "ice-box" where prisoners were punished in solitary confinement. *This time, I'm done for.* As had occurred before in isolation, all sense of time left Nick. Minutes might be hours;

hours might be days, or vice versa. The windowless room remained dark; no one came to offer any kind of relief. The dank air reeked of sewage and vomit. Now and again Nick heard a shout from somewhere outside, then a rifle shot. Once it was a whole volley of rifle fire. He didn't want to think about what that might mean but couldn't shake the image of a pale but determined Tony Zee facing a firing squad. He also thought of his friend Cy.

"What have we done?" He asked Cy, but of course, no answer came.

VIII

Northern Light

An ill-fitting door provided the only source of light in Nick's earthen and cinder-block cell. Slender beams of daylight shot through the gaps between hinges and frame. Dust specks floated in those beams, drifting gracefully as if they basked in the light, completely immune to gravity. Many times, with nothing else to occupy his hours, Nick focused on one mote, following it with his eyes as it spiraled in the beam. It had a hypnotic effect on him, and he could feel tension leave his body. Sometimes it seemed he could trace the movement of a dust speck for a long time, ten or fifteen minutes he supposed, though time no longer seemed measurable to him. For a man isolated in dark or semidark with nothing but his thoughts to occupy him, a day could feel as long as a week or as short as a few hours.

Eventually, of course, every speck of dust he studied disappeared from the light. He surmised that it continued to float about, but sometimes he wondered where it ultimately ended up. Did it fall to the floor, adding to the grit already there? Did he inhale it with a deep breath, and now it drifted about in the further confines of his lungs? Did it continue to float away toward whatever little crack or chink that might be its way out? *A way out*, Nick mused then. *I'd like to be as insignificant as a speck of dust and just drift out.*

Sometimes, there was only a narrow slit of dim light between the door's hinges. One time Nick stared at the light so long that it began to seem like a rip in the dark fabric that enshrouded him, but it was an opening that he couldn't get his fingers inside to tear his way out; it seemed an impermeable fissure between worlds, a hole . . .

" . . . in the bottom of the sea." He sang the familiar line aloud. The sound of his voice surprised him, ragged after a long period of silence. He cleared his throat, then tried again, "There's a log in the hole in the bottom of the se-e-ea." Nick chuckled, wondering if solitude might have driven him just a little closer to madness. He questioned, *would a sane man in this situation sing?* Shrugging, he cleared his throat again. Sane or not, at the moment, Nick simply felt like singing. His bass tones grew lustier with each silly verse of the ditty, and when he finished the song, he sighed, then started again, this time with lyrics of his own.

"There's a hole in the bottom—no—in the heart of Germany!" Nick added a new line after every chorus, singing each one louder than the line before, until he practically shouted the last verse, stomping his feet and pounding the walls with his fist in emphasis: "There is *dust* in the *lungs* of a *kriegie* in a *cell* in the *stalag* in the *hole* in the *heart* of Germa*ne-e-e-y* . . . There's a *ho-o-o-ole*, there's a *hole* . . . There's a *hole* in the *heart* of Germany!"

When his last note dwindled, silence resumed. No shouting or pounding or any other sign of protest came in response to Nick's singing. He stared at the door, willing someone—anyone—to break it down.

"Come and get me!" he challenged, then reduced his defiance to a whispered plea, "Someone—please—come and get me."

Daytimes, no one came. Each night the door would open once, and only far enough for someone to deliver the skimpy rations of water and bread or gruel, and to retrieve and empty the bucket that served as Nick's toilet. In the first few days—or hours—of his confinement, Nick's heart pounded each time the door opened; he feared the crashing entry of guards that might lead him away to face a firing squad. His fear of the door opening lessened with time, however. Now his fear was that it might never open wide again.

The last time Nick had been in solitary confinement, he had dreamed of the warmth and softness of home. This time, he thought no further and desired no more than his bunk in the barracks, the Red Cross rations, and the companionship of his fellow prisoners.

Where are they now? He wondered about the others who had been participants in the Kid Russki incident. In particular, he worried about Chef, such a lost kid himself, dependent and frightened to the point of panic. Since their capture, Chef's dependency had often felt burdensome, almost smothering. Now Nick missed it. He wanted again the strength he felt in being needed, and not to be the one in need.

Feeling powerless, Nick didn't want to think anymore about the futility of his situation. Sitting on the cold ground with his back against the wall, he hugged his knees and once more started a nonsense song he remembered from childhood.

"*Ist das nicht ein Schnitzelbank?*" He began smoothly, then shouted the response line off-key, again beating the rhythm with his fists. "*Ja, das ist ein Schnitzelbank!*" Nick stopped focusing on the slash of dim light near the door. Instead, he closed his eyes to sing in complete darkness.

Ist das nicht ein kurz und lang?
Ja das ist ein kurz und lang!
Kurtz und lang, Schnitzelbank!
Oh du schöne, oh du schöne
Oh du schöne Schnitzelbank!

After he finished the song the first time, Nick began again, adding more of his own verses. When he could think of no more, he started from the beginning, and so passed the time until his voice grew hoarse. Sometimes he nodded off, but each time he awoke, it was with silly song lyrics on his mind.

Then the door squeaked open—wide open—and Nick saw a German guard silhouetted in the entry.

"*Ist er nicht ein Schweinehund!*" Nick heard the words, but he wasn't sure at first who had said them, he or the guard. He squinted in the glare of the German's flashlight, and cleared his throat, but before he could say anything, the guard ordered, "*Komm' mit! Mach schnell!*"

Nick struggled to his feet, stretched his stiffened joints, and followed his captor. The night air felt damp, but not as cold as Nick expected. Maybe, he thought, his blood had already turned to ice water. He deeply inhaled the fresh air, then almost without thinking, stepped away from the guard and headed toward the familiar barracks.

"*Nein!*" The guard shouted, nudging him in the opposite direction to the kommandant's headquarters, where Nick saw other prisoners being hustled inside. When he drew closer, he recognized them all: John and Johnny, Red, Foul Mouth, and much to his relief, Chef. Kid Russki, however, was not among them. Haggard and grizzled after many days in solitary, most of the men nodded or blinked recognition of each other, then stood with eyes cast down. The kommandant faced them, a snifter of brandy in his hand.

"You all are troublemakers," he announced. "Here we cannot allow for troublemaking." He strode in front of the men, glaring at each in turn. When he reached Chef, he stopped, studying the young American through narrowed eyes. "*Ein kranker Kriegsgefangener bekommt erger!*"

At that, Nick studied Chef's face. The kid did look sick. Purplish shadows ringed his eyes, and his mouth twitched uncontrollably. Nick offered a faint *ahem*, hoping to get Chef's attention, offer a little subtle warning or at least silent encouragement, but the kid didn't lift his gaze from the floor.

"You will be transported to another prisoner facility—perhaps not such a nice one as you had here." Kommandant swallowed the brandy, then handed the snifter to one of his underlings. "That is the price of your . . . ingratitude—"

"*Entschuldigen Sie—,*" Nick spoke up, wanting to ask about the Russian youth. Actually he wanted to shout, *Where is he! What have you done to that kid!* A warning look from Red Murphy made him change his mind. Maybe it would be better never to know.

"*Was wollen Sie?*" The kommandant asked, his tone inviting Nick to test his authority. "What have you to say?"

Nick hesitated, then shook his head. "*Nichts. Es macht nichts.*"

"Good," the kommandant smiled. Gesturing to the soldiers who stood at attention near the door, he ordered, "If there is any trouble en route—any trouble at all—do what you have to do! Now take them away. I do not wish to see them again."

The men didn't talk as they crossed the compound toward the waiting transport. Nick kept his eyes down, concentrating on the movement of one foot in front of the other. He looked up only once when they passed nearest the Russian section of the camp. He knew that none of the Russians would be outside their barracks after sunset, yet in his mind he saw a montage of gaunt, shivering men, featureless except for the dark hollows of their eyes. Even in his imagination, however, he could not see Kid Russki among them.

An open-back truck hauled the small band of prisoners out of the compound. Finding it impossible to be heard over the rumble of the engine, they communicated with raised eyebrows and shrugs. They huddled close together, bracing for one more bone-jarring drive over rough, frozen ground.

Nick suddenly thought about the brandy the kommandant had been drinking. He would give almost anything for a powerful swig of that to kindle a fire in his gut, to warm him from the inside out. He leaned back against the cab of the truck and stared up at the stars that seemed close enough to pluck right out of the velvety night sky. He recognized the pattern of one of the constellations, though he didn't know its real name.

White Lightning, he sighed, sketchily remembering another cold night when he and his brother had named the stars.

"Damn, I'm freezing!"

"Shhh!" Nick whispered. "Do you want the folks to hear us?"

As stealthily as they could, the boys led Dotty, the spotted mare, out of the barn. She nickered once, but Nick quieted her with a scant amount of Ma's precious white sugar he held in his palm. If Ma ever caught him swiping her sugar, there was no telling the extent of her anger and disappointment, probably worse than if Pa caught them in their current activity. It wasn't the first time he'd engaged in this nocturnal escapade, but the excitement of sneaking out of the house with the sugar and stealing away on Dotty's back with a jug of Pa's moonshine had not diminished. This time he had special occasion for making the trek over the north pasture, beyond the plum thicket, across Willow Creek, up Schiltz's Hill past the schoolhouse, and down to the river. Tomorrow was Marcus's fifteenth birthday, and as his older brother, Nick wanted to initiate him.

Descending Schiltz's Hill, they saw flames of a small fire on the bank above the frozen river.

"Good," Marcus said. "They're already there. Now we don't have to freeze to death out here."

The others consisted of Norm and Henry Schiltz, twins Nick's age, and their year-younger cousin Erich. All three huddled around the fire, rubbing their hands or slapping at their arms to keep warm.

"Finally!" Henry called out when he spotted Nick and Marcus approaching on Dolly. "We thought maybe you wasn't coming."

"Ma was up a long time with Jacob," Nick explained. "The little guy's got the croup again."

"Well, c'mon down offa that horse and let's have something to take the chill off or we'll all be crouping too!"

The five of them gathered around the fire and passed the moonshine jug around. When Marcus took his first swallow, his eyes widened; he gulped hard and coughed.

"Whoo-ee!" He sputtered when he caught his breath. "This stuff is burnin' my insides out!"

The others laughed, swatting Marcus on the back. They encouraged him to take another drink, then shared the boon themselves. The whisky warmed their insides, and the fire helped stave off the cold outside, though every now and then they had to turn around to keep their backsides from freezing. They talked of all manner of things: girls and getting off the farm and staying on the farm and girls and finishing school and looking forward to summer and girls.

"Hey," Erich interrupted once, "tha's the las' drop. Ol' greedy ol' Henry drunk the dregs."

"Time fer reinforcements," Norm said, elbowing Nick who shook his head and stepped closer to the fire.

"I don't think so," Nick refused. "I think I'm too drunk already. We should probably go home now and stay there."

"Ah, c'mon," Marcus goaded. "It just barely turned my birthday. I ain't ready to quit celebratin' already."

"Well then maybe you should go," Nick argued. "Besides, how'm I s'posed to find the way when I see two of everything. I won't know which turns to take."

"Just hang on to Dolly. She'll head right home."

"Yah, she will," Nick conceded, "but she won't head back here on her own!"

"Take Sheriff along," Erich offered. "You can ride Dolly on your way home, and Sheriff on your way back here. You won't even have to be awake. Let these horses do the work!"

After one more futile protest, Nick reluctantly left the fire and struggled onto Dolly's back. Erich brought his own horse close, and Nick grabbed Sheriff's rope halter. As he rode away, his brother and friends teased.

"And don't worry if you have trouble on the way. After all, you got 'the Sheriff' with you!"

"And we all know what he is!"

Nick grinned and shouted the expected response to their old joke, "He's just another horse's ass!"

The ride wasn't very pleasant at first. Nick leaned his head against Dolly's neck and closed his eyes as she headed straight for home, but that made him dizzy and queasy. He felt a little better with his eyes open, in spite of double vision. The cutting cold slowly revived his senses, and by the time he reached the home place, everything started to fall back into proper focus. He fetched the second jug of moonshine, then climbed onto

Sheriff, who instinctively headed back to the Schiltz property, with a somewhat more reluctant Dolly trotting along behind. Back at the river campfire, the boys continued their party but, this time, didn't have the stamina to polish off another whole jug.

Much later on the way home, Marcus' head kept bouncing against Nick's shoulder, sending the younger brother into paroxysms of laughter.

"I'm sh-shakin' so mush I'm gonna foam over," he tittered.

"Not on my back!" Nick warned. "Now for cryin' out loud, be quiet!"

They rode quietly for a while longer. Finally Marcus whispered, "Jus' lookit all them stars. There's the Dipper stars an'"—he stifled another giggle—"there's the Sipper stars an' the Nip—oh my gosh—there's one jus' fell plum outa the sky! Poured right out of the Dipper!" He gasped, then started to cough.

"Marcus, what the hell—?" Nick turned to get a better look at his brother. "You're not gonna be sick now, are you?"

"I . . . think . . . I . . . swallowed it," Marcus hiccupped when he finally caught his breath.

"Swallowed what?"

"That sh-shootin' star! It burned goin' down, and now it's burnin' in my gut—oh, it's gonna burn comin' up! I don't feel so good."

"Whoa," Nick murmured, halting Dolly. "Marcus, you didn't swallow no shooting star. You swallowed a whole bolt of White Lightning!"

It took several minutes for Marcus to recover enough to get back on the horse. By the time he did, both boys shivered and Nick fought an almost-overwhelming desire to sleep. *Only a little farther,* he told himself. *We're almost home.*

"Take us home, Dolly."

"What did you say?" Drummond asked. "I didn't catch that."

"Nothing," Nick answered, shaking his head.

The truck roared and bounced along several more miles of rutted-up road before it finally came to a halt at a railroad crossing. A train waited there, consisting of engine and a few cars. The prisoners stood up, resigned to the next leg of their journey in livestock cars, but this time there were none.

"Will you look at that?" Foul-Mouth stood amazed. "Passenger cars!"

"Yeah," Red added, "and will you look at *that!*" With a tilt of his head, he gestured toward several rows of German troops heading for the train. "There must be a couple hundred Nazis here to accompany us!"

One of the guards in charge of the POWs ordered them to board the first car and stand at the rear. After them, scores of soldiers jumped on the train. When the seats in the first car were filled, soldiers climbed into the remaining cars until they too were filled. More soldiers filed into the already-filled cars, nudging their compatriots to make more room, until at last, the train was filled almost to overflowing with human cargo. The Germans seemed lighthearted in spite of the discomfort, and when the train began to move, they sent up a loud cheer.

"What the hell is going on here?" Foul-Mouth whispered.

"They're going home on temporary leave," Nick translated what he heard the soldiers talking about. "They've been given a few days to celebrate the New Year with family."

Until he said the words, Nick hadn't even been aware what day it was. Christmas had come and gone while he was in solitary, not that he would have found much to celebrate in the season this year. Now they were on the verge of—or a few days into—a new year.

"Wow," Red echoed Nick's realization. "It's 1944."

Frequent stops marked this leg of their journey. At one of the stops, they were allowed off the train to get a drink of water and to relieve themselves. Back on board, soldiers pushed and crowded them again. The car became oppressive with the closeness of bodies, the mingled scent of scores of men too long unwashed. For so many days Nick had been cold; now the closeness made him sweat. The soles of his feet ached from standing so long.

I never thought I'd miss riding in a cattle car, he thought. *If I could just get to a window for some air.*

"Hey! Hey, Bremer!" An urgent whisper broke into Nick's thoughts. He turned to see Drummond and Matthews trying to keep Chef from falling to the floor. The kid's ashen face glistened with sweat. Remembering the kommandant's warning about troublesome sick prisoners, Nick edged closer. When his foot came down hard on a Nazi officer's boot, he tried to correct his step, then lost his balance and fell forward against a German soldier who sat at the edge of the nearest seat. Instinctively he lifted his hands to break his fall.

"*Was tun Sie!*" The soldier shouted, shoving him back, and the buzz of conversation among all the other soldiers stopped, replaced by the sound of the guards' weapons snapping into readiness.

"*Entschuldigen Sie, bitte!*" Nick straightened himself slowly. Glancing toward his fellow prisoners, he saw that they had managed to revive Chef—at least for the time being. Still he hoped the Germans wouldn't notice the kid's sickly appearance. In a voice much louder than he needed, he continued, "Excuse me. *Ich bin müde. Ich muss eingeschlafen sein!* I just fell—I mean—I fell asleep!"

Shouting eased to swearing and grumbling, and finally to a few derisive laughs. Not long afterward, the train slowed again. When it came to a full stop, many of the soldiers disembarked. Since no new passengers came on board, one of the guards directed the prisoners to sit.

Nick almost fell into the seat near the window. He leaned his head against the pane, relieved for the first time in weeks to feel the cold. Chef sat next to him. Nick offered to trade places so the kid could get closer to fresh air, but Chef shook his head.

"I'm already f-freezing," he stammered. "I f-feel real sick. Bremer, I don't think I'm gonna m-make it this time."

"Don't you say that!" Nick urged. "You're going to make it! You're going to make it to wherever it is we're going, and you'll make it while we're there, and you'll make it home again! Don't you dare give up now!"

Chef attempted a smile. "Okay," he sighed. "But if I don't—"

Nick felt the weight of Chef's head on his shoulder. He shrugged and nudged, trying to jostle him back to consciousness.

"Kid? Chef? Don't you die on me now!"

"He's sleeping, Nick," Ames assured. "Just sleeping. Let him be."

For a long time Nick stared at the blackness outside the window. He stopped wondering where they were or how far they were going or what they would face when they got there.

There's only now, he told himself. It was the thought that he fell asleep with, and the same thought woke him what seemed like only moments later.

Only now. The train had stopped. Low murmuring followed by deep silence in the car unnerved him and he looked around. Chef seemed to be in a deep sleep, his breathing heavy. All the other prisoners gazed out the windows. Outside, several of the German soldiers stood near the tracks, looking northward. Nick turned to see why the Germans still in the car were so quiet; he noticed all of them focusing outside as well.

"What's going on?" he asked, peering through the window to see what they looked at. All he saw was blackness, the blackness of a deep night that it seemed would never end. Just then a brilliant flash and a yellowish glow lit up the horizon.

"What is it?" Nick asked a smiling Foul-Mouth Matthews. "What—the sun coming up?"

"Not unless the sun rises in the north," Matthews answered. "But I think it might be as good as the sun."

"What—?"

"Well, I don't understand German, you know," Matthews whispered, but it seems to me that words like *bombardieren* and *Berlin* mean pretty much what they sound like. I'm pretty sure those lights are the Brits bombing Berlin."

Nick looked into the night again. Faraway light roiled against the darkness. White flashes preceded orange or red afterglow. The light shifted intensity, sometimes appearing harsh and then muted. Once Nick thought he saw the lightninglike streaks of anti-aircraft fire, then wondered if maybe it were lightning. Though he had been awed by prairie fires and electrical storms and a few times even by northern lights, he had never seen anything quite like this. It seemed that there should be sound accompanying such a light show, thunder or fiery roar or at least a crackle in the air. The silence itself was heavy and seemed to grow more menacing right there in the car.

We're in danger here, he realized, almost certain he could feel the air spark with the German soldiers' unspoken resentment. *They'd like to kill us all right now.*

One by one, his fellow prisoners turned away from the window, as they, too, realized the threat. Here, in the very bowels of Germany, they were the enemy; they were the ones responsible for this destruction of Berlin. They were the ones whose lives had no value to the Nazi soldiers guarding them, and whose deaths could go unrecorded.

For the first time, Nick envied Chef, who remained in a fevered sleep. With any luck at all, the kid would never know what hit him.

Part Two

Stalag IIB 1944

IX

Lucky Strike

Dumb luck. That's what kept us alive that day, Nick decided. Dumb luck had kept the prisoners under the watch of German soldiers unflinching in military deportment. The soldiers had their orders to deliver live prisoners to their internment, and they'd carried out those orders, despite any sore temptation they might have felt to do otherwise, especially when the train finally passed through Berlin. In daylight, the results of Allied bombing were glaringly clear: buildings reduced to mounds of rubble, streets pocked with craters, fires raging. Though he had never witnessed the aftermath of an earthquake, Nick thought that only a catastrophic earthquake could result in similar deadly destruction. Here and there, he noticed, civilian women and children searched through debris. He saw one little girl pick up and wave something silvery. In the sunlight it glistened like tinsel on a Christmas tree. Maybe it had been from a Christmas tree, but Nick suspected it was nothing quite so festive—more likely some of the aluminum strips Allied planes sometimes dropped before bombing in order to confound ground radar. Nick saw the woman swat the strips out of the child's hand, no doubt cursing the cause of the devastation around them—their enemy. As enemy representatives, however, the band of prisoners posed little threat, and Nick recognized the dumb luck in that as well. Filthy and hungry, they railed safely through Berlin, finally arriving at their destination physically weakened but alive. Even Chef had rallied some, enough to stand on his own, though he tired very quickly. At least his fever had broken.

The town they reached appeared to be a fairly bustling community where several rail lines converged. Herded past the main station toward a waiting truck, the prisoners caught sight of a signboard with place-names and distances in kilometers: Neu Stetten, Konitz, Tempelburg, and Jastrow. Another sign indicated that the town they were in was called Hammerstein.

Exactly where, Nick wondered, *is Hammerstein?* One of the other men pointed out a more familiar city name.

"Danzig," Ames voiced, "We're damn near in Poland."

It didn't take long to reach the stalag. Nick estimated that they traveled less than two miles west of Hammerstein along a highway. Shortly after the road curved

northward, the truck pulled off the highway, veering easterly again on a narrower
road before entering the prison grounds.

Stammlager IIB, or Stalag IIB as the Americans called it, looked enormous, covering
more than twenty acres of land and surrounded by two barbed-wire fences. Inside, the
compound was subdivided into four sections, each separated from the others by more
barbed fencing. Four towers rose above the compound, one near each of its corners.
Two guards with machine guns watched from the tower nearest the entry. Nick assumed
that all the towers were similarly manned. Many Nazi soldiers with rifles patrolled on
foot, and large, hungry-looking dogs wandered the grounds, unleashed.

The section for American prisoners held three one-story stone barracks, plus
several additional buildings that housed canteen and workshops, areas for recreation,
dispensary, showers, latrine, and delouser. The latter buildings proved to be the
prisoners' first destination. In Nick's experience back home, insects had not been
a problem in winter, but recently he'd found that lice survived very well within the
climate of the human body during any season of the year.

After delousing, guards watched as working prisoners handed the recent arrivals
their new clothes, uniforms supplied by the International Red Cross, and other
garments furnished by the Germans, including raglike socks, coarse undershirts that
Nick could swear had been spun from some kind of processed wood, shoes—some
pairs were made of leather, others were wooden clogs—and to each man an old
overcoat that already hosted several tiny, leaping insects. Nick looked at the clothes
and picked up the wooden shoes handed to him.

"Where's my boots?" he asked, "And my other clothes?"

"Old clothes are confiscated," came the reply. "You can register an official
complaint if you want, but the last guy who followed that procedure ended up walking
into a bayonet."

With mumbled protest, the prisoners picked up their clothes and dressed. At
least the garments were clean, with the exception of the bug-infested overcoats. Nick
slipped his feet into the wooden shoes, surprised at how comfortable they felt. By the
time the men reached their newly assigned barracks, however, he began to realize the
inflexibility of his footwear.

"Well, here we are," Red mumbled as they entered the barracks, "home at
last—again."

The building looked very much like what the men had already grown used to,
except here the floor was made of brick instead of wood. A center washroom separated
units A and B. Three stoves provided some protection against the cold in unit A,
the front, while two stoves seemed to be losing the battle in the rear unit. Nick saw
that several of the windows were cracked, and some had breaks sloppily plugged with
rags. Triple-tiered bunks lined the walls, each bunk with its moth-eaten, rough-wool
blanket over a thin mattress, which, on closer examination, turned out to be more
like a large papery bag filled with wood shavings. Nick did a rough calculation as they

passed through the barracks, estimating a total of 240 bunks in each half, almost five hundred men per building.

"This is it, guys, home sweet home," announced the prisoner in charge of the newcomers. "Looks like you guys lucked out—got here at the right time. There's a few bunks available. You won't have to sleep on the floor."

"Pretty sizable accommodations," Drummond remarked. "What's our count here, about twelve hundred?

"Oh, there's plenty more around," announced their guide. "By the way, my name's David Bartell." Nick and his companions introduced themselves, claimed their spaces, and then gathered around Bartell again.

"So what's the real lay of the land?" Foul-Mouth asked.

Bartell sat on one of the wooden tables, picked up a pack of Old Gold cigarettes and, after offering one to each of the newcomers, opened a packet of matches, lighting each cigarette with one match. In minutes, the group felt more at ease, sheltered in a haze of smoke. Bartell explained the workings of the stalag.

"This is a pretty new prison camp," he began, "opened last August for all of us lucky bastards. You probably noticed the compound divisions." He pulled deeply on his cigarette and slowly exhaled before continuing. "The krauts got us sorted by nationalities: French, Serb, Belgian. They put us Americans and the Brits together in one section. Must be a language thing. We're allowed to mix some with the other sections, though, except for the Russians. They're a couple of miles from here. Be glad you're not one of them. All together, there's thousands of us."

"Thousands?" Chef looked around in disbelief. For a camp occupied by thousands, the place didn't seem to be overcrowded.

"Prob'ly close to three thousand Americans alone. This here is base camp, a kind of center for work detachments mostly for farm labor. Most of the guys are out on kommando now. There's a hundred and some work detachments. Some of them are a ways away—as much as 350 kilometers."

"What kind of work detachments?" Ames asked, suspicious. "They can't force prisoners to work for the Wehrmacht."

"Well, now, that seems to be a matter of opinion," Bartell explained, lowering his voice. "See, the officer in charge of kommandos is one cream-of-the-crop Nazi asshole bastard—Hauptman Klaus Erbst. You don't want to mess with him."

"What about Geneva Convention?" Nick asked. "I thought the regulations made it a voluntary act to work."

"Yeah. Yeah, that's what a couple of the guys claimed a few months ago. They chose not to work. Erbst said he didn't care what came out of the Geneva Convention. He ordered the complainants to fall in, give their names and numbers, and when they didn't—hell, I don't know exactly what happened. Somehow, I don't know, a bayonet charge, couple of guys wounded—"

"What happened then?" Chef asked. "To the ones who chose not to work?"

"Went out on kommando like they were told. Came back dead a week later. 'Shot while attempting to escape' was the official report. According to some of the other men, all their 'escape' really amounted to was stepping behind a couple of bushes to take a piss."

"Damn!"

Bartell continued his narrative, "That's not the worst. On another kommando, another couple of GIs got themselves shot—again for 'attempted escape,' but that was just more bullshit. It was murder pure and simple. Then that asshole Erbst ordered a special warning for the rest of the camp. He had the dead men's bodies stripped, and left them for a couple of days, lyin' naked in the latrine. He threatened that anybody who attempted to move them would be shot and left in there with them. He meant it."

For a long time, the men sat quiet, taking a few final puffs on their cigarettes. Nick began to doubt the dumb luck that brought them here. He crushed his cigarette against the edge of his wooden shoe, then dropped the butt into a tin sardine can on the table. Finally he asked, "What about you? How come you're not out on kommando?"

Bartell smiled, closed his eyes, and shook his head. "Just pure luck," he said. "Some guys are needed at base camp: medics, basic staff for general housekeeping chores—those benefiting prisoners, you know—and some aren't physically fit enough to work kommando. Me? I got here with a severe case of grippe. By the time I got over it and was fit for kommando, I'd managed to become useful right here at home. I'm one of the lucky *living* stiffs on latrine duty, and there aren't many guys lining up to do my chores. But I don't mind. It could be worse, I could be on dump duty."

"What's that?"

"You don't want to know."

Bartell let his sketchy information sink in, then shook several more cigarettes from the pack. The men lit up once more, eyes squinting as smoke rose around them.

"Hey, you don't have to worry about it right now," Bartell assured. "It'll be a few days before the next kommando assignments. You've got some time to get used to this place."

It didn't take many days to get used to the camp regimen since it followed pretty much the same routine the prisoners had already grown accustomed to. The day began at seven with an insistent summons to *appel* or morning count out in the yard. Satisfied with the tally, the Germans raised their flag on the pole near the main headquarters between sections.

Nick lowered his eyes as all the German guards barked a crisp *Heil Hitler* accompanied by a stiff-arm salute to their flag. Though he'd grown accustomed to seeing that black spidery emblem on every German officer's uniform, the hoisted flag unnerved him more every time he looked at it. Averting his eyes helped him to ward off unwanted what-if thoughts: *what if the Nazis win this war?* In his mind's eye he envisioned stars and stripes, an image he found reassuring, much more uplifting than the encircled, twisted cross on a blood-red field.

After the first salute, the German radio came on, amplified through loudspeakers mounted on guard-tower support poles. Through crackles and hisses, radio voices reported in German, then English and French, the latest victories for the Third Reich, apparently on all fronts of the war. Sometimes the reports included editorial comments. More than once, Nick heard official remarks about Roosevelt and Churchill, "induced by a Jewish plutocracy," having betrayed the ideals of America and England, resulting in the current "bloodbath that claimed so many of their common citizens." Most of the prisoners knew better than to believe the reports, and so they considered the radio announcements more of an exercise to boost the morale of the guards than to reduce that of the prisoners.

Announcements for the day followed the radio report, then came another *Heil Hitler* chorus, which some of the prisoners joined, though they twisted their words just a bit.

"Go to—" they began under their breaths, then finished with a shouted drawl, "h'ell, Hitler!"

Occasionally, when they were sure the guards weren't watching them too closely, some of the prisoners also joined in the salute, though their more subtle gestures usually presented a message that was a far cry from allegiance. Nick realized that these were rather mild forms of dissent against the controlling power, but to a degree they met a need for the men to show that, though detained, they were not yet defeated.

The transferred prisoners fared no better at Stalag IIB than they had at previous camps in terms of warmth and nourishment. Insufficient coal supplies made the barracks consistently cold, and while the prisoners joked about getting "three squares a day," the meals were anything but adequate. Breakfast, served immediately after count and dismissal, consisted again of ersatz coffee, an even worse concoction than the men had grown used to in their last internment.

"Christ!" Foul Mouth swore, spitting out his first swallow of the brew. "What the hell is this shit?"

"Supposed to be ground grains and acorns," Red answered, sipping in mock daintiness with his pinky finger extended.

Chef swilled a little of the drink in his mouth before swallowing it. He lightly smacked his tongue against his lips, exploring the aftertaste.

"Coal," he concluded.

"What?"

"No way! What are you, some kind of swill connoisseur?"

"You telling me this 'coffee' is made out of coal?"

Chef shook his head, coughing. "No. Well, maybe. Maybe it's just the water," he explained. "I used to spend summers with my grandparents in Virginia. Pops was a miner. I just remember everything at their house—even the air—tasting kind of like this, to me at least." He drank another swallow. "It's awful stuff, it tastes a little bit like the worst of home." He drained his share. "Funny, though. The worst doesn't seem so bad to me right now."

At midday, POWs on mess duty brought the main meal into each of the barracks. It came in a large steaming kettle that hung from a pole, which the soldiers balanced on their shoulders. The contents never varied much: most often it was a watery cabbage or rutabaga soup; sometimes instead of soup, each man received two boiled potatoes. If the soldier receiving them were lucky, both potatoes were entirely edible. Most often, however, he had to discard rotted portions—sometimes up to a third of his ration—not always a serious loss, thanks to queasiness induced by the foul-sweet stench of rotted potatoes. Three times a week, the prisoners were treated to meat, barely a mouthful per man from a source they chose not to guess. The main staple continued to be the bread they now referred to as *kriegsbrot*, coarsened with sawdust. A dab of oily margarine per man enhanced the bread's flavor only a little.

Nick found the evening rations at Stalag IIB even sparser than they had been at the transit camp. After their seven o'clock curfew, prisoners had to remain in their barracks where all they received was hot water, which they could use to mix with the coffee or cocoa that came in the Red Cross parcels.

"When I get home," Nick vowed, "I'm going to donate whatever I can to the Red Cross. If not for them, we'd all starve."

"Amen to that," Drummond responded, adding, "How in heck are we supposed to do work detachment if we can barely keep our strength up?"

"Oh you eat a little better out on kommando," Bartell informed. "Kriegies definitely need their strength if they're going to be picking rocks or digging potatoes all day. They get an extra uniform too because they really need it, and leather boots."

Hearing that, Nick decided he might do all right on kommando. Hard labor was not new to him, and if it allowed him to fill his belly a little fuller and wear clean clothing more often, it could be worth extra physical effort. Hunger, it seemed, was his worst demon. His decision faltered somewhat several days later when the first of the work detachments returned to base camp for a couple days of rest.

These men trooped into the barracks, their hands and faces grimed, and their clothes looking more like beggars' rags than uniforms. Some of them nodded greetings to those in the barracks, or raised their brows in unspoken question of the newest detainees. Most, however, stumbled in without acknowledging the others, heading immediately for bunks, or finding none unclaimed, for tables and even the floor, where they lay motionless for several hours, ignoring mess times and waking only when they were summoned to the showers.

Nick's bunk was in a middle tier close to the far end of unit B. The first night after repopulation of the camp—after he recognized that there were indeed several thousand British and American POWs incarcerated—he glanced at the soldier who had climbed, then virtually fallen into the bunk next to his. Since returning from the showers, this man had not moved, though he lay with his eyes open, staring at the bottom of the bunk over his head. Nick turned on his side, leaning on his elbow. Not quite sure how to begin, he cleared his throat.

"Looks like you've had a tough week," he finally offered. "How long have you been here?"

The man didn't answer, didn't even turn his head. Nick tried again.

"My name's Nick Bremer. I just got here a few days ago. I was captured in—"

"He don't talk," a voice came from the bunk below Nick.

"What? Not ever?"

"Maybe to hisself once in a while, but not to anybody else. Not since I known him, and we been here since they opened this fine resort."

"Is something wrong with him? Battle fatigue? Or—something?" Nick queried.

"I dunno. He don't say."

Nick felt a little uncomfortable talking about the man as if he weren't there, but his questions elicited no response from the silent soldier. As a matter of fact, the man didn't so much as blink.

What's a guy in his condition doing out on work detail? Nick wondered. Aloud he remarked, "Seems like he should be in a hospital or at least at base camp under a medic's care."

"I don't think he'd much care for that," the soldier in the lower bunk eased on to his feet, turning to face Nick. "His name's Luke Allen. Least that's what I was told. The guys he come in with—well, a couple of 'em ain't with us no more."

"Attempted escape?" Nick hazarded.

"You already heard that, huh?"

"Is that why—?"

"Nah. Luke was already the strong, silent type before that all happened. It was something else brought this on. We'll prob'ly never know. Anyway—they tried keeping him here at first. Turns out, he's too damn stubborn to sit here and rot. Would rather work out whatever his problems are out there." He held out his hand. "I'm Royal Glover—Roy—your downstairs neighbor. I'd love to spin the yarn with you, but I am plumb wore out so I'm gonna get me some sleep now, okay?"

Roy returned to his bunk, and within minutes, loud, heavy breathing indicated that he had already reached deep sleep. Nick looked at the immobile Luke Allen one more time before he too turned onto his belly and succumbed to sleep.

The soldiers on work detachments were allowed only two days of rest. During this time they got warm showers, had their uniforms cleaned, complained about the meager rations, and slept. Some of them talked about the work they'd been doing: hauling rocks, mucking out barns, picking and digging at frozen ground to unearth any potatoes that might have been left in the field after harvest.

"Is that where our fine fare comes from?" Red asked.

"Hey, if you're starving," someone responded, "even a puny, pocked, soft spud starts to look good."

Hearing the details of work detachment, Nick knew he could do the work all right. It didn't seem much different from what he'd known growing up on the farm, and he seemed in no worse condition than many of the regulars. Any kind of activity, it seemed, would be better than the hours of hungry tedium the prisoners faced in base camp, hours of little to do but evade the dogs and remember kinder times in finer places with friendlier people. Rugged work detail would at least keep those thoughts at bay.

The inflated prison population made morning and evening *appel* last much longer than usual as guards counted and recounted the prisoners, checking the numbers against the official internment lists. The evening before detachments were to go out once more, Hauptman Erbst joined several of the other guards. Referring to papers in their hands, they called roll of new detainees, ordering them to remain in place after count. The men stood for what seemed like hours, awaiting their assignment to various details. At first Nick tried to keep track of who would end up going where, but after a while, the damp wind and incessant ache in his feet and legs distracted him.

When at last a guard barked dismissal, the prisoners stumbled back to their barracks, some feeling relieved, others apprehensive. Nick himself felt a little disappointed. By some luck of the draw, not one of the six men who'd been together since capture back in early November ended up assigned to outside detachment. Appropriately enough, Chef wound up being assigned to base-camp food detail, which included delivery of rations to barracks, oversight of distribution, and general cleanup. The others, however, were not relieved at being assigned to sanitation detail, especially after Bartell warned them of some particulars.

"Sanitation?" He grinned, shaking his head. "That's dump-and-dig detail. What'd you guys do? Piss somebody off?"

"What do you mean?" Drummond inquired.

"Thing is, dump-and-dig is more of a punishment than a regular chore," Bartell explained. "See, what I do on latrine duty is keep the latrine clean—or as clean as a place like that can be in a place like this. You know, I wash it down twice a day. It can be some pretty dirty work, but you guys got a real shitty job—and I mean that in every sense of the word because one thing you'll be doing is hauling shit."

"Aw, come on!" Nick protested, hoping Bartell were only joking.

"Hey, this ain't no bullshit," Bartell snickered, delighted in his own word play. Nick and Drummond looked at one another, then back at Bartell. Finally, Drummond just shook his head, elbowed Nick, and declared, "I think he's just japin' us. David Bartell, you're full of it."

"You'll see," Bartell ragged between guffaws. "It ain't me that's gonna be full of it! Besides that, they'll have you diggin' the fields to cover the sewage you dump there—and probably digging any graves that might be needed." He paused long enough to draw a deep, audible breath. "But there's a bright side. You'll probably get some extra clothes, and maybe even overshoes."

In the next few days, the men learned just how filthy their job was. The latrine, a long, narrow building, held forty-eight outhouselike stalls. Beneath the building, a full, concrete basement collected the waste. When the basement was full, its contents had to be pumped out and hauled away into nearby fields. Fortunately, hauling and dumping waste was not a daily chore; however, Nick discovered that the one thousand to fifteen hundred Allied prisoners housed constantly at base camp could fill a basement with their own by-product soon enough—this in spite of a near-starvation diet. Matters worsened whenever various work detachments returned to camp.

After his first day on dump-and-dig detail, Nick welcomed the monotony of regular prisoner routine. He couldn't quite rid himself of the smell of his work, however. The pungent human-waste odors seemed to seep inside him. Even after scrubbing fiercely at the cold-water taps in the washroom, after sudsing away half a cake of soap to scour the odor from his body, after sitting bundled in his blankets while his clothing soaked and then dried near the coal stove, it seemed he still carried the smell. Like a bad memory, it came to him whenever he breathed deeply. The already-unsavory food he ate seemed laced with an even more acrid taste.

The next time Nick worked in the field shoveling earth over the dumped sewage and spading to mix it into the hard soil, he folded a handkerchief in half diagonally and tied it around his face, covering his nose and mouth. He wasn't sure if this actually reduced the odors, or if the mere suggestion of reduction lessened his senses somewhat. It didn't take long for the other men to follow suit.

Nick hated dump duty. The best way he knew to get through it—until he could convince the guards that he'd be much better suited for kommando detachment—was to do the work as quickly as possible. He used the best method he knew for fast-pacing tiresome chores: listening to music in his mind. The kind of work they engaged in required forceful, martial music, a rhythm that drove the muscles to do the work in quick time. Hearing the marches in his mind, Nick scooped and shoveled, dug and turned the soil in a kind of frenzy that annoyed those working with him.

"Christ, Bremer! You enjoy this? You in some kind of race or what?"

"Yes, I'm in a race," Nick answered, breathing hard. "The faster I go, the sooner I get done. The sooner I get done, the more time I'll have before I have to do this again."

"Well, you're making me tired just watching you."

Nick didn't slow his pace. "So don't watch," he instructed. "Just do it. It helps if you move to the beat of the drum."

At this, several men stopped what they were doing, looked at one another and again at Nick. Warily Drummond asked, "What drum?"

Finally Nick paused. He explained, "Look, guys. I've shoveled manure before, but this is—well, this—it makes me sick. I have to get through it as fast as I can. So I do it to music."

"What music?"

Nick adjusted the handkerchief around his nose. Gripping the shovel in both hands once more, he said, "Like this," and began roughly to sing. He swung the shovel in sharp, insistent rhythm, matching that of the song.

Over hill, over dale
As we hit the dusty trail
And the caissons go rolling along.
In and out, hear them shout,
"Counter march and right about!"
As the caissons go rolling along.

At first, the other prisoners just watched Nick as his movements gained momentum to match the increasing tempo of his song. Then one by one, they picked up the tune, matching their own labor to the pace Nick set. Before long, the entire crew shoveled madly as they very nearly shouted the familiar army tune.

Then it's Heigh! Heigh! Hee!
In the field artillery.
Shout out your numbers loud and strong!
For where e'er you go
You will always know
That the caissons go rolling along!

As the song increased in fervor, some of the guards dared to stride closer, raising their rifles. Usually they kept watch from some distance upwind of the prisoner activity. Observing a sudden behavioral change among the prisoners, they spoke among themselves for a moment, gesturing widely and shaking their heads. Nick saw that some of them even laughed. He could only assume that they didn't entirely disapprove of the more rhythmically regimented toil.

I guess they probably hate this job almost as much as I do, he thought.

When the prisoners finished their work in less time than usual, Murphy slapped Nick on the back. "Good work, buddy," he smiled. "Now we got ourselves a little more time before the tank's full again. Even better—it's our turn for warm showers!"

Hot showers were allowed only once per week, though the water never reached a degree that Nick could accurately label as "hot." Still, even a tepid shower made him feel so much cleaner than did the cold-water tap baths in the washroom. Afterward, Nick relaxed on his bunk, smoking a Lucky Strike. He exhaled and watched the smoke spiral away, then dissipate into the air. The army marching song still played in his head, this time with a new opening lyric:

Feelin' clean; feelin' good,
as a showered Kriegie should
and the hours just keep rolling on!

The life of a prisoner of war became a series of repetitions. Almost any break in monotony provided momentary relief, triggering refreshing conversation rather than the same old reiteration of stale topics. Sometimes the sameness was broken by nature, a vicious blizzard or a fickle winter thaw. Other times, breaks came as a result of war: new prisoners, whose latest news from various battlegrounds provided a gut-twisting mix of pride and misery, or sudden changes in stalag procedures. Most often, however, the POWs themselves broke tedium through a variety of creative channels, from playing practical jokes on each other, or on the guards—whom many referred to as "goons"—to surreptitiously making wine using Red Cross-supplied prunes or raisins and sugar.

For Nick and the rest of the sanitation crew, the worst routine came with recurring dump-and-dig detail. They much preferred boredom, even to the point of inertia. Their only relief in the course of their labor came in discovering and appreciating the irony of burying Hitler's German fields in American waste. Drummond, a natural musician and sometime songwriter, diverted the crew by creating new lyrics to the army theme song. Gloating, the men sang the new rendition softly at first, so as not to be overheard by any English-speaking guards. When their lyrics attracted little attention, however, they dared to sing louder, the words as motivational as the cadenced melody.

Feelin' mad, feelin' mean
As we clean the old latrine,
All us kriegies will keep going on!
In and out, here us shout,
"Goddamned Nazis all about!"
Still us kriegies will keep going on!
Then it's Heil! Heil, Hitler!
We will bury him in shit fer
Everything he has done here is wrong.
Then we'll send him to hell
Where they'll know him by his smell
And we'll send all his henchmen along!

Nick kept his eye on the guards, watchful for any sign that they registered the prisoners' sarcasm. He paid closer attention to one German soldier, whose wary demeanor he had noted before. The man appeared to be in his forties or fifties, roughly the age of almost all the prison guards. Nick assumed this was because most of Germany's younger, abler men bore the brunt of warfare on the battlefields. This particular soldier appeared to listen harder, to be more closely—yet almost furtively—attentive to the activities he watched over. Nick had seen him up close during *appel*, even looking him directly in the eye, a somewhat puzzling experience since the German's eyes didn't seem to work together, and Nick couldn't really tell if the soldier looked directly at him or not. The right eye appeared to, but the left eye listed. It seemed fitting, and somehow unnerving, that the Germans would have a walleyed guard who could focus on two locations at once.

When the crew repeated their song yet again, the guard approached them with long, determined strides. Breaking into the song, Nick warned, "Goon approaching!" Gradually, the lyrics died away, replaced by self-conscious whistling.

The guard trudged through the field to stand directly in front of a burly prisoner known to the others as Bull. For a long moment, he stared at Bull, who tried to meet his gaze equally. Nick watched the scene from a short distance. In a way the two men facing each other seemed unreal, like ridiculous characters from a bad comedy film: a sinister soldier lifting his rifle to confront a masked outlaw wielding a shovel. Bull was the first to break gaze, a move that surrendered any attitude of defiance. Nick guessed that it was because Bull also couldn't tell which of the Nazi's eyes to stare back at. The guard was the first to speak.

"*Was bedeutet das Lied? Erklären Sie, bitte!*"

Bull shook his head and shrugged. Matthews, standing a short distance from Bull, glanced quickly at Nick, and head gestured for him to come over. At first Nick shook his head. He didn't want to get further involved. Every time he got caught up in someone else's ideas or acts, it seemed he and whoever was with him ended up in some kind of difficulty.

"Goddamit, Bremer," Foul Mouth swore. "What's this guy want? Talk to him!"

Reluctantly, Nick moved closer, translating, "He just wants to know what we've been singing—what the words mean." To the guard he said, "*Es bedeutet nichts—nur Spass.*" The guard squinted, studying Nick.

"*Spass*—" he echoed, his tone acid.

"*Es hilft uns schneller zu arbeiten,*" Nick explained quickly, clarifying to the other prisoners, "I told him the song means nothing. That it's just a bit of fun that gets us to work faster."

It felt like a pretty flimsy explanation, and Nick didn't expect the Nazi to be at all satisfied with it, but at the mention of working faster, the guard nodded. His gaze swept from Nick to the other prisoners on detail, then he looked down at his own begrimed boots.

"*Sie können weiter zu singen,*" he instructed almost amiably, then warned, "*Aber es wird verboten den Führer zu verspotten.*"

Again, the prisoners looked questioningly at Nick. The guard nodded his permission for him to translate.

"He said it's okay to go on with the singing. I guess he'd like to get off this detail as much as we would. But," Nick cautioned, "it is forbidden here to poke fun at Hitler."

The men acknowledged the warning with a string of insincere agreements, nodding all the while.

"Not a problem."

"Wouldn't even think of it."

"Gotcha!"

Inwardly Nick cringed, certain that the artificial tones would only anger the guard, and so it came as no surprise when the German ordered Nick to accompany him. *Shit,* he thought, dreading yet another stretch of solitary confinement in the Clink. *Here we go again!* As he accompanied the German soldier back to the guard position further upwind, he heard the prisoners begin to sing again, a little quieter this time.

We'll send him to hell
Where they'll know him by his smell
And we'll send all his henchmen along!

That evening, long after curfew, Nick returned to the barracks, dressed in a clean uniform and wearing—at last—leather boots. As he walked through unit A, several POWs acknowledged him, having heard something of the event in the fields. Drummond looked at him quizzically, and Chef hovered near. By the time he reached one of the tables in unit B, a number of fellow prisoners flocked around him.

"Nick," Matthews sounded almost apologetic. "I didn't mean for you to—hey, you don't look like you've been in trouble. You look like the cat that swallowed the canary!"

Nick pulled a stool out from beneath the table and sat down. He couldn't keep from grinning.

"Boys," he announced, "I won't be working dump detail with you anymore."

"You on detachment?"

"Nope."

"What then?"

"I've been given a new job. It seems that this camp needs another interpreter, and all of a sudden—maybe even thanks to you—I'm the man."

Matthews considered this, then grinned himself. "Damn it, Bremer, how do you manage to come out on top?"

"I don't know," Nick admitted. Reaching into his overcoat pocket, he pulled out an onion and two slightly wilted carrots and laid them triumphantly on the table. "Just dumb luck, I guess."

X

Fritz

As interpreter, Nick got to know a little more about the German personnel. Already forewarned about Hauptman Erbst, he also learned to avoid as much as possible several of the officers whose view of camp discipline tended toward the extreme. Two junior officers in particular, Wagner and Nauman, seemed to enjoy keeping prisoners in line through brutality. POWs out on the kommando details were most at risk of severe beatings, but occasionally someone in base camp "fell ill" as a result of assault. As for the highest in command, Nick could say that the camp kommandant and his immediate assistant appeared correct in their dealings with prisoners, but none of the prisoners believed them ignorant of their junior officers' methods. Another German soldier despised by the prisoners was the chief censor. Whenever Nick was called on to interpret POW letters, he offered the most innocuous translations he could, hoping the brief notes prisoners wrote might reach their loved ones without deletions. Even so, a letter rarely made it past the censor, who fanatically inked out words with his pen as if he were disemboweling a demon.

The only German officer actually liked by POWs was the medical officer, Hauptman Kessel, who treated them with dignity and was meticulous in his assessment of physical fitness before approving prisoners for kommando details. Though his definition of fitness differed somewhat from the American medics' definitions, he didn't completely disregard diagnoses or suggestions made by the American medical officers.

Nick felt most at ease interpreting for the German noncoms, even with the intimidating, lazy-eyed guard Friedrich Janos Immelmann, or Fritz, as Nick began to think of him. Through Fritz, Nick came to value American cigarettes for more than the smoking pleasure they brought. For the prisoners, cigarettes worked like cash, which they used to purchase a variety of items from each other. A general barter system emerged in camp. When a prisoner desired another prisoner's recently received fountain pen or harmonica, the going rate for such an item was anywhere from thirty to sixty cigarettes. Occasionally a prisoner dared to trade with one of the guards, though discretion in these partnerships was crucial. If caught, a German faced severe punishment; prisoners who traded with the enemy also risked being accused of disloyalty.

Nick preferred to barter for food items, most of which he could obtain only through the Germans. He discovered that Fritz attempted a little outside black market trade where American cigarettes were highly valued. Though Nick disliked the man intensely and couldn't completely trust him, the two began surreptitious dealing. He didn't ask what Fritz ultimately purchased with the cigarettes, but ten to fifteen of them might buy Nick an extra quarter loaf of black bread; for only three he could purchase a parsnip or a carrot, and five cigarettes might get him a very rare treat—a real hen's egg. In most cases, Nick shared the bounty from his deals, usually with the same group of men: Chef, Foul-Mouth Matthews, Red Murphy, Bartell, Johnny Ames, and John Drummond. After some murmuring in the barracks about "Nick's clique" and "special treatment," he offered to try negotiating deals for others as well.

Nick found his job as interpreter to be relatively undemanding. He was not the only prisoner at Stalag IIB who spoke German, but one of many. Another inmate, a British private called Ian Kent, was fluent in the language Nick referred to as "high German," a seemingly purer dialect than what he'd grown up with back in North Dakota. Others could understand the language, but could not efficiently speak it. Nick also learned that quite a few of the Germans could speak English in varying degrees of fluency. Because his new role kept him off dump duty and kommando, he didn't question why the Nazis needed him as an interpreter, but speculations rose among some of the other prisoners.

"It's prob'ly a check-and-balance kind of thing," Bartell offered. "You know. In case what you tell them we say isn't really what we say, some other interpreter could report it different. And vicey-versey, of course."

"I bet it's more than that," Foul-Mouth insisted. "I'm thinkin' there's at least one guy in this camp—hell, more likely one in every barracks—that's a stoolie."

"What are you saying? That I'm—?" Nick objected, but Matthews topped in.

"I know it ain't you, Bremer." He leaned in close to Nick and whispered, "But not every prisoner in this camp knows it ain't you."

Murphy reckoned, "I guess you're no longer just one more sardine in the can, Nick. You're a different kind of fish now."

"Then I better be careful where I swim."

Nick tried to be cautious, spending most of his hours with those he knew best and interpreting for those he trusted most. This included several of the permanent camp staff: Pvt. Hank Miller, the Man-of-Confidence, or MOC, whose job was chief negotiator between captives and captors; Pfc. Pete de Luca, the Red Cross representative; S.Sgt. Ray Dickerson, one of the NCOs in charge of mail and parcel distribution; Cpl. Bruce Wyman, Protestant chaplain; and Pvt. Tom Connelly, Catholic representative. Nick also came to respect the four American medical captains, the only commissioned officers imprisoned in the stalag. Their dedication kept the health at Stalag IIB generally good. Save for rare cases of malaria and diphtheria, they mostly treated minor illnesses like grippe or diarrhea. Nick felt the greatest admiration for these men.

"Ah, we're not doing that much," one of the medics responded to Nick's praise. "You can give most credit to the tenacity of our soldiers. Without that, we'd be facing a nightmare here, especially considering that we never have enough quinine or Atabrine—or even aspirin—on hand."

"The requisitions went through Miller to Kessel," Nick offered. "If he wired the Red Cross, supplies should be on their way."

"That's a big 'if,' Bremer," Captain McAndrews explained. "Kessel's only one link in a long chain of procedure. By the time our requisition gets to the end, somebody has decided that we don't really need what we're asking for, and even if we did, it wouldn't look good for the Germans. You know—it gives the wrong impression, like they're not taking very good care of their prisoners."

"I see."

"We requisitioned a thousand Phenobarbital tablets awhile back and got ten. So far that's our only success, if you can call it that, but we keep on asking. What else can we do? You wouldn't happen to know of another source, would you?"

Assuming that the question was posed in jest, Nick shrugged, shaking his head. What he knew of medicine or how to get it wouldn't even fill the dropper used to dispense it. He was somewhat surprised, then, when a second medic, Captain Whitlow asked, "You're sure?"

"I'm sure," Nick claimed. Only then did he realize what must have been intended as a subtle request. As the two medics gazed at him, Nick fidgeted; he trusted these men, but wondered if they trusted him. He cleared his throat before finally responding.

"What? You mean—Fritz?"

"Well?"

"Aw, come on," Nick objected. "I don't deal—you know there's a big difference between finding a few carrots and asking for a shipment of quinine!"

"Couldn't hurt to check, could it?"

"I don't know the guy that good," Nick reasoned. "He's a Nazi through and through. He's just—what—*hungrier* than some I guess. It's not like we *like* each other. He's just as apt to turn nasty as to—"

"Okay. Okay, just thought it might be worth looking into," McAndrews said. "You gotta play it the way you see it. Meanwhile, we'll just keep bugging the MOC to get to Kessler to reach the adjutant kommandant to—well, you know."

"Yeah," Nick mumbled. "Yeah. I know." As he left the infirmary, he felt the challenge laid to him, hefty as a shovel. "Dammit," he murmured, heading toward his barracks. "Feels like I'm still shoveling shit!"

Almost a week passed before Nick found opportunity to do a little preliminary negotiating with Fritz. During a random barracks inspection, the German ordered Nick to accompany him. They sat at a table near the stove while the other guards rifled through the prisoners' meager possessions and bedding. For a long time they didn't speak. Nick occasionally tried to establish eye contact, but as usual, the German's walleyed glance confused him. Finally, they both spoke at once.

"I was wondering—"

"There is something—"

"I'm sorry—what?"

"You wanted to say—?"

Nick chuckled and held up his hand. One corner of Fritz's mouth twitched a little, the closest thing to a smile Nick had seen on the German's face. It didn't do much to soften his natural scowl. Fritz reached into his overcoat and pulled out a cloth-wrapped bundle. He opened it, displaying a small wheel of yellow cheese. A few spots of mold dotted the outer edge.

"*Fünf Pakete*," Fritz said, "*Ein hundert Zigaretten.*"

Nick tried not to look too eagerly at the cheese. He hadn't seen a decent article of food in that quantity in a long time. He drew a deep breath, uncertain if he could actually smell a milky, slightly moldy aroma or if he just imagined it. Though his mouth watered at the thought of biting into a hunk of that cheese, Nick shook his head.

"*Zu viel*," he protested. "Too much. I'll give you twenty-five cigarettes."

"*Nein, nein,*" Fritz objected in his turn. "*Das ist nicht genug!* Four packs!"

For a while both men debated about the value of the commodity and the exchange, then dickered until they reached a stalemate, Nick unwilling to pay more than two packs for the cheese, and Fritz refusing to go below fifty cigarettes. When Fritz began to rewrap the wheel in its cloth, Nick reached out his hand to stop him.

"Wait," he murmured. "What price for the cheese—and for something else?"

"What else?" Fritz sneered. "You want now a good sausage with this?"

"No—well—" Nick hesitated, tempted at first, then shook his head. "No, I'm thinking more of something like atabrine—or quinine. Not for me, you see," he added quickly, "for the sick prisoners. The docs need it."

The German's sneer faded, replaced by a more familiar, cold expression as he declared, "Medical supplies are more than adequate in this stalag. What you ask is impossible."

"They're not adequate," Nick argued. "They're needed to treat the malaria and dysentery, possibly diphtheria. Our docs go through the proper channels with their requests, but their requests are denied, or else the supply is far below what they asked for."

"Eggs, carrots, cheese from the farm—this is one thing." Fritz stood to finish wrapping the wheel of cheese, then tucked it back inside his coat. "Medicine is something else. You would have me rob our soldiers sickened, wounded in the field to give aid to the enemy? I am no traitor. We have finished here."

For weeks Nick had no further dealings with Fritz. He hated admitting his failure to the captains and felt he'd let fellow prisoners down. For himself, he missed the occasional parsnip or slivers of dried beef he might have bargained for. During a particularly cold spell in late February, Nick approached Fritz after evening appel, hoping to find out about the availability of just one extra hod of coal, but the German, on seeing him approach, turned his back and marched off.

Then came a day in March when a gentler breeze blew in from the west. Sun warmed the ground, releasing puddles from the ice. When allowed outdoors for exercise, POWs walked more spryly in their 50 x 50 yard space at the rear of the barracks. They removed their tattered overcoats, stretched their arms, and lifted their faces to the sun. Though morale among the prisoners had always been fairly good, the spring preview lightened their spirits even more. Broader smiles, sillier jokes, and heartier laughter replaced the tight-lipped banter the men had grown used to during the long winter. Nick stood outside with others, lifting his face to the sun. With his eyes closed he could easily imagine himself back on the Dakota prairie, hearing meadowlarks and smelling earth freshly turned for spring planting. For several minutes at a time, the war seemed like something very far away, his imprisonment a memory.

"You Americans," a voice broke into Nick's reverie, "you are so—what is your word—khaki?"

"I think you mean cocky," Nick corrected, recognizing Fritz's voice immediately. He didn't open his eyes, unwilling to return to reality.

"Perhaps."

When Nick didn't respond, Fritz nudged him. "Come with me," he ordered. "I have something I think you will like."

"What is it?" Nick finally did open his eyes and looked into Fritz's left eye. "Medicine?"

"Don't be foolish," Fritz huffed. "Come."

They strode toward the building where Nick occasionally interpreted for the chief censor. Other guards on the grounds paid them little heed. Once inside the building, Fritz motioned for Nick to sit in the chair near a table that held one pile of blank capture cards and another of handwritten—and ink-blocked—letter forms. Nick sat down, surprised when Fritz pulled up a second chair and placed it opposite him. The German removed the papers from the table. He selected two metal cups from a cabinet near the door, placed them on the table, then sat down.

"Here it is," Fritz lifted the canteen from over his shoulders and uncapped it.

"What is it?" Nick asked again.

"*Kaffee.*'

"That's it? That's what you have that I'm supposed to like? Hell, I get this swill—"

"This is *real.* Only good beans." He began pouring the coffee slowly. As the liquid steamed into the cups, a deep, rich aroma filled the room. Both men inhaled, neither able to stifle an appreciative grin. Fritz's grin created deep, curving lines around his eyes and from the edges of his nose to the corners of his mouth, lines so deep they seemed more like crevices. It gave Fritz an almost clownish look.

"What's the occasion?" Nick asked.

Fritz lifted his cup. "Let us drink to an end of the war," he toasted. "To our final victory."

"To *our* final victory," Nick lifted his own cup. They stared at each other, their smiles equally defiant. Fritz was the first to sip. When Nick took his first taste, he knew he'd never had better coffee in his life. For a while the two men drank without speaking, slurping softly and sighing an occasional "ahh." After they'd drained the cups, Fritz refilled them, tapping the last drops out of the canteen.

"I have relation in America," Fritz announced after his next sip.

"Is that right? Whereabouts? Where in America?"

"I don't know. We do not communicate."

"I see."

They both drank again. After several swallows, Fritz spoke again. "Maybe Chicago. Where the gangsters are, *nicht wahr?*"

"I wouldn't know about that."

"You wouldn't know?" Fritz's voice altered a little, the smile disappearing from his face. "You wouldn't know that you rich, cocky Americans are paying gangsters to fight for you? As much as $50,000 to bomb Germany?"

"That's nonsense."

"Sure, sure. You wouldn't know about that," Fritz reasoned. "You are here. How could you know about that?"

"You're here too," Nick challenged. "How could you know?"

"Unlike you, I am in a position to hear things. To know things."

"About gangsters?"

"About Allied atrocities: bombing passenger trains, peasants working in their fields, children on playgrounds, hospitals, even funeral processions."

"That's not true." Nick emptied his cup and put it down hard on the table. "We wouldn't do that. That's just plain—not true."

"Not true? You *know* this is not true?" Fritz lifted the canteen again and shook it. "You want more coffee?"

"It's empty."

"How do you know it is empty?"

"I saw you empty it the last time you picked it up. I know it's empty!"

"Aha! This you can *know* because you have seen. The other you cannot know."

"That's bull—," Nick started, then changed his mind. "We *kriegies* are in a position to hear things too, you know."

"What things?" Fritz leaned in, his lazy eye shifting rapidly. Nick swallowed, suddenly aware that he probably shouldn't have said that. Hesitating, he recalled some of the observations and rumors that prisoners in kommando detail reported.

"How about things like murder of prisoners on kommando detail? Shooting downed pilots? How about rounding up old people, women, and children like cattle and sending them to labor camps? We hear about these things."

"From whom do you hear them?" Fritz demanded in a low voice.

"From—," Nick began, still uneasy. "We just hear them."

"Such stories are propaganda," Fritz dismissed the accusations with a wave of his hand. "These stories are not true."

"How can you *know* they're not true?" Nick taunted.

"I have not seen any evidence of such things."

Nick leaned back in his chair. He felt an urge to laugh. "Seeing is believing, is that right? Have you ever seen a Chicago gangster?"

"I have seen films, read newspapers." Fritz sounded smug.

"Well, Fritz—" Nick slipped, uttering the nickname for the first time. The German lifted his chin and frowned, but Nick continued, "I can say exactly what you said a little while ago. Propaganda. These stories are not true."

At that moment, a small cloud passed over the sun, dimming the room. It sent a shiver through Nick, a chill that didn't end when sunlight brightened the room once more.

"Perhaps it is time you returned to your barracks," Fritz announced.

Nick rose and headed toward the open door. Just before stepping outside, he turned around, remembering. "What is it you wanted for the coffee? More cigarettes?"

"No, no *zigaretten*," Fritz said. "This time I ask nothing for the coffee. I believe for now I have what I want." He smiled crookedly, his left eye focusing on some indeterminate distance. "You may go now."

Nick left. He stepped over puddles on his way back to the barracks, uneasiness adding an icy feel to the spring day. *What did I tell him?* Nick wondered, replaying the brief conversation in his mind. *What did I say that he wanted to hear?* Uncertainty gnawed at him as he suspected—though he wasn't quite sure how—that he had been played for a patsy.

XI

Goon Baiting

"Do you think this is enough?" Chef dumped the last of the raisins into a rusty three-gallon pail he'd managed to scrounge up while on KP duty. "I tried to chop them up finer this time."

"It's gotta be enough," Nick said. "That's all we have this time around. How's the water coming?"

Bartell stood next to the coal stove where an assortment of metal pots and cans began to steam. Gazing into a large open-top teakettle, he announced, "Not boiling yet, but I got my eye on it. Hey, you know what I just realized? My grandma was right about a watched pot. I wonder if that means she was right about everything else too."

"Like what?"

"Like you got to have yeast in order to make wine."

Nick picked up packs of sugar saved from weekly Red Cross parcels and emptied them into the pail of chopped raisins. "As usual, we don't have any yeast," he said. "I guess it's not something folks think we need, like the raisins. Besides, you can make wine without it. All you really need for good fermentation is sugar."

Bartell harrumphed, then reported, "Oh, wait! We got a bubble here. That's close enough to a boil, ain't it?" Without waiting for a response, he grabbed the handle of the teakettle and carried it to the bucket.

"Bartell, I thought we were going to do it right this time," Ames drawled as he watched Bartell pour the water. "The water should be boiling, not just steaming."

"Oh hell, what difference does it make? We still don't have no yeast!"

The men bantered through their third attempt at wine making, hoping for a little more success than their first two ventures had proven.

The first time, they had merely repeated the procedures others had already undertaken but had forgotten to take necessary goon-protection measures. Before their first bucket of wine had had time to ferment, guards discovered the operation and dumped the brew. As punishment for their moonshine activity, all the offenders had been confined to barracks for a week without parcel or mail distribution.

By the time they had amassed enough ingredients for a second attempt, they had devised a plan to keep guards from destroying their efforts. Instead of trying to hide

117

the container, they kept it right out in the open near the stove in the B unit of the barracks, obvious to anyone who came that far into the building. Next to it, they also kept an open packet of laundry powder—something the men occasionally received in packages from home—and a small wooden crate filled with tattered but clean socks. Whenever the cry "Goon-up" came through the barracks, whoever was nearest the fermenting brew dumped several clean socks into the wine. Plunging his arms in up to his elbows, he rubbed one sock against another as if scrubbing out a stubborn stain. If a guard seemed too curious about the activity, the prisoner reached for the packet of laundry soap and added a small handful of powder to the brew. Since the Germans usually showed scornful disinterest in the laundering of filthy socks in a barracks where foot ailments and infections were common, they never drew close enough to notice that the laundry powder was, in fact, white sugar. To cover any possibility of aroma giving their venture away, the prisoners smoked even more heavily in the barracks, until the room was rarely without a swirling, gray haze. For added good measure, a couple of the less meticulous guards had been distracted by offers to taste some of the canned meat products from America.

The first sharing of the wine occurred during a late-winter ice storm. Driving, stinging sleet deterred stalag personnel from making more than a rudimentary barracks inspection. Afterward, the prisoners brought their cups or tin cans to the vat where Chef took charge of ladling the new wine. When the cups had been filled, Foul-Mouth Matthews gave the ceremonial toast, "Let's all raise a glass. If this wine has a kick, may it kick Hitler's ass!"

"May it kick Hitler's ass!" The men echoed and swallowed.

"Phew!" Nick exclaimed, nearly gagging on the cloying taste. "Somebody send this brew to the War Department. I think we've discovered a secret weapon."

"Kind of like drinking syrup, ain't it?"

Bartell took another long swallow and grimaced. "Okay," he said, "what'd we do wrong?"

"I bet we used too much sugar every time we gooned up," Chef claimed. "A pound of sugar to a pound of raisins, wasn't that the ratio? We got way too much sugar in here."

"That's not it," Nick countered. "I think it just isn't ready yet. It's too soon."

"So what do we do? Wait some more? Dump it out?"

"Hell no!" Foul-Mouth protested. "A few drinks and we'll be too pissy eyed to know it tastes like shit. C'mon, the Krauts are in bed, it's fuckin' freezing in here, and we got no place to go. I don't care how it tastes. I'm gettin' drunk."

As it turned out, there wasn't enough of the raw wine for all the men in the barracks to get blind drunk; its potency, however, did cause a few to experience blurred vision and rather odd behavior. After only two drinks, Chef claimed to have lost peripheral vision. He began to move like a marionette, turning his head and body sharply to face whatever he tried to focus on. Red Murphy tried to teach a few of the prisoners how to do an Irish jig. They hoisted their knees as he whistled an Irish tune off-key, until one of the men, claiming to have seen a vision of both his ex-wives, tripped over his own feet, fell against the stove, and burned his ear. One of the original internees at Stalag IIB, Bernard Olsen, sat on the floor between bunks, cradling a scrawny, mangy cat—a pitiful, half-wild beast he'd coaxed from the garbage dump his first week of internment—and sang to it over and over.

You are my shunshine, my only shunsine,
You make me h-happy when skies are blue—I mean—graaaay!

"Hey, Bernie," someone called hoarsely. "Bernie, shut up! You couldn't carry a tune if it had handles!"

"You just shuddup yerself," Bernard answered. "BC likes my singing, don't you, buddy?"

"Then he must be as deaf as he is ugly."

Nick agreed. He had never seen a homelier cat, nor heard a sourer tune. BC, short for Bernie's Cat, had a pointy face with ears that seemed too large for its head. With a bent tail, patchy fur, and numerous scars, it looked to Nick like something a cat would drag in, rather than like a cat itself.

"Why in hell you keep that creature?" Matthews asked. "It's not like there's enough food for us humans here and you go and feed a goddamned cat!"

"BC cashes—catches—rats and mice." Bernard enunciated. "You b'grudge him that, do you? Anyhow, he was here before you were, so don't you tell me—"

"Never mind about the cat," Drummond called out. "Just don't let Olson sing anymore!"

After his first cup of the syrupy liquid, Nick's gag reflex wouldn't allow him to swallow another gulp. His stomach turned, threatening to disgorge its contents. He swallowed several times in an effort to get control over the queasiness, then inhaled deeply, which only made him cough.

"Whatsamatter, old man? Too much for you?"

"No, it's not that," Nick said. "I'm not much for drinking wine. I'd rather have beer or something hard. This just doesn't set well—oh boy, I gotta get some air!"

Nick stumbled from unit B through unit A, then without even checking to see if a guard were posted outside the door, he slipped out. Wind-driven sleet felt like needles against his face. Shielding his head with his arm, he crept along the wall the entire length of the barracks, until around the corner in the back he found some shelter from the wind.

"Son of a bi—" He bent over and vomited, then dry heaved until he felt gut punched. After the sickness eased, he leaned against the barracks wall, sliding down until he sat hunched on the ground.

"Feeling better?" The smooth, clipped voice startled Nick.

"Wha—?"

"It's what you Yanks call 'rot-gut,' isn't it? You really should stick to something a bit more . . . refined. Here, try some of mine. Bremer, isn't it?"

"Yeah," Nick responded, recognizing Ian Kent. He reached for the flask Ian offered, sipping first, then taking a hefty swallow of the smoothest whisky he'd ever tasted.

"*Das ist viel besser, nicht wahr?*" Kent asked.

"*Ja, dank*—," Nick began, then caught himself. "Thanks. It's very good. Where did you manage to get this?"

"Like you, Bremer, I have my connections. Here. Have another drink—something to brace you against the cold."

Nick allowed himself one more taste. He closed his eyes as he swallowed. "Very smooth," he announced. "A guy could get real used to this. It might make him forget about more than just the weather."

"Yes, perhaps we should suggest it for the next war, as part of every soldier's kit—on both sides."

Nick chuckled, feeling warmer. "So who's your source? And what'd you have to trade for this?"

Ian Kent sat on the ground beside Nick. Their backs against the barracks wall, they remained out of the wind where the driving sleet didn't reach them. Warmed by the whisky, they felt no immediate urge to return to the barracks.

"As you know, they're not all bad."

"What's not all bad?"

"Not what—who. The Germans. They're not much different from you and me, except that they started something we apparently have to finish."

"They shouldn't have started."

"Yes, well. That's beside the point."

Nick frowned, facing Ian. "What is the point? What are you doing out here anyway—hell, what am I doing out here?"

"Well, Bremer, as I see it we have a bit in common. We're both prisoners in the same stalag, both translators, and dare I say, we both have some empathy for our enemy."

"What do you mean empathy?"

"You wouldn't be making deals through Immelmann—Fritz—if you didn't have some empathy for his situation."

"*His* situation?" Nick huffed. "Even if I would make deals, as you say I do, it would be because of *my* situation, not his. It could be that I—that he is just someone I could connect—"

"Exactly," Kent interrupted, "someone you could connect with. You have an empathic relationship."

"Nuts to that!"

"I am sure," Kent continued, "that you are both driven by the same motivations. What is most important in your life? No, don't tell me. I believe I can guess: it is home, family, freedom—autonomy, right?"

"So?"

"What do you think Immelmann is fighting for? For that mustached buffoon they call a führer?"

"Yes, that's exactly what I think he's fighting for, except that Fritz isn't exactly fighting."

"Serving then. He's serving a cause of home, family, autonomy—in a country that has had those values weakened since the last war by—shall we say—certain segments of the population."

"What segments?" Nick asked, though he thought he knew what Ian meant.

"You know—communists," Kent once more offered his flask to Nick, "and Jews."

Nick pushed the flask away, shaking his head. "I don't know what you're getting at."

Ian Kent capped the flask and tucked it into his coat pocket. Getting to his feet, he offered a hand to Nick, helping him up. "I'm not getting at anything, actually," he said. "I just thought you knew—would like to know, for example—that our very own MOC, Hank Miller, you know, the man representing us prisoners, is Jewish."

"I didn't know that, but so what?"

"You didn't know that?" Kent echoed, "But you know it now."

"I guess—I mean—no." Nick felt that all-too-familiar uneasiness come over him, suspicion that he was being tested, or maybe tempted. "All I know is what you just told me. And that will hardly pass as confirmation."

"Oh, I wasn't looking for any confirmation," Kent laughed. "I was just curious about your loyalties, you see. One can't be too sure where one stands—or with whom one stands. In this hole, one must always beware of a mole."

Nick shook his head. *Is it the wine and the whisky,* he wondered, *that makes this conversation suddenly confusing?* He knew where his own loyalties lay, and at first he was dubious about Kent, but now he wasn't sure. Or was it Hank Miller he was supposed to be unsure of? His instinct told him to disengage.

"Yeah, well. I'll keep an eye out," he said and turned the corner into the wind. Behind him, Kent called, "There's a radio, you know, in the barracks. There's a connection to the outside—" but Nick pulled the collar of his coat up close and pretended not to hear.

Later, Nick lay awake in his bunk, while those around him snorted, snored, or moaned in their sleep. Unit B reeked of smoke and vomit. Apparently several prisoners had reacted strongly to the wine.

Hell, it's not the wine, Nick told himself. *It's the place, the empty bellies!* He closed his eyes, trying to force himself to sleep by recalling details of life before the war. He visualized the USO Club where he used to dance with Helen. He remembered how she looked the last time they danced there, just before they had—*he* had—decided not to marry. Behind his eyes he saw her again, wearing that sleek green dress that draped her form so elegantly, saw the way it fluttered around her legs when she walked away from him.

Stop it! Nick groaned and turned over. The edges of his eyes ached, the effort to keep them closed exhausting muscles he didn't even know he had. He tried to recreate another image, one without any hint of regret: Ma's garden—the rows of cabbages and peppers and beans; new peas that bulged in their pods; tomatoes so ripe and juicy, they nearly split their skins; new potatoes pushing up through the soil. He imagined himself once again hoeing weeds away from the plants, flicking potato beetles off the leaves and into a can of kerosene, picking up a hefty potato and holding it to his face, inhaling, then suddenly seeing it shrivel and shrink in his hands while a great rumbling sound came from somewhere within his own body. He dropped the potato, and it fell with a splash by his feet. Nick looked down to see the pristine, white, sandy bottom of the clear aquamarine sea he swam in. He had never seen water this color, a color he could breathe like clean air. He inhaled harder and harder, then noticed that with every inhalation, the dropped potato swam nearer, its shape now torpedolike. He held his breath, but the potato still came nearer, and now Nick could see that along with eyes, it also had teeth, arrow-shaped teeth in a maw that gaped wider and wider. Nick thrashed in the blue, his movements slowed by the weight of the water. He tried to find footing on the sandy bottom, to push away from the shadowy, hungry creature gaining on him. He saw peripherally that a small dark island lay near behind him, if only he could reach it. The potato, now recognizable as a shark, spewed a bubbling laugh, then clamped down hard on Nick's kicking foot.

Aaaiiiii! Sharp pain in the sole of his left foot woke him. Nick sat up, breathing hard. He rubbed the stinging sole of his foot.

"Ouch, dammit!" His fingers pushed against a thick splinter that had lodged in the tender arch of his foot, a splinter from the crosspiece of his bunk. He must have been kicking and scraping against that to get away from his nightmare. In the predawn gray light of the barracks, Nick tried to see the splinter end and grasp it between thumbnail and fingernail, but its edge was just below the skin so he couldn't get a hold of it.

Just then, the door at the end of unit A banged open, and a guard's voice ordered morning roll call. Nick wondered how most of the night could have passed in the few minutes of his dream. Many of the other prisoners moved slowly this morning, some moaning and clutching their heads. Nick swung his legs over the edge of his bunk and stood up, wincing. He sat down again to pull on his socks, adding a second sock to his left foot. This cushioned the sole a little, though he could still fill the needlelike pierce whenever he put weight on his foot.

Fully dressed, Nick limped out of the barracks to line up with the other prisoners. His left shoe pinched, two layers of thick knit too much for a comfortable fit. Hoping for a short count this morning, Nick put most of his weight on his right foot and tried not to think about the irritant under his skin. He concentrated on the tedious process of head count, then on the propaganda report—shorter this morning than usual.

"Thank God!" Nick sighed when the men were dismissed. He limped toward Chef.

"Chef, we gettin' anything besides sludge this morning?"

"Why would today be different?"

"Wishful thinking, I guess. Must be something I dreamed last night." Nick shuddered, now remembering only the last few seconds of his dream. "I got to check with the doc, okay? I gotta get a shark tooth out of my foot."

"What are you talking about? Are you still drunk?"

Nick shook his head, waving Chef away, then limped across the compound to the building used as an infirmary. He waited there, listening to the coughing and moaning of men who still battled grippe or malaria. It seemed a long time before McAndrews came in.

"Well, well," the doc greeted Nick. "Haven't seen you in here for a while. Looking for a little hair of the dog this morning?"

"Is nothing secret around here?" Nick sat down to tug off his shoe and socks.

"No, I don't need any hair of the dog. I had some pretty fair medicine last night—compliments of Ian Kent. You know him?"

"The stiff-upper-lip Brit interpreter? Sure."

"You trust him?"

"Shouldn't I?" McAndrews examined Nick's foot, then whistled. "Wow, what were you up to last night, barefoot tunneling? I'd advise against that."

"Believe it or not, I was fighting off a potato," Nick joked. "One with teeth."

"Right. I keep telling you guys—you're living with shrunken stomachs, you're on different metabolism now. You have to go easy on the sluice." The doc opened a drawer and pulled out a pair of tweezers. "Can't get a hold," he said after a minute. "If you want this out, I'm going to have to dig it out. It'll hurt like hell for a few minutes."

"Better than hurting like hell for a few hours. Go for it."

Nick clenched his jaw as McAndrews worked, needling the splinter out of Nick's foot. When he finally got it out, he held it up.

"Son of a gun," Nick grimaced as he flexed his foot. "That's no splinter, that's a shim."

"Yeah, it's going to give you one sore foot for a while."

"Got any kind of poultice for it?"

"Poultice," McAndrews considered, chuckling. "My great-grandmother used to put a mix of mud and manure on open wounds. I wouldn't advise that, though. A bread poultice might work, but most of the men would rather eat their bread rations than wear them. Let me just bandage it up good for you. Keep it as clean and dry as you can. You know the drill—the same practice to prevent trench foot."

His foot wrapped, Nick pulled on one sock and slipped back into the shoe. He thanked the doctor and, stepping lightly on the sore foot, hobbled to the door. Just as he reached for the handle, the door opened from the outside and Hank Miller started to enter.

"S'cuse me, Bremer." He stepped back to let Nick pass, then called after him. "Wait!"

Nick turned. When the MOC beckoned him, Nick returned to the infirmary. The two men, joined by McAndrews, made their way past the sick prisoners, into a more private area behind makeshift screens.

"Have you had any luck with your guy?" Miller asked. "Any chance we'll find a supply of meds here soon?"

"I'm afraid that connection's gone cold—for now," Nick said.

"Oh? How come?"

"If I knew that for sure, I might know a lot of other things." Nick answered. "Like why Kessel is ignoring your requests for supplies—"

"It's not Kessel who's ignoring them. That goes higher up. His wires aren't reaching the Red Cross."

"Do you know why?" Nick asked Miller. "Are they ignoring Kessel, or are the requests ignored basically because they come from you?"

"What the hell is that supposed to mean?"

"Bremer," McAndrews intervened, "what's this about?"

Nick moved toward one of the wooden chairs that sat next to a small table. "Mind if I get off this foot?" he asked, sitting down. Hank pulled out the other chair and straddled it, leaning against its back. McAndrews sat at the edge of the table. Nick told them about the unusual interrogation by Fritz, and about Ian Kent's cryptic comments. He explained his uncertainty to the doc and the MOC, two men whom he trusted implicitly, raising his concerns about being mistaken for a stoolie or unwittingly informing a stoolie. He didn't want to mention the remark about Miller being a Jew, but since he'd already implied a problem between Miller and the Germans, he could hardly sidestep the issue. Miller was first to bring the subject back to that.

"What did you mean before, about med requisitions being ignored? You said that I had something to do with it."

"I didn't say you did, I said—"

"He said," McAndrews interjected, "that they're ignoring requests that come from you. Isn't that right, Bremer?"

"Look, I don't know if that's what's going on. I just thought that maybe—if they know—"

"Know what?"

"Know that you're a Jew."

McAndrews snorted, much to Nick's surprise. "Hell's bells," he said. "That's not exactly a state secret. I know it, your chap Kent knows it. There's other prisoners in this compound who happen to be Jewish. I'm sure plenty of guys know that Miller's Jewish. It's not so surprising that the Germans would learn it too."

Miller nodded. "So far I've been treated like any other prisoner. I didn't mention a religious preference on my capture card—not because I was afraid to—I just thought it wasn't their business. And so far—"

So far, they knew Miller had been admired and respected as the American Man-of-Confidence. They knew that some anti-Semitism existed among the prisoners—it had to among such a large and mixed contingent—but that it had not affected Miller's position so far. Nick hated to accuse anyone, especially since he wasn't certain there was anything sinister to accuse him of, but he wondered about Kent.

"You think Ian Kent's a plant?" he queried.

"Maybe. Maybe not," Miller answered. "Maybe we need to find out."

"How?"

"Bait him. Just like you bait the goons."

Goon baiting had become one of the prisoners' favorite methods of tormenting their captors without suffering direct retribution. It took a variety of forms, but the favorite scheme was to lure a German guard into stealthy eavesdropping, then when he thought he was on to a swell of secret information or stash of smuggled goods—like a radio—to sully him in some way.

Nick's first experience with goon baiting had been as a bystander. At first he wasn't aware that the whole incident had been set up. Olsen, Bartell, and a cocky young New Yorker Alex Symmington seemed to be in a serious bunk-side discussion about tunneling activity within their own barracks. Nick had observed through the rag-patched window that a German soldier leaned against the building just beside the window, casually smoking a cigarette. Nick tried to warn the three men with a gesture, but they just grinned, brushing his concerns aside as they continued their much-too-audible chatter. Later when several Nazi soldiers explored the ground just outside the barracks where they assumed the tunnel to be, Symmington stealthily approached an open window inside the barracks, a heavy bucket in his hands. When the guards stood together in just the right spot, booting a slight depression in the ground, the young American casually announced over his shoulder, "Well, *my* laundry's done!" He hoisted the bucket and tossed the contents out the window, dousing three of the Nazis with dirty water.

Since then, Nick learned that a couple of the guards had been drenched with hot water, one with cold, and rumors flew that a few unlucky Nazis had been befouled by the swill called soup, and even by urine. The prisoners never confessed more than just accidental responsibility for sullying a guard, and always implied that the guard had been most careless in his duty. So far, goon baiting had brought punishments of a few days' confinement to barracks without light and once in a while, if the guard were of particular standing, without coal for a day or two. Since the men felt they already inhabited hell, they willingly risked occasional punishment just to see their enemies besmirched. As a morale booster, goon baiting worked wonders.

Since Ian Kent had to be aware of the practice, Nick had no clue how to lure him into a situation that would either confirm or disprove his loyalty. He didn't feel clever enough to devise some sort of trickery. Maybe the clique—those few men he felt closest to—could help him come up with something.

Nick waited a few days before he finally brought up the subject. On the mildest evening the prisoners had known in months, they idled outdoors just before evening appel, breathing in the earthy scent of spring. Casually clustered together, Nick's clique listened to what he had to say. When he finished, they seemed hesitant to speak.

"So Miller's a kike," Foul-Mouth finally blurted. The others glared at him; as Drummond shushed him, he protested, "What? Aw, c'mon, it's a nickname for chrissake! Miller's a kike, Fancy over there by the post is a frog, Kent's a limey. You and me are yanks, and the bad guys are krauts. So Miller's a kike, Murphy here is a—what the hell are you, anyway?"

"In your circles, I believe I might be referred to as *mick*," Red responded dryly.

Nick shook his head. "Listen, guys, we're getting off the subject here. This is what I want to know. Is Kent a Nazi stoolie, or does he think I'm the stoolie and he's just feeling me out? Remember my last deal with Fritz? I told you guys about that. He thinks I know something, and he seemed pretty eager to find out what. Is Kent after that something too?"

"Or does he think you've been selling out?"

"Exactly," Nick said.

The men thought awhile, offering suggestions for baiting either the Englishman or the German, or both. They dismissed most of the suggestions as impossible, ineffective, or incomplete. Finally, they agreed that it would take some time to uncover the information they wanted.

"Time," Nick offered, "I guess we got plenty of that." After their discussion, Nick felt more certain that the only way to find out what Kent stood for was simply to ask him. The time had to be right for that too.

"I think it's going to be pretty good this time, Nick." Chef dipped his finger into the wine and licked the tip. "Not too sweet, not too dry."

"Just too . . . raisiny." Nick tried a drop himself. Both Nick and Chef had spent most of the day outside in the yard, taking in the sunshine, as spring finally seemed to instate itself. Cool mild air smelled rich with earthy dampness. Though the grounds were too muddy for engaging in ball games, many prisoners wandered from barracks to barracks, bored with inactivity, but reluctant to leave the welcome sun. Nick and Chef would still be outside if both hadn't misjudged the depth of a wide puddle near the hut where worship services were conducted. Back in the barracks, they took off their wet, muddied socks, tossing them in a pile to launder later. Nick removed a bandage from his foot and casually tossed it onto the laundry pile. Carefully he dried the slightly infected wound on his foot.

"Seems like the only way I'll keep my feet dry around here is to carry them around in my pocket."

They removed their pants and hung them over chairs near the stove. A few coals from the night before still glowed faintly in the stove's belly. Waiting for their pant legs to dry, the men tested the wine, made small talk when they could think of any, and read articles from the premiere issue of *Barbs & Gripes*, a POW newsletter detailing camp activities and complaints.

"Look at this," Chef called Nick's attention to a particular blurb. "Says here that German citizens 'will celebrate *der Führer's* birthday this month in a strong show of support for the cause, demonstrating their gratitude to soldiers serving the Reich . . .

could that mean extra rations for our hosts, and maybe for their starving guests as well?' You think that's possible, Nick?"

"Hah," Nick dismissed the notion. "I wouldn't get my appetite in a stir if I were you."

"No, I s'pose not." Chef put the newsletter down and stared at the stove. After a few minutes, he reached for his pants and dug in one of the pockets. He cupped a small item in his hand, studying it for a while, then showed it to Nick.

"See this? You have an idea what this is for?"

Nick glanced at the tiny, notched, hat-shaped knob and started to shake his head. He frowned, picking it up between his thumb and index finger.

"Where'd you get this?"

"While I was working mess, that Englishman, the interpreter?, he dropped it and I picked it up. I tried to give it back to him. I thought maybe it was his lucky piece, you know, like I have my lucky spoon. But when I held it out to him, he acted like he didn't understand me. You know what I think it is?"

"A radio dial." Nick handed it back.

"Yeah, what should I do with it?"

"Better put it somewhere safe," Nick directed, adding quickly, "No, not in your shirt pocket. Somewhere else—"

"Bremer! You in here?" A voice called from unit A. In a moment, Ian Kent himself stepped into unit B. Nick stood up, blocking Kent's initial view of Chef and hoping the kid would somehow get rid of the dial. More and more he suspected that Kent was a German plant in the stalag, that Chef finding the radio dial was no accident. What he didn't know was why Kent would plant incriminating evidence on someone as naïve as Chef. What could be the purpose in putting the kid in peril?

"What do you want?" he asked.

"Oh good, your young friend is with you." Kent stepped over the box of dummy laundry and kicked the small pile of muddied socks closer to the stove. He crouched beside Chef, gazing intently at the young man, who himself stared into the bucket of wine.

"How is the latest brew?" Kent asked, a little too loudly, Nick thought. The Englishman dipped his finger into the liquid. He licked the tip of his finger, then smacked his lips as if savoring something fine. "Not bad, not bad at all. You chaps have obviously improved your technique."

"What do you want?" Nick asked again.

"Very well, we'll have done with the small talk." Kent stood, looking again at Chef. His voice dropped to an intense whisper. "I came here to collect something that belongs to me. It's very important, and I need it now."

Chef looked at Nick, who shook his head ever so slightly.

"I don't know what you mean," Chef answered with more composure than Nick thought him capable of. "I don't have anything of yours."

"Don't be obtuse. You know very well that you picked up something I dropped earlier. Hell, you made such a big deal of it then, I had to ignore you! Didn't you notice that you'd begun to attract attention?"

"I don't have anything of yours," Chef said again.

"Then you must have given it to your—patron," Kent spat. "Bremer, I need that piece. It is vital to more than—"

"I don't have anything of yours either," Nick announced.

At that Kent became more agitated, glancing over his shoulder toward the doorway between units, and then toward the window nearest them. Again he crouched low, motioning Nick and Chef to lean in close as well.

"Listen, you fools! I'm part of an underground. We have a radio—tune in to BBC London every night, then dismantle the radio immediately afterward. The parts were smuggled into camp in marked bars of soap. Prisoners each carry a piece of it until we can reassemble it just before—look, I wouldn't be telling you this if I weren't on the up and up. Goddamit! I need that piece before tonight!"

"Maybe you lost it outside somewhere—carelessly," Nick baited.

"Keep your voice down," Kent ordered intensely, then added in a loud voice, "How long have you allowed it to ferment?"

Chef glanced at Nick, puzzlement on his face. Kent darted his eyes quickly toward the window as a signal that someone might be outside eavesdropping. At that moment, Bernard Olsen entered the unit, cradling his cat under one arm. He too gave a slight nod toward the window and lifted a finger to his lips. Sidling close to the window, he remarked jovially, "I heard you guys got some fine brew here ready for the palate. Whew! I hope that ain't the wine I smell. You guys oughtn't stick your smelly feet so close to the goods!"

Olsen's next move came so quickly and so gracefully, that afterward Nick would always remember it as a kind of dance. Bernard whispered tenderly to his cat, then with one hand, hoisted the window open, while his other hand, the one holding BC, swung back in an arc, then forward. As if he'd done it a hundred times before, he pitched the cat through the window. BC yowled, his mouth gaping in an evil, terrified grin, claws flexed as he sailed through the window.

"*Jesus Gott!*" A voice roared outside as a German soldier suffered the pointed results of BC's terror. Olsen grinned, nodding at Kent.

"I had to give them something," Kent whispered to Nick and Chef. "If you don't trust me about the radio, ask McAndrews. He knows, he's carrying too."

Foul-Mouth Matthews and Red Murphy hurried into the unit as a commotion arose behind them in unit A.

"Goon up! Goon up!" Murphy whispered, dashing to the wine bucket; he shoved Kent out of the way. Grabbing a handful of socks, Murphy plunged them into the bucket, then began frantic scrubbing. He tried to cover his breathlessness by whistling an irregular tune. The rest of the men arranged themselves casually around the barracks, just as three Germans entered the unit.

Fritz led the trio; one of the other guards bore fresh razor-thin scratches on his cheeks, chin, and forehead. In the next few minutes, Nick noticed that the German's wounds blossomed into angry red welts.

"*Was haben wir hier?*" Fritz toed the bucket of wine. Murphy lifted a discolored sock out of the wine, its brownish stain looking suitably filthy.

"Just catching up on my washing," Murphy grinned. "You know us Americans. We like to keep clean, no matter how dirty our surroundings."

Fritz half smiled, shaking his head. "*Werdet ihr nie lernen?*" he asked, then in a clipped tone, added in English, "Do you think you are dealing with fools?" He snapped his fingers and the cat-scratched guard stepped forward. The guard used his bayonet to fish the remaining socks out of the bucket, then carelessly tossed them onto the stove. He gripped the handle and began to carry the bucket toward the washroom that separated the barracks units. Fritz looked at Kent then, who returned his gaze without flinching. Nick couldn't tell if their eye contact communicated something or not.

Just as the guard reached the washroom, Fritz called out. "*Halt! Kommen Sie zurück.*" He then nudged the other guard, ordering, "*Bringen Sie mir ein Glas.*" When the soldier hesitated, Fritz gestured toward the table where the prisoners' collection of metal cans and cups sat. "*Eine Tasse,*" he added impatiently.

The soldier brought him a cup with a handle. Fritz dipped it into the bucket of wine now at his feet. He sniffed it for a moment, wrinkled his nose, and sniffed again with his eyes closed. He sipped, swishing the liquid around in his mouth as if he were rinsing out a bad taste, then spat the wine out onto the floor. He sipped again and swallowed.

"It is not fine," he judged. "The officers would not like it. But it is not distasteful. Perhaps"—here he gestured again to his companions—"we might provide our soldiers with a libation of their own tomorrow, a special toast on a special day."

He dismissed the two guards and as they exited the barracks with the wine, Fritz looked first at Kent, then at Nick. Nick had a sick feeling in his stomach. Though he had not seen it happen, he was certain that Chef had dropped the radio part into the bucket when Kent first entered the room. He glanced at Chef, raising his eyebrows in question. The kid looked tense and flushed, as if he would burst.

Fritz, shifting back to his native language, instructed the two interpreters to inform their men that they were confined to the barracks for twelve days, without lights, without parcels, without mail, and without coal. Any further infractions would bring more serious reparation. Nick allowed Kent to relay the information, keeping his eyes on Chef, mentally encouraging the kid to hold his tongue awhile longer.

After the Germans cleared the barracks, the men remained silent for a time. Nick, feeling sheepish that he'd faced the enemy with his pants off, hurriedly dressed. Chef also reached for his pants, then clutching his stomach, he rolled onto the floor and howled.

"What the hell—?" Matthews jumped back, startled, and Red reached for Chef's shoulders to shake him.

"It's okay, kid," Red assured. "They're gone—we're okay."

"Wait a minute." Matthews frowned. "He's *laughing*! What the hell is so funny? We're locked in here for damn near two weeks, and we can't even get drunk to help us through. What is there to laugh about?"

"Didn't you see?" Chef choked, reaching into the box of dummy laundry. He pulled out a sock and handed it to Kent. "Here's what you were looking for."

"I don't get it," Murphy said. "What's so funny about Kent's sock?"

"No, no." Chef caught his breath. "Murphy, when you gooned up, you reached for the wrong pile. You didn't put any of the clean socks in the wine. You rinsed out Nick's and my dirty socks—and his foot bandage—in the wine. And Fritz thought it tasted pretty good!"

"Well, well," Matthews chuckled, then laughed loud. Nick laughed until his stomach hurt, until he felt his face would crack. Kent too guffawed as he surreptitiously extracted a small item from the sock in his hand.

"I have just one thing to say," Red announced. He stood and raised an imaginary glass. "Happy birthday, Herr Hitler! Drink up, you Nazi bastards!"

XII

Food for the Soul

Earlier in the year, lockdown in the barracks might not have been so hard. In the grip of winter, with nothing better available to them, the men would have spent the time as close to the stoves as possible, telling stories or playing cards or dominoes. This time, however, the walls of the barracks seemed to close in even more than usual. Poker or pinochle games lost their appeal as the men gave in to distraction, gazing wistfully at the windows through which they could see other, less-confined prisoners exercising in the yard, or strolling toward one of the buildings where Yankee ingenuity had created means of battling agonizing tedium.

You don't miss the water till the well runs dry, Nick acknowledged, not for the first time.

Now that there were other things he could do, he felt an almost unbearable itch to get outside, to do something with his hands—maybe work in the hobby area where he might ply his carpentry skills to build more shelves for the camp's growing library—or take advantage of one of several means of keeping his mind occupied. He estimated that shipments from America had already endowed the camp with well over a thousand books. Some of the prisoners used these books for informal classes, even though the kommandant generally disapproved of that, apparently deeming educational endeavors to be outside the work-base function of Stalag IIB. Still, the prisoners who were not on kommando details managed to hold classes in math, literature, history, and even law. Fortunately, many of the guards preferred that the prisoners keep themselves occupied in such a way. It made their jobs a little easier, curbing what might otherwise be a dangerous restlessness.

In addition to various hobbies and the library, the newly established *Barbs & Gripes* newsletter kept some of the men busy writing articles or drawing cartoons, which others reproduced for the next distribution. Recreation opportunities in camp had increased in the last few weeks as well. Outdoors, the men were still restricted to a rather confined area near the barracks, but they managed to do daily calisthenics or throw a ball around now and again. One of the best improvements, however, had been created in the French sector of the stalag, a small theatre shared by all. With hours of time available to them every day, prisoners exhaustively rehearsed musical talent shows and comedy skits for camp performance. A phonograph and records, even a film projector and screen supplied by YMCA just before spring, offered both prisoners and captors some very welcome hours of entertainment. So far, in one of his minor roles as an interpreter, Nick had announced to the barracks and to the Germans the showing of two films, also compliments of YMCA: *Andy Hardy's Double Life* and *Judy Garland presenting Lily Mars.* Up to three hundred men could crowd into the makeshift theatre at one time, so every film or concert or stage play was presented up to five times to accommodate all the prisoners—and guards—who wished to see it.

Having tasted these soul-nourishing tidbits in their otherwise drab and depressing lives, the men felt in their punishment an even deeper craving than they'd known in almost half a year. As they fed their bellies with the "slop and sawdust" of standard prison fare, they longed for the flavor of chocolate or chewing gum or Spam from their withheld Red Cross parcels. Not allowed to occupy their minds or bodies with intellectual or physical pursuits, they found themselves wandering in potentially perilous territory: their own morose thoughts. Mail also being withheld, some of the men tried to keep their spirits up by rereading older letters, but this only made them hunger for more. After nearly six months of incarceration, Nick had still received no mail, though he had written three letters to his parents, two to his brother, Marcus, and two to Helen. Having any chance of mail withheld as punishment only made his desire for word from home more wrenching.

On the eighth day of barracks lockdown, the men's morale seemed to have sunk to its lowest. Most of them lay on their bunks, closing their eyes to their surroundings or staring vacantly into the air. Foul Mouth Matthews marked time tapping his fingers against one of the boards of his bunk. *Tap. Tap. Tap.* The steady rhythm reminded Nick of the pendulum clock that hung in his mother's kitchen. There had been times in his youth when the clock's steady *tick tick tick* had driven him into another room, or outside where no discernible pulse announced the slow, ceaseless passage of minutes. Even when it had bothered him back then, at least the ticking in some way had announced the certainty of today passing into tomorrow, creating in him a restive anticipation for something else—whatever his future held in store. Now, however, Matthews' unremitting *tap tap tap* seemed only to confirm that time was leading them nowhere. Today would become another today and then another, unchanging, a hellish eternity of nothing. *Tap. Tap. Tap.*

"Damn it, Matthews!" Nick finally barked, "You're making me nuts with that tapping. Knock it off already!"

"You got something better I should do?" Matthews muttered.

"Bacon." The word came from Red, and both Nick and Matthews sat up, exchanging puzzled looks.

"What?"

"Aw, I almost had it for a second," Red moaned.

"Had what?"

"What the hell are you talking about?"

"I've been workin' on this for a while now," Red explained. "If I think hard enough about something—bacon, for instance—if I concentrate on it really hard and try to see it in my mind, I think I can actually remember how it tastes and smells."

"You're crazy!" Matthews dismissed him and lay down once more, though this time he refrained from tapping.

For Nick, however, an image of bacon entered his mind so sharply, it was almost as if Murphy's words had conjured up something tangible. He visualized a thick slice of home-cured bacon sizzling in a charred skillet, the white fat and pink meat slowly crisping to a deep golden-brown. He imagined taking it in his fingers, the hot slice dripping grease, and lifting it to his mouth to take that exquisite first bite of salt-brine, smoked-meat flavor, crispy and at the same time juicy with rich fat. He sighed, then chuckled.

"You know what would be real good next to that?" Nick offered. "A stack of buttermilk pancakes big as a pie plate, just oozing with melted butter and chokecherry syrup."

"Huh-uh," another voice joined in. "Pure maple syrup. There's nothing like it."

"Don't forget the eggs," Matthews contributed. "*Real* eggs, three or four of 'em, fried sunny-side up and sprinkled with salt and cracked peppercorns. That would be heaven."

"Not without some orange juice," Bernard Olsen added. "A big glass of it, squeezed fresh, and thick with bits of orange."

One after another, men involved themselves in enhancing the imaginary menu. One added a glass of milk—served cold and fresh from the farm, with swirls of cream still floating at the top. Another included real coffee, strong and black. Their heavenly breakfast grew to include bowls full of strawberries and cream, "Grandma's caramel-and-nut sticky buns," a banana, and even kippered herring.

"Not on your life!" The last suggestion met with strong veto. "No sardines! We aren't having anything that comes in a can that we can get in POW parcels!"

"Only real food. That's the rules."

Just like that, the men made a game of teasing their appetites with fantasy foods. Each man tried to outdo the others in his descriptions, to bring about the loudest moans of desire. After only a little further discussion to establish ground rules, they decided that the winner of the game would be he who finally made one of the others plead for them all to stop.

"Then what?" Bartell asked. "What does the winner get for winning? There ought to be more incentive here."

"The winner can have my evening rations," Murphy joked.

"Oh, he's a funny man," Matthews scorned. "How about this: the winner gets his choice of one item out of everyone else's next parcel."

"Aw hell, Matthews, that's still at least four days away!"

"So? Gives the lucky bastard something to look forward to, don't it?" After the others added their reluctant agreement, Matthews continued. "Okay, that's it then. Let's do lunch."

During the competition of courses, time seemed to lose its excruciating pace. The men moaned their way through visions of fried chicken, cheese-filled dumplings, a steak, sizzling outside, but "rare enough to moo" on the inside. They smacked their lips over home-made raspberry ice cream, chocolate cake the size of a hatbox, a peppermint stick, spring-cooled watermelon, fresh ears of corn roasted in their husks, and mugs of cold, frothy beer. Occasionally, a friendly argument broke out over adherence to the rules. When Murphy introduced a succulent baked ham smothered in a sweet raisin sauce, Olsen protested.

"Wait a minute. Raisins are prisoner food. You can't be using raisins."

"They don't come in a can," Murphy argued.

"Don't matter. They come in the parcel. No prison food, that's the rules. You lose! Next contestant!"

"Oh, I got a good one," Matthews spoke up again. "For my first meal when I get home, I'm gonna have some of those tender, wafer-thin slices of juicy roasted beef, with a thick, dark gravy covering a mound of mashed potatoes, light and smooth as whipped cream—"

"Hold on," Murphy objected. "No potatoes. We get that here. Potatoes are out."

"We don't get *mashed* potatoes!"

"Hey, if I can't have raisin sauce, you can't have mashed potatoes. That's the rules."

"Well, what the hell am I gonna put my thick, dark gravy on if not mashed potatoes!" Matthews glanced around, looking for a little support from the other men. Finally he focused on Chef, who throughout the game had lain silent but watchful in his bunk.

"You! Chef, you gotta help me out here. You more than anybody here should know—"

"Leave me alone," Chef mumbled and turned away. His response surprised the others into silence. They looked at Chef, then at each other. Finally Bartell leaned forward and whispered, "Is that a give? Does that mean that Matthews won?"

This raised a new volley of protests, and the competition resumed. Nick listened awhile longer but kept glancing at Chef. The kid had been quieter than usual in the last four or five days, but this was the first time he'd actually spurned their camaraderie. Usually Chef would cling to the group, or at least to one or two members of the group. Nick edged around to the other side of Chef's bunk.

"You okay here, Chef?" he asked.

The kid shook his head, his eyes reflecting a misery Nick had not seen there before, not even in the early days of their capture when they didn't know from one minute to the next if that would be their last. Then, the look in the kid's eyes had been one of sheer terror, but now it was the dullness of absolute despair. Before Nick could voice his next question, Chef reached out and grabbed him around the neck, pulling him closer.

"It's like they know something," Chef whispered intensely, and Nick could feel a trembling in the hand that gripped his neck. "Listen to them. They all feel that they'll be going home sometime. They can actually see all that food in their minds, practically taste it too!"

"It's just a game, kid. Just a way—"

"But I can't see it!" Chef's voice, now slightly above a whisper, shook with a barely subdued panic. "I used to go to sleep nights thinking about—seeing—home, but I can't see it anymore. I try and all I see is where I am! I want to join in with you guys here, but no matter how I try, I just can't *see* anything in my mind, can't even imagine the taste of anything but stale crumbs and flavorless, watery soup."

"Come on, Chef," Nick tried again, but the boy wouldn't let him finish.

"You guys . . . you all have some kind of . . . I don't know . . . a well full of hope that we're gonna make it outa here. I don't have that. I thought I could make myself believe it, but I can't anymore. I *know* I'm not gonna make it back home—that I'm destined to die in this place."

Chef's insistence unnerved Nick, but he chose not to give sway to the kid's fears. Instead, he loosened Chef's grip from around his neck.

"That's just the hunger talking now," he said, "and the boredom. Don't give in to that. You've already bucked some pretty serious odds here. Besides, lots of us guys in here are counting on you to get us through." With his knuckles, Nick rapped lightly against Chef's chest, where he could feel the metal object tucked inside Chef's pocket. "You're the one with the lucky spoon."

Chef tried to smile but failed. He sat up, lifting his own hand to his pocket, fingering the bowl of the spoon. In a moment, he gave Nick a conciliatory nod, then said in a flat voice, "I suppose a person could have a nice rice pilaf—wild rice—instead of potatoes, I mean."

At Nick's urging, Chef repeated his suggestion loud enough so the others could hear. During the subsequent jibes of *Pee-laff!* and *ooh lah-dee-dah!* Chef made an effort to join in the laughter and teasing. Nick could see, however, that pretense at levity did nothing to replace the dull look of misery in the kid's eyes.

The men continued with their game until their rations were brought into the barracks. Then the insipid smell of acorn coffee and the coarse texture of the dry bread silenced them. They chewed and swallowed their portions without any pleasurable exchange, once again without humor, almost without hope.

Two days before the expiration of their barracks confinement, the men went through the motions of falling in for morning count, their spirits dimmed, but not quite extinguished. Nick kept his gaze on the ground during the raising of the Nazi flag. Though he heard the propaganda report of the day, he realized immediately afterward that he had not listened. When Drummond, who stood next to him, whispered for clarification of one of the announcements, Nick shook his head, remembering nothing of what had been said.

After the general prison populace had been dismissed, the men from Nick's barracks waited in formation as they had every morning and evening for the past nine days. They waited for the escort back to their confinement, where guards and dogs would make sure that none of them exited the barracks and no one from other barracks entered. When the escort didn't immediately appear, Nick began to pay a little more attention to the scene around him. As he scanned the dwindling crowd of prisoners in khaki or gray, Drummond nudged him.

"What do you s'pose is goin' on over there?" He nodded toward a scene somewhere to the distant right. Nick followed the gaze and noticed for the first time that Fritz and Ian Kent seemed locked in an in-your-face kind of conversation. After a few brusque gestures from the Englishman, the German stepped away, then abruptly spun back. Nick could hear nothing of what was said, but the stances of the two men told him some kind of argument had reached its peak.

"I think we might be about to find out," he murmured to Drummond as Kent and Fritz together made their way across the compound toward the men still in formation. Fritz seemed even more out of sorts than usual, and his walleye darted wildly as he growled his orders to the prisoners. Before Nick had time to translate, Kent stepped forward.

"You men are to resume your normal activities and duties," he announced, a little too triumphantly, Nick thought. "The confinement is lifted." Kent and Fritz exchanged one more heated glance before Kent continued, "And you are advised to remember the—ah—'leniency and fairness of your treatment here by the personnel at Stalag IIB.'"

Matthews snorted, a sound that turned into a series of coughs after Olsen elbowed him in the ribs.

"Yes, well," Kent continued. "On that, I believe you are dismissed. Wait! Before you fall out, I am also informed that you will receive last week's and this week's parcels and mail sometime before the day is out."

This brought relieved sighs from the men, who collectively had no intention of returning to their barracks—not when they might engage in some activity, relieved from the inertia of the last several days. As they departed, Nick and Kent remained. When they felt they could speak without being overheard, Kent put his hands in his pockets and nodded, indicating that Nick should walk with him.

"The intelligence is out," Kent finally pronounced in a low voice.

"What?"

"We heard confirmation—coded, of course—on BBC several nights ago. They know what's going on here."

"You mean our being confined to quarters is news?"

"No! God, Bremer, sometimes—," Kent complained, then added, "You can quit playing these games with me. No matter what you think of my methods, I am not a kraut. I'm an Englishman through and through."

"Okay." Nick kept his tone noncommittal.

"What I meant is that the outside has the word—about the inhumane rations, the lack of necessary medicines, the brutality, the murders of men on labor detail. Fritz telling you to be honest about your treatment here means that they're probably hosting a rather unexpected Red Cross inspection team today or tomorrow—soon at any rate. If it happens that some Swiss gentlemen should show up and ask questions about your treatment here—go ahead and play along. Tell them everything's swell. They already know the truth. As I said, the intelligence is out. You should probably inform your friends about the details."

Details. When it came to details about most developments, Nick felt he never had quite enough of them. When pressed for more detailed information, he typically found himself providing the sketchiest of answers, marked with frequent *I don't knows* and *maybes*. Often it made him feel out of the loop, whatever the loop might be. Other times, he felt protection in partial intelligence, in knowing just enough to be alert, but not enough to be a threat, either to the Nazis or to his fellow prisoners.

Nick spent most of that day away from the barracks. He wandered the grounds, engaging in small talk with several prisoners whom he didn't know very well. He spent a few hours in the makeshift shop area, sanding rough boards under the careful watch of guards. Later, he went to the library to set up and stock some of the new shelves. Quite a few men occupied the area; some studied from books, while others wrote letters. Toward evening, Nick stopped in at the infirmary, but noticing that the docs and orderlies seemed pretty involved in their work, he shuffled back to the barracks. The only good thing about going back to that unit was that once inside, he didn't feel so closely shadowed by a weapon-wielding soldier, or an unfriendly dog.

The next few days proved to be considerably gentler in camp. A surprise "bonus" Red Cross parcel made it to each prisoner, and the Germans announced the recent arrival of a shipment of quinine. In a most unusual move, they also extended access to a field at the center of camp, where prisoners might engage in athletic activities: softball, basketball, football, or volleyball. What's more, POWs of all nationalities were to share the field and could use it freely every evening after 1700 hours.

Nick supposed these events were results of the intelligence Kent had told him about. He began to feel that he might have misjudged the Englishman. Anyone who could bring about such a boost in general morale couldn't be too bad. *Of course, he only reported the news*, Nick cautioned himself. *He didn't exactly make the changes.*

Whatever covert actions Kent might have been involved with, he had nothing to do with Nick's best morale booster. On what seemed to be the finest day a May morning could promise, after months of anticipation and subsequent disappointment, Nick finally received mail, not just one letter, but five.

He held them in his hand like a long-sought treasure. There was his name, five times, written in five different scripts. He recognized his mother's precise style, Marcus' scrawl, and his father's detailed swirls, lettering no doubt influenced by the exotic German script Pa used for keeping accounts. He didn't recognize the writing on the other two letters.

Impatient to read, but at the same time reluctant to tear open the envelopes, Nick looked around for a private area. Nowhere seemed very private or inviting, and so at last he simply sat on the ground in the sun, leaning his back against the wall of one of the barracks adjacent to the playing field. He didn't know which letter to open first, which to save for last. Finally he chose the letter that bore his mother's handwriting. At the top of the page, just before the heading, was the date: March 25, 1944. The airmail letter had been written six weeks ago. Nick read on.

Dear Nick,

At last our prayers are answered. Since November until now we have waited for news from the War Department, better news than the "missing in action" telegram we received then. Your letter to Marcus is the first we have heard of you, and thank God Marcus dashed into town to share the news with us as soon as he took the letter out of his mailbox and saw who it was from. Thank God you are out of the fighting now. I pray that the prisoner camp where you are is watched over by decent men and that this war will be ended soon so you and all the men and boys can come home. You should know that your brothers and sisters are well and your little nieces and nephew too. We had a letter from Jacob. He could not tell us where he is, but we think his XXXX is somewhere near XXXXXXXXXXXXXXXXX. Mrs. Darschon, you remember her, she used to live on the Fox place? She is a gold-star mother. I don't ever want a gold star for being your mother or Jacob's, so you stay safe. God bless you and keep you warm.

Your loving mother.

Nick couldn't keep his bottom lip from trembling as he read the short letter. When he finished, he folded the missive carefully and simply held it for a while. He couldn't help but think of what his mother must have gone through in those first four months. She hadn't even known that he was alive until six weeks ago—months after report of his capture should have gone out. Since his family hadn't learned until March that he was a prisoner of war, Nick felt especially lucky that the letters—five letters—had all reached him in a relatively short time. He knew by what other prisoners experienced that it took up to four months for surface mail to reach camp. Airmail took only five weeks. His folks had paid the cost for airmail.

Nick looked at the two letters whose handwriting he did not recognize. He assumed, because of the perfection of the script, the spacing and shaping of letters, that these had also been written by women, but definitely not by the same woman. He hoped one of them was Helen. Choosing one, Nick's fingers felt clumsy as he opened the letter. He couldn't help glancing first at the signature. *As ever, Helen.*

As ever. Not *love*, not *affectionately*, not even just plain *yours.* Nick swallowed a lump in his throat, trying to quash that sense of dread that so easily lodged in the pit of his stomach. He took a deep breath, then read.

Dear Nick,

> *First I want you to know how relieved I am that you are all right. In spite of everything, I have worried about you and prayed for your safety every day since I heard that you'd gone missing. You have to know that, no matter what, I will always care deeply for you.*
>
> *Because I care, I have to tell you that I have been seeing someone else. You were right not to commit to a relationship with so much distance and uncertainty between us. I met Charlie at the hospital where I've been doing volunteer work since you left. I read to him and wrote his letters as he recovered from eye surgery, necessary after severe shrapnel wounds. For the rest of his life, he will wear one glass eye, and though vision has returned to his right eye, he will never again see the world clearly. We discovered that we have a great deal in common; we like the same foods, listen to the same music, enjoy the same books.*
>
> *I know that you will like Charlie, especially his great sense of humor, which is so much like yours. We are going to be married before the end of the year. I hope hearing this will not make you think any less of me. I would very much like us to remain friends, and when this war is over, if you come back to Cleveland, you will always be welcome at our house.*
>
> *As ever, Helen*

Nick read the letter a second time, hearing Helen's voice in her words. He couldn't blame her. After all, it had been his idea to delay any commitment until after the war. Still, he felt an awful finality, like a door slamming closed or a light extinguishing. Suddenly the pleasant May sunshine lost its warmth. Nick got up, tucked the letters into his pocket, and walked back to the barracks.

Apparently he wasn't the only one who had received less than happy news in the mail. Olsen alternately boiled and bragged about his wife taking a factory job; a guy named Slade wept into his mattress. Nick didn't ask why. Johnny Ames sat at one of the tables, staring intensely at a photograph. As he walked by, Nick noticed the picture of a pretty woman with her arm around a little girl.

"Your family?" Nick asked, his voice rough. He cleared his throat.

"She's growing up so fast," Ames sighed. "I'm missing so much—"

Chef sat on his bunk, absently turning something through the fingers of his right hand. In his left hand, he held a torn envelope. When Nick drew near his own bunk, Chef looked up but said nothing. Nick lay on his back, then took the three remaining letters from his pocket. He chose the one written by his father, but before he could open it, Chef called.

"Bremer? You ever get—you ever hear of someone getting something like this?"

"Like what?" Nick asked, without bothering to look. Chef stood up and walked over to Nick's bunk, his hand extended. Nick saw that the object Chef had been fingering was a feather.

"Throw it away," he said without waiting for Chef's next question. "It's nothing. Just throw it away."

"This came in an envelope—all the way from my hometown. There wasn't any letter or anything. Just this feather. I don't know who sent it."

"It doesn't matter. Just throw it away."

"They think I'm a coward, don't they? They think I gave up on purpose—"

"Look, kid. You're no coward. Everybody here knows that, and your family back home knows it too. If this was sent as a message from someone at home, then whoever sent it is the coward, not you. Take my advice and throw it away."

Chef clenched his jaw, nodded, and turned away, but as he did, he tucked the feather back into its envelope, folded it, and pocketed it in his shirt, right next to his lucky spoon. Nick returned to his letter from Pa.

Dear Son Nikolaus,

Your mother and I are much relieved at the news that you are yet among the living and that you suffer no injuries. You should also know that I am proud of you, and of your brother Jakob. We turn on the radio every night hoping for heartening news. It seems we must be patient awhile yet. God willing, Jakob is as yet well. Marcus and his wife are good farmers on the home place, and the land is producing again. We are sorry to say that Frank and Agnes and young Jimmy moved to Montana, and Elsie is engaged to a bespectacled teacher who wheezes. Another Roosian, but not like Frank. Your mother and I wish they would wait until after the war to marry, and so far they obey our wishes. If the war lasts a while yet, God forbid, we have hope that Elsie will find someone better. Take care, son, and know that you are in our daily prayers. We will send a package.

Your father, Nikolaus G. Bremer

In spite of the ache he felt over Helen's letter, Nick couldn't help smiling at the news from his Pa. What an odd mix the old man was: proud and humble at the same time, stubbornly clinging to his old attitudes, yet showing near resignation to what he could not control.

"You know what, Bremer?" Chef interrupted Nick's thoughts again.

"What?"

"I'm not gonna let this get to me. I'm not a coward! Sure I get pretty damn scared a lot of the time, but that doesn't make me a coward!"

"No, it doesn't."

"They'll see. I'll show them yet. Even if I never get home, they'll see—"

Nick folded Pa's letter and began to open the one from Marcus. In an even, but firm tone, he assured Chef, "Look. The real coward is the one at home sending feathers to prisoners without so much as signing his name. And as for being afraid—what the heck, Chef, only a fool isn't afraid. I'd put more trust in a frightened man than in a fool!"

Chef clenched his jaw again, his lips tight with a new determination. Nodding slightly, he patted his shirt pocket where his spoon and the feather were. Nick realized that the kid would never throw the feather away, not now. Just as the spoon symbolized good luck, from now on the feather would represent some kind of willpower. Maybe receiving the feather was the best thing for Chef.

Nick read the letter from Marcus. He couldn't help smiling, even chuckling aloud at Marcus' words.

Dear Brother Nick,

> *You had us perty worried there for a while. It sure is a releif to know that you are alright. I don't know if its because you are lucky and blessed or stubborn and stupid! Ha Ha. Whatever it is, you just keep it up and when all this is over, I hope you come on back home to North Dakota. The folks sure would be pleased if you lived here again. Our little girls would like it too if their Uncle Nick came home to teeze and play with them on a reglar basis. Molly and Theresa are growing like weeds! You mayn't even know them anymore except for their Bremer marking—that black hair and those blue eyes, like you and me see every time we look in a mirror. Dora sends her love. God bless you and keep you safe.*

> > *Marcus*

Only one letter remained. For a minute Nick thought he just might put the last one away to read at a later time, when loneliness or tedium became almost unbearable again. Almost immediately after he thought of the plan, he felt doubt. What if the letter were like the one from Helen, not exactly bad or unexpected news, but nothing pleasant either. Reading that on a day when his spirits were low would only make him feel worse.

He tapped the envelope against his palm, studying the handwriting. It was very neat, slanted perfectly, just the way all his teachers' had said good penmanship should be, a style he never seemed to achieve himself. He knew the letter wasn't from either of his sisters. Elsie's bold and Agnes' spidery strokes were easily recognizable.

Finally Nick decided he could not wait.

Dear Nick,

    Your brother told the folks in church on Sunday that your family had finally heard from you after almost five months. He said that you wrote that you were well, but that you apparently longed for word from home. I thought I would drop you a line to let you know that not just family, but also friends and neighbors at home are thinking of you. You remember me, don't you? We went to country school together. You used to ask me to help you study for your vocabulary tests. Do you still remember that "dethrone" has nothing to do with "de outhouse"? Oh, how we laughed about that when we were kids!

    I returned to North Dakota just after you enlisted last year. For almost two years I had been working for XXXXXXXXXXXXXXXXXXXXXXXX in XXXXXXXXXX, California, where three of my sisters and their husbands now live. California is an exciting place, but when Ma and Pa had a hard time finding help on the farm, I thought I'd better come back and give them a hand. I've always preferred working outdoors to working indoors. I guess that makes me a tomboy still. Unfortunately, on my trip home, I lost my watch on the train. While I teach (can you believe I now also teach at the place where we used to go to school?) I wear Ma's watch. I guess you could say I'm living on borrowed time.

    Everyone here prays for your safe return. We'll "keep the home fires burning" for you!

                              Your friend and neighbor, Carolyn Pater

Nick did remember her, one of ten siblings of the Pater family who lived near the country church. Back when Nick's family still lived on the homestead, they used to get to church early on Sundays, just so they could see the Pater girls—all nine of them—walking to mass in their Sunday best, each girl wearing a different color or hue. Ma used to call them the "Pater parade." In school, Carolyn was always the fastest reader, the best speller, but Nick remembered that two of her younger sisters were prettier.

Smiling, Nick took all five missives out of their envelopes, piled them one on top of the other, then read them all again—more slowly this time, imagining the faces of his loved ones as they might have looked when they wrote the lines. It felt good knowing that people missed him and prayed for him. Even Helen's letter, though discouraging, helped to feed a deep kind of hunger that no mere food could satisfy.

XIII

On the Town

On a rainy afternoon late in May, Nick sat at the table in his barracks unit, shuffling and reshuffling a deck of cards. Snapping them into formation on the table, he then counted out cards by three and slapped the trio face up, creating a discard pile. The top card was a ten of hearts. Nick picked it up and placed it on the jack of diamonds in the formation.

"Hey," Ames remarked, "you can't put red on red."

Nick counted out another trio—no play—then three more cards.

"Bremer, you can't put red on red," Ames said again, but Nick ignored him. Ames stepped closer, thumping Nick's shoulder with his knuckles. He leaned over the table close to Nick's right ear and pronounced, "I *said*, you put a red ten on a red jack. That's cheating. You deaf or somethin'?"

Without looking up from his game, Nick mumbled, "Or somethin'."

"Christ a'mighty, shut up already!" Matthews, trying to sleep, grumbled from his bunk. "You guys always gotta yammer like that?"

Nick carried on with his game. When the cards came up right, he placed black on red or red on black as the rules dictated. Several times when they didn't, he played color upon color. Again, Ames kibitzed.

"Geez, Bremer, either you don't know how to play the game, or you're a lousy cheat. You gotta be a lot smarter to be a good cheat."

"You know what this game is called?" Nick asked. "It's called *Solitary*. Do you have any idea what solitary means?"

"Actually it's called Soli*taire*," Ames shot back, "and I sure do know what it means. It means you want to be left the hell alone. Well fine, you just pretend the rest of us aren't here."

Just then Bernard Olsen strode into the rear unit and called out, "Any of you seen my cat?"

"Nope." The answer came from various directions. Even if someone had seen the mangy beast, Nick figured that no one would say so. Everyone but Bernie, it seemed, hated that creature, resenting it for its ability to roam freely and its stupidity for not roaming free of Stalag IIB.

"Damn cat ain't got the sense to come in outa the rain is what I'm thinkin'. Stupid animal! Wonder where he could be." Dejected, Bernard stuffed his hands into his pockets and headed back outside.

Nick collected all the cards, thumped the deck loudly against the table, then stood up. Without a word to the other men, he also strode outside the barracks. He knew he shouldn't be so testy among his compatriots, but an indefinable malaise had put him on edge for the past several days. The euphoria he'd felt upon finally receiving mail dissipated quickly, as he realized the likelihood that it could be many months before further word from home reached him. He still hoped for the promised care package from his folks but suspected that the parcel of food items or clothing intended for him had already been claimed before it reached the prison camp. Captive for half a year already, Nick chafed at the thought that the war's end could still be a long way off. More frequently he had to remind himself, *there's only now*, but that didn't keep the unanswerable questions from creeping into his thoughts: *How much longer? What if? What's next? When?*

The tension Nick felt was not his alone, though certain others seemed to feel it as more of a sense of anticipation. It could be because of the change of seasons, Nick supposed. The end of what had seemed to be the longest winter of his life brought such relief, even on cloudy, damp days like this one. He guessed, however, that something else also lay under the general attitude, basing his guesses upon subtle clues: the lift of an eyebrow from one, the slight nod from another, the occasional overheard word. He could have been much more in the know. All he had to do was pose the right questions to the right people—Ian Kent and Hank Miller, among others that he thought of as "the radio ring."

He didn't ask. Whatever might be in the offing—talk of escape, some hopeful reports from the front—didn't account for the sudden, almost-benevolent manner of the Nazis, their tolerance and even encouragement of prisoner activities within the compound: sporting games, lessons, entertainments. It just seemed that the morale among the troops—both prisoners and captors—might be inordinately high. He didn't trust the Germans' easing of restrictions, even if it had come about as a result of a negative report from the Swiss Red Cross inspectors. He also felt uneasy about the optimism indicated by his fellow prisoners. It just seemed too sudden, too unpredictable, and Nick feared that it might lead to a lapse in vigilance or good sense. With his bilingual understanding, it was impossible for Nick not to pick up tidbits of information, but he took care not to know—or seem to know—too much. To achieve a kind of middle ground, Nick honed an old skill from childhood—an *I-dunno* kind of detachment, a feigned deafness, even dullness. It allowed him to listen carefully when it appeared that he couldn't hear, or didn't care, or was too preoccupied or witless to understand. In this way, he figured, he would know more than he appeared to know and could convincingly play ignorant if he needed to.

What exactly do I know? he asked himself more than once. *Something big is coming, but for who? Why are both Germans and allies in high spirits?*

Nick walked across the compound in rain that had dwindled from the earlier downpour to a steady drizzle. He'd had no particular destination in mind when he left the barracks but now thought he might as well visit the French-sector theatre and sit in on one of the rehearsals for the next stage show. Maybe that would lighten his mood a bit. He noticed that many prisoners had selected to brave the rainy weather rather than stay cooped up in the barracks. Some even enjoyed a very soggy attempt at football.

"Hey, Bremer!"

Nick looked into the drizzle to see John Drummond sloshing through the mud toward him.

"You seen Ames around?"

"Yah, he's kibitzing back at the barracks," Nick answered dryly.

"Huh?"

"Never mind. You just come from the show hall?"

"Yup. That's why I gotta get Ames. I got this great idea watching some of the guys practicing. We could be a pretty good duet, me and Ames. Both of us aren't too bad as musicians—even on those shoddy guitars from the YMCA, and we harmonize real sweet too. I even got a great name for us. Bet you'll never guess."

"Uh"—Nick played along—"Hummer and Strummer? John and Johnny? Two Johns?"

Drummond chuckled. "No, but you're getting warmer. We're both over six foot tall, and we're both named John, so how about 'A Pair of Long Johns'? Pretty clever, don't you think?" Without waiting for a response, Drummond slogged on toward the barracks, and Nick made his way to the makeshift theatre.

Stepping into the building, Nick saw that he wasn't the only one to sit in on rehearsals. While some of the men found these practices to be nearly as tedious as doing nothing at the barracks, many came to enjoy behind-the-scenes antics that never made it to the stage on talent nights. Currently, those antics included several prisoners wearing loose, belted tunics that passed for dresses and wigs made of bound straw. They struggled not to laugh as they practiced an inharmonious version of a tune popular in America just a couple of years earlier, "Boogie-Woogie Bugle Boy of Company B." Nick couldn't help but chuckle, and he appreciated the sudden lightening of his spirits. The men's falsetto voices butchered the melody, and their efforts at synchronized dance had some onlookers in tears of laughter. Hairy legs kick stepped to the tempo. With each bounce, the men's grossly exaggerated bosoms gave in a bit more to gravity.

"Hey, Bull," a voice called from somewhere in front of Nick. "Don't look now, but I think you're about to lose your kajoobies!"

Without missing a clumsy kick step, Bull manipulated his descending breasts, lifting them until they formed a rack just below his neck. As he bobbed his chin from the left one to the right and back again—all in tempo with the music, his audience rewarded him with hoots, whistles, and catcalls.

Bernard, who had entered the building not long before Nick, apparently found the act a little more promising than searching for his cat. He also whistled and grinned as he strode toward the front to take a seat with the jeering audience. Nick edged into one of the back rows of benches and chairs where he felt equidistant between the other prisoners and the several groupings of guards. He noticed that most of the Germans laughed and heckled with the prisoners; a few, however, remained stony. His eyes adjusting to the dimness of the room, Nick recognized Fritz in quiet conversation with Hauptman Kessel, the German medical officer. At just about the same time, Fritz noticed Nick and gave an almost-imperceptible nod.

Fritz continued to be Nick's primary source for barter, usually accepting American cigarettes or Red Cross commodities for extra rations or stale produce, sometimes for some kind of meat or an article of clothing. For whatever reason, with the slight easement of restrictions and even slighter increase of rations came greater vigilance in black market trading. Nick had not managed to barter anything with Fritz in the last two or three weeks. The German's nod seemed to indicate that at last he might have something to offer. Nick focused once more on the stage business and waited.

He sat through three more acts: a juggler, who couldn't keep his balls of wadded up socks in the air; a jokester who kept bungling punch lines; and a singer who crooned almost as artfully as Bing Crosby himself. During the last repetition of a very slow-tempo version of "Don't Get Around Much Anymore," both Fritz and Kessel took a seat in the row behind Nick.

"*Das ist ein sehr trauriges Lied, nicht wahr?*" Kessel observed.

Nick turned. In English he answered, "I guess it is a kinda sad song. The saddest thing about it is that it's so true." He waited while Kessel, whom he knew to be proficient in at least three languages, remarked on his response. Thereafter, the three conversed in either German or English, or a fractured blend of both.

"Perhaps my news will be not so sad," Fritz offered.

"What have you got for me?"

"Oh, this is not for you alone." Fritz's tone seemed arrogant, triumphant. "It is for all the prisoners, at least for those in base camp."

"Oh?" Nick couldn't resist a sarcastic tone. "You're surrendering? We can all go home now?"

"*Das Vaterland* will not make the mistake of surrendering a second time," Kessel put in. "However, it would appear that there is cause for a little—what shall we call it—beneficence?"

"What kind of 'beneficence'?" Nick queried.

"*Ein Film.*"

"Cripe. Is that all? Do you know how many times the men have already seen those movies? Half of 'em can spew every line of *Andy Hardy's Double Life* and the first two reels of *George Washington Slept Here*. By the way, we never *did* get the other reels. Heck, we even repeat the lines in our sleep!"

"*Nein, nein, nein!*" Fritz objected.

"I think you will find this to be much better," Kessel added. "It is quite a pleasure, and it proves that Germany handles its—guests—with great generosity. We are not the 'mad dogs' your propagandists would have everyone believe."

"Just what kind of film is going to prove that?"

"You will see," Fritz gloated. "*Sie werden zu Hammerstein gehen, den Film zu sehen.*"

Nick shook his head, uncertain that he'd heard correctly. The two Germans actually grinned. As usual, Fritz's grin twisted his features and crinkled his walleye in such a way that he looked sinister rather than satisfied. Nick chuckled, shaking his head even more.

"Oh no. Now I know you're pulling my leg. You think I'm going to believe that you'll let more than a thousand men out of confinement—just send us off into town to the motion picture show, like we're—what—your good little kids? You guys oughta do this act up there on the stage. It's almost funny."

Fritz's grin disappeared, but Kessel kept smiling.

"I understand your disbelief," he admitted. "It is quite obviously not something your countrymen would do for their German prisoners, is it? Perhaps *der Führer* is of a more humane nature than are your Roosevelt and Churchill."

Nick didn't respond to that. Instead he remembered the phrase Kessel had used to introduce this ridiculous enterprise.

"You said there's cause for this. What cause?"

"Our military is always one step ahead of yours," Fritz boasted. "When yours thinks it is taking a great step, ours is always greater. Soon you will know that—"

A blood-chilling scream interrupted his words.

"Jesus Christ! What the fuck was that!" A voice erupted from the area in front of the platform stage, startling everyone in the building. Prisoners jumped from their seats, jostling one another, some tripping over others in a defensive reaction to get out of the way; guards reacted quickly, drawing their weapons. Suddenly it seemed that almost everyone was shouting and shoving; some commanded order while others demanded to know what had occurred. Fritz and Kessel immediately rose, Fritz gesturing for other Germans to bar the building exit. Nick felt his heart pumping hard in his chest. In the first row of benches, one of the prisoners had leaped up on the bench, ranting. Others tried to pull him back and quiet him down. On the stage, several men froze in the midst of what must have been a vaudeville-type skit, gaping at weapons now aimed at them.

"It's all right, it's okay," a voice called. Nick saw Bernard attempt to subdue the panic as he declared "*ist nichts*" to the guards. Bernard crouched to retrieve something from beneath the bench where the panicked soldier flailed his arms and grabbed at his crotch. Hoisting the cause of the commotion over his head to show it to the others, Bernie added, "It's only BC. I just found my cat."

An uneasy silence followed, broken eventually by moans, a few awkward chuckles, and guttural murmurings. The soldier who had caused the stir now stepped off the bench, still swearing, "Damn! That scared the shit out of me! I'm just sitting on the bench here minding my own business and right from under me that—*thing*—reaches out a paw—a fucking *claw* and grabs me right by the—*shit*, that hurts!" He winced as he rubbed himself and sat down again.

Though the prisoner's panic was under control, his outburst had seriously intensified the atmosphere in the room. The smattering of laughter didn't lighten the mood, and none of the German guards laughed, nor even smiled. Worse, the sound of purposeful boot strides indicated someone new had entered the building. Nick turned to see the silhouette of Hauptman Erbst, the most-hated guard in the compound, in the doorway. Silence descended again as everyone waited for whatever would follow.

Erbst lifted his left hand and wordlessly scratched an itch just below his collar. The *scritch-scritch-scritch* of his fingernails against the fabric of his uniform reminded Nick of the intense seconds that followed the unpinning of a grenade. He struggled to resist an urge to dive for cover from the explosion that he was sure would follow.

Finally, Erbst barked orders to empty the building at once. Within minutes, it seemed, the POWs were outside, roughly herded back to their respective barracks. Rain fell hard again, and Nick lost sight of Fritz and Kessel, whom he'd hoped to question further. While the troops trekked across the muddy compound, guards rounded up others from other buildings, marching them all back to barracks. As they moved, the announcement passed from group to group, "Confinement to barracks until further notice."

Well, Nick inwardly smirked, *so much for them being one giant step ahead of us.*

Oddly, confinement this time lasted less than twenty-four hours, long enough for the sky to clear, and the men to hear the announcement from the camp kommandant himself as they stood, many almost ankle-deep in mud, at morning's *appel*. The kommandant paused frequently during the announcement so that his statements could be translated into both English and French.

"In a most magnificent display, of civility and humanitarian interest, for which all German peoples are known, enemy prisoners of the Third Reich—"

"Blah, blah, blah," muttered Bartell as he lifted first one foot, then the other in a vain effort to keep the mud from seeping inside the cracks of his shoes. Nick shushed him.

"—demonstrating to the entire world, the lies in deceitful reports, of brutality in prisoner labor camps—"

What had been introduced as merely an announcement turned into a lengthy, broken oration. The kommandant's effusive praise of *der Führer* and his many ministers, generals, ranking officers, and soldiers became a litany of Nazi devotion. The prisoners' attention lapsed, and they grew restless, whispering and shuffling. Nick, too, stopped listening, until a guard nearby snapped, "*Achtung!*"

At last, the kommandant arrived at the purpose of his announcement.

"—and so, as proof of our benevolence, in less than a fortnight, soldiers shall escort prisoners into the town where they shall be allowed to view a very excellent and amusing film."

So it's true, Nick thought. *They really are going to go through with this.* He saw the disbelief register on his fellow prisoners' faces; soon the murmuring began as the men wondered about the unprecedented luxury.

Further instructions followed: In a few days, the men would be divided into three units. Under heavy guard, the first unit would march the two-plus miles into Hammerstein, attend a showing of the film *Baron Munchausen* at a city auditorium, and return immediately afterward to the stalag, while a second unit under a second battery of guards would set out. As the second unit made the return march, the third unit would set out.

At first, most of the men felt excited about the promise of stepping outside the barbed-wire boundary, even for just a few hours. Some, with almost-childish anticipation, imagined additional possibilities.

"Maybe there'll be civilians there," Bartell offered. "Maybe we'll even see a pretty face and figure."

"I wonder if they'll have candy for us, or peanuts—"

"There's still a war on, you know," Matthews sneered. "Don't go thinking this is like some kinda family picnic. I just wonder what they're really up to. It can't be they just want to make nice."

Speculation continued through the day; by evening, however, suspicion and disappointment replaced the earlier enthusiasm as prisoners discovered what really lay behind the sudden act of kindness.

"Not only are we to see a film," MOC Miller reported to a group of men as they awaited nighttime lockup, "we're also going to *be* a film."

"What do you mean?"

"It's nothing more than propaganda," Kent added, his flushed face showing an anger that didn't quite touch his voice. "They expect to use us as part of their latest campaign of half-truths. The poor, disheveled, and *weak* Allied soldiers totted off to their *generous* weekly entertainments like schoolboys! Bloody bastards!"

"We could—probably should—refuse to go," said Miller. This brought silence as the men thought about what a mass refusal meant. They would not only sacrifice those few precious hours of change and pretended freedom, but also set themselves up for more retribution from the Nazis. Miller sympathized with the regret he could read in the others' faces.

"Unless—," he hinted.

"Unless what?"

Miller became pensive, his concentration evidenced by the lines that deepened above the bridge of his nose. The others waited, certain that their Man-of-Confidence would come up with a practical compromise, relieving the men of complicity in a Nazi propaganda film without denying them a simple privilege. Miller thought awhile longer; soon the wrinkles between his eyebrows smoothed, and he laid out his suggestion.

"How about this? The men *do* go on this little—field trip, but we go as soldiers, not as prisoners."

"How we gonna do that?"

"Attitude. Demeanor. We won't be a straggling bunch of ragged, underfed prisoners. We'll be three massive units of soldiers, uniforms clean and pressed, bearing ourselves with pride, marching in step like a regiment on parade. By God, we'll out-propagandize the ministry of propaganda."

"I ask again, how we gonna do that? Look at us!"

The men glanced at one another. As they did so, Nick realized that their dishevelment would be difficult to erase, or even disguise. They stood in their RC-issued uniforms, wrinkled and mud spattered. Some of the men had lost so much weight since incarceration that the uniforms hung too loosely on their bodies. In addition, most of their footwear was inadequate for hiking across the compound, much less for marching in step for over four miles.

"Well, gentlemen," Kent finally broke in. "It looks like we've got our work cut out for us—and not much time to do it. I'm game to give it a go. Are you?"

Not one soldier said no.

The work began that night as groups of men took turns in the washrooms, scrubbing their uniforms in the cold water with whatever type of soap they could gather: liquid shampoos, powdered soap, and soap bars from RC parcels, as well as the slivers of harsh lye soap provided by the Germans. With the damp weather, drying took many hours, and in the morning, almost all the men appeared for *appel* wearing their initial, course, prison garb instead of their more-favored uniforms. To press their clothes, they used whatever method they could, from placing high demand on the prisoners in charge of laundry, to devising crude flatirons from pots and cans, even to pressing their clothes between mattresses as one might press a flower in a book. Since not all the men had appropriate footwear, one group was placed in charge of inventory and repair, to determine if a thousand men might be adequately shod at one time, through a kind of check-out system if necessary. They patched and cleaned shoes, the closest to spit-polish they were likely to get.

With the tonsorial preparations came physical preparations as well. The men spent more time than usual in the yard, stretching their limbs, engaging in rigorous calisthenics. Though malnourishment caused them to tire quickly, morale encouraged them to test their mettle just one more step. Now it wasn't just the prospect of stepping outside their barbed-wire prison that motivated them; they looked forward to showing their pride, unity, and determination *not* to be cowed.

Fortunately, the chosen day arrived sunny and temperate, with just a slight breeze. As the first unit stepped into formation, several trucks grumbled into the compound. Some of the trucks carried armed guards, mostly middle-aged and older men. One truck carried a film crew, who immediately set to work recording.

"Seems kind of crazy to me," Nick mentioned to the man next to him. Not included in the first wave of privileged prisoners, they watched the proceedings from just outside the infirmary. "I don't see how putting this on film is going to interest anybody. Just shows a bunch of guys in formation, and a bunch of other guys watching a bunch of guys in formation." Just then, Captain McAndrews stepped outside, carrying a sheaf of papers. He, too, stood awhile to watch, then shuffled through the papers.

"Same kind of craziness I got here," he commented. "I don't know why I keep doing this. Written request for requisition forms, copies of requisitions, copies of requisitions denied, and for what? These people"—he nodded toward the nearest German officers—"I think they just love to see themselves in print."

"And on the screen."

In spite of what he thought of as craziness, Nick couldn't help feeling proud as he watched his fellow prisoners—soldiers—march out of the compound.

"Soldiers, march!" A prisoner's voice commanded after the initial German order to move out. "Left . . . left . . . left." In unison they moved with measured stride, all faces forward, and arms swinging in time with their steps. Also on foot, German guards flanked them or followed behind; many were interspersed with the prisoners, and they too picked up the rhythm of the march. The people filming captured it all, then hurried to the waiting truck and hopped aboard, followed by other truckloads of Germans.

With a "see you later" kind of nod, Nick strode off to join some of the other men who, like him, waited for their opportunity to strut their stuff.

A couple hours later the second unit marched through the gates of Stalag IIB. Nick felt another swell of pride as he unison stepped with almost five hundred other men. Eyes focused forward, he could see many rows of khaki-clad soldiers, all bearing themselves with chest-out, shoulders-back dignity. Their rhythmic steps provided a percussive sound, like the pulse beat of a single massive being. *Five hundred men*, Nick thought, *more than ever before, one body*.

Save for the occasional "left—right" calls to keep them apace, the unit marched in silence. Once they had passed several hundred yards beyond the compound, Nick eased his face-forward rigidity a little and turned his head every once in a while to see what surrounded them. They marched past a field that looked newly turned and sown. Nick heard warbles and chirps of birds that reminded him of the meadowlarks, robins, and barn swallows he'd known back on the prairie. About a mile into the march, Nick observed two women in a distant farmyard, chasing something. A faint but irate squawk identified the prey as a rooster.

I'd give almost anything to be there, he yearned. Envisioning a whole pot of hearty chicken soup, or even a scrawny, tough rooster crisp fried, Nick clenched his right hand, twisting his wrist as if he were wringing the rooster's neck. When he realized what he was doing, he broke pace for a second, corrected himself with a graceless little skip-hop move, then fell in line once more.

Halfway to Hammerstein, they met the first contingent of prisoners marching back to the stalag. As the companies passed each other, men nodded subtle greetings and frowned or rolled their eyes, indicating mixed reactions to the outing. Some looked pensive, even glowering, making Nick wonder just what kind of film he would be seeing.

Hoping to march into a bustling town, Nick was a little disappointed by the somber quiet of the streets. Hammerstein being a rail-line junction, the chuff and screech of trains pervaded, but Nick saw only a few automobiles, and even fewer pedestrians. Some civilians stood in open doorways or behind windows. The men could see curtains being pulled back as curious eyes peered out. When the prisoners neared the auditorium, more civilians began to appear outside, singly and in pairs or small groups. Many put their heads close and whispered, gesturing toward the prisoners; others watched, silent and expressionless. They were a mix of old men, women, and young children.

Nick found himself staring almost hungrily at the women and children. A pang of homesickness and regret hit him right in the gut as he thought yet again of family and the fairer sex, of his curly-haired little nieces, of Helen, now lost to him. He longed for the voices of women, soft and smooth tones, soothing, and the squealing giddiness of children, sounds so long unheard.

Suddenly, one dark, stringy-looking woman broke from a civilian group, dashed out into the road, and began shouting. Clad in a patched, flowered housedress that looked like it had seen too many washings, she lifted both bony arms and, shaking her fists at the prisoners, screamed, "*Schweinehunde! Verdammte Amerikaner!*"

The prisoners pretended not to hear. German soldiers suddenly shouted at the film crew, ordering them to stop filming. Guards tightened their jaws. Their steely glares persuaded bystanders to hustle the woman away, but she continued to scream invectives at both prisoners and guards. Nick had never before heard a woman rail in such language. She continued to hurl abuses so foul that Nick wondered why they didn't cloud the air like rank smoke.

"*Dumme, dumme Amerikaner!*" Her outraged shrieks faded only after she was yanked through a doorway, and the door slammed her into silence.

It took quite a while to usher the massive audience into the auditorium seats but finally the lights dimmed and the projector cast its beam onto the screen, revealing flickering images of Hitler addressing a crowd of thousands who waved and wept and cheered. The men groused as the newsreel played but relaxed once the actual film began.

Nick had already discovered that watching films in prison was not like watching them back home, where the audience sat quietly in a darkened show hall. The prisoner-audience usually carried on strident conversations with each other or with the characters on the screen as the film played. The same occurred now during the showing of *Baron Munchausen*. Several times, men called out, "What's he saying?" and those who understood translated. Nick too translated for the men surrounding him, but eventually he grew tired of repeating lines and, caught up in the story, barked, "Just watch for a minute!"

The story unfolded in color rather than in black and white, and told of fantastic and romantic adventures in all kinds of exotic locations: in Russia as the lead character had a dalliance with Catherine the Great; in Turkey during a battle; even—and here Nick thought the story a little too incredible—on the moon, where moon children grew like fruit upon moon trees. He didn't believe the scene about the frozen horn either, though he did like the thought of a cozy hearth fire thawing the music out of it.

When the last scene faded, and the music finale waned into the *thwack-thwack-thwack* slap of film on still-spinning reel, Nick became aware that audience chatter had ended some time ago. Apparently almost all the men had been drawn into the story, and whether they understood the words or not, the colorful images captivated them. They broke into applause; then, recognizing prideful looks on the faces of the Germans, some of the prisoners stopped clapping, nudging or shushing those around them to stop as well.

Outside the hall, formation of the troops seemed to occur too quickly and precisely. Nick wanted to linger, but in what seemed like moments, the five hundred men were once again in unison stride, heading back to the stalag. Just outside Hammerstein, they passed the final group of prisoners, whose faces showed an almost-naïve optimism. Nick now understood the frowns and scowls he'd seen on the earlier corps. How different he felt now, heading back to the prison compound than he had felt marching into the town. Though the men still bore themselves with pride, it felt strained somehow, much harder to maintain than it had been earlier. As before, birds twittered in the spring air. Nick envied them, whose songs now seemed to clash with the crunching thud of prisoners' measured footfalls. He envied even the worms and spiders that could crawl, unnoticed, almost directly from beneath a Nazi's boots.

The sun still fairly high in the western sky, it, too, seemed to have lost some of its radiance. Longer shadows added to Nick's growing sense of gloom. As they passed the farmstead he had noticed before, he felt resurgence of that earlier desire to march over there. By now the rooster was dead and stewed, but maybe not entirely eaten. Nick's muscles felt taut, and his skin prickled with the itch of dust and sweat—and something else.

What if I just walked away? he wondered, marching left—right—left.

XIV

Backlash

While the base-camp prisoners enjoyed their few hours of special privilege, four POWs on kommando detachment about thirty kilometers away made a break for freedom. Nick learned of the escape when detachment forces came back to the stalag. Some of the men had been severely beaten.

MOC Miller summoned several of the German-speaking prisoners, Nick among them, and they trooped to the kommandant's headquarters, where detachment officers gathered to make their reports.

"With their penchant for record keeping," Miller grumbled, "they'll probably be documenting for quite a while. We should be able to get the skinny from them."

"Why should they tell us anything?" Kent posed, adding, "Or anything like the truth."

"Seems like we could find out more by just questioning our men," Nick observed.

"I want to know what this side has to say before they have any more opportunity to manipulate their stories."

Nick realized that the reported escape might be just another cover for out-of-control brutality. He had not forgotten what Bartell had told him when he'd first arrived at the stalag, particularly about the bodies left in the latrine for a couple of days, a gruesome reminder of what might befall anyone else who attempted escape. Of course, in those earlier situations, according to Bartell, no actual escape had been attempted. That was merely the official report covering what the prisoners felt to be cold-blooded murder.

"*Halt!*" The order came from the block tower nearest headquarters. Alerted by the call, several German soldiers turned from their own intense discussions, lifted their weapons, and barked orders for the POWs to return to their barracks. Two of the sleek, dark dogs that accompanied the guards bared their teeth and growled. The Americans stopped.

"Tell them we need to talk to the kommandant." Miller directed Ian Kent. "You're a smooth talker. Tell them we need to know exactly what happened to our men."

The Germans responded to Kent's request with sneers. One of them muttered something derisive, drawing laughter from the others. Nick hoped no one would translate the cruel remark, but he knew that even though Miller didn't understand German, he most likely recognized the word *jüden*. Hank Miller's face reddened. Kent arched a brow and opened his mouth as if to speak, then changed his mind and said nothing. Kent's general attitude toward Jews was no secret, nor, Nick remembered, was his doubt in having a Jew as the prisoners' Man-of-Confidence. Fortunately, the majority of inmates admired and respected Miller, despite what Kent felt to be a real detriment in relations between the Germans and the Allied prisoners.

Once again, the men made their request to hear from the Germans exactly what had happened on kommando detail. Then the headquarters door opened, and Hauptman Erbst stepped out. As usual, he stood quiet for a long moment, slowly raking his gaze across the faces of all the men in front of him. Nick marveled at the man's talent for intimidation through silence. Finally Erbst spoke.

"*Was willst?*" He directed his question at Ian Kent, his tone a mix of impatience and condescension.

"Just what happened out there?" Nick blurted, but Erbst kept his eyes on Kent and waited for the Brit's response. Nick felt an annoying tic around his right eye. *Funny how these guys can make my skin crawl,* he thought. *They're like snakes that way.* He included Ian Kent in his assessment. The Brit might be an ally—a so-called good snake that might help curb the population of rats in the world—but he was a snake nonetheless. Try as he would, Nick just couldn't bring himself to trust the man. He realized that Miller didn't completely trust him either or he wouldn't have requested more than one interpreter. With several men listening and translating, chances of a mistranslation—accidental or intentional—were reduced. Nick listened. Kent didn't bother to ask what had happened.

"Where are the bodies?" he demanded.

"Bodies?"

"The men shot for supposedly escaping."

"No one has been shot—not yet." Erbst growled. "But they will be. They cannot hide for long."

So they actually did make it. Nick was surprised, not only by the successful escape attempt, but also at his unexpected feeling of resentment and envy. While he had merely thought about walking away, other men had actually done so. Nick had dismissed the notion out of a strong instinct to stay alive. Stalag IIB lay very close to the border between Germany and Poland, and Nick felt that he alone was most unlikely to stumble upon friendly assistance in a stealthy trek toward the western front—wherever that might currently be. How would the escapees fare? He wondered if he knew any of them, or if they could pass for Germans.

Before the Americans had a chance to pose another question, the headquarters door opened and the kommandant himself stepped out, accompanied by an elderly civilian gentleman and another officer in a black uniform, with high boots polished so that light glinted off them. This man glanced at the group of prisoners, then turned steely eyes on the kommandant and muttered something Nick could not hear.

The kommandant saluted, ordered his soldiers to escort the Americans back to their barracks and to shoot any who hesitated.

Surrounded immediately by Nazis, the Americans made no further demands. Nick felt a blunt nudge in the small of his back as a soldier urged him to "*mach schnell!*" One of the dogs nipped at his feet.

Just before he was out of earshot, Nick heard an additional order for an immediate and in-depth barracks and grounds inspection. Kent must have heard it too, for Nick saw that he picked up his pace, faster even than the guards had commanded. *Of course,* Nick realized. *The radio. They need time to hide it—or destroy it.* He wondered what he might do to help. He didn't know where the radio or its pieces were, nor did he know how many prisoners might be involved in the ring, but he did know that whoever they were, they might need at least a few minutes more time than they were about to get.

A flurry of activity grew around them. Whistles blasted, and from every corner and building of the compound as far as Nick could see, soldiers gathered, hurrying from whatever activity they had been engaged in. Following orders now crackling over the loudspeaker, they split into groups, each group heading for a specific location. One contingent, the group Nick snidely thought of as the *dog soldiers,* immediately proceeded toward the kennels. Though some dogs and their handlers were on constant patrol of the compound, the most skilled scent dogs remained kenneled until called upon for specific duties. Apparently this was to be an inspection the likes of which they hadn't seen in some time. If the men had just a little extra time to warn their fellow prisoners, they might prevent discovery of any contraband, and most particularly of the radio. Without such warning, however, something—even the smallest, overlooked item—could lead to full discovery, and the inevitable punishment: solitary confinement or in the worst case, death by firing squad for all perpetrators. Nick racked his brains trying to think of something he might do to delay the inspections, since it appeared that none of the others with him had an idea.

Maybe I'm worked up for nothing, he considered. *Maybe whatever there is to hide is so well hidden, not even the smartest Nazi goons can uncover it. Or maybe right now there's nothing to hide.* He was not convinced.

Guards moved too quickly toward barracks and other buildings. Nick scanned the area frantically but saw nothing that might serve as a diversion.

Somebody needs to do something, he agonized. *What can we do? What should I do?*

Then, without design or consideration of consequence, he did something he'd never done before, not even back home on the farm. He turned abruptly and kicked the dog that continued to bite at his heels.

The initial surprised yelp preceded a storm of snarls and ferocious barks. As if his senses contracted inward, Nick heard and saw nothing but the monster that now seemed to roar through its slobbering jaws. As it sprang for him, Nick shielded his face with his arms, but not before he saw a reddish glare in the dog's eyes. The animal knocked him to the ground. Nick kicked furiously to protect himself as best he could.

He didn't notice the outbursts from guards and prisoners. When his kicks seemed ineffective against the dog, he curled his body into as tight a target as he could, lying facedown in the damp dirt.

Again, Nick lost a sense of time. The attack might have lasted only a few seconds, or it might have gone on for many agonizing minutes. He didn't know. When at last the sounds of human voices topped the dog's ferocious barking, Nick dared to turn his head a little. The tastes of dirt and blood blended in his mouth. He must have bit his tongue during the attack. He tried to spit but ended up coughing hard, each spasm bringing back into his body sensations that sheer terror had dulled. Pain seared through his flesh and muscles where the dog's jaws had clenched and ripped: his foot, thigh, shoulder, and neck.

"Bremer! Nick, you okay?"

Nick heard the voice but didn't answer. Warily uncurling his body, he rolled over onto his back, wincing as fresh wounds met the rough ground. He looked into what seemed to be a swarm of faces above him.

"Christ, Bremer! What the fuck did you think you were doing?"

"Get him to the infirmary," an authoritative voice ordered.

"Can you walk?"

Several hands lifted Nick to his feet, then continued to support him when he nearly fell, unable to put weight on his right foot without torturous pain. He glanced down. His shoe gone, his sock hung loose and tattered from the end of his foot except where it stuck to and blended with torn flesh. Nick felt woozy. Gasping deeply and swallowing hard several times, he managed to keep from passing out, then leaned heavily against the men who half lifted and half dragged him toward the infirmary. Only then did he recognize that one of the men helping him was Chef.

"Hey, k-kid, where'd you—agh—c-come from?" Nick rasped.

"Miller alerted us."

"Miller? He was with me—" Nick grimaced as a new wave of pain throbbed in his left thigh.

"Maybe at first," the other prisoner remarked. "But him and the Brit must've skedaddled when the guards started pulling you and that dog apart. What did that dog have against you anyway?"

"I k-kicked him," Nick admitted, coughing.

"Shit, Bremer. You're fuckin' nuts, you know that?"

"Yeah," Nick answered, "I do now."

Captain McAndrews met them at the infirmary and directed the two prisoners to help Nick onto one of the cots at the far end of the ward.

"Not you too," McAndrews said. "We're getting way too much business in here lately."

"Sorry, Doc," Nick moaned. "I just thought I had to—" Again he winced, then continued in a tight voice, "I thought I had . . . the upper hand with a dumb d-dog."

"Well, you sure didn't have the upper foot, did you? Thanks, men." McAndrews dismissed Chef and the other POW, adding, "There's sorry business going on. You best get back to your barracks before—"

He didn't have time to finish before the door burst open and four guards traipsed in. Though Nick felt light-headed with the pain and aftermath of terror, he was alert enough to recognize Fritz's voice ordering the Germans to search the infirmary thoroughly, including the patients. Chef and the other able POWs in the infirmary were searched first before soldiers roughly escorted them to the door where other guards waited to take them back to their barracks. Doc McAndrews was allowed to stay. He staunched Nick's wounds as Fritz questioned him about the bedridden men in the infirmary.

"This man"—Fritz gestured at last to a heavily bandaged form in a cot next to the one Nick occupied—"what is his injury?"

"He was beaten," McAndrews answered, "almost beyond recognition."

"Ah yes. One of those attempting escape."

"So you say."

"Will he live?"

"Probably, no thanks to—"

"Then he is most fortunate. He may count his blessings."

Fritz turned his attention to the next bed. Standing at the foot of the cot, he looked down on Nick for a long moment before asking, "And this one?"

"I think you know," McAndrews replied. "And his injuries need bandaging, so if you don't mind—"

"You have stopped the bleeding, so his injuries can wait a few minutes more," Fritz scoffed, "so if *you* don't mind, I will have a talk with this man."

Nick didn't know how serious the bites were, but just then he wished they had been even worse—at least bad enough to somehow knock him cold. *Why didn't I pass out when I had the chance?* he thought, groaning.

"Why did you do it?" Fritz wasted no time. When Nick didn't answer, Fritz asked again, forming his English words slowly. "Why did you attack the dog?"

"The dog attacked me!"

"Come now. I already know what happened and how."

"Then why do you ask me?"

"I want to know *why.*"

Nick closed his eyes. He wasn't sure he had an answer to why. Sure, he'd been desperate for some distraction to allow Miller and Kent a little extra time to alert their cohorts, but he didn't remember actually planning to kick the dog. It had happened so suddenly, so completely without thought, as if the act had just burst from him.

"I don't—I'm not—" He faltered, then blurted, "Damn dog wouldn't stop biting at my feet! It just made me mad."

"Mad," Fritz considered. "Yes. Yes, I think perhaps you are mad. I just wonder if you are also clever?"

Nick shrugged. The burning sensation in his foot had lessened, but the pain now throbbed more intensely. Instead of answering Fritz, he lifted his head enough to see the torn and angry red flesh. He'd seen injuries before, but knowing the wounds were his own made him queasy. He was glad he couldn't see the other bites. Their pain gave him image enough.

The three soldiers who had entered with Fritz completed their searches. One carried a box that held an assortment of small bottles, vials, tins, and packets.

"You can't take that stuff," McAndrews protested. "Those are all medicines—*requisitioned* medicines—for treating the sick and wounded."

Fritz casually pawed through the materials, studied McAndrews's face for a moment, then directed his men to replace the medicines. He dismissed them, suggesting that they assist in the grounds inspections. To McAndrews he said, "You may bandage the wounds as we talk."

Stepping to the other side of the cot so McAndrews had space to work, Fritz removed his hat and tucked it under his arm. His right hand in a fist, he extended it toward Nick's face, then loosened his fist and fingered something in the palm of his hand. At last he opened his hand, showing both Nick and McAndrews what lay there. It was a metal coil, about the size of a fingertip.

"This was on the ground beneath you," Fritz announced. "Perhaps it fell from your pocket?"

Nick met McAndrews's gaze. He could read nothing in it, though he sensed a kind of urgency. The doc calmly reported that he needed to bandage the upper leg bite, if Nick would turn on to his side. Doing so, Nick saw only Fritz in his field of vision.

"What is it?" he finally asked about the coil held out for him to see.

"That is what I expect you to tell me."

"It looks like a piece of junk to me."

"Junk. Yes," Fritz murmured. He tossed the coil into the air and caught it, tossed it again and caught it. The third time, he tossed it higher. This time he missed the catch, and the coil fell to the edge of Nick's cot where it bounced, then landed on the floor. Instead of stooping to pick it up, Fritz appeared to move his foot a bit. Nick froze. He thought Fritz had just toed the coil further under the cot. *Can that be?* he wondered. If McAndrews had noticed, he gave no indication.

"You are a lucky man, *Herr Bremer*," Fritz said at last. "Nauman is very fond of his dog. In another instant, he would have shot you for assaulting his pet."

"Yeah," Nick grunted, "I feel real lucky right now."

"I can give you a little something for the pain," McAndrews offered, adding, "You are a lucky son of a bitch. That Nauman takes such good care of his dogs, we can be pretty certain you don't have to worry about rabies."

"Well—good!" Nick hadn't even thought about rabies—until now.

Fritz stared down at Nick a moment, or at least Nick felt his stare. Finally, the German replaced his hat smartly and gave a curt nod to McAndrews. "This man is confined to the infirmary," he ordered, "until I notify you otherwise." He strode toward the door, then turned once more, adding, "And clean this place. It is in disgraceful condition, bloody rags and—debris—lying about." He left, and the brisk sound of his footsteps disappeared when the door slammed. Nick and McAndrews exchanged a puzzled look before Doc reached under the cot to pick up the small piece of junk.

Nick missed the evening count that night, and after he struggled to his feet in the morning to line up in the yard with the other men, two guards blocked his exit from the infirmary. He limped back to his cot, sat down, and stared at the badly beaten prisoner in the next bed. The man's head was swathed in bandages; the parts of his face that showed had a purplish, bloated look and at first Nick didn't see that one of the man's eyes was open. The other eye, swollen shut, couldn't have been pried open, Nick was sure. He leaned forward.

"Can you hear me?"

The man's torn and ballooned lips parted just a bit with a soft "pwhhh" sound as he exhaled. The open eye stared straight ahead, unfocused at first. Nick stood again and leaned directly over the prisoner. This time the eye seemed to focus on him. Again the man's lips gave a plosive sound as he exhaled.

"Do you need something? Water?" Nick looked around. The medics weren't in the building; only a few other sick or injured men peopled the room. Some coughed softly or moaned. Others lay quiet, either asleep or pretending to sleep. Nick hobbled to the washroom at the back of the building. He used the urinal, then limped to the deep rust-stained sink where water dripped from a corroded tap. A twist of the handle brought a trickle of cold water. Nick leaned over, cringing as he felt some of his wounds stretch. He washed his hands, noticing for the first time the red welts that crisscrossed the backs of his hands. Tooth marks? Claw marks? He couldn't remember. The abrasions were not deep, piercing only the top layer of skin, but they were enough for Nick now to feel the stinging. He splashed water on his face, then cupped his hand and sipped water from his palm.

Nick found a small, chipped jar beside the sink. He rinsed it out, then carried it half full back to the cot where the beaten soldier lay.

"You want water?" he asked a second time.

"Don't give him that," a voice came from one of the other cots. "That's not drinkin' water. That's just washin' water."

"Oh?" Nick sensed a metallic taste in his mouth. "I thought it all came from the same place."

"Maybe, but the docs usually boil it first. They keep the drinkin' water in a covered pail back there. Cuts down on the chance of more sickness, they say."

The soldier struggled to sit up. He lifted thin bony hands to rub his gaunt and grayish face.

"What're you in here for?" Nick asked.

"Aw, I got the runs. I got 'em so bad I'm like a dang sieve. Shoulda dried up by now, but I just keep on pissin' and shittin'."

"How long have you been here?"

"What day is it?"

"Thursday. Oh, you mean—ah, I think it's the twenty-first—no, twenty-second of June."

"I come in with the last detachment." He nodded toward the beaten soldier. "With Luke there."

"Luke?"

"Yeah, Luke Allen. Big silent type. Guy never talks. That's why he looks like he does now. Four men got away, and the krauts are so damn sure the quiet guy knows all about it. Every question he didn't answer, they beat him for it. They asked a lot of questions."

Nick looked again at Luke. Of course he remembered him; because of the disfigured face, he just hadn't recognized the man who always lay motionless on a bunk, staring at the air when he came in from kommando detachment. Upon first arriving at the stalag, Nick had tried to talk to him, but he'd soon learned that Lucas Allen admitted no one into his silent world. Nick turned again to the other soldier.

"What's your name?"

"Jimmy. Jimmy Perry."

"Nick Bremer." They shook hands. Nick continued, "So those guys really made it then?"

"Far as I know. Heck, I was too busy shittin' to know what was goin' on. I think that damn Kraut potato farmer was poisonin' me." Jimmy smiled thinly. "But I think I got him in the end. I give him a present before I left—a whole handful of chocolate. 'Finest chocolate from America,' I told him. 'Best et all at once,' I told him, 'on account the Nazis kill for goods like that.' Dumb ass didn't know they was all laxatives. Well, he'll be the one shittin' his innards out for a while."

Just then the infirmary door opened, and McAndrews and Whitlow entered, followed by Chef, Bartell, and Slade, who carried morning rations for the sick prisoners. Guards stood in the open doorway, watching and listening. Chef immediately went to Nick, gesturing for Bartell to follow with the coffee.

"Oh goodie," Nick mocked. "Coffee's on." He waited as Chef filled a tin can with the dark, bitter brew, then asked, "You didn't bring anything else?"

Chef glanced toward the door before whispering, "They took everything away—all the Red Cross foodstuffs. And they say they're not giving us parcels until those guys are caught. Like starving the rest of us is gonna help." Chef offered another tin of coffee to Jimmy, who waved it away and lay down again, grumbling, "No thanks. It'll just leak right out of me anyway."

"We're all being punished," Bartell added, "but it ain't just because of the escape. We all pissed 'em off."

"Now what'd we do?"

"Complaints from civilians," Bartell said. "Word has it we looked so good when we was marching to Hammerstein and back—all spit-and-polish and pride—we made the

Krauts look pretty shabby. Some guy from town—do Germans have mayors?—anyway, whoever he was, he came out here to complain, learned at the same time about the escape on kommando, and now the Germans are just mighty pissed. Soldiers *and* civilians."

The guards snapped orders for the men to hurry, to stop talking. Without further word, the three prisoners poured rations for those men who were able to drink, then left. Chef turned back in the doorway and lifted his hand in a half wave. One of the guards grabbed him by the arm and shoved him, hard enough to send the kid sprawling into the dirt outside. The door slammed, cutting off Nick's view.

"Best get back to your cot," McAndrews warned. "If you're well enough to be visiting, they'll consider you well enough for real solitary."

"Solitary?" Nick was surprised.

"You're on ice, Bremer. So are Miller and a few other guys too. Thought they'd throw me in too, but I guess I lucked out. Eight days in the clink at least."

"What for? Was it—?" He didn't voice the word and knew that McAndrews didn't need to hear him say "radio."

"No, oddly enough. And that piece of 'junk' that Fritz found? It really is just a piece of junk. It could've been there since before this place opened." McAndrews waited for Nick to lie down, then sat on an empty cot nearby. "Or," he continued, "it might have recently landed there—during your dogfight."

"Landed. You mean like someone else just threw it? If it's just a piece of junk, what's it matter? Pretty flimsy excuse for solitary confinement."

"Maybe it doesn't matter," McAndrews admitted. "Can't help wondering why Hank Miller's on ice, though, and at least one other who was with him isn't." Nick pinched his mouth, about to protest when the doc assured, "Not you, Bremer. You *are* sentenced to solitary confinement. You were just lucky enough to bleed."

"Kent?" Nick asked. "Is he the one not in solitary?" McAndrews nodded.

"The other interpreters?"

"Solitary."

It didn't make sense to Nick. Apparently the men who had attempted to question the kommandant about the escape were all confined in the clink, except for Kent and, by sheer stupid luck, Nick himself. Why not Kent? Yet again Nick questioned the Brit's loyalty. He seemed to be on the same side, seemed to be involved in the radio ring and perhaps even secret communication with the outside. Still, his special status among the Germans led Nick, and surely others as well, to suspect him of being a stoolie.

Confinement in the infirmary made Nick itch with restlessness, though he thought he might be better off than those in complete solitary. How the slow passage of time could torture a man! With nothing to do, little to talk about or plan or look forward to, Nick found himself passing tedious minutes by counting. He counted the number of cots in the infirmary, then the number of cinderblocks in each wall; he counted bottles and vials, panes in the windows and cracks in the windowpanes. Sometimes he counted his sips of coffee, spoonfuls of soup, or bites of bread, even the crumbs that dropped in his lap. After a few days, he counted without even thinking about counting. With every repetitive act or sound, numbers simply came into his mind: twenty, twenty-one, twenty-two paces to the toilet, ninety-three, ninety-four, ninety-five—the tap dripped relentlessly.

Sometimes Nick sang; often he tried to talk with the other sick prisoners, but those who were truly ill didn't do much talking, and those who were well enough to converse were quickly sent back to barracks. He was most grateful to the medics who allowed him to help out. He took it upon himself to assist in the care and feeding of Lucas Allen. He spoke to Luke whenever he spoon-fed him, though he knew the man would not respond.

"Here you go. You gotta get your strength back. That's it. One more sip. Yeah, I know. It tastes like a barn floor, doesn't it? Come on. You keep on trying. The day will come when we'll all go home. I know you want to stick around for that." Luke swallowed every mouthful, staring at Nick with his one good eye.

After a couple of days, Doc McAndrews let Nick help get Luke on his feet. Though Nick's bite wounds still ached, he bore much of Luke's weight and the two men lumbered several paces back and forth. *Eleven, twelve, thirteen*, Nick found himself counting again.

On the sixth day of confinement, the afternoon brought a change in routine. It began with the rumbling return of trucks, bringing men back into camp from their detachment labor. A horn blared, followed by shouting and shrill whistles. Nick hurried to the nearest window but could not make out the cause of the unusual uproar. McAndrews moved in behind him. Before he had a chance to speculate, the door burst open. Fritz entered, followed by Wagner and Naumann. The latter looked around curiously; his eyes narrowed when he spotted Nick.

"All able-bodied men, out!" Fritz called. He strode into the room, pointing. "Him." He gestured first to Nick, then looked toward Luke. "And him. He is not so helpless—you!" Here he pointed to Jimmy. "Enough weakness. Out! All of you, out!"

The prisoners headed toward the door, Luke leaning on Nick's shoulders. As they passed the guards, Naumann spat in Nick's face.

"*Schweinehund*," Naumann said under his breath.

Nick's face burned. He had borne indignity and near starvation, threats and physical and sensory deprivation for many months. He'd endured, and knew he would continue to endure, but being spat upon just then filled him with such hate, the intensity of it surprised him. Still, he was grateful when Luke leaned even more heavily against him, preventing him from thrashing out against Naumann.

Nick paused a moment, glaring at the officer. He didn't attempt to wipe the spittle away from just below his eye. Instead, he forced himself to smile icily.

"I wish I would've choked that damn dog, you son of a bitch!" he murmured to the man who didn't understand a lick of English.

Fritz cleared his throat gruffly, commanding the men to move out faster. If he had heard Nick's comment, he said nothing. Nick, Lucas, and Jimmy were first out the door, followed closely by Doc McAndrews, who supported a man sick with grippe. Outside, the grounds had begun to fill with POWs in their usual morning or evening count formations. Whistles continued to shrill as Germans shouted orders for faster formation or for silence.

Nick's gut tightened. This was not just another prisoner count, and he knew the Germans would not hurry them into formation only to inform them that barracks confinement had ended. Something else was up, and he felt pretty sure it meant bad news. Appel proceeded more quickly than usual, most likely because none of the men attempted to mess up the count as they typically did. Soon after guards reported an accurate count, the kommandant's voice crackled over the loudspeaker, followed by a translation in Kent's familiar though trembling voice. The Brit sounded frightened—or angry—Nick couldn't be sure which.

"By authority of the highest command, prisoners attempting escape are to be shot," Kent interpreted, then waited for the kommandant to continue. Nick understood it all without Kent's translation. He felt taut, as if every muscle in his body fought to burst through his skin. The ugly report unfolded curtly; civilians had discovered the escaped prisoners of war and tortured them before turning them in to the nearest military garrison. Two of them had been summarily executed; the other two lay near death in a German hospital—all the result of a "foolish and impossible plan."

The men listened, stone-faced, to the fate of their fellows. *It could have been me.* Nick remembered his temptation to walk away and inwardly blessed his decision to resist it. He stood in the compound, a little sore, weary, bitter, and hungry, but alive. The war would have to end sometime, he thought, and when it did, he would go home to people he cared about, to another life. The dead prisoners would not. Nick wondered about their families. Would they ever know what had happened?

Before the kommandant dismissed the prisoners, his tone altered. He announced that Red Cross parcels would once more be distributed—sparingly, and that some regular activities might resume come morning. Lockdown, for the time being, was over. So were the solitary confinement sentences. He then informed the prisoners that they should feel very lucky and grateful for his generosity in the light of what had happened. Nick felt sure that he wasn't the only one who seethed, hearing the kommandant's words.

Still acting as a crutch for Luke, Nick looked for some of his close circle when the men broke formation. Foul-Mouth Matthews and Bernie spotted him first, however.

"Let me give you a hand there," Matthews said. "Bernie, get on the other side. Bremer, you just let us carry this guy back to the infirmary."

"Wait," Nick protested. "No, he's—we're all kicked out of the infirmary. Fritz's orders. It's back to the barracks for us."

"Shit, Luke don't look so good."

"He's better than he was."

With Luke propped between them, Matthews and Bernie headed to the barracks. Nick followed. They hauled the weak man to their rear unit where they managed to convince another prisoner to relinquish his lower bunk, at least for the time being. Gently, they eased Luke back onto the bunk. He lay there unmoving. Both eyes now open and vacant, he seemed to stare at the air.

"How's he doing?" Nick heard Ian Kent's smooth voice.

"What do you care?" he snapped, moving in close to Kent, his fists clenched.

"Hey—hey, easy there, soldier. I'm not the enemy, remember?"

"What do you want?"

"I thought you'd like to hear some good news for a change."

Nick's eyes narrowed as he studied the Brit's face. He wondered what possible good could come out of the recent events. Curious, but unwilling, he remained silent. He would not ask. Let Kent spill his guts first.

"I know the reason for all the crackdowns."

"So do I," Nick sneered. "Four guys escaped—"

"Yes, right, but that's not all of it." Kent's eyes seemed to gleam in the dimness of the barracks, and his voice took on an excited intensity. "They're scared. They're pissed off. They've been caught with their pants down, so to speak."

"What the heck are you talking about?"

Kent looked triumphant as he whispered, "The invasion has begun. Couple of weeks back, we think. We are taking back France."

XV

Gospel According to Luke

As the rumor of a huge Allied offensive spread through camp, morale among the prisoners lifted once again. Their hunger for news equaled their physical hunger. New prisoners to the stalag found themselves besieged by the veteran inmates desperate for signs of liberation.

"Where were you in the fighting?"

"How far have we come?"

"How much longer?"

"Are the Huns finally on the run?"

The current of hope drew speculation away from the recent escape and resulting execution, and hope ran high for many days. It made those days more bearable, even when guards required prisoners to stand during *appel* for hours at a time while they counted, miscounted, and recounted captives, and broadcast their twice-daily propaganda reports.

"Seems like the Germans always have such victories," Chef observed, standing just left of Nick in formation. "It's funny they haven't won this war by now."

"That tells a lot right there, doesn't it?" Nick responded. He kept a careful eye on the man at his right, watchful for any signs that Luke might not bear up. The silent soldier appeared to be physically healing from the brutal beating he'd suffered. However, most of the men who had assumed protective responsibility for Luke—Nick's clique—worried that the beating had resulted in some other kind of damage, that which couldn't be treated with medicine or patched with bandages.

"How's he doing?" Chef asked.

"Holding up," Nick answered, wishing Chef would quit talking around Luke as if he weren't really there. "Ask him yourself."

No one asked. Most of the men thought Luke suffered the severest case of battle fatigue. Some guessed that he had seen things in combat that had broken something inside; others felt he was just too weak in the mind to bear the rigors of warfare and captivity—especially of Nazi abuse. Nick didn't know what to call Luke's ailment, but he was sure that Luke was anything but weak-minded. He actually admired the taciturn man, certain that Luke had created a kind of impenetrable armor through silence. Nothing could hurt him or worry him or make him afraid, certainly not the propaganda that echoed across the compound. By all German accounts, the Nazis continued to be victorious on all fronts, defeating the Russians in the east and the Americans and English in the west, while still withstanding assault in Italy.

With every glorified report and fervent *Sieg-Heil* salute, prisoners inwardly cheered, confident that truth lay opposite of whatever the Nazis told them. Morale continued high for a couple weeks, until all hell seemed to break loose.

On an oppressively hot afternoon, most prisoners lolled in the barracks or strolled from place to place in the compound. A few worked up a sweat in a ball game, grateful for the slightest breeze to cool their bodies. Nick stood at a sink in the center washroom of his barracks, letting tepid water from the tap trickle over his wrists. Only a few months ago, Nick had felt that he might never get the ice out of his bones. Now he longed for ice or snow—just a little that he might rub against the back of his neck or on his itching sores and the dry and cracked soles of his feet.

Boom! The barracks door crashed open as two guards barged in, one piercing the quiet afternoon with repeated blasts of his whistle.

"*Alles raus! Schnell, schnell, schnell!*"

"What the—?" someone said sleepily.

"Every man outside! Now!"

The order came in hard, choppy English. Nick turned off the tap and patted his face with his wet hands. On the wall above the sink, a cracked sheet of glass painted black on one side passed for a mirror. Nick saw his dim reflection, distorted in the rippled glass. It didn't matter how many times he had already looked in that mirror; the reflection always surprised him. The face that looked back had such pronounced cheekbones and jawline. His eyes seemed overly large in a face that appeared hollow.

The whistle blasted just behind Nick.

"Son of a bitch!" he cried, putting a hand over his ringing ear. "I'm coming!" He faced the impatient guard. "Just keep your shirt on!" The guard looked at him oddly before pushing him through the washroom.

Outside, men scrambled from various locations, trying to get into *appel* formation fast enough. They held their questions until they stood next to their fellow prisoners in their usual configuration.

"What's going on?"

"Do you think this is *it*?"

"I knew it! Liberation at last!"

The news that greeted them had nothing to do with liberation. When the shouts and whistles ended, the kommandant ordered silence, which another German officer repeated through a megaphone; gradually the speculative murmurings among the men stilled. The kommandant's voice sounded tight, as if he barely controlled his rage. The prisoners listened, their spirits sinking with every word. Apparently the "kindnesses" that had recently been shown to prisoners of war were to cease immediately due to the "ingratitude and insubordination" of prisoners in various POW facilities.

"Rumors of daring and fantastic escapes are false," the kommandant pronounced; here and there among the prisoners, translators flatly repeated the words.

"All reported escapees have been caught and sentenced for their foolish crimes. Orders from the highest command in Berlin tell us that execution for the crime of escape is compulsory."

The kommandant paused, nodding to one of the soldiers near him. This soldier in turn stepped forward, broadly waving a signal. The prisoners heard the familiar growl of a truck engine rumbling to life. The military truck approached from the compound gates slowly, its massive tires crunching and spitting bits of gravel. The driver maneuvered the truck so that its gated end faced the prisoners. Two Germans on the ground approached the truck and unlatched the tailgate. The engine stopped.

"Once more," the kommandant continued, "a warning sharper than words seems to be required. Let *this* suffice!" Again he nodded, then with low-voiced instructions to his underlings, he stormed away. The soldiers in the back of the truck kicked two heavy bundles off the truck bed. The bundles thudded on the ground. Nick couldn't see them from where he stood, but it didn't take long for gasps and curses to ripple through the rows of prisoners.

It seemed then that every guard in the compound—including those who watched from the towers—aimed his rifle at the prisoners. The order came for all POWs to march past the truck, look at the two bundles on the ground, and head quietly back to their barracks, not to any other building in the compound.

"What is it?" Chef whispered to Nick. "Did you see what it was?"

"No." Nick had not clearly seen, but based upon the kommandant's words, he had a sickening idea of what they were about to witness. He put a hand on Chef's shoulder.

"Prepare yourself, kid. Or better still, just look at the ground when you go by."

Chef swallowed hard, and he nodded as understanding dawned in his eyes. A slow and graceless parade of silent soldiers passed by the back of the truck. Men who initially refused to look at what lay in the dirt at their feet were manhandled by the Nazis, forced to see. Nick felt beads of sweat run in rivulets down his back, caused by more than the climate. He looked up at the cloudless sky, surprised to see it so blue. It seemed that the swelling sense of revulsion and bitterness should actually be visible, darkening that blue sky.

Wordlessly, with lips tight against any outburst that might incite the guards to more brutality, the prisoners streamed past what turned out to be the bodies of two men. The foul sweet smell of death reached Nick while he was still some distance away. A bitter taste of bile rose in his throat, and he tightened his abdomen as he felt his stomach wrenching. Ahead of him, Chef faltered, cupping his hand over his nose.

"*Schauen Sie hin!*" Germans repeated the order to look every time a prisoner attempted to close or avert his eyes. Nick kept his gaze on the ground until he too received the direct order. His breathing felt shallow, and he tried to focus on the air between him and the two bodies that lay with limbs grotesquely splayed. Nick didn't want to see, but part of him felt compelled to look. As soon as he did, the sick feeling left his gut, replaced by a heated, throbbing sensation just under his skin. The top of his head felt hot and tight, as if the blood in his body were expanding and threatening to explode. Once again, he truly felt and tasted what it was to hate.

One of the dead prisoners lay facedown. A hole gaped at the back of his head, bordered with dried blood and brain matter. A fringe of dirty, knotted, once-blond hair lifted in the slight but stifling breeze. That gentle movement kept a fat blue-green fly from landing on the wound. The second soldier lay face up, and Nick cringed when he saw another fly light on one of the man's open and cloudy eyes. Part of this man's face had been shot away, leaving him with a ghoulish death grin.

Nick stepped away at last. With the sight branded in his mind, he caught the sickening whiff of vomit on top of the stench of death. He wondered how the Germans could all stand by seeing this, smelling this—the odor so pervasive they might actually taste it. How could any human beings be so utterly without mercy?

"*Hinschauen! Hinschauen!*" The order came furiously behind him. Nick turned to see one of the Germans grab hold of Luke's head, twisting it so that he faced the dead soldiers. When the guard couldn't force evidence of awareness into Luke's vacant face, he spat at him and pushed him hard. The momentum forced Luke against the prisoner in front of him and the two together fell hard on the ground. Nick stepped in to offer a hand, as did several other prisoners. The fallen men ignored assistance and picked themselves up. They followed the prisoners in front of them, at first in single file, then bunching in groups. Luke, Chef, and Nick made one silent trio.

Nick looked into the faces of the Germans as he walked past them; most of them stood as if they were made of stone. Not even the slightest hint of compassion or shame marked their faces. When Nick saw Fritz in line with the other guards, he paused briefly, narrowing his eyes, almost daring the officer to speak. Like the others, Fritz stood with his rifle aimed at the prisoners; his leathery face seemed to have deeper folds than usual. Nick stood in that awkward space between Fritz's walleyed focus and the direct gaze of his good eye. Just before turning away, Nick thought Fritz shook his head ever so slightly. He glanced back once, uncertain if that movement had been a warning to Nick or a subtle hint of Fritz's humiliation.

Is there a man under that monster? he wondered.

Entering the barracks, Nick saw men crowding near the windows, forcing themselves to watch the grisly parade. Their voices subdued, they cursed, cried, and conjectured.

"I wonder who they are—were," Chef whispered.

Nick didn't answer. He simply watched Luke shuffle to his bunk, sit down, and then lie on his back, staring. Nick and Chef sat on the floor between bunks, their backs against the wall. The brick floor offered the only coolness in the barracks.

"Those weren't the two prisoners supposedly executed a few weeks ago," Matthews stepped in between the bunks, but he remained standing.

"No, of course not," Nick agreed. "They couldn't have been more than two days dead. But with this heat—" He swallowed the bitter taste in his mouth. Matthews continued.

"I think it's the two that were supposedly in a German hospital. Remember what they told us? Damn lying sons of bitches! They hadn't recaptured all the escapees. Those two were still out there somewhere."

Nick didn't want to think about the dead men, but he couldn't help it. Soon enough all the camp would learn their names; some would remember one or the other or both of the soldiers.

"Kraut bastards!" Matthews muttered. "To treat human beings like that—even dead ones—it's . . . hell, it isn't human at all!"

Nick agreed. He still felt that pounding, burning sensation under his skin and knew it was anger, bottled up, building pressure. If he didn't find a way to release it, who could tell what it might lead to? Nick flexed his hands, wondering what it would feel like to choke the life out of a Nazi. Closing his eyes, he imagined a German soldier in the grip of his hands, almost heard the dying gurgle as the Nazi struggled to breathe, saw in his mind's eye the hideous, leathery face, its walleyes popping—

"Shit!" Nick mumbled, realizing that he had imagined killing Fritz. Breathing deep, he knew he'd have to do something physical—anything—to burn away the anger. Without a word to Chef or Matthews, Nick stood up and strode out of the barracks. The sickening parade of prisoners had not ended yet. Nick looked through the line of men returning to the barracks, hoping he might see Hank Miller. He waited for what seemed ages.

"Miller!" Nick called as the MOC made his way to his quarters. Miller turned and waited for Nick to reach him.

"We gotta do something!" Nick blurted. "*I* gotta do something! I want to volunteer for grave detail. Those men deserve a decent burial, we can't just let—"

Miller nodded but said nothing. His eyes followed the stream of prisoners, then studied the placement of guards. He looked down at the ground, kicking a small stone with the toe of his boot. Nick could hear his exhalation, like a shudder.

"This is a hell of a way—" Miller hesitated, and for a moment Nick thought he'd said "a hell of a wake." Breathing in, gaining control, Miller continued, "You're not the first to offer, Bremer. I'll bet there's a thousand guys here who all want to help out somehow." He looked up at last, meeting Nick's eyes. "It looks like we've gotta face the kommandant one more time, demand answers, satisfaction. I just hope he'll listen."

Nick started to say something, but Miller shook his head, then put his hand on Nick's shoulder.

"I'll come get you when it's time," he said, his voice sounding very tired. "I'll see that you get a shovel."

Back at barracks, POWs wondered if the two dead soldiers had in fact been those that the Nazis claimed to have killed a few weeks ago. Had the Germans lied about the escapees being found? Were the two that still lay in hideous display on the grounds those the Nazis claimed to have taken to a civilian hospital? If so, why had they bothered to treat them in a hospital only to execute them now?

"Has anybody heard yet who those two are?" Johnny Ames asked. "Somebody's gotta remember them. Somebody's gotta tell their families—some day."

"Tell them what?" Matthews spat. "That their son or brother was treated like a rotten carcass?"

"Aw, come on, Matthews," Nick rebuked. "Nobody would say that to their families."

The men became silent. For the first time in a long time, Nick thought of his kid brother off in the Pacific somewhere. What if this kind of thing had happened to Jacob? He groaned, trying to erase the image of his brother's blond hair blowing about over a gaping head wound. His stomach tightened again; his eyes burned.

Just then, a quaking sigh broke the silence, followed by a sharp, rasping intake of breath. Prisoners turned or stepped around others to seek the source. The sound came from the bunk where Lucas Allen lay. Luke took another deep, ragged breath before exhaling a long, airy word.

"Chri-s-st!"

"He talked!" another voice cried.

Luke's sudden awakening brought other prisoners into the rear unit of the barracks, and they crowded around, demanding and encouraging the man to say something.

"Luke. What happened to you?"

"How come they beat you?"

"What did you see that made you go cra—?"

"Ssshhh, for Chrissake, he ain't nuts!"

Luke lay still, but his eyes darted from one face to the next, and this time they didn't have a vacant look. Several times he opened then closed his mouth. Each time he did so, the prisoners around him hushed their murmuring, waiting. Nick looked at the men. If his heart and mind weren't still so black with hate and anger, he thought he might have laughed. The guys looked so eager, as if they expected Luke to say something fantastic, or heartening. What Luke said next didn't make sense at first.

"They burned 'em."

"What did he say?"

"Burned what, Luke? Who burned what?"

Luke sat up, gasping as if he couldn't breathe. With his elbows resting on his knees, he covered his face with his hands, then rubbed his eyes. He rubbed harder and harder until Chef gently reached out and stopped him. Luke raised his head, his breaths still rasping, and looked with reddened eyes at the men around him. When at last he seemed to have enough air in his lungs, he began to speak, words pouring from him as if a floodgate had opened.

"The guy with me, we were buddies—him and me—right next to me in the foxhole—he stood up to toss a grenade. Next thing he's falling back on top of me. I swore at him, yelled at him to get offa me, but he didn't move. I shoved him and I—he didn't—God!" Luke's breaths came in short gasps again, and his whole body began to shake.

"Hey, hey, easy there, Luke," Bartell soothed. "You don't have to talk about it if you don't want to."

"No—I gotta tell it." Luke clenched his fists. His entire body stiffened. Nick had never seen anyone work so hard just to remember. It seemed to take every muscle and sinew Luke possessed to express what had for so long been buried in his silence.

"I was w-wearing his *face*! His twenty-three-year-old *face* oozed all over my chest. I wanted to scrape it off, but I couldn't—touch—there was an eye—!"

"Stop," Chef, white-faced, pleaded. "Don't say any more."

Luke was unstoppable now.

"I couldn't move," he continued. "I know I tried, but nothing w-worked! The Germans overran us then. I was lyin' there at the bottom of my foxhole, and I remember seein' the sky, smoky and dirty, but every once in a while there was a spot of blue, and it didn't seem right somehow. That blue piece of sky and the explosions and shouts and my buddy's . . . b-blue eye . . . . on *my* chest, lookin' at me like it was my fault! Then the Germans were pointing their rifles down at me, and it seemed like the rifles had eyes, and all of them were staring at *me*—and then they laughed. They fuckin' *laughed*."

Luke stammered, remembering that the Germans continued to laugh as they pulled him from the foxhole. Made to keep his hands together at the top of his head, Luke had stumbled along with other captured GIs, carrying the remnants of his friend's face on his chest. He didn't remember how long. He did remember waking up hours, maybe days later, on a prisoner transport. He felt numb and cold, as if his whole body were made of ice. That's when he'd slipped into his silent, blank world, where for over a year, nothing had reached him.

When Luke's story ended, the prisoners remained quiet for several minutes. Finally Matthews, in an unusually gentle voice, asked the question Nick had in his mind but dared not ask.

"You said they burned 'em, Luke. What did the Germans burn? Was it . . . your clothes? You know, with—" He left the sentence unfinished. Luke fell back on his bunk, sighing.

"No," he said, all emotion gone from his voice. "The POWs. The ones that escaped from kommando detail. Four walked away. Two were found within hours. Krauts shot them in the back of the head and burned the bodies. They ain't nothing but ash in a goddamned German field. The other two musta been in hiding for a few weeks. You know where they are now."

"Good God," Murphy interjected. "How do you know this, Luke?"

"I seen it. I seen lots of things, and I remember, and I'm gonna remember for the rest of my life!"

"But if you were a witness to all this," Murphy continued, "how come you're still here to tell the tale?"

Luke raised his left hand, and it shook as he tapped the side of his head. "They think I'm not *here*. They think I don't know—don't feel nothing. But I seen it all. I seen those two guys last year too, the ones shot for escaping. Escaping? All they did was cross the potato field to get behind some bushes. Dysentery. They shouldn't have been on detachment. They just wanted a little bit of . . . dignity . . . there was German women in that field. One of those women points and yells, and the guards shoot—bang! bang!—they're dead. Shot dead for wantin' to shit in private."

"Why didn't you say something then?" John Drummond asked. "Report it to the MOC next time you came in?"

"Like you said," Luke answered, his voice colorless, "I gotta *live* to tell the tale. Long as they think I can't think or see or feel, I'm alive."

Just then, someone from the front unit called, "Goon up!" The men broke from their circle, taking seats in bunks and chairs, or leaning against the walls. They watched quietly, suspiciously, as Fritz entered unit B. Fritz scanned the gathering, one of his eyes finally lighting on Nick.

"Come with me," he commanded. By the sound of his voice, Nick realized that Fritz would tolerate no protest. With an uncertain glance at his friends, he began to follow the German officer.

"Wait." Fritz halted, turning. "Select three men to accompany you." He briefly looked at Chef before adding, "Strong men, if possible."

Not sure what he might be selecting the men for, Nick hesitated. He didn't want to be responsible for bringing further misfortune on anyone else.

"Now!"

"All right." Nick swallowed, looking about, but he didn't have to choose. Several men raised a hand; four simply stood up and began to follow: Matthews, Drummond, Bull, and Murphy. Fritz glared, prompting Nick to ask one of the men to step back. At first the four didn't move. Then Matthews thrust Drummond back a few steps and said, "Sorry, John old boy. It just ain't your time."

The men followed Fritz outside. The sun had just sunk below the horizon, sending orange and pink flares into the western sky, while purple darkness blanketed the east. The grounds were empty of prisoners, but German patrols and their dogs continued their sentry duties. Nick and his companions glanced at the area where the dead men had lain, but the bodies had been removed.

"*Wo sind sie?*" Nick asked Fritz, but the German didn't tell him where the bodies were. Instead he escorted them toward the compound entry where another contingent of guards waited. In addition to their rifles, four of them carried shovels.

"It is a long time since you have dug dirt," Fritz observed, taking the shovels from the guards and handing them to the prisoners. "It is my understanding that you have volunteered. Out there." He gestured toward a field across the road. "Two graves. Three feet by six feet. Six feet deep."

"Six feet!" Murphy started to protest, then changed his tone, "But it'll be dark soon."

"You will have enough light. Go."

The four spent the next several hours digging, two men working on each grave. Sometimes the ground came away easily; other times the men grunted and sweated as they struggled to get through clay or stones. In their weakened physical condition, they tired easily, but none of them hinted at a desire to quit, or even to rest. Slowly the holes widened and deepened as the men dug by the light of a lantern. When they reached a depth of approximately four feet, Fritz appeared at the site with two five-gallon buckets and two lengths of rope. Two diggers filled the buckets with dirt, which their partners hoisted to the surface and emptied onto a growing mound. Their work took on a rhythm, accented by grunts, sighs, and wheezes. Nick thrust the shovel into the ground, twisted to unearth a hefty load, then dumped it into the bucket. Thrust, twist, dump; thrust, twist, dump. His movements constrained by the dimensions of the grave, he soon felt deep, throbbing pain in muscles that hadn't been worked so hard in some time. Partnered with Nick, Bull also moved rhythmically, breathing hard and resting while Nick filled the bucket, then grasping the rope: pull, pull, pull, lift, dump—over and over again, until they decided to switch places.

"Enough," one of the guards called at last. In the dim light, Nick eyed the grave, estimating its dimensions. It would do, he agreed, but just as he reached out a hand to assist Bull to the surface, Matthews spoke out.

"No, no it ain't enough. These graves ain't deep enough, and they sure as hell ain't square enough."

"Hey now," Murphy uttered, "you don't want to kill yourself here, man. It's enough. These here graves will hold a man sure."

"I don't care! Them two guys deserve it. It's the least—the *last* square deal we can give 'em."

So they continued digging to the prescribed depth measured by the height of a man. At one point one of the guards wearily demanded that the prisoners conclude their work at once, but Fritz countered his order with a sharp, "*Nein!* Let them finish."

With the blades of their shovels, they shaved the dirt along the sides and corners until each wall looked straight to the eye, and the corners met at right angles. Nick was certain that if they had a level to test the straightness, the bubble in the glass would rest at center on every wall.

At last they admitted their job was done. In predawn twilight they trudged back to the compound and into their barracks, where they virtually fell onto their bunks. Though his body ached unmercifully, Nick fell asleep. He slept through their reveille and through appel, and didn't know until later that Chef—that timid and terrified kid—had ducked through rows of POWs to place himself so that he might be counted twice. Others had done the same for Murphy, Bull, and Matthews.

"We just thought you needed to sleep," Chef explained.

"You might want to go back to sleep after you hear the latest," Bartell put in.

"What? What's happened now?"

"Hank Miller's being replaced. He's no longer our Man-of-Confidence. He's off this morning. Probably spend the rest of this war on kommando detail—if he lives through it."

"Shit!" Matthews swore. "Miller's a good guy, the best. Why in hell—? I thought we were supposed to decide who our MOC is, not the Germans."

"There must have been some complaints," Chef replied. "And the Germans are only too happy to oblige."

"Another thing," Bartell interrupted. "About Luke over there. If too many guys hear about his sudden awakening, it won't be long before the Nazis find out he's all there—uh, mostly all there—that he actually saw what they done. He'll be back on kommando detail just like that." Bartell snapped his fingers. "And chances are real good the next time we see him, he'll look a lot like those guys we're burying today."

Nick glanced at Luke who had taken his usual position lying on his back. Luke looked back at the men, his eyes moving slowly from one face to another.

"What are you saying?" he asked.

"You gotta keep it with you, Luke," Bartell warned, "bottled and corked up inside, no matter what. For your own survival, you gotta go back to what you were, frozenlike."

Luke shook his head. "I don't know if I can now. It's like a wall's broke down. I don't think I can just build it back up."

"Well you have to build it back up no matter what it takes! Remember your friend? You have to keep wearing his face on your shirt so you can live to tell it later. You have to!"

Luke draw in his breath as if to protest further, then changed his mind. He heaved a deep sigh and nodded, then turned away, staring until his eyes took on a vacant look, almost like a curtain drawn against the light.

The next morning, all prisoners stood at attention, six long rows of men standing straight and facing forward. A slow and silent procession moved past them, eight prisoners bearing each of two rough-board coffins, an honor guard of four preceding and following. As they passed, the prisoners in formation raised their right hands in salute, creating a slow tide of movement down the ranks. Only one prisoner did not lift his hand. Lucas Allen gazed into the space in front of him, seeming not to see or to hear, withdrawn into his silent world.

XVI

The Weight of Darkness

"Listen, you blighters, it was nothing of my doing!"

Kent glared at the men surrounding him and attempted to get up from his chair. Rough hands pushed him back down and held him there.

"Stay put!" Bull ordered. "You're not going no place yet."

"Well, Mr. Kent, it's just a little hard to believe, that's all," came from another British prisoner, his voice chilly. "I mean, it's quite a coincidence, isn't it, that you lately have been making very—shall we say, incendiary—remarks about Miller, and the next thing we know, he's no longer our representative."

Kent huffed. "Should I be flattered that you think I have so much influence over the enemy?"

"No, you bastard," another GI warned. "You should be afraid."

Kent licked his lower lip. His eyes darted here and there, seeking someone in the group of prisoners who might speak for him. His gaze landed on Nick, who sat on a lower bunk just outside the group, watching.

"I'm not the only one here who deals with the Germans," Kent said.

"You're the only one here who has made it plain that you don't trust a Jew representing the prisoners."

"It's true. I don't," Kent pronounced defiantly. "And from what I have seen firsthand at home, I have good reason. But that doesn't mean I'd do something to get rid of him. Besides, I'm not at all convinced that Miller is going off to his death as you claim. Thousands of men are working kommando detail, yet we're not assuming that all those thousands are going to be murdered before this war is over. If something does happen to Miller—well, I'm sorry. I wouldn't want that. But I will not deny that we need to be represented by someone who doesn't immediately stand for everything the Nazis hate. How much influence do you think a Jew has with them?"

"I'm curious about one thing, Ian."

This voice also came from outside the group gathered around Kent. Sergeant Ray Dickerson—Whitey—stood up and ran his knuckles over his head, a habit indicating he had something important to say. Nick liked Whitey, so named because of the bristles of white hair that sprouted from his head. He knew that all the prisoners appreciated Dickerson because he was the one who distributed the wonderful gift of mail. A reserved, soft-spoken man, Whitey Dickerson wasted no words.

"What is that, Whitey?" Kent asked.

"Do you have someone else in mind who has the prisoners' confidence *and* the Nazis' trust?"

"As a matter of fact, I do."

Whitey nodded, pursing his lips. He looked at the others, his eyebrows arching, as he waited for someone else to pick up the questioning.

"And who would that be?" Bull inquired on cue.

Ian Kent squared his shoulders and stood up. He looked each man in the eye before stating, "I think we all know that I am the man for the job. I seem to have some powers of persuasion, even with the enemy. I am fluent in German and in French, and I know things that most of the prisoners in camp don't know. As it happens, I have access to certain informa—"

Thwap!

Kent reeled, his neck twisting from the unexpected punch to his jaw. As he fell, the stunned prisoners around him gawked at Captain McAndrews who now rubbed the knuckles of his right hand. Nick stood up and took a step forward, but stopped when Whitey laid a hand on his shoulder.

"Sorry, Kent," Doc McAndrews muttered, then offered his hand to the downed man. "Don't know what came over me there." Hesitating, Ian Kent allowed the doc to pull him to his feet.

Nick heard someone mumble "bloody arrogant bastard" and knew that the sentiment had nothing to do with Doc McAndrews. He couldn't help feeling a little pleased with the doc's Sunday punch and with the general attitude the other prisoners showed. Apparently he had not been alone in his dislike of the self-important Ian Kent. The murmurings even from Kent's fellow citizens showed that the man did not have the support he may have supposed he had. Nick suspected, however, that McAndrews's quick wallop had not come as an angry reaction but as the quickest means of silencing the Brit, who might have been on the verge of disclosing just a little too much.

"Let's put this off a while longer," McAndrews suggested. He offered his arm as support for the dazed Ian Kent. "When we've all cooled off a little, we can choose our MOC. It doesn't have to be done today."

With that, he led Kent outside. The other prisoners murmured or whispered, and some even laughed as they gradually dispersed. Nick left the barracks, relishing his satisfaction at seeing Ian Kent put in his place, knowing that the prisoners would choose the best man available to replace Hank Miller as Man-of-Confidence, and that the choice would not be Ian Kent.

In the weeks that followed, it became clear that it didn't matter who the new MOC was. Though the British prisoner who was ultimately chosen, Anthony Burton, did his best to negotiate with the Nazis for the benefit of the prisoners, his efforts usually failed. Nick wouldn't have thought it possible, but conditions continued to worsen as the Nazis forbade many of the activities the men had come to appreciate so much. No more *Barbs and Gripes* newsletters passed from barracks to barracks; group studies were curtailed in the makeshift library. Entertainments were limited due to the "ill-mannered and impudent nature" of some of the songs and skits.

The little information Nick managed to garner from Doc McAndrews proved disheartening. As the summer wore on, it seemed that the progress of the invading Allied forces faltered in the face of strong German defenses. At the stalag, the guards proved that they had not yet reached the depth of their hate and cruelty, but their malice took an inward direction as well; fellowship among guards weakened, and distrust of each other seemed to grow as guards questioned each other's loyalty. Unfortunately, most of them attempted to prove their loyalty to the Reich by dealing harshly with the captives. The Germans' wariness made sense to Nick only after word came through channels that some months earlier, members of Hitler's inner circle had failed in an attempt to overthrow their leader. While it had been Germany's own who'd made the attempt, retribution was felt strongly among prisoners of war. Listening to the Nazis' daily propaganda and sometimes even subtly eavesdropping on conversations between guards, Nick also learned that changes in treatment of prisoners came about because someone new was in command in Berlin; a man named Himmler, apparently fairly high up in the Nazi organization, had taken control of all decisions regarding prisoners. Whoever this Himmler was, the prisoners speculated that he possessed little in the way of compassion.

This became obvious early in the fall of 1944 as the Nazis withheld still more privileges. Chaplain Bruce Wyman and Tom Connelly, the Catholic representative, announced to the prisoners that the building they had been using as a chapel would no longer be available to them. Any religious services would have to be confined to individual barracks. The men resented the commandeering of their place of worship, but they allowed their hope a little renewal when rumors flew that the building would be used for storage, primarily of Red Cross supplies.

"You wouldn't believe how many parcels have been withheld," Pete deLuca, in charge of Red Cross distribution, told the prisoners in barracks one night. "There must be thousands—hell, tens of thousands of packages just waiting, and my guess is that they've been waiting for a long time."

Except for occasional denial of parcels as punishment, each prisoner continued to receive only one Red Cross package per week. Nick felt it was the only thing that kept the men from starving to death. The tins of sardines and Spam, the crackers, raisins, sugar, coffee, and tea provided necessary supplement to the watery swill that passed as soup, the tiny wrinkled potatoes, and the dreaded *sauerbrot* that tasted too much like sawdust.

"Maybe we'll get double rations," Red Murphy guessed. "Maybe the Nazis have to fatten us up a bit more so we don't look so bad when liberation finally comes. What do you think, Chef? Think we'll all be eating a little better in the next few weeks? You know, before freedom?"

Murphy tried to pull Chef into conversation. Nick had all but given up on trying to boost the kid's morale, which had plummeted after the murder of the escaped prisoners. Chef continued to shadow Nick, to rely on him for assurance, though he was not likely to accept that assurance when it was offered. Chef's constant need for encouragement sometimes overwhelmed Nick, and in recent days, he'd tried to distance himself from the kid's dejection.

"I doubt it," Chef responded to Murphy in a flat tone. "I bet they'll put all those food packages in that building, shut the door and padlock it, and shoot anybody who tries to open it."

"Or they take it for themselves," Foul-mouth Matthews offered. "Them sons o' bitches ain't looking so healthy anymore either. Be just like them to steal provisions meant for prisoners. Why else would they keep them? What have they got to gain by starving us?"

The rations were not distributed. Days of waiting for the hoped-for double portions turned into weeks. Prisoners pressured deLuca, who made a request to MOC Burton, who in turn petitioned the kommandant for weekly release of the parcels. The kommandant's response came quickly: By order of the highest command, captives were to be "treated like prisoners of war and not like pampered guests." There would be no more inspections by Swiss representatives. In addition, because Pete deLuca's service as Red Cross representative and parcel distributor would no longer be required in base camp, the order came for him to be reassigned to a labor detachment outside the camp.

Several days later, Pete stepped out of appel formation to join a workforce as it returned to the field. Several men around him called encouragement.

"Take care, Pete."

"Be strong."

"At least you'll eat better out there."

Just before appel dismissal, Chef muttered, "That's the last we'll see of deLuca."

Nick just shook his head, refusing even to comment on Chef's prediction. The white feather Chef still kept in his pocket next to his lucky spoon seemed to have lost its power. The defiant determination it had briefly given him had diminished, leaving the kid with the certainty that he would never again know freedom, that every time he walked the prison grounds, he walked over his own grave. Nick couldn't stand to be near such pessimism for very long. He feared it might be too contagious.

The days crept by, each one a repetition of the last. With less nourishment in their bodies, the men had little energy for exercise, and even their creative innovations dwindled. Their primary activities, it seemed, were reduced to sleeping and to waiting. Grateful for every minute erased through sleep, the prisoners spent the tedious, waking hours speculating on the progress of the war.

"Where do you reckon the front is now?"

"I'm guessing by Christmas . . . by the new year at the latest . . . we'll see our guys comin' over the rise."

"Wonder why it's taking so long. Don't the Germans know their cause is all but lost?"

"Once we're on their ground, they'll fight to the last man standing. Count on it."

The days grew shorter, at least in terms of light and warmth. Cooler nights reminded the prisoners that winter would come around again, that their battle against hunger would be compounded by their struggle to stay warm. At the first sign of frost, the prisoners stoked up the barracks stoves, hoping to beat the cold before it even arrived. The Germans thwarted their efforts, however, by severely reducing coal rations.

On the night of the season's first snowfall, a light dusting, Nick lay quietly in his bunk trying to recapture what it felt like during the sweltering days of summer.

It's all wrong, he thought. *We ought to be able to bottle the heat or the cold so we can use them when they're needed.* Just then, Nick heard Chef's low, gloomy voice.

"You know what tomorrow is?" After a moment of silence, Chef spoke again, a little louder. "Hey, Nick. You know what tomorrow is?"

"Just another day as far as I know."

"Uh-uh. Tomorrow's November tenth. You know what that means?"

Nick didn't answer. Of course he remembered that date. He remembered as clearly as if it were just yesterday, waking up to look into the barrel of a German soldier's rifle. He remembered fear, revulsion, physical exertion the likes of which he'd not known before. He remembered it all. What came as a surprise was the sudden awareness that an entire year had passed since that day, an entire year of existing rather than living, of surviving rather than thriving.

"My God," Nick blurted then. "I'm thirty years old!"

He wondered how he could have forgotten his own birthday back in August, how a full year of family birthdays and holidays and just ordinary days could even have taken place during his time of incarceration. Surely time on the outside should have stopped on the tenth of November 1943. Nick realized that his year as a POW was time he would not get back again, that as he shivered and sweated and starved and ached, the people he cared about back home worked and prayed, aged and changed. His little nieces and nephew probably weren't as little as he remembered them; his folks very likely looked older, maybe grayer, and more stooped. Were the people he'd worked with back at the Cleveland tool company still there? What about the elderly landlady who'd rented him his rooms? Had she survived the year? How many of his relatives and one-time neighbors had died? Or wedded, started families, found jobs, made homes—all the things that normal people experience in a normal time? He thought about Jacob, who had just wanted to see the world and ended up fighting the Japanese in some obscure corner of it. He too would be a year older now—if alive, and like Nick, a lifetime changed. Nick closed his eyes.

"God let this be over before another year goes by," he prayed. He didn't know he'd said the words aloud until Chef echoed him.

"Just let it all be over."

The following week brought a much-too-early cold spell. The rationed coal wasn't nearly enough to warm the barracks, and even though the sun broke through during the day, it seemed far too powerless to warm the interior of the cinder-block buildings. The prisoners bundled themselves tightly in as many clothes as they had, wrapped thin blankets around themselves, and huddled so close together that if one man sneezed, the next man's ribs ached.

Though he appreciated the warmth generated by body heat, Nick came to hate the tight crowding of men. At times, he felt as if he couldn't breathe, and whenever that feeling came over him, his heart pounded hard, which ultimately did affect his breathing. He could take it only so long.

"I got to get out of here." A simple trip to the latrine usually calmed him down until the chilly wind drove him, shivering, back to the groups in the barracks. Aware that winter had not even arrived yet, that the cold that seemed so debilitating wasn't near the intensity of the cold they had experienced during the last winter, Nick wondered how the men would make it through the coming months.

We've lost all our insulation, he realized. Their clothes hung loosely around their bodies, cinched up with rope or twine or scraps of cloth. Nick's arms, once taught and muscular, looked like they belonged to an old man.

Nick left the latrine. Heading back to the barracks, he passed the former chapel building. He noticed that the door wasn't padlocked; in fact, it stood ajar. He wondered if it were true that thousands of packages of food, socks, scarves, and mittens were stored in there. Without actually planning to, Nick drifted closer to the building, then hesitated as several guards looked his way. When one of them approached with a leashed dog, Nick turned away from the building, trying not to walk too fast back to the barracks.

"*Halt! Was tun Sie da?*"

Nick stopped, every muscle in his body tense as he turned to face the guard and the dog. Since his earlier encounter with a vicious dog, Nick tried to avoid close contact with the animals.

"I was just at the latrine and was on my way back—," Nick began before realizing that would not explain his proximity to the chapel building. He wet his lips and tried again.

"They told me to wait outside," he gestured toward the open door, not even sure if anyone were inside.

"*Warum?*"

"I don't know why; I'm just supposed to wait out here, but I tell you I'm getting damn cold, so I guess I'll just go back to where I should be—in our nice, comfortable barracks."

The German narrowed his eyes, then chuckled.

"I know who you are," he finally said, leaning in close and whispering. "And I know who you're dealing with."

Nick pulled his blanket tighter. Now what had he gotten himself into? Puffing a steamy breath, he faltered, "Yes, well—I'll just—"

Without finishing the statement, he turned but took no more than two steps before the guard ordered him to stop.

"You will not go back to your barracks! If Immelman has ordered you to wait outside here, then that is what you shall do. Go on!" He pointed toward the chapel door. "Go over there and wait."

Nick obeyed, his throat tightening. If Immelman—Fritz—actually were in the chapel, Nick would have a very hard time explaining his lie.

"Not so close," the guard ordered when Nick stopped just outside the door. "Step back and wait."

"May I at least wait by the corner? Away from the wind?"

The guard snorted, then turned on his heel, pulling the snuffling dog with him. Nick stayed in place, knowing well that the guard would continue to watch him. He wondered how on earth he was going to get back to the barracks unseen.

After a few minutes, Nick had something else to worry about. Voices from inside the chapel indicated that at least two Germans were inside, and they were moving toward the front of the building. Nick crouched down below one of the front windows, hoping they wouldn't see him. He was amazed at how well he could hear the Germans' voices, until he remembered that the building had originally been erected for the use of the prisoners' church services, that the thin walls had been built of the crating from around Red Cross parcels—an intentionally weak structure so that Nazis had no trouble hearing what might be spoken within. Now the reverse was true, and Nick clearly heard Fritz and another guard in conversation. The Germans spoke a dialect slightly different from Nick's native tongue, but he missed very little.

"What will you do?"

"There is nothing to be done. If the end would come sooner rather than later, perhaps they would not—but what can I do?" Nick recognized Fritz's voice.

"Still, thirteen years old. Such a one should be studying, or playing with balls and sticks, not carrying a gun into a battle."

"And the old one too. What can they expect my father to do, almost seventy now?"

"Everyone must do his part. The führer needs every muscle of every man, old and young. He will not fail his people or his country."

"Do you still believe that?"

Silence followed until Nick heard Fritz answer his own question.

"Of course, of course. We all believe what we are told. It is death not to. Like you, I prefer not to die, but if I must, it will be in loyal service to my country, and not against it."

"I am glad to hear you say it, Friedrich. I only hope that you mean it—whatever comes."

Nick forgot about being watched. He felt a strange mix of excitement and dread as he listened. The conversation implied the certainty that Germany's war was indeed lost, that it was just a matter of time before surrender. It also carried the warning of last-ditch efforts. When the offensive armies met the defensive forces head on, the battle surely would be some of the fiercest fighting of the war.

And we sorry, starved band of prisoners will be in the thick of it, Nick understood.

Before Nick was ready for it, the door opened wide and the two Germans stepped outside. Fritz spotted Nick immediately. Expressionless, he aimed his rifle. Nick slowly stood up. He waited for the guard to speak first. For what seemed like a long time, Fritz appeared to consider his options. Finally, he spoke over his shoulder to the second guard.

"Take the report to headquarters. I will deal with this man."

Nick and Fritz faced each other, unmoving, as the other guard saluted and left. Though he thought he should say something, anything at all, Nick couldn't help being silenced by the weapon pointing directly at his chest, by the Nazi's hand and fingers so poised to fire.

"Step inside," Fritz spoke first, and then snapped as Nick hesitated, "Now!"

Nick followed the order, not even speculating on what would come. He felt his entire life bound up in the moment and didn't dare to think about the next minute, or the minute after that. Once both men were inside the building, Fritz closed the door.

"Sit," he said, gesturing to a nearby bench.

Fritz placed his right foot on the bench next to Nick and leaned the rifle more casually across his bent leg. Feeling just a little less tense, Nick glanced around the room. Except for a few empty benches and chairs, the room was filled with boxes. He didn't see the familiar red symbol anywhere on them, however. Nick swallowed.

"Yes, quite a few supplies," Fritz said, as if reading Nick's mind. "They will not go to waste."

Fritz pulled a packet of Old Gold cigarettes from his coat pocket, lit one, and offered the pack to Nick. Nick took one, allowing Fritz to light it. The two puffed and exhaled slowly, Nick keeping his eyes on the weapon, Fritz's eyes seeming to watch both Nick and the door.

"You must know, it will not be long now," Fritz finally spoke. Not sure how much he should or shouldn't know, Nick didn't reply.

"Two, three months perhaps." Again, silence as the men warily studied each other's expressions.

"You have family? Children?" Fritz finally queried.

"No, I'm not married," Nick answered.

"Ah. You are fortunate then. You do not have them to worry about. But then you Americans have no need to worry about your families, do you? You do not fight a war on your own ground." When Nick didn't respond to this, Fritz added, "I have two children. Maria and Kurt. And my wife . . . Hannah."

"Do you . . . see them often?" Nick ventured further small talk.

"Not for a long time. They stay with my parents until—"

He paused, lifting the cigarette back to his mouth, then stopping to watch a thin wisp of smoke rise from it. He pulled his foot from the bench and strode a few steps to stand near a window where he laid the cigarette. He leaned the rifle against the wall and pulled out a pistol, a Luger, from inside his overcoat. Idly examining it, he continued speaking.

"I had hoped to send all my family west before Christmas. Now, it seems, that is not likely to happen."

Nick cleared his throat. "How old are they?" he asked. "Your children, I mean."

"Maria is ten. Kurt is now thirteen—as I'm sure you already know." He thumbed the handle of the revolver, looking first at Nick, then through the window. Finally he turned, and with his back to the window, asked, "What were you hoping to hear out there?"

"Nothing. I wasn't—" Nick faltered. "I saw the open door is all. From the latrine."

"And you are like the cat, *nicht wahr*?"

Nick was momentarily taken aback, as he thought Fritz referred to BC, Bernie Slade's scrawny, ugly pet. He wasn't sure how he and that animal might be alike except perhaps in their thinness. He certainly didn't have the liberty to come and go as he pleased, like the stupid cat had.

"Curiosity," Fritz clarified. "A sometimes deadly trait . . . in the world of cats."

"What are all these supplies?" Nick blurted, surprising himself. "If these are—fifteen hundred men here are practically starving! Thousands more out on detail. You claim this war will be over soon—if it were you, or your son or your father in a prison camp, wouldn't you—?" Nick stopped, aware of the changed look on Fritz's face. The intimidating sneer Nick was so accustomed to wasn't there. Instead, the man looked weary.

"I am a soldier. I do what I am told to do when I am told to do it, and I expect the same of those who serve with me. It is the duty of all who serve, no matter whom they serve. We are a proud people, Herr Bremer, and we do not relish the shame of defeat. The truth is we are like cornered animals—"

"And we're caged animals!"

"A caged animal is already checked. The cornered animal must fight with every tooth and claw, and that is exactly what we will do."

"No matter how wasted the effort?"

"A man—a soldier—is not well remembered for giving up, even if giving up is the wise thing to do."

Fritz replaced his pistol and picked up the cigarette again. A long cylinder of ash hung from the end of it. He flicked the ash on the floor, then swept at it with his boot. Picking up the rifle, he gestured with his head that Nick should get up and move toward the door. Nick rose. At the door he stopped, turning to face his captor and feeling suddenly quite brave.

"We aren't giving up either, you know. We might be caged—checked, as you say—but we'll do whatever we have to do just to survive. You can starve us or freeze us or beat us down, you might break some of us—you might break me—but you'll never break us all. When this is over, maybe we won't be heroes, but—"

Fritz burst out laughing. He strode to the door and opened it.

"Herr Bremer," he said, "you are right. You are no hero, you give me no cause to shoot you. Go on. Go back to where you should be."

Nick returned to the barracks to the tight group of shivering men. He squeezed in among them and gradually felt the warmth of their closeness, the increased beating of his heart, the difficulty breathing.

The hoped-for liberation did not come by December. As the men realized they faced still another Christmas in prison, their spirits sank again. They tried not to think about family or feasting or memories of happier times. They forced themselves not to speculate on how their loved ones might commemorate the holiday without them. Christmas would be just one more day like all the other days, a day of cold, hunger, boredom, and as always, waiting.

The only bright moment for Nick came a few days before Christmas when he received a package during mail distribution—supposedly the care package that his parents had sent almost nine months earlier. The brightness faded quickly, however. The box could hardly be recognized as a box, its corners crumpled and ragged. Loose and frayed string barely kept the box in one piece. When Nick tore it open, the only thing he found inside was a tin of crumbled honey cookies. He stared at the crumbs, then picked up a sizable one and put it in his mouth, biting down hard. It crunched, so dried and solid, Nick felt almost as if he were chewing on gravel. He sensed only a slight sweetness, nothing at all like the delicious cookies he remembered. Whatever else his parents had included in the box had disappeared, very likely pilfered long ago. Nick imagined a Nazi soldier enjoying the warmth of a pair of his mother's hand-knitted socks or mittens. The thought made him ache.

On the twenty-third of December, just after the customary evening count and propagandized war report, the men heard an unfamiliar voice over the loudspeaker. It was that of a prisoner who spoke in French, then waited for his words to be translated into English and German.

"There will be a special Christmas service tomorrow at midnight at the show hall in the French sector. With permission of the kommandant, prisoners who wish to attend this service should gather here by twenty-three hundred hours. This is not compulsory."

As the men settled in after lockdown that evening, Matthews wondered how the show hall would accommodate all the prisoners who would choose to attend the services.

"Maybe not so many will go," Chef offered. "What's the point after all?"

"Are you nuts?" Matthews retorted. "Who's going to miss an opportunity for a break from the ordinary? Besides, you never know, a little praying on Christmas maybe couldn't hurt."

"If all it took for this war to be over was a little praying, it would have ended before it began," Chef argued.

Nick had heard enough. He wheeled, facing the kid with fire in his eyes.

"You know what, Chef?" he rebuked. "There is no one here who needs to go to this service more than you do. And you're going to go, if I have to drag you there myself!"

"I'll help." This from Bull.

"Thanks," Nick said, "but I thought you were an atheist."

Bull grinned. "You know what they say: There ain't no atheists in a shithole."

"That's 'foxhole,' Bull," Murphy corrected. "No atheists in a foxhole."

"Foxhole, shithole, it don't make no difference. Come midnight tomorrow, me an' the kid here, we're gonna do us some prayin'."

Nick just shook his head. If reverence were a requisite for communicating with the Almighty, no wonder God seemed so unresponsive.

At 11:00 p.m. on Christmas Eve, almost every prisoner in camp showed up on the grounds. The show hall allowed seating for only about 250 men. Almost twice that many managed to squeeze themselves in, claiming every square inch of sitting, standing, and clinging space. Nick stepped away from the line of men still clamoring for entrance. He knew he wouldn't make it through five minutes in such cramped conditions.

The remaining prisoners gathered outside as close to the open doors and windows as they could get. As the service began, those closest repeated some of what they heard for the benefit of the men out of range. Nick saw that quite a few Germans also stood around listening, their heads bowed.

An English chaplain and a French priest led the service, but the priest alone delivered the sermon, amplified through a loudspeaker.

"And the Word was made flesh and dwelt among us," he began. "Yes, among people like us, so that God—even with all his greatness and goodness, majesty and might—would experience firsthand what it is like to be human."

The night held a crisp stillness. As the reverend continued his sermon, prisoners inside the building and out stifled their restless murmuring and shifting. Men bowed their heads and closed their eyes; some simply looked at one another and nodded. Each seemed to be absorbed in thought or memory evoked by the simple words.

"Jesus, the son of God, knew helplessness. He knew fear and goodness, injustice and hope, cruelty and love. It is his knowing that entitled him to call all the poor in spirit blessed."

Nick turned his gaze to Chef, considering him one of the poorest in spirit. Standing slump shouldered, with eyes cast downward, Chef didn't look particularly blessed, and Nick was sure he didn't feel very blessed either. Nick only hoped that the profound words spoken on this profoundly cruel and beautiful night would somehow reach the kid, to ignite even a little spark of hope.

" . . . and so let us remember on this Christmas night 1944, the song of the angels themselves: 'Glory to God in the highest, and peace—*peace*—to his people on earth.' "

At that, as Nick somehow knew they would, the men began singing "Silent Night." He joined in, the sweet, familiar melody sung by a thousand harmonized voices—maybe more—made him shiver. Nick heard German words mingling with English:

> *Sleep in heavenly peace—*
> *Schlaf in himmlische Ruh.*

Because they had been on the outside of the crowd, Nick and Chef were among the first to get back to the barracks. Coming from the harshly lit grounds into the dimly lit building, both men stumbled into something that blocked the aisle between tiers of bunks.

"What the—?" the man behind Nick exclaimed, bumping into him.

Eyes adjusting, the men sidled carefully around two wooden crates heaped with coal. More exclamations came as more men entered.

"Well, I'll be damned," Matthews uttered. "You'd think it was Christmas or something. And look at that! We even got ourselves a Christmas tree!"

In the rear unit, Lucas Allen, who had not attended the church service, paced around a bucket that held an odd arrangement of dried and crooked twigs. Every few seconds he paused to wind or tie something around one of the twigs. Nick saw that Luke's decorations consisted of small twists of paper from cigarette packages, metal "keys," and tiny coils of tin from Spam cans, and knotty strands of wool—probably the unraveled threads from a worn sock.

Bernie whistled low and asked no one in particular, "How long has he been collecting this junk, I wonder?"

Matthews walked up to Luke, patted him on the back, and said, "Nice work, Luke. You just made this place a little bit cheerier. Merry Christmas to you, you crazy son of a bitch."

Ignoring the men, Luke continued his meticulous decoration of the bare twigs.

Later, when the men gradually began drifting off to sleep in their slightly warmer barracks, thanks to the extra coal, Nick lay awake remembering the Christmas tree he'd bought two years ago for his recently widowed landlady. It too had been a scrawny thing, barely strong enough to stand straight, yet she'd accepted it with such tearful gratitude that Nick had felt embarrassed. Now, two Christmases later, he understood what it was to be grateful for seemingly small blessings.

He turned over to lie on his stomach, using his arms like a pillow. *I don't know what 1945 will bring*, he thought just before falling asleep, *but it's got to be a better year than the last one.*

Muffled sighs interrupted Nick's thought. Tracing the sound to Chef's bunk, Nick raised himself on one elbow.

"What is it now?" he asked, immediately regretting his impatient tone.

"Oh boy, Nick—it's just that—just that," Chef's voice trembled with a mingling of wistful sighs and little hiccups of laughter. "When I was a little kid, I was always scared to death of finding nothing but coal in my stocking. I just never dreamed I could feel so darn good . . . getting lumps of coal . . . for Christmas!"

Part Three

To The Western Front: January-May 1945

XVII

Out of the Box

The New Year came without liberation, intensifying the awful restlessness of waiting. The men grew weary of speculating; they became more impatient with their situation and with each other as well. Always battling hunger, once again defending themselves against winter, they frequently snapped at each other.

Just a few days into the new year, Nick and several other prisoners clustered around the stove. The extra coal they'd received on Christmas night had burned fast, and now they were back to typical rations—far too short a supply to make the unit comfortable. Only by getting close to the stove for a period of time could the men get the numbness out of their fingers and toes, the sting out of their cheeks and noses. To be fair as possible to every man, they took turns closest to the heat, though frequently one group's turn seemed too short, while another group seemed to occupy the warmest places for too long.

Bernie Olsen sat on the floor by the stove, his contented cat draped around his neck. From where he sat, Nick could hear the animal purring, not smoothly as he'd known cats to purr, but roughly, with a low popping sound. The cat also showed its satisfaction by occasionally flexing its claws, gouging Bernie's shoulder and neck. Each time it did, Bernie grabbed hold of the offending paw and squeezed it.

"Ouch, BC, don't do that."

M'rowww. The cat answered every reprimand with a scratchy, throaty cry. The sound jangled the men's nerves. Even Lucas Allen stopped staring at nothing and turned toward the sound, focusing almost studiously on the cat. After a time, Bernie became twitchy under Luke's gaze. He reached behind his neck to stroke the cat.

"BC is not depriving you of your rations," he answered a charge that had not been made, at least not for a long time. Luke did not turn away. Instead, his steely eyes narrowed as they made contact with the cat's dilated and fiery eyes.

"Ouch, ouch, ouch," Bernie repeated as the claws dug at him. The cat hissed, opening its mouth into an evil-looking grin. In a flash, BC pounced from Bernie's neck to Allen's chest, and from there he leaped to a third-tier bunk, where he lay down, his body tense and his eyes glowering at the men below him. In spite of three fresh claw marks at the base of Luke's throat, the soldier's mouth twitched as if he might smile.

Just then Nick felt someone nudge him from behind. He turned to see Johnny Ames wrapped in a flea-ridden blanket.

"Shove over there, can't you?" Ames tried to squeeze in closer to the fire. "You guys are soaking up all the heat, you know that? You should let it spread around a little."

"Ain't enough here to spread around."

"C'mon guys, you're hoarding the hot spots," another man complained.

Sighing, Nick stood up and backed away from the stove, allowing another man to take his place. He would have needed to get up and out of the barracks soon anyway. Nature's calls didn't stop just because the weather turned cold.

Nick could have used the night-use-only urinal at the back of the barracks, but he elected to go to the latrine instead. As he walked through unit A of the barracks, he noted that an even greater number of men huddled close to their somewhat-larger stove. One small group tried to ignore the cold by playing or kibitzing a game of dominoes. From somewhere in the background came the plaintive sound of harmonica notes.

Outside Nick inhaled biting air and felt the hairs inside his nose freeze together. Still, he savored the freshness. One thing winter could not deaden was the constant odor of staleness and filth that permeated the barracks. Making his way to the latrine, Nick passed Ian Kent, apparently returning from that very place. Kent seemed to be pretty much a loner now, shunned by most of the other prisoners. As the men passed each other they made eye contact; Nick gave a nod, but Kent ignored the greeting and looked away.

You made your bed, Nick judged. *Now you have to sleep in it.*

Other prisoners also meandered the grounds; some exercised for warmth and strength—what little of either they could build. As usual, guards patrolled, though Nick observed that there didn't seem to be quite as many of them as there had been before Christmas. He had not seen Fritz since their conversation back in December and so was surprised when that familiar voice reached his ears just outside the latrine.

Focusing on his own footfalls, Nick passed the walleyed German, hoping not to catch Fritz's attention. At the door Nick measured his breathing, taking one long and deep breath before entering. Inside he exhaled slowly, emptying his lungs completely before taking another breath, a shallow one this time. He continued with the shallow breathing as long as he remained in the building. As soon as he could, he left the building, gasping for fresh air.

"The next crate of coal that comes in, you should not also burn the crate." The peculiar order came from Fritz.

"What?" Nick faced him.

"Keep the crate. Don't burn it, as you have been doing."

"Why—do you think the wood is giving us a little too much heat?" Nick asked. As Fritz's lips tightened, Nick tensed, waiting for an angry response to his undisguised cynicism. The German grumbled words Nick couldn't quite discern. He waited a little while before daring to ask again, "Why should we hang on to the crate?"

"Not for everyone. That is not possible," Fritz replied. Enigmatic as usual, he added in a low voice, "Your armies will not come to you, you know."

Nick shook his head. *What is this?* he wondered. *What kind of party line blather is he trying to give me now?* Aloud he began again, "What are you—" but Fritz cut off the question with an impatient wave of his hand. He leaned his face in close. Nick's eyes darted from Fritz's right eye to the left, as he tried to determine which one he should focus on.

"You must know that no German will surrender to Russians—if there is any way at all to prevent it." With that, Fritz walked away, joining another German in patrol of the grounds.

"What the hell was that about?" Nick asked no one in particular.

Later, he shared with his companions Fritz's puzzling words—all except the instruction about needing the crate. It didn't take them long to put an explanation on the event.

"Hell, it's obvious," Foul-mouth claimed. "The Germans have lost this war. That means they have to surrender sometime, but they'll do anything they have to do in order not to surrender to the Russians."

"So they'll surrender to our guys," Chef offered.

"Right. But this stalag is on, or almost on, their *eastern* border. Our troops aren't going to get here before *theirs* do—the Russians, I mean."

They imagined possibilities: Would the Germans simply disappear one night, leaving the Allied prisoners free to try joining with the Russian forces? Would they attempt to transport all the prisoners west, perhaps keeping them as some kind of collateral? What if the prisoners attempted some kind of revolt to expedite their liberation?

"Don't be insane." Drummond nixed the last idea. "Hell as it is to wait, that's exactly what we have to do now. If we start some kind of uprising, then a lot of us aren't going to make it out alive. I can't speak for the rest of you, but I for one have a couple of damn good reasons for staying alive."

"You know, it's a prisoner's job to try to escape," Bartell observed. "So far we haven't been doing our jobs."

Drummond countered, "It's our job to be strong and hang on, and not complicate the war for our buddies still out there fighting it!" The others nodded. Though they didn't know how much longer it would be, most felt the end finally within sight.

"I'd say, it's more like within sight of being in sight," Murphy cautioned. "But by God, we're getting there. What do you say to that, Chef? We're going to make it."

Chef offered a weak smile. With eyes shut, he moved his hand to the pocket on his chest. Through the fabric, he fingered the bowl of his lucky spoon. The men watched him. Their silence made Chef open his eyes again. As he looked around, a sheepish expression dawned on his face.

"I guess so," he finally said.

By the middle of January, there still seemed to be no sign of immediate surrender, though the men noted changes, some subtle, some fairly obvious. For one thing, distant rumbling sounds drifted in whenever the wind blew from the east. In addition, the guards appeared more temperamental than usual. Even more promising, the Germans had stopped their usual propaganda reports. Though *appel* continued, the twice-daily count didn't take as long as it used to. Prisoners stopped trying to foul up the count, and if a discrepancy in number occurred, certain guards began to ignore it, assuming that the captives continued with their little deceptions. Soon, a few of the men simply refused to fall out for the count.

Nick continued to show up, if only because it used up some of the time that hung so heavily. Most of his closest buddies did, too, though Luke usually remained behind in the barracks. His setback to shell-shocked silence had become so complete and unbreakable, that even the prisoners who knew him best forgot he'd once spoken lucidly. Luke was an empty man, usually easy to ignore—until a few nights later.

Traipsing into their quarters after evening count, Chef and Bartell were the first to notice an unusual odor. They stopped, lifted their faces, and sniffed. Nick, close on their heels, did the same.

"Come on, guys, move it," a voice urged from the door.

"What's that smell?" Bartell asked. "You guys smell that?"

"Something in here actually smells *good!*"

The aroma grew stronger as the men passed the central washroom and entered unit B. There they spied Luke, hunched before the open belly of the stove. A soft, sizzling sound came from within and as the men drew closer, they saw that Luke was roasting something at the end of a stout twig.

"Luke?" Chef asked. "What are you doing there? What have you got?"

Of course Luke didn't answer, didn't show any sign of recognition that others were in the room. The embers lit his face, where the men saw a serene smile.

"That's meat!" Matthews announced. "Lucas Allen, where the hell did you get meat?"

As word spread, others gathered around; some came in from unit A demanding to know the source of the smell, asking for their share of the supper. When it became clear that this was not a sudden blessing from the Germans, their demands subsided.

"Oh what's the big deal?" Slade asked. "It's probably just rat again."

"Can't be," Bernie answered. "There haven't been any rats in this building since my BC showed up. He's awful good at—"

Bernard stopped, his mouth open and his eyes widening. He dashed to his bunk and thumped the scant bedding. Getting down on his knees, he looked under the bunk, then scanned beneath the entire bottom rows.

"BC? Where are you? Here, kitty kitty!"

No yowl or meow came in response.

"You guys seen my cat?" Bernie asked. No one remembered seeing the animal since sometime the previous day. Bernie wheeled on Luke. He grabbed the man's shoulders, shaking him.

"What have you done with my cat? Goddamn you to hell, Lucas Allen, is that my goddamned *cat?*"

Just as his hands circled Luke's throat and began to squeeze, several POWs scrambled forward to pull him away. Bernie flailed against them and swore as Luke coughed. In the tussle Luke had not loosened his grip on the stick. Turning it slowly, holding it just far enough away from the coal embers so it would not ignite, he simply stared at the hunk of meat that roasted at the end of it.

"Jesus Christ, Luke," Matthews uttered, "you didn't really cook Bernie's cat, did you?"

No response. Luke pulled the stick from the fire and brought the meat close to his nose. Inhaling, he closed his eyes, a look of ecstasy on his face. As he bit and then chewed, he began to moan. He didn't open his eyes until after he'd swallowed. Then he looked around at the astonished men who watched him. Straightening up, he turned and moved toward Bernie. The two men stood face-to-face, one panting and glaring, the other wearing a blissful expression. Luke extended the chunk of steaming meat toward Bernie. With a simple move of his head, he encouraged Bernie to take a bite.

"No, damn you!" Bernie struggled against the men who still restrained him. His voice quivered. "I ain't gonna eat my cat, you—you butcher!"

"Easy there, Olson," Murphy said. "I'm sure that's not your cat he cooked. It's probably—well—something else. Isn't it, Luke?"

Luke withdrew his offer, considering. In a moment, he held the meat out to Bernie again. Nick watched, almost mesmerized by the scene. All the men grew quiet. The tantalizing aroma of roasted meat hung in the air.

So tempting, Nick thought. *Just one taste.*

Others must have felt the same urge. Nick saw several men wet their lips and look achingly at the steaming meat. Even Bernie grew calmer. What followed seemed unreal to Nick. He knew he would always remember the extraordinary moment when Bernie took a bite of meat, choking back a sob. It felt like a bizarre kind of communion when Luke offered a bite to all the men around him. Some turned away appalled, but others accepted, their appetite too strong to resist. When Luke finally drew round to Nick and offered him a taste, Nick bit off a morsel. The meat was tough, stringy, and tasted a bit gamy, a little sweet.

When all the meat was gone, Luke broke the stick into small pieces and laid them across the coals. Little flames erupted where greasy wood rested against glowing coal. Luke closed the stove door. The squeak and clank seemed to break a spell. Wordless, the men turned away, refusing to look at each other. Nick crawled into his bunk and pulled the blanket tight around him. He tried to shut his mind to the muted sobs that came from Bernie, and the mournful words that accompanied them, "Poor old BC. He never hurt anyone."

Nick didn't sleep much that night, and he could tell by the restless stirrings that many of the other men in the unit lay awake too. In fact, they were already alert before first light the next day, Sunday—January 28, when they heard trucks rumble into the compound. The stalag siren wailed followed by the shriek of many whistles as the prisoners were roused for a much earlier than usual morning count.

Nick felt his pulse quicken at the base of his throat. Murmuring in the barracks increased as the men readied themselves to fall out. They gathered in the compound, a larger group than usual. Nick realized that several labor detachments had arrived on the trucks. As he took his place in formation, he scanned the crowd of men, hoping to recognize Hank Miller or Pete deLuca among them. He saw neither and stopped looking when he heard the announcement over the loudspeakers.

"Tomorrow morning, relocation will begin. Those who are fit will march to the new location, anyone not fit will remain here until—"—the speaker hesitated, as if he had trouble saying the next words—"until the arrival of the Russian forces."

Barely avoiding immediate pandemonium, the Germans ordered prisoners back to their quarters to prepare themselves, to gather sufficient clothing, blankets, and their few personal belongings. That afternoon, Anthony Burton proved himself a worthy MOC when he somehow convinced the kommandant to release the hoarded Red Cross parcels and distribute them to the men. Word came that distribution would take place in the center of the compound. When he heard more trucks pull in, Nick headed to the center and nearly ran into Fritz, who spun around shouting orders to other guards and prisoners. Fritz didn't see Nick until the two bumped shoulders.

"*Schnell!*" Fritz shouted. Only then recognizing Nick, he grabbed him by the shoulder.

"You did what I said?" he asked. "You saved a crate?"

"Well, no. There's still some coal in the one—"

"Foolish—!" Fritz began. He turned his head and spat on the ground, then continued. "Go, get what you can. There are suitcases of goods. You will need them." Fritz pointed to the trucks where guards and prisoners alike were now clamoring for Red Cross parcels.

"Maybe I'll just stay and wait for the Russians," Nick declared.

Fritz almost growled with impatience, "You also know Russian?"

"No."

"But you do know German. Therefore you *are* a German." Fritz lowered his voice, speaking close to Nick's ear. "There is such history of hate—the Russians, barbarians—they will just shoot. Now go and get ready! At dawn we depart."

Nick needed no further encouragement. He couldn't help remembering his own pa's words, "You can't trust the Rooskies." He remembered Kid Russki's stories about Russians treating their war prisoners as traitors. He decided he would be better off reaching the western front. Nick hurried back to his unit, relieved to see that no one else had bothered to grab the wooden crate. He dumped the remaining chunks of coal, then rifled through his meager belongings, seizing only what he needed or couldn't bear to be without: his single change of clothing, his three pairs of socks, the prisoner-issue clogs, blanket, soap and shaving materials, and his letters from home. He had just put the latter in his overcoat pocket when he heard Chef behind him.

"I don't think I'm fit for this," the kid blurted. "I think I'll stay behind—"

"The hell you will," Nick ordered. "We haven't come through this much for you to drop out now. You're coming along with the rest of us. Get your things together."

Nick carried the crate out of the building. Squeezing through the crowd near the chapel, he managed to get close enough to the parcel distribution to see the enormous supply. For so long these packages had been denied; now thousands were available, not just the food parcels, but the captive parcels every prisoner should have received upon arriving at the stalag. These parcels—simple, cardboard suitcases—came packed with many items that would have come in handy during the past year. Every prisoner who would make the westward march received an entire carton of food parcels as well as the captive parcel. Nick managed to grab two of the suitcases, which he packed into the crate, adding the food carton on top. He lugged the crate back to the barracks and opened the captive parcel. Inside he found a knitted sweater, pajamas, a pair of house slippers, a pair of woolen socks and two pairs of cotton socks, woolen underwear, towels, chewing gum, pipe and tobacco, a shoeshine kit, playing cards, and a sewing kit. He ran his hands over the sweater, couldn't help thinking how often he could have used it during two winters. Nick laid the sweater on his bunk, then repacked the other items and squeezed the suitcases and food parcels as tightly as he could into the crate. He then invited others to add theirs until they could stuff no more into it. Nick studied the result. The pack was far too big and awkward for one man to haul.

"I can help with that." Red Murphy lifted one end, but before Nick could grab the other, someone flung several lengths of rope at them. Both men looked up to see where it had come from. Chef stood there.

"That guard—Fritz—he just chucked me this rope."

Murphy winked at Nick. "Pays to have friends in high places, don't it?"

Hauling the crate back outside, they knotted the rope ends around the top slat at one of the narrow sides of the crate. They tried pulling it. It moved with difficulty through the snow, finally getting stuck when too much snow lodged in front of it.

"Here, let's try something else," Murphy suggested. He undid the knots and retied the rope ends to a lower slat. When the men pulled on the rope, the crate lifted just a little at the bottom, making it slightly easier to pull. Meanwhile, other prisoners around them also began making similar sleds out of the cartons the parcels had come in, tearing strips of blankets or prison uniforms to use in place of rope.

His last night in the barracks, Nick sat with Luke, who had made no effort to ready himself for evacuation.

"Luke, you're part of our group. You're coming with us, aren't you?"

For the first time in months, Luke broke his silence. Shaking his head, he spoke, his voice hoarse and gravelly.

"No. Better off with Russians than with Germans."

"Come on, Luke. We're moving west—soon we'll be meeting up with our side. You won't have to be so cautious anymore."

Again Luke shook his head. "Soon?" he coughed and cleared his throat. "Be safe in Russian hands before you make it to the west."

Nick argued well into the night, but Lucas Allen would not change his mind. He vowed to stay at Stalag IIB—along with the sick and injured who were too weak to be moved—and await liberation from eastern forces. Finally Nick could do no more than shake Luke's hand and wish him luck.

Monday dawned with a wild northerly wind, but it did not alter the plans to begin the mass exodus. Divided into several large groups, the men lined up. Nick and his buddies felt lucky to be in the first group of about five hundred men. He grabbed the rope of his sled but found that it took quite an effort to pull it. Two men pulling made the work a little easier. They had barely joined the columns of prisoners when they realized that while the box slid fairly well through snow, it was unwieldy at best over bare ground, jamming up against rough terrain.

"Maybe we shouldn't take so much," Chef offered. "Maybe we don't have far to go."

Nick didn't know how far they had to go, but he was not willing to lighten the load, not after hearing Fritz's urgent suggestions, and certainly not after having spent so much time without these simple good things.

"We'll take turns," he decided. "Couple guys pull from the front, couple at the sides can lift whenever it gets hung up."

Getting through the gates proved to be a slow process as every man passing out of the compound was given a loaf of bread and block of margarine. Receiving his share, Nick paused, then turned to look back. Scanning the compound one last time, he filled his lungs with the cold air. An early-stage blizzard already blurred much of the stalag's layout, but Nick didn't need to see it clearly, knowing that he would remember this place for the rest of his life.

A short distance outside the compound, Nick glanced at the snowy field where the murdered prisoners were buried. Passing the snow-covered mounds, he said a little prayer for the dead soldiers and for those physically unable to make this march to freedom. The prisoners moved under constant watch by armed Germans on foot or clumsily pedaling bicycles. Some guards had boarded trucks of supplies, which headed out of camp gradually, then sped up as the marching columns moved too slowly. Soon the trucks moved beyond sight.

"How far you think we gotta go?" Chef asked.

"No idea," Nick clipped his answer. Talking used up his breath, and he knew he and the men with him didn't have the strength they once had. They'd have to pace themselves, not waste any strength on idle chat.

The blizzard made the going rough. Blinded by stinging snow, the men frequently stumbled over rough ground and into one another. Bone-chilling wind intensified; exertion of the march helped them allay the cold for a time, but any little pause made them feel it more. Nick appreciated the added layer of protection the knitted sweater provided. It didn't take long for the weak men to tire, but every time a prisoner showed signs of faltering, a German descended on him, ready to kick or club him. The prisoners tried hard not to break the pace.

Nick thought about the men who were not on this march. He remembered Cy Popp—the Rev—who had been killed nearly a year ago. Once again he recalled Kid Russki, hoped the boy had somehow survived and that his liberation by the Russians would be a good thing, and not more torment. Nick wondered about some of the other men with whom he'd spent the early weeks of his capture. Were they also being relocated now, or had American troops already reached and liberated their camps?

That one, he always quoted from books, Nick tried to remember the name. *Van something. Vander—?* He couldn't remember and felt bad that he didn't.

Onward the men trudged. Most often they stayed on roads, but once in a while they took to the fields and hills, making their movement even more difficult. Nick felt the strain of pulling the supplies, and knew that his partner on the rope must also be close to exhaustion.

Thank God we know how to work together, he thought as several pairs of men took turns relieving each other of the burden: Nick and Chef, Murphy and Drummond, Matthews and Ames, Bartell and Olson. These eight men created a partnership, a "combine" as Matthews called it. Conserving breath, they spoke very little, simply moved. Before they had marched five miles, Nick began to notice a few food packages scattered along the way. Apparently, burdens had already become too much for some of the men, and they were forced to relinquish them or to fall behind and risk the severity of the Nazis. Hating to see the waste, Nick thought about picking up a few of the items, but with their crate already full, he simply had to leave the abandoned items. Soon he stopped seeing the waste, concentrating only on placing one foot in front of the other.

Before he was aware of it, Nick had begun to count his steps. He couldn't seem to help it. When he stopped counting, it was because a new thought had entered his mind, and he might walk many yards or even hundreds of yards before he became aware that he'd begun counting again—sometimes picking up where he had left off, sometimes starting anew.

A little after midday, an order came down the line to stop for a brief period of rest and food. Nick let himself drop right where he had stood. Wanting something more than the crusty bread, he pulled a packet from the crate. When more hands reached for other parcels, he swatted them away.

"Hey—let's not use everything up at once!" he snapped. "We've still gotta ration ourselves."

His seven partners mumbled a little but agreed. Nick tore into the parcel. He rummaged for the edibles, proffering a small tin of sardines and a tiny pack of crackers. After the men ate just that little bit of salty food, they realized their thirst. None of them carried anything like a canteen and no offer of water appeared to be coming from the Germans.

"Good thing it's winter," Murphy said, gesturing toward a somewhat dirtied drift of snow that had not yet been trampled into slush. The men slaked their thirst as well as they could on handfuls of gritty snow.

Rest period didn't last long. Though muscles throbbed and feet felt numb, the men were glad to move again, physical effort being their best method of battling the storm. As they struggled, they tried to focus on anything but their discomfort. Nick began to repeat song lyrics in his head, every song he could think of from his earliest-remembered childhood lilts to recent battle songs, from church hymns to the filthy ditties he'd learned at boot camp.

The man in front of him fell, and Nick nearly tripped over him. Immediately others tried to help the man to his feet, but guards pounced as if they had hovered in the air over them. They pounded on the man, swearing at him and shouting orders. When he didn't make an effort to rise, one of the guards kicked him hard in the lower back. Finally, even they gave up.

"Leave him! Just move on!" Nick translated the command to those with him, who objected.

"We can't just leave him," Chef said. "Somebody's got to help him."

"Go! Move on! He will be seen to!" One of the Germans shouted, his words hardly reassuring.

"Seen to how?" Chef whispered to Nick, who didn't want to speculate. The guards seemed too eager with their clubs and rifle butts, reminding Nick of what Fritz had warned about cornered animals. If the Nazis had to fall, it appeared that some of them would take down with them as many of their enemies as they could.

Nick felt that the prisoners had only one choice: to move on. He almost hated himself for choosing to survive and began to avert his eyes whenever another prisoner fell. He didn't see when one man, desperate and exhausted, tried to fight against the guards, but he heard a muffled whack and the stillness after it. Soon it seemed that those who fell behind were simply swallowed up by the churning snow. As Nick forced one foot in front of the other, pushed every ounce of his strength into one more step forward, he occasionally heard the rumble or squeal of a truck.

Surely someone will help them, he told himself. *They'll haul 'em back to camp or to a hospital somewhere. Maybe they're the lucky ones, getting a free ride outa here. Maybe I should just stop and wait for my ride too. I could just drop. I could sleep.*

He did not stop. He didn't dare risk the chance that he might be wrong.

By nightfall, Nick was actually grateful for the abysmal weather that helped to numb his pain. The men had marched the last few hours in the dimness of a snowy night. Nick had no idea how long or how far they had marched.

Orders came through the storm that the men should find space to rest for the night in a large barn, and that they should refrain from lighting any campfires or torches. Seeing only the vague shape of a structure through the snow, Nick thought it far too small to house the number of men who needed shelter. Again he lowered his head, watching his footsteps until he thought he should have reached the barn. Still the men marched on. It seemed to take forever to close the distance, until Nick realized that it was a much greater distance than he'd first thought. The barn was not a tiny structure on the landscape, as Nick had assumed, but loomed enormous as the men drew closer.

When he finally walked through the wide doorway, Nick felt dizzy with the shock to his senses. His body had been buffeted by wind for so many hours, that he almost lost his balance with the sudden cessation of it. Moving from dim white night into complete blackness made his steps tentative. More than once he bumped into another soldier or someone else's sled. As prisoners crowded inside to claim their own few square feet, voices called in the darkness.

"Ouch! You're stepping on my hand!"

"Spot taken. Move on."

"Move your damn boxes!"

"Over here. That's it. A few more feet left—we got some room over here."

Before long, prisoners and guards alike dared to defy the orders against light. Little flares began here and there offering guidance in the dark and ultimately little enclaves of warmth for the men who huddled around them. The barn smelled of animal waste, moldy straw, and smoke. Nick and his company stumbled along, finally picking up their sled to make the going easier for men who came in after them. They squeezed into the corner of a stall, lodged the sled tight into the corner, then dropped to the floor next to it.

"I don't think I will ever get up again," Chef mumbled.

"I can't feel my feet!" Matthews spouted.

Nick couldn't find the energy to speak. Dropping to the floor, he leaned against the box-sled, drew his knees up, and rested his head against them. Now that he stopped moving, he felt the strain of the march: his leg muscles ached, his feet stung with cold, his shoulders and back felt as if they were on fire. He wanted to stretch out, to lie down and wrap himself in bales of straw and sleep and sleep and sleep. As more men stumbled into the darkness, however, Nick felt even his little bit of space shrinking. He would not be able to stretch out those painful muscles. Hearing the sound of moaning, he didn't even realize until someone elbowed him in the ribs that the moans were his own.

Nick lifted his head. His eyes finally adjusting to the dark, he watched Bernie Olsen strike a match and light one of the prisoner-crafted, sardine-can candles someone had had the foresight to bring along. In the little flicker of light, the men chewed their bread, too tired even to rummage in the parcels for something more edible. Nick swallowed only a few bites before drowsiness finally overcame him. He fell asleep with a bittersweet image in his mind, the luxury of cold and drafty barracks; a rough, wood bunk; and a thin, lumpy mattress.

XVIII

Foot Soldiers

Located near a town called Hinton, the barn provided shelter during the following day of rest. In spite of the discomfort of the quarters, the prisoners welcomed that break, especially after learning that they had marched approximately twenty-five kilometers through blizzard conditions. For twenty-nine hours, they rested as comfortably as they could in the crowded barn or just outside it when smoke from forbidden fires made the air too close. Sheltered from bitter wind, they savored some of their Red Cross stores.

Shouts roused the men at one in the morning on the last day of January. The early hour darkness made preparations difficult as the men had to feel around the stall for items of clothing they had put aside to dry and now scrambled to find. While Nick's group gathered and reloaded their belongings, they heard voices from the other side of the stall.

"I can't. I just can't do it. You're going to have to leave me behind."

"No, we won't do that. They're shooting anyone who falls behind!"

"You don't know that."

"You want to take the chance to find out?

A guttural moan followed. "I'm gut sick. I'm telling you, I just can't do it."

Nick's whole body felt stiff, though without the severe throbbing he'd known the day before. Beside him, Chef stirred, slow to get his things together.

"Did you hear that?" Chef asked Nick. "That guy's staying behind. Maybe somebody should stay with—"

"Get up. We gotta move. Don't even think about staying behind."

"But—"

"I said *move!*"

Stepping outside the barn, the men saw stars overhead. Only the gentlest night breeze blew, and best of all, the temperature seemed milder. Nick hoped that they had already experienced their worst day of marching.

The men labored through the first mile or two, stumbling over rough ground. Finally reaching a road, their steps became a little easier and they picked up their pace.

"Either today is less strenuous," Ames remarked then, "or I'm just getting used to this."

"Probably a little of both," Nick answered, noticing that talking didn't take quite as much breath as it had two days earlier. Throughout the day they continued, this time not even stopping for food or rest. Usually they traveled on roads or at least next to roads. Sometimes they cut across fields. Nick wondered if these detours were a measure of safety or shortcuts to their next resting place. If the latter, they may have saved miles, but uneven terrain slowed their progress. Their steps became much more cautious on frozen, furrowed fields or grass-stubbled ground. Here, snow hid occasional dips and rises in the landscape, and many times the men stumbled or snagged their sleds. The prisoners at the front of the group set the pace for all, and it slowed considerably over such uneven terrain.

Just before dark, the troops reached a paved road flanked by watery ditches where a thin layer of ice proved easy to break. Here the Germans allowed only a brief pause so that the prisoners could drink from the ditches. Nick cupped his hands and drew some of that icy water close. He wrinkled his nose at the odor and, rather than drink, let the water trickle through his fingers. Others did the same. Nick heard someone swear and accuse the Nazis of forcing their captives to "drink from their own latrine." Throats dry, most of the prisoners chose to forego the brief rest stop, though a few did drink the rank water.

Marching on a paved road once more, the men traveled faster. Sore and aching, all of them wanted to reach their destination as soon as possible. Where that was or when they would reach it, they still didn't know, but they believed every step led them just a little closer.

"Eichenberg," Chef said at last, pointing to a road sign.

When they drew closer to the village, Nick saw smoke rising from chimneys of several houses. It looked so familiar, even cozy, and made him feel homesick for the prairie town in North Dakota where his folks lived, where he knew they waited and worried. Passing through the village altered his feeling, however, as several civilians awaited them, calling vile words and throwing stones.

On the other side of Eichenberg, the group stopped in a large farmyard. Waiting for orders, the prisoners watched German soldiers speak to a woman who appeared to be in charge of the farm. Nick couldn't hear their conversation, but by the several shakes of her head and finally a shrug and fearful look at the ragtag crowd of prisoners, he assumed that she had little choice in providing a portion of her property for their bivouac.

The men claimed their spaces, preparing as well as they could for an unsheltered night. Instructions and reports spread from one cluster to another.

"No fires allowed in the farmyard. It'll be a chilly night, men."

"They say only three or four more days of this."

At that, the cold and discomfort of sleeping on the ground didn't seem so bad. Combines of men huddled together, leaning against each other's backs. This time

Nick didn't yearn for a bunk or barracks. Lying under a canopy of stars, the same stars that twinkled at people he cared about in another part of the world, Nick drifted off to sleep, comforted by the thought: *four days to freedom.*

At 8:00 a.m. on February 1, the men were eager to begin the day's march. This time, none elected to stay behind. Before pulling out, the Germans commandeered a farm wagon from the owner, though she could provide no horses to pull it. After learning that the wagon would be used to haul the sick or injured, teams of prisoners volunteered to yoke themselves and pull the wagon.

Once again a mild day unfolded with a thawing wind. At first they welcomed the warmth, but before two hours had passed, the wind began to melt the snow. By noon they marched through increasing slush, wet up to their knees. It became more difficult to pull the makeshift sleds.

Early in the afternoon the troops stopped only a few minutes while Germans argued about routes, just long enough for a few bites of bread. Immediately, the slightest breeze seemed like a frigid blast as it blew against their wet clothes. The men didn't protest when orders to resume marching came down the lines and welcomed the little warmth generated by exertion, gladly taking every step closer to liberation. In truth, it felt better to keep moving than to sit or lie still and feel the damp cold in their legs and feet.

At one point late in the afternoon they overtook a group of British prisoners who veered in another direction, pressed by their German guards. Several men called greetings.

"Limeys," Matthews remarked. "Wonder where they're going?"

"Shouldn't we all be heading in the same direction?" Chef posed.

"Who knows? Maybe it all depends on who's fighting where." Murphy voiced what the others were guessing. "Or maybe it has something to do with some international protocol."

Matthews pondered, then said, "One thing we probably shouldn't forget is that the krauts haven't actually surrendered yet. We're still at war, and maybe we're all hostages, some kind of bargaining tool—all of us: Yanks, Limeys, Frogs, all of them others. We'll get to where the best deal can take place. That's what I think."

He might be right, Nick thought. It made some sense. So far the men had heard no report indicating exactly where they were headed. The only place-names mentioned were those they reached as they trekked across, or around, Germany. Every once in a while during the day, Nick wondered if they went in circles. That day, after marching a total of fifteen kilometers, they camped outside a place called Altkoprieben. Finally the Germans encouraged the men to build small bonfires so that they might warm themselves and especially dry off, precaution against trench foot and pneumonia.

"Nice of them to think of that now," Matthews grumbled. "Must be their own feet are finally starting to feel the wet."

Rummaging through the captive parcels, Nick and his partners pulled out extra pairs of clean, dry socks. When Nick removed his soiled and wet socks, he wrinkled his face at the sight of his feet. They seemed so white and puffy. On the soles, layers of dead skin outlined his heels. He pinched the dead skin, feeling nothing. He then scratched at it and a gummy residue collected under his fingernails. He rubbed his feet with a towel until he felt every little bit of moisture had been absorbed, then pulled on the dry socks. Stretching out by the fire, he began to feel warmer, though not quite comfortable.

The Germans distributed small, wrinkled potatoes to the men that night. Chef concocted a kind of stew with the potatoes and slivers of Spam. Nick also ate the last bit of his bread, now so dry and stale, even the margarine couldn't make it palatable. It crunched when he chewed it.

"I hope we're not getting too low on goods," Murphy said after swallowing his last crust of bread.

"Still a bit of stuff in the boxes," Chef assured, looking through one of them. "Except some of it we can probably do without. Anybody need the pipe or tobacco? Cards? What about this—here's some letter paper and a couple of pencils."

"We should get rid of that stuff we don't need," Olsen counseled. "Why carry that extra weight? It's getting harder and harder to pull this thing."

Agreeing to reduce their load to absolute essentials only, they spent the next couple hours going through every package in their crate and suitcases. Only food, clothing, and a few items for personal hygiene were deemed necessary. Nick eyed the pile of refuse. The tedium of internment behind them, he now saw little use for the playing cards or dominoes, the extra hairbrushes and combs, the harmonicas and house slippers. Some of the men felt they needed to keep the cigarettes, if not for smoking, then for possible barter with the Germans, though Nick didn't know what they might barter for on this march. Even Fritz wouldn't dare being caught trading so openly, and even if he would, Nick was quite certain the German currently had little to offer.

On a whim, Nick reached toward the refuse and grabbed a few sheets of the letter paper and a couple of the pencils. Bartell raised his eyebrows.

"What, you gonna write home *now*?" he asked.

Nick shrugged, tucking the items into one of his coat pockets that didn't have a hole in it. "Might want to jot a couple things down," he said. "You know—to tell the folks about when I get home."

"Jot this down," Drummond instructed, "February first 1945: only three days till liberation."

Any sense of relief and optimism drained from the men during the next day's grueling trudge. As usual, they began at 8:00 a.m. Within only a couple hours, all the snow was gone and the sleds that had at first seemed so functional became useless. The men could no longer pull them.

Unwilling to leave any crucial food parcels or items of clothing behind, they now attempted to carry their stores in their arms or lashed together and slung across their backs. In his left hand Nick carried one suitcase—the one that still had a handle; the other suitcase without a handle he tucked against his body under his left arm. His right arm clutched a sizable Red Cross box. Setting out, he thought his burden wasn't much different from what he'd done in active duty: lugging the ammo for his machine gun squad.

The group marched at a much slower pace that day, and when they stopped for an unusual midday respite, they could barely find the energy to scrounge for a bite or a drink of water. Nick's back and shoulders throbbed, and his left hand had become so numb grasping the suitcase that it took a long time before he could let loose of the handle.

"It's only a couple days more," Chef panted. "Maybe we don't need to load ourselves down like this."

"True," Drummond said, but no one offered to leave his burdens behind, and when the marching orders came again, the men reloaded themselves without question or comment. For too long they had done without sufficient food; no one wanted to take the chance that they might have to do without again.

Nick struggled during the afternoon, having to take frequent pauses to catch his breath or to readjust his load. He began to fall behind. Again he noticed boxes, parcels, and personal items lying by the way, discarded by men who could no longer carry them.

You can do it. Just one more step, he encouraged himself. *One more. Now another.* Again he fell into the habit of counting. At one point he reached a number in the seven thousands before a misstep interrupted him. He lost his balance and fell even further behind in the time it took to right himself and to rearrange the box and suitcases.

He began again: *One. Two. Three . . .*

Nick held on for almost the entire day, but finally the burdens simply became too much. He didn't dare ask any of the others to help, for they all fought to hang on to what they had. He stopped. Regret knotting his stomach, he put the bundles down. Should he leave them all behind? Try to stumble along with just one—maybe two? His arms tingled in their numbness, and the fingers of his right hand now had no feeling. He flexed them, and it was as if they belonged to someone else. He brought his hand to his face, tried to scratch at his stubbly beard. He felt the sensation on his chin, heard the rough *scritch-scritch*, but his fingers felt nothing at all. He might not be able to carry anything much longer.

"Move on," a German voice ordered. Nick recognized the tone immediately. Fritz.

"You there," Fritz called from a few feet behind Nick, who turned to face him. For a few seconds they said nothing further, Nick breathing too hard to talk. Fritz hung on to the handlebars of a bicycle, walking next to the bike on land too rough for riding. He eyed the suitcases and the box, then turned his head away, considering. Finally he faced Nick again.

"Fasten what you can to the bicycle," he said. Working together, Nick and Fritz tied the packs onto the bicycle. Once they were secure, Nick offered to help push the bicycle now too awkwardly laden to ride. Fritz grunted, shaking his head.

"It would be best for both of us," Fritz spoke quietly, "if we did not seem to work together." Fritz moved away from the prisoners. Eventually he requested one of the other Germans to help push the bicycle. Unburdened now, Nick soon caught up with the others in his group. Foul-mouth Matthews saw that Nick no longer carried packages. He started to say something, but then caught sight of Fritz and the other German pushing the loaded bicycle. He arched his brows in unspoken question.

"Well, well," he said. Then, stuck for other words, he added, "Well, well, well."

Nick didn't know whether he should gloat or feel shame.

The daily distance of fifteen kilometers brought them to a town called Klaushagen. Nick estimated it to be about the size of his hometown and again a kernel of nostalgia for that quiet, friendly place lay in his gut. That night he took out a pencil and one of the sheets of paper and wrote a simple record of the last six days. He continued to jot notes down on succeeding days, a terse record of miles hiked, places reached, and any circumstances he felt he should remember.

> *3 February 1945—Out of bread for a day already. Received another loaf and some cheese before starting out at eight o'clock as usual. Passed a group of Russian prisoners going east. Looked like they were starving. Much worse for wear than we are. Gave them most of our cheese. Moldy anyway. Fifteen kilometers—Gerdorf.*

> *4 February—Need food. More men failing. Beyond that, no experiences today. Heard rumors that Russians have passed Sagan and that Hitler has ordered all prisoners of war to be moved to Bavaria, used as hostages. I think we're headed in a different direction. Some say he's ordered all shot. Hard to know what to believe. Walked fourteen kilometers to Klutzhow. Klutzhof?*

> *7 February—Two days ago, made it to Shivelbein—fifteen kilometers. Promised two days rest. Needed it. Staying on hog farm that has big boilers for steaming potatoes for hogs. Helped ourselves to some pig food, ate boiled potatoes. Yesterday and today the Germans also provided soup. This is to give us pep for the next leg.*

> *8 February—Started at 8:00. Must want to make up for lost time. Marched twenty-two kilometers today. Bypassed a good-sized city. Resting at a German Cavalry camp in Labes. More food and better this time! Think we might be getting close to front. Saw two big railroad guns and other heavy mechanized weapons. Passed a couple of factories—war plants. Going strong.*

By Friday, the ninth of February, the men stopped talking about the days till freedom. They had already passed their much-anticipated fourth day and seemed to be no closer. As Friday's march began, many of them grumbled, noting that they now backtracked toward the city they had passed just yesterday.

"I think we're being led around the bush," Bartell complained.

"Maybe it's time to risk a little side trip," Olsen added. "Anybody for just disappearing into the next woods?"

No one took him up on the offer, but no one vocalized a protest either.

Nick observed that more and more civilians were also on the move. Some went one way and some another, pushing or pulling carts of personal goods. It seemed that they didn't know where to go. He felt a little sorry for them, but at least they were in their home country, and their movement from one place to another was a personal choice. They traveled without threats of being shot by the Germans or abandoned to the ruthlessness of the Russians. Most of the civilians avoided looking at the prisoners as they passed. Their faces—as much as Nick could see—reflected combinations of misery and fear, and sometimes, he thought, of pride and hate.

The days ran together, each repeating the difficulty of the day before. The troops marched no fewer than ten kilometers per day, usually averaging fifteen. Soon Nick's attempt at keeping a record turned into a simple list of towns: *Farbenzin . . . Friedricksberg . . . Batzfall . . .* and finally, *Wiedsock.* Here he wrote: *Two days of rest. Thank God! Seems like we're lost in hell. Will this never end?*

XIX

Luck of the Spoon

The two-day rest period at Wiedsock proved necessary, more for preparation than for recovery. Germans informed the prisoners that when they set out again on Friday, the sixteenth of February, their next destination would be a grueling thirty-four kilometers away and they would have only one night of rest after that. Nick began to worry about the state of his boots. Thin spots on the soles soon would wear away, leaving holes. The tops showed cracks and tears at the seams, having been through successive days of wet, muddy trails followed by nights of drying near open fire.

Nick also had doubts about the condition of his feet. His soles had thickened with the spread of white dead skin. They weren't callus-toughened as they used to get after he ran barefoot on the prairie when he was a kid. He sniffed. The odor seemed no more offensive than the usual tired, enclosed-foot smell. Remembering some of his training lectures and the grotesque photographs he'd seen of the Great War's trench foot sufferers, he felt reassured seeing no unusual redness or telltale bluish cast, prominent signs of trench foot. Luckily, he had so far managed to avoid frostbite. Still, the deadening flesh worried him.

Always a difficulty during internment, cleanliness became an even greater challenge on the march. Each night the men washed themselves as best they could, not a simple activity. As usual they found their water sources in snow or water-filled roadside ditches, sometimes in frozen creeks where they had to chop at the ice with blunt objects. Melting the ice or snow in whatever containers they could come up with resulted in rather small amounts of water, which the men were more likely to want for drinking than for scrubbing. When they found sources of open water, they simply used that without first heating it. Washing up and shaving almost always proved to be a stinging experience, one that they endured for as short a time as possible. During two-day rest stops, the men also tried to scrub the grime off their clothes, an effort that gave Nick new respect for the work his mother and grandmother always did. The prisoners' attempts at laundering did not defeat the tenacious lice and fleas, however.

Mild weather greeted the prisoners the morning of their prolonged march. The burdens of their packs now considerably lightened, the first few miles seemed almost easy. Nick once again carried his own load, down to just one suitcase. The food stores would not last much longer.

Just a couple hours into the march, the temperature plummeted and the wind rose, but fortunately it blew at their backs and they didn't have to lean into it. As usual, the guards allowed no rest stops. Prisoners who needed to pause for breath dared take only a minute or two before they risked a clubbing. When they had to relieve themselves, they did so at the side of the road or in midfield.

Just before midday, one of the prisoners who had been coughing for several days fell. On hands and knees, he gasped and hacked, his back arching with every cough until, exhausted, he just lay his face against the ground. Those around him pulled him to his feet and supported him. Unable to take even a single step, his feet dragged.

"Leave him for the cart," one of the prisoners ordered. "We can't carry him."

"We leave no more behind!" another commanded.

"Come on, buddy. He'll be okay. They'll get him to a hospital if that's what he needs."

Nick kept moving. He didn't wait to see the man loaded onto the farm wagon; prisoners who pulled the wagon assured others that the sick men were in fact delivered to hospitals or internment facilities in the towns they passed. Between such locations, the sick men had to remain on the back of the open wagon, cold and groaning at every bone-jarring jolt. The moans seemed more constant that day, and able prisoners grew uneasy, even impatient at the sound. Trying to be sympathetic, they were thankful when the yoked prisoners veered away from the group to haul their human cargo into a town named Hagen. Because of the number of sick, it took eight prisoners to pull the full cart; three guards accompanied them. They would rejoin the troops later, catching up when the group finally stopped for the night. Meanwhile, the other prisoners kept marching, determined not to fall. Even Chef no longer voiced any temptation to remain behind. In spite of assurances, most doubted that the sick and injured would receive appropriate care. The Germans too readily kicked, clubbed, punched, or slapped a prisoner who faltered, until he became incapable of righting himself and ended up on the back of the cart in worse shape than when he'd first fallen. With that kind of preliminary care, what might possibly await the sick and injured at the Germans' so-called hospitals?

On the road past Hagen, Nick once more drifted into a kind of numbing reverie. Placing one foot in front of the other over and over, he calculated the number of days he'd spent in captivity.

November tenth to November tenth, he began. *That's a whole year, three hundred and sixty five days. Plus twenty days. Add December and most of January. That's—um—four hundred and forty four days.* He visualized the numerals: 4-4-4. *Four days to freedom. Huh! Probably more like forty days!* His thoughts continued to drift. *Forty days and forty nights. Forty years lost in the desert. Forty years across Germany? Thirty-four kilometers. Four steps . . . four more . . . four hundred and forty four.*

Nick's thoughts repeated themselves, echoing the steady rhythm of the soldiers' pace. Then, when the tempo of their movement abruptly altered, he became more alert.

Nothing grabs attention like a broken pattern, he realized as guards shouted orders to abandon the road immediately. They began to cross a vast, bare field, treading quickly but carefully over the frozen clumps and ruts. Nick didn't have time to ask questions about the urgency. Before long, no one had to wonder about the altered course. With the wind blowing out of the east, the men saw the planes before they heard them, tiny, dark blemishes above the western horizon.

"The Germans got us running. That means those ain't their planes," Matthews cheered. "All right. Hot *damn!* Here they come at last. Our boys are comin' to take us home!" Several others added cheers of their own, but these died down when they noticed that the planes continued away from them in a southerly direction. Some of the POWs stopped to watch, then uselessly waved their arms and shouted. At that, guards fired warning shots into the air. Again the prisoners hurried toward a tree line in the distance, keeping an eye on the planes.

"They're turning," Chef panted. "They're gonna fly right over us I bet."

Nick saw three of the planes break from the formation and begin a straight approach right toward the field. Again prisoners broke into cheers.

"What are they? Spitfires?" Drummond wondered, then added, "God bless the RAF!"

"Those aren't Spitfires," Bartell corrected. "They're American fighters." He squinted, trying to identify the shapes. "Mustangs, maybe?"

As the planes came closer, the men noticed distinctive details. All three aircraft had yellow tails and red nose cones where the props spun almost invisibly. Seeing the cockpit bubble about midpoint on the fuselage, Bartell wondered, "How can those guys see what's in front of 'em anyway? They'll never notice us!"

Compelled to hurry toward the shelter of the trees, yet not wanting to go unnoticed by the flyers, prisoners loped clumsily, trying to watch the approaching aircraft. As the distance shrank, however, a horrible reality dawned.

"Son of a bitch, this ain't a friendly flyover!" Matthews shouted. "They're diving!"

"They think we're German reinforcements!" another voice exclaimed.

As the sound of the planes crescendoed from a drone to a roar, Germans shouted for the men to keep running, while prisoners yelled out their identity.

"Allies! Americans! We're prisoners, not Germans!" Although they knew their calls were useless, they couldn't keep from trying. They ran faster, many stumbling. Nick ran hard, lifting his knees, pushing himself more than he thought he could. His lungs felt raw as he rasped for breath, leaving a bitter taste of metal somewhere at the back of his throat. Part of him wanted to halt, to turn and face the oncoming aircraft, lifting his arms in a sign of surrender. His instinct for survival, however, compelled him to run away from what should have been the source of his deliverance toward the shelter of a tree line he knew they'd never reach in time.

"We'll never make it," Ames gasped. Nick looked over his shoulder. In that moment he saw a flash from the wings of the lead plane. A second later, sound followed the light.

"They're firing! Hit the dirt. Down, down!"

Nothing protected them. Nick realized that unless they could somehow signal the pilots, the whole lot of them would be mowed down like hay, if not this time, then when—not if—the pilots came in for a second strafing. Some men threw themselves onto the ground, tightening their bodies into the smallest targets possible; others ran left or right, trying to evade the path of the shooting. Nick veered sharply, then dropped to the ground, his heart thudding. He felt more than heard a roaring sensation in his ears, and the metallic tang in his throat now tasted more like blood. Any second he expected to feel metal rip through his body. He closed his eyes, wordlessly praying, then felt his shoulder muscles tauten, is if they would snap.

When the sound changed Nick dared to look up. He saw the planes rise steeply. The men scrambled to their feet, looking around to see who had been hit. Shouts for help indicated that several had been wounded; some bodies remained, unmoving. Nick watched in relief as one by one, the men of his combine rose to their feet. Only Chef remained on the ground, curled in a fetal position, with his arms crossed over the back of his head.

"Chef!" Nick called, nudging him. "Kid? You all right?" Grasping Chef's shoulder, he turned the kid over. Chef looked up at him, his face and limbs trembling.

"I'm not dead?"

"No," Nick affirmed. "You're not dead yet. C'mon. Get up. We have got to move. They're sure as heck gonna come back!"

Even as he said it, he knew he didn't have the strength to run anymore. His throat and lungs hurt as if they'd been scraped raw, and he had a hard time drawing a deep enough breath. His legs barely felt strong enough to bear him up. By the gasps and groans around him, he knew that none of the men were up to another all-out dash. Besides, they couldn't just leave the injured behind.

The men knew they'd have to try somehow to show that they were not German soldiers. Some scrambled through their meager belongings, hoping to find anything with the Red Cross symbol. Though many still carried their RC suitcases, the crosses on these were faded and much too small to identify from any distance, much less by a pilot traveling at great speed. From what Nick had observed about the airplanes themselves, the pilots didn't have a very clear view of what was in front of them anyway. They needed something huge, something viewable from a distance and at high speed that would unmistakably identify them as Allied prisoners.

"Over here! You there—you men, this way! No, *this* way. Just stand *here*!" These orders came from a small group of prisoners who had begun to direct other men to stand in particular formations. When guards threatened them, an argument arose, half in English, half in German.

"Bremer!" One of the arguing prisoners called to him. "Tell these assholes that we have got to get the men in formation!"

"Formation! *Now?*"

Nick listened to the ideas, translating to the Germans as he heard them. In moments, the guards nodded understanding and helped direct the men into place, mingling in with the troops themselves for their own safety. Nick found the men of his combine, taking his place with them, nudging one or another into position.

"This might not work, but it's about the only thing we can do in the little time we have," he said. "We're going to spell it out for our friendly flyers up there."

"How we gonna do that?" Chef balked.

"We place ourselves where those guys tell us to be. Like right here!" Still gasping for breath, he forced Chef into position. "This might be crazy, but hundreds of guys forming the letters P-O-W should be visible from the air. I hope."

In the curve of the *P* formation, Nick was amazed at how quickly the exhausted men took up the positions indicated; he even began to feel optimistic until he heard a curse from one of the organizers.

"Shit, our clothes are the color of dirt! They aren't going to distinguish no message. We're sitting ducks!"

"Take off your shirts," another command came. "Bend over. Show them your backs!"

Too late to question these orders, the men tore off coats, sweaters, and shirts, baring their backs and shivering as the frigid air raked their skin. Most of them pale-skinned, they hoped that they created a stark contrast to the brownish-gray dirt of the field. The next seconds felt endless. Bent at the waist, clutching his knees, Nick felt too vulnerable. Tension thickened, and his ears again hummed with the deafening silence of dread. When Foul-Mouth Matthews spoke, it was as if a knife pierced the strain.

"I sure as hell hope there ain't any Eye-talian boys flying. They might not take it too kindly if they buzz us from the wrong direction."

"What?"

"What if they see a great big WOP spelled at 'em down here?"

Several men groaned. Bartell thumped Matthews hard across his back, causing Matthews to wince at the sting and release a whole barrage of curses. Chef chuckled, at first in quiet little hiccups. Soon his shoulders quivered, and the giggles turned into guffaws that grew into such intensity, he gasped for breath. Losing his balance, he fell to the ground, rolling over onto his back. Nick watched, stunned, as Chef's face purpled and tears rolled down his temples and into his ears. Still Chef hooted uncontrollably. He clutched at his gut.

"Jesus, kid, it ain't that funny," Matthews uttered, then "Oh fuck, they're coming."

Buzzing turned into droning, then roaring once more as the planes flew nearer and began their sharp descent.

"Oh, geez!" Chef's watery eyes grew so wide that white showed all around them. His laughter ending as suddenly as it had begun, he cringed, his torso tightening so much that for a moment Nick thought the kid would shrink himself right into the frozen ground.

"Don't watch," he warned. "Close your eyes. Breathe!"

Bent low, he wondered if he could take his own suggestions. Nick's skin tingled; he felt spasms in his leg muscles as his body tensed against this new level of helpless terror. The growling death machines dove in, piloted not by enemies, but allies. *Shot by our own side,* he couldn't help thinking. *It doesn't matter. From friends or enemies, the shots still kill. Oh God, let this work!*

It took every ounce of will to resist the urge to run or dive out of the deadly path. Again came the awful anticipation of bullets riddling through flesh and bone, again the taste of blood. If he'd had any satisfying amount of food in his system, Nick knew, he'd be losing it all right now, puking or pissing or shitting.

Then he yelled—a long, throat-rasping bellow—echoing the deafening roar of the engines. He couldn't hear himself, could hear only the din of what he knew might be the last few seconds of his life. He hollered until he ran out of breath and his forehead pulsed with the strain. Taking another quick breath, he yelled again, determined to drown out the machine gun fire that would mow them down any minute, any second, *now*!

No blood; no pain.

The roaring peaked; the fighter planes passed over without firing. Nick dared to straighten up. He saw the lead plane tip its wings as the pilot acknowledged recognition of their message. All the men straightened, amazed at their success. A cheer rose, picked up by all, even the Germans. Forgetting the cold, they slapped each other's backs; some embraced while others hopped or danced in jubilation. They couldn't help grinning.

"Hot damn we're good!" Matthews crowed.

Finally the guards remembered themselves and their duty; shouting for order, one of them fired his pistol into the air to get attention. Subdued only a little, the prisoners donned their shirts and coats, still exclaiming over the miraculous success of a seemingly hopeless plan and their astonishing quickness in carrying it out. It had to be a miracle, they deemed, in such a short amount of time to have achieved something so improbable, so impossible.

As the Germans shouted orders for marching formation, Chef clapped his hands against his shirt pocket. Smile fading, he sidestepped first one way, then another, frantically eying the ground under his feet.

"My spoon!" he cried. "I lost my lucky spoon!"

Again the Germans shouted, prodding at the men with their rifle barrels. German words drowned out the hum of excited conversation, and soon it seemed as if the moment of relief and joy had never happened. As if oblivious to the commands, however, Chef continued his reckless pacing of the ground, ranting.

"I gotta find it! I can't leave without my spoon!"

"Leave it, kid," Nick cautioned. "You don't need it. It's just a spoon. Come on. You're calling too much attention—"

Nick stepped outside of the formation, roughly grabbing Chef by his upper arm.

"No!" Chef continued to resist. "Leave me be. I gotta find—"

"Damn it shut up! You're just making it worse—"

Click.

This time Chef stopped. Still gripping the kid's arm, Nick slowly turned. He looked first into the barrel of a pistol, then into the coldly amused eyes of the German who pointed the weapon, cocked and ready to fire. Nauman. The guard's lips slowly widened into a sinister smile. Not for the first time, Nick felt as if he were looking into the face of a snake. He had somehow managed to avoid confrontation with this German since the dog attack months ago. Nauman looked too pleased about their meeting now.

"I would very much like to shoot you," the German stated flatly, his grin now showing crooked, stained teeth.

Nick could sense a restless tension from the other prisoners. He knew that some of them considered rushing the guard but hoped they wouldn't try anything heroic, not as long as he remained the direct target of Nauman's loathing. The German didn't need much incitement to carry out his desire. Nick was almost relieved to hear the quick snap of rifles from other guards, keeping any insurrection at bay.

"*Zurück!* Back away!" they ordered as Fritz moved in, speaking directly to Nauman.

"*Halt! Sie werden nicht schiessen.*"

"*Ich habe nichts zu verlieren,*" Nauman argued.

"Unlike you, I have a great deal to lose," Fritz countered, repeating, "You will not shoot."

The smile didn't disappear from Nauman's face, nor did he lower his weapon. Nick couldn't take his eyes from the gun barrel. He knew that contrary to Fritz's suggestion, Nauman intended to shoot him.

Just then, Chef wriggled, still in Nick's grasp, and exclaimed, "My spoon!" At the very second Nauman's weapon discharged, Chef dove into the dirt by the German's feet, pulling Nick down with him. Pain seared through Nick's right shoulder as he hit the ground. He heard another gunshot, followed by German words calling for immediate order. Nauman's pistol dropped to the ground as the hated German fell to his knees, clutching his own right forearm tight against his chest. Fritz towered over all three men. He bent to pick up Nauman's weapon.

"Get up," he ordered the two Americans. Chef rose, gripping the spoon he'd just rescued from under Nauman's boot. Nick stood up slowly, his shoulder still burning, his arm numb. Assuming that he'd hit a nerve against a rocky clump of frozen ground, he winced as he flexed the arm.

"It is most unfortunate that your weapon misfired," Fritz directed at Nauman. Hearing this, Nick understood that the German version of the event would hereafter be "accident." He knew well that Nauman had meant to kill him, knew as well that Nauman's subsequent wound had not been the result of misfire from his own weapon, but of quite deliberate fire from Fritz's. Nick massaged his throbbing shoulder, an effort that only sharpened the pain. Withdrawing his hand, he noted with some surprise the blood on his fingers. At the same time, Chef pronounced, "Nick, you're bleeding!"

The bullet had torn through the outer, fleshy part of Nick's upper arm, ripping skin and muscle, but not coursing deep enough to meet bone.

"I think it just grazed me," Nick grimaced. "I'll be okay."

Fritz called for a German medic to see to Nauman and ordered one of the prisoners to assist Nick.

"We will not turn back," he informed the men. "We will support the injured as best we can, continue on to the next village where they will remain for medical attention."

"No!" Nick blurted, causing Fritz to glare at him. "I mean, not me." Nick didn't want to end up in some German hospital, and especially not with Nauman. "I can make it. It's a flesh wound, that's all."

At this, Drummond stepped close. Placing his hand on Nick's uninjured shoulder, he said, "You know, your stoicism is admirable, but you don't have to be a rock. You need to get that arm looked at."

Stoicism? Nick wasn't even sure what that meant, and he certainly didn't feel at all like a rock. In fact, he felt an absolute coward, afraid of what might befall him if he turned back or lagged behind. All he wanted was to continue on with the men he knew and trusted, to reach their liberation without additional delay.

"No," he insisted. "I just need to stop the bleeding and patch it up. It'll be okay."

Fritz nodded, then turned away. He rejoined the other guards in their effort to reorganize, arranging for the injured and the dead to be assisted or carried.

The medic, Captain Whitlow, had his hands full with those more seriously injured from the strafing incident. It took some time for him to get a chance to attend Nick. When he finally did, he announced, "Well, it isn't life—or limb-threatening, but it's going to hurt when I try to close it. I don't have anything to spare—for the pain, you know."

Nick clenched his jaw as the medic cleaned his wound, then winced at the rough-and-ready suturing. He bit down hard, feeling something solid and gritty crunch between his molars. He spat.

Great, he thought as he realized a back tooth had crumbled. *This too?* No pain accompanied the broken tooth, at least not enough to compete with the fire in his arm. For that little blessing, Nick felt grateful. The medic covered the injury with a bandage, then fashioned a sling to keep the arm immobile.

"Might not hurt as much if you don't move it," he instructed. "Keep it clean. Watch for swelling, discoloration—you know, sign of infection. That's about all we can do for now."

By the time the troops headed out, most of the day was spent and they still had a long way to go. Already behind their planned schedule, they lost even more time as they moved at a slower pace, burdened with injured or dead men, and then even more slowly with uncertain steps in the growing darkness. After only a couple hours marching, the prisoners and guards with the farm wagon caught up with them. It helped a little to surrender their burdens into the back of the wagon. When Nick was offered a space, he simply shook his head.

He had found the pace and body position that gave him the least discomfort. No longer carrying a suitcase—Chef toted it for him—Nick simply concentrated on keeping up with the other men. His arm continued to throb and burn; he imagined a flame beneath his skin, a sledgehammer pounding his muscle into mush. Every time he felt the burn, he tried to visualize water dousing the flame and to hear a soothing hiss of steam. At the throbbing, he imagined a bolt of lightning shattering the sledgehammer into bits, igniting the flame once more. The pattern continued, almost in measure with his stride: burn . . . hiss . . . throb . . . crack . . . burn. The visualization gave him a second of relief for every few seconds of hurting.

Every step took them a little further away in place and time from the strafing incident. After countless of those steps, the event already began to lose its significance as it smoothed into memory. The day now too long, it felt more like weeks than hours since the men had resumed their march.

At last they reached the town of Wollin. Here the cart broke from the rest of the troops. Nick wondered who in that town would bury the dead, who would remember them. At first, he assumed that the whole group would rest somewhere in the village. He needed the painkilling effect of deep sleep, even if it were for just a few hours. His disappointment when marching orders came again felt like a rock in his gut.

Beyond Wollin, they reached a wooded area. Here at last the Germans allowed them to rest for the night. In a short time, several campfires blazed, and men huddled close around them, slurping bitter brews of coffee and munching on remnants of parcel food. Some speculated on the distance they'd marched that day; most felt it was more than the threatened thirty-four kilometers; others agreed that they'd reached just that distance.

"You know these krauts," Matthews offered, firelight reflected in his eyes as he imitated, "You *vill* marchen today *twenty-zree* miles *schnell, schnell, schnell, eins, zwei, zree,* four! *Nein* stoppen! *Nein kaputten!*"

Chef chuckled. "You look like a demon with that light in your eyes."

Matthews laid two fingers beneath his nose and cocked his head sharply first left, then right, his way of impersonating *der Führer.*

"*Jawohl,* ick bin the very devil himself!"

Chef laughed harder. Feeling a little woozy, Nick turned to gaze at the kid. Chef seemed to have taken on an entirely new personality since the strafing. He spoke eagerly rather than timidly as he had done since the beginning. He seemed more open and confident in his talk with the other men, not as frightened or as burdened with despair.

"What happened to you today, kid?" Nick finally asked.

Chef smiled. He reached into his pocket and pulled out the spoon, not even noticing the ragged feather that came out with it, that drifted gracelessly right into the fire and burned without additional flash or spark.

"Today I found out that I was right about this spoon," he announced. "It is my lucky charm, and it's going to get me home."

"Yeah," Matthews mocked, "we were *real* lucky today—some a little luckier than others—blown away by our own side. Huh."

"Me and Nick were especially lucky," Chef insisted. "If this spoon hadn't jumped out of my pocket during all that, I wouldn't have been looking for it like a crazy person. And if I hadn't seen it when I did—almost like it just popped out from under that Nazi's boot—well, one or probably both of us would be dead right now."

Chef looked so self-assured, Nick didn't bother to remind him that it was his panic about the spoon that had brought Nauman to them in the first place. Besides, Chef's impromptu dive for the spoon had in fact pulled both of them out of the way, though Nick did feel the bullet.

"Know what I'm going to do when I get back home?" Chef asked. He didn't wait for a response. "I'm going to open a fancy restaurant, and I'm going to call it the Lucky Spoon."

"Sounds more like a greasy-spoon diner," Murphy observed.

"No, no, it won't be like that. It'll have the best food you can imagine, and you know why? Because I'm going to cook it myself!" He nudged Nick's leg with his boot before continuing, "And, Nick Bremer? You get to eat free every time you come in."

"Hey! What about the rest of us?" Bernie Olsen demanded. "We want the best food we can imagine too!" This produced a wide grin on Chef's face.

"Sure, why not?" he said. "Long as you don't show up every day."

"Course not. A man can't handle so much good food."

"And long as you give a hefty tip to the chef."

Chef laughed again at the barrage of good-natured protests. Nick couldn't help smiling along with the rest of them. What a relief it was not to have to buck up the kid's attitude. When the laughter died down, the men grew quiet. Nick began to drift off; he came alert again when Ames brushed his elbow.

"You know, this place could be worse. Anybody know where we are?"

"Yeah, I heard, "Matthews responded, yawning. "Spitzer—Fritzer—some kind of itzer woods."

"Pritzerwoods," Nick clarified, having himself heard the place identified earlier. He supposed it might be fairly nice as woods go, but it still provided little comfort for tired, starving, aching men. He realized that Ames' sense of pleasure no doubt came with the relief of having survived the day. As if Nick's thoughts made Ames suddenly aware that not everyone shared the same level of relief, the man said, "Yeah. Too bad about—well—how are you doing, Bremer? You gonna make it?"

"Yeah, I guess." Nick admitted, then not wanting to be labeled as a *stoicist* again, he added a suitable complaint. "Hurts like a son of a bitch, though."

"You know what you got there, don't you?" Murphy asked. "You got yourself a citation! Fine way of getting yourself a purple heart! Now you'll have something to tell your grandchildren, won't you?"

Nick offered a half smile. He tried to imagine himself years from now, surrounded by an assortment of boys and girls admiring his medals—for some reason he imagined a lot of them.

Grandpa, tell us about the time you got shot in the war! He imagined airy little voices pleading. What would he tell them?

Well, kids, it's like this, you see. I was in the middle of a minefield . . . it was a horrible battle . . . bullets were coming from all sides . . .

Just before he drifted off to sleep, Nick imagined the eager question once more. *How did you get your purple heart, Grandpa?* He shook his head, a sardonic smile creasing his face.

"Diving for a spoon," he muttered, and fell asleep.

XX

Notes

1 *7 February—Arm hurts. A little swelling, but not too bad. Moved eighteen kilometers today, slight distance compared to yesterday, though ended up crossing pretty big body of water. Nearly froze afterward. Sure glad for the barn to sleep in. Pretty drafty though. Right now guys are drying clothes around fires. We sit bare under blankets, guys are picking lice off each other. We must look more like apes in a zoo than men. Wonder if I'll ever feel clean again.*

*   *   *

21 February—Made seventy kilometers since last time I made notes. Swelling in arm down, but wound looks angry red. Maybe that is a good sign. Still hurts like the dickens when I move my arm, but I gotta move it now and then, sometimes just to keep my balance when we march over rough ground. Much prefer the roads. We're held over in this place, I think called Klempenow, until tomorrow. It's good to have a whole day, but sure would be better if we got some food in our bellies. When I look down at my chest, I can see my ribs through the skin. It's not just me. All the others too. I'm surrounded by racks of ribs. Seems like there's no meat on our bones anymore.

*   *   *

1 March—Have been interned at Dahlen for a week already. Looks like we'll be here another week. Some of the Germans are no longer with us but seems no shortage of others to take their places. Fritz still with us. Have to admit, I'm glad. I feel I can trust him some, though he growls and threatens and says things that might mean one thing or they might mean another. Replacement guards are odd lot. Some are barely more than kids themselves, but they sure do have a hard look about them. The older ones, and some of these are quite old, I don't know about them. One day they are harsh in their treatment of prisoners, another day they look as if they would apologize if they dared to. Have heard regular guards refer to the whole mess of them as Volksturm. *It is a good word for them, for they sure are stormy kind of folks, and we can never be sure if they'll carry on with thunder and lightning or just blow hard and clear away. A good thing about this break. We have had showers and delousing (seems sometimes a useless effort, though), but as for food, only one Red Cross parcel per man has been allowed for all this time. It's not enough. I am now glad for the occasional rat or—yes—even cat that finds its way to the end of a stick at our fires. I guess Luke A. wasn't so crazy. Hunger makes a man desperate. Sometimes a guy gets so desperate for something to eat, he'll chew up bits of dried grass, but a little better than that is when we find a handful or two of grain to swipe, though that's pretty hard on the teeth these days. Today promises better yet: Chef just came in with a goose—where he found that I don't want to know, but it sure looks good to me, and he's the one to roast it. Can hardly wait till Chef's goose is cooked!*

*   *   *

2 March—How grown men can become animals when they are starving. Before the goose was done yesterday, the guys asked for it, then demanded it, and next thing that goose was pulled at and torn apart and eaten up raw—bones and everything. Broke another tooth, darn it.

*   *   *

7 March—On the road again, it was hard to make today's twenty-two kilometers after two weeks doing next to nothing. No end in sight. I remember when they said only four more days. It is since then a month. How big is this country anyway?

*   *   *

11 March—Day of rest after over 70 km since my last note. At Lanow. On our way here we passed by a farm where someone had just slopped hogs. We took food from the pigs. I can't say it was good, but it was food. My shoes are worn through, and now the socks are wearing through as well. I have blisters and bleeding where the skin isn't dead. I'll have to watch out. Medic reports several cases of gangrene among the men. Sure wouldn't want that.

*   *   *

13 March—Overheard Germans talking about the winter, saying it is endless and coldest they remember. Just our luck. They sound exactly like the folks at home complaining about the weather. Just wish we could do something about it. Today the sky closed in, flat grayish-white cover. Smells like snow coming. Made 18 km today.

*   *   *

14 March—I sure didn't expect any of my guys to go missing. Woke at the usual time this morning, and Olson and Bartell were not around. Seems they just walked away during the night. They must've gone before the snow came because there were no tracks in the fresh snow—and there was a lot of fresh snow! It made today's march pretty rugged. Fritz is fuming. He seems to think I know something, says we're so close, why would the men make a run for it now? Close? I wonder about that. They didn't send any guards after the men because they didn't know which way to send them. Hope those two do all right. Afraid they'll stand out like sore thumbs, sickly, starving, tired men.

*   *   *

16 March—Resting in Tramm. Rough encounter today with civilians. I see why we skirt past villages whenever we can. These people are like minefields; a guy just doesn't know which way to step. We were quiet coming through, and at first the people lining the road were pretty quiet too, just watching like they're at a parade. The way some of them watched, though, could give a guy gooseflesh. If looks could kill, we'd all be dead. All it took was one fellow to go off the deep end and next thing we knew the whole mob was throwing rocks and sticks, downright attacking. I done my best to stay out of the way—get past as quick as I could. It got real ugly when the guards tried to step between and a couple of them took the brunt of the blows. It didn't hurt my feelings when some of them got beat up worse than the prisoners did, but when Fritz went down, well, that's a little different. He's sure unpleasant, but I think he tries to be fair. He was struck pretty bad but refused to stay behind for medical attention. If he won't stay behind, I sure as heck feel I was right all along—it's just plain dangerous to stay behind. Someone had to help him along when we moved out of the village. Guards were too busy putting down the uprising, seeing to it that the prisoners didn't fight back. Me and Matthews ended up helping Fritz. I even had his weapon over my shoulder. Maybe I should've—I don't know—done something different. Some of the POWs didn't look too kindly on this, like I'm giving aid and comfort to the enemy. I don't see it that way. Seems a guy just needed help, and somebody had to give it. Matthews sure spouted a colorful stream of words afterward. I guess nobody will suspect him—

*   *   *

17 March—Three men on a parcel now. Can't remember what real food is like. Fritz is moving fine on his own now, has his weapon back, but my shoulder hurts bad again. Guess I should not have helped. Thought I was pretty much healing. Ugly scar, though. Matthews still bitter. Boy, I hope Bernie and that old Bartell don't encounter local folk like we did. They wouldn't stand a chance. Wonder where they are, how they are.

*   *   *

18 March—Today made 26 km. Tonight the Germans told us that tomorrow we'll be moving only ten kilometers, a light march, and that is as far as we'll go. Why we didn't just go for the whole 36 km today I don't know. I'm worn-out as usual, but this close to the end of the line, why I'd hike another six hours if I had to just to reach that place, though I bet our guys aren't there yet. We can't be so close to the front yet. Sounds of battle are still too patchy and distant. At night sometimes we see a glow in the west—but we're not even close enough to see flashes or explosions. More now we see aircraft flying over, most likely on bombing missions. Thank God, no more direct attacks on us. It must still be rough going for our guys on the battlefield. I've been called a stubborn German in my time, and I'm seeing that stubbornness in the real German people and soldiers. They'll hold out to the very end. Why don't they just put down their weapons when the results are so clear already? Why won't they give up? Over a year ago, one of their soldiers told me "for you the war is over." I guess they need someone to tell them that now.

XXI

Waiting Out the Night

The prisoners expected a kind of excited prelude to liberation when they reached Hagenau; they did not expect to find themselves in a situation almost identical to that which they'd marched away from: confined in prison buildings, restricted in their movements, rationed in their supplies, and still ordered about by Nazis. Nick's heart sank when he saw the Swastika banner flying high and the snap of stiff-armed salutes to a distant leader who still would not give up.

When they'd begun their relocation march, they had numbered roughly five hundred men. By the time they reached Hagenau, the forces were down to a little over half of that. So many had fallen ill and incapable of completing the march, or had been wounded; a few had died, and a handful had escaped—at least Nick hoped the disappearances meant successful escape. He realized that he might never know the fates of Bartell and Olsen.

Nick also wondered about the thousands of other men who had been interned at Stalag IIB or assigned to its labor detachments; he assumed that almost all had formed groups that began the westward march that long-ago day in January. Nick had been in the first contingent to leave the stalag. Would the others arrive at this place too, or had they been led in different directions? What about those physically unable to make the trek? Were they now trapped in frontline battle? What about Luke? Did he make it safely into Russian hands or was he now mingled with the German prisoners of war, not so safe somewhere in the cold regions of the Soviet empire?

Relief at being closer to the western front came with a measure of apprehension as well, particularly when the prisoners noted their proximity to an air base. Further misgiving arose when they learned that they once again would be assigned to work detachments.

"Better not be war work," Red Murphy observed. "Against conventions of war, you know."

Nick harrumphed. How often had they challenged their captors' maneuvers as contrary to the Geneva Conventions? What good did it do?

Rules of war, he thought, not for the first time, *as if it were a game.*

"Seems to me," he ventured, "that the first rule of warfare ought to be that there aren't going to be any rules."

"You know, I don't like this at all," Ames said. "We might as well have a bull's eye painted on our backs. This air base is gonna be a primary target if these guys don't hurry up and surrender."

The men realized that German surrender and Allied liberation might be close, but that they probably would not come without some final deadly confrontation. Yet again prisoners would be in the thick of that clash, trying to resist enemy forces while dodging their own allies. For now, however, all they could do was wait and hope, as Ames suggested, for a quick and quiet surrender.

After tepid showers and delousing, the men headed toward two long buildings very similar to the barracks they'd known at Stalag IIB. They settled in for the rest of the day, trying not to think about the danger in being so close to an air base. At least for the moment they had beds to sleep in, such as they were, and shelter from the elements, though they'd already struggled through the worst season. Nick sat at the edge of his bunk massaging his feet. In the last few days the blisters had broken, leaving little flaps of dried skin that he methodically peeled off. Tiny scabs covered sores that had bled, and he scratched at these, then rubbed the now-whitened scars around his ankle where Nauman's dog had bitten him. Contemplating his feet, Nick didn't notice Chef standing near the foot of his bunk until the kid spoke.

"I got a good feeling, you know?"

"Do you? Well that's good."

"No, I mean it. I just got a feeling it won't be long now."

"Chef, I sure hope you're right." Nick lay down on the thin, straw-filled mattress, clasping his hands behind his head. "We'll just see what tomorrow brings." He, too, couldn't help feeling somewhat optimistic: their long, merciless march had ended; he felt almost clean, and the hard bunk provided more comfort than he'd known in a month and a half.

The triumph at having successfully endured so much diminished later that evening when other prisoners returned from labor. Newcomers watched these exhausted men trudge to their bunks. Eying each other warily, some nodded their greetings, while others answered requests for any word about surrender with shrugs and shakes of the head.

The next morning the prisoners stood in formation for count, an all-too-familiar process. Afterward they lined up yet again at the infirmary to be checked by a German doctor who would determine their fitness for work. Waiting his turn, Nick observed his fellow prisoners, noticing that none of them looked physically capable of any kind of labor; they were far too thin, faces sunken. Still they had already pulled off what should have been impossible: a weeks-long trek of more than five hundred kilometers, facing brutal forces of nature and threat from enemies as well as from allies. Nick marveled at their endurance, but hoped they wouldn't have to test it much longer.

A guy can be only so tough, he thought, stepping a little closer to the infirmary door.

"After this war is over," Matthews commented, "I ain't never *ever* gonna stand in another line—ever! I don't care if there's a thousand bucks or a Greta Garbo waitin' for me at the end of it. I ain't standing in line."

Gradually the line grew shorter. Once determined healthy enough to work, the men were directed to one of the trucks that had already returned from hauling prisoners to their work detail and now sat idling in wait for the newcomers.

The examination proved to be superficial with the same diagnosis for nearly everyone. Men systematically breathed and coughed as a German listened to their heartbeats with a disdainful expression on his face, particularly as he brushed lice away from their chests.

Damn lice, Nick cursed the creatures he'd had to live with for too long. *Just can't seem to delouse a louse!*

"Fit for labor," the doctor droned, dismissing one prisoner and beckoning another. Waiting, Nick scanned the inside of the infirmary. Only a few beds were occupied. By the persistent, gravelly hacking that came from the men lying in these beds, Nick assumed they represented the worst cases—probably pneumonia or even consumption. Just then, one of the patients turned his face toward the men in line. Nick recognized Lucas Allen at once. Luke, in turn, saw Nick and raised his head as if to speak, but a spasm of coughing prevented it.

"Remove your shirt, please," the doctor's words broke into Nick's thoughts. Nick undressed, inhaled, and coughed as he was told.

"Fit for labor," the doctor announced. "Proceed in that direction. Next!"

Before the nearby guard could direct him back outside, Nick spoke.

"*Darf ich mit ihm sprechen?*" He pointed toward Luke, surprised at his own impulsiveness. The guard stared at him, and then looked at the doctor as if waiting for permission. The guard displayed a kind of resigned attitude. Meeting his gaze, Nick concluded that the man very likely came from the *Volksturm* forces. Craggy and worn, the old German had stooped shoulders and tired eyes.

Here's one who's just waiting for the end, Nick speculated. *Not much fight left in this cornered animal.* It was good to know.

"*Warum?*" the doctor demanded. "What have you to speak about?"

Nick replied that he just wanted to know how his friend was doing, that they had come from the same location. The doctor shook his head; when Nick pressed for just a five-minute visit, the doctor spoke impatiently.

"That one—he is not all in his mind. However, he recovers from pneumonia and soon will be strong enough for labor! Then you may talk!" The doctor sounded defensive.

"Can you just tell me how long he's been here?"

"How long? *Ich weiss nicht. Vier—fünf—?* Four or five weeks perhaps. What does it matter? Now go!"

Nick trudged outside. He couldn't help thinking that it mattered a great deal. He knew that Luke had chosen to stay behind when the rest of the able-bodied prisoners evacuated. How could he have made it to Hagenau five weeks ago?

Nick could not dismiss from his mind the images of sick, shivering, injured, or dead prisoners. He thought of his own damaged feet, his shoulder wound, and his absent friends. Memories of the rigors, exhaustion, danger, and degradation left him with a bitter taste. The entire ordeal now seemed like such a mockery—not just for the prisoners, but also for the Germans who had overseen them.

Why didn't they truck or rail all of us and be done with it? Stupid! Senseless!

With difficulty, he swallowed his anger and joined the others waiting to be assigned to one of three work details: sacking potatoes at an enormous storage mound a few kilometers away; cutting, splitting, and hauling firewood from nearby woods; or digging trenches around the grounds for air raid protection. Chef, Matthews, and Ames ended up on potato duty, while Drummond found himself in the firewood brigade. Handed shovels, Nick and Murphy joined the company of diggers.

The first day they toiled hard, pushing themselves as the Germans insisted they dig faster and deeper. By nightfall, Nick felt too exhausted to care that there would be no showers, or that evening rations did not come close to restoring the energy they had spent during the day. His shoulder throbbed again, a hot arrow of pain darting just beneath the scar. His belly also ached, not only with emptiness, but also from the disappointment in knowing that the next day, and the next—and very likely more days after that—would bring more of the same.

Within days, Luke was released from the infirmary, still coughing but no longer considered too weak to work. His voice hoarse—either from the illness or from lack of use—he told the men about the Nazis' very sudden change in plans back at the stalag, how they managed to evacuate most of the sick and wounded on trucks and then train just ahead of the Russian army. Most of the prisoners had been delivered to internment hospitals along the way. Luke, however, not considered physically unsound, made it all the way to Hagenau, where he'd been on the prison labor force until pneumonia took him down.

"What about the others? McAndrews and the other medics?" Murphy asked.

"I don't know about them," Luke rasped. "Lost track of them after only a couple days. And I didn't dare ask." He pointed to his head, adding, "Still crazy, you know. That couldn't change."

Some changes did occur in the next few weeks. For one, the Germans altered their labor assignments so at least prisoners didn't face the same duty every day—and on a few foul days they didn't have to go out on detachment at all. They also paced themselves better, creating an illusion of grueling work while slowing their progress, a deception that didn't take a great deal of skill considering their physical condition. Another difference came as faint rumbles during the day and far-off flares in the nighttime proved that the battlefront was indeed inching closer. When planes took off from the air base, prisoners counted them, disappointed if the same number returned later, pleased when fewer returned than had set out. Finally, several of the men who'd been sacking potatoes succeeded in smuggling some of the better specimens into camp, an act made easier by guards who conveniently turned their heads. They hid the potatoes in bedding, under bunks, or in their clothing, cooking up a few each night to supplement their meager rations.

"Finally a good solid potato that doesn't taste sour," Murphy declared, sprinkling a little salt onto his. He added a dollop of oleo and watched it melt. "A genuine feast!"

"Think we'll get sick of these?" Chef wondered.

"Sicker than we are of that stinking soup we've seen too much of?" Nick vowed that once he got back to his life he would never eat another turnip, not even a fresh one.

One morning just as they finished their rations of bread and coffee, a lone guard entered the barracks. Nick recognized the worn-down German he'd spoken to in the infirmary earlier. The man said nothing, just strolled, looking left and right at the prisoners, shaking his head every few paces. Reaching the far end of the barracks, he stood facing the wall for a few minutes. As if he were involved in a debate with himself, he shook his head again, then nodded before turning around.

"There will be a 'surprise' inspection tonight—or perhaps tomorrow," he warned and Nick translated. "It seems that there is a question over inventory. I suggest"—he lowered his voice, darting his eyes to windows and door—"that if you have something that you should not have—something you may have taken—you conceal it so that the searchers do not find it." Clasping his hands behind his back, he waited for some response. None came.

"Fall out for detail in fifteen minutes. *Das ist alles*," the guard finally announced, and then strode out of the building.

Once the men determined that the German was out of earshot, they began to discuss ways to hide the only contraband material they had—the potatoes. They had very little time to do it, and no places within the buildings that would not be examined during an inspection. Finally they agreed to gather the smuggled goods, conceal them however they could on their persons, and dispose of them sometime during their workday.

"The diggers can hide them best," someone offered, and so they decided that those on foxhole duty would bury the potatoes. They could then create some kind of inconspicuous mark, allowing them to retrieve the spuds later, perhaps a few at a time.

"I wonder why the sudden inspection," Matthews considered. "Over a few missing potatoes? Yesterday those guards didn't give a damn that we swiped a few spuds. Why would they care today? Hell, it's a damn *mountain* of potatoes out there in the spud dump. What are they gonna do now—count 'em?"

When inspection actually did take place that night, the Germans found nothing, though they seemed determined to uncover something. They left the barracks, disappointed, but easing their disappointment some by confiscating cigarettes. The prisoners had little else worth taking.

"Is it just me or do the Germans seem a little bit more—I dunno—eager lately? Like they were early on?" Drummond asked.

The others agreed that the inspection and the day's increased labor demands indicated a shift in attitude, a kind of renewed vigor. They worried that the Allies at the front might have met with fierce resistance, turning them back. Not until count next morning did they learn what gave the Nazis fresh resolve, hearing the announcement delivered in an ugly, gloating tone.

"The Fatherland has been given a great victory. Roosevelt, the Jew-leader of America, is dead."

Germans cheered. Prisoners stood in stunned silence. Then a few of them smirked, shaking their heads at this last-ditch propaganda attempt. Nick listened as the announcer praised the persistence of *der Führer* in the face of enormous odds and assured the German soldiers that this world event would turn the tide of the war, that the Third Reich would now, at the eleventh hour, fulfill its destiny.

"This isn't propaganda," Nick murmured, convinced by the self-importance of the announcer's tone. "This is true. My God. The president is dead."

Breathing seemed hard as if he'd been kicked in the gut. He'd known heart-sinking sensation before, but seldom had he felt it so literally. What would happen now? How would the fighting forces carry on without their iron-willed commander-in-chief?

The prisoners did not go out on work detail that day, though Nick almost preferred that they would have. Laboring and sweating their misery might be a better way of dealing with the shock than commiserating on base in the face of the Germans' satisfaction and relief.

Like most of the other prisoners, Nick spent the day in thought, moving from feelings of stunned disbelief to dejection in the face of the awful truth. With the others, he prayed for his country, his family, for the soldiers, and for the new president. Finally, near sunset, the men gathered in the compound and held a brief, simple memorial for their fallen leader. A few men spoke; one led the group in prayers, and afterward, a prisoner, lacking a bugle, blew "Taps" on his harmonica. The prisoners stood straight, their arms raised in crisp salute as the song played in gliding tones, sounding wistful and forlorn. Nick's throat ached. He had difficulty swallowing. In the distance, the rumble of battle continued.

The next day, Nick, Matthews, and Chef joined the firewood brigade. Again commanded to increase their amount of product, the detachment now was larger than usual, and they found themselves crammed into the backs of the trucks. Nick grimaced as he wedged himself closer in, his sore shoulder pressed hard against the side of the truck. For most of the journey, the men remained silent, still caught up in the anguish of yesterday's reality. Finally, someone spoke.

"That's what we're doing! Son of a bitch!" The man paused only briefly before continuing. "All this firewood, it's not just to sell to civilians or to keep us warm. It's for the damn war plants! We're helping to keep them in business!"

"Factories don't run on firewood," another man protested. Silence again. Nick frowned, realizing, *They do if there's nothing else to burn.*

Again the men spent the day working hard to look as if they worked hard. Still, the mounds of firewood they produced seemed far too large. The Germans, however, scowled their disappointment in the output. One of them threatened to cut food rations if the men didn't improve their production. At this, several prisoners sneered.

"Tell them that would be fine," someone instructed Nick. "Tell them that will only make us work slower."

Nick didn't have to translate. A second guard observed that men made even weaker than they already were would be most unlikely to work harder. The two Germans began to argue; the prisoners felt pleased. Finally Fritz scrambled out of one of the trucks waiting to transport the prisoners back to the base. He shouted to break the argument and commanded that the men load up.

"Let's get in Fritz's truck," Nick urged Chef and Matthews, and the three of them scrambled to hop aboard. The truck box filled; men stood so close together that every breath stung with the acrid smell of sweat. Fortunately there would be showers that night.

For three days they went through the same schedule: up early, prisoner count, distribution of bread rations, then loading on to trucks. By the fourth day, almost all the men worked the woods. Some hewed dead or dying trees; others cut logs into shorter lengths, while still others split and stacked firewood onto growing piles. Every other day, trucks hauled the firewood away, presumably to one of the factories in the area.

Then the air raids came, mostly at night, stirring captors and captives alike from their bunks or nightly watches. They fled out of buildings and headed for the nearest foxholes where they lay low against the earthen walls opposite the direction of assault. Occasionally a day raid occurred, driving men into foxholes, behind buildings and trees, or under vehicles. One strafing raid came when the men were on their way back from working the woods. The trucks stopped; Germans ordered the prisoners to clear out of the backs of the trucks. As machine gun and anti-aircraft fire burst out around them, men dove beneath the vehicles or ran for any cover the landscape provided: trees, brush, gullies, ditches, hillocks, and buildings.

"Christ, this would be so much better if the damn krauts would just give the hell up!" Matthews panted as he took cover next to Nick under a truck. "I'm getting goddamned tired of running away from our own side."

They watched plumes of dirt rise as machine-gun fire pocked the ground only a few yards away.

"That was too close," Nick pronounced, aware that the truck's fuel tank might take a direct hit in the strafing. He didn't feel at all safe, knowing that they could be directly beneath a fiery explosion, but until the planes passed, he dared not try to emerge from beneath the truck.

Finally "all clear" shouts came, and the Germans hurried the prisoners back on to their transports. As Nick climbed into the truck box, he spied Chef curled up in the far corner.

"Chef? What are you doing in here? Didn't you take cover?"

His face the color of chalk, Chef stammered, "C-couldn't get—out—in time. Right over my h-head." He tried to laugh but coughed instead. Nick dropped to one knee beside him. He noticed a thin line of redness between Chef's lips.

"You okay?" he demanded, checking the young soldier for injuries. "Chef you been hit?" He didn't see it right away. Only when he tried to help Chef into a more comfortable position, did he feel the sticky wetness at Chef's back. He pulled his hand away, stunned by how red it was. Nick struggled to open the kid's jacket and shirt.

"Jesus!" he exclaimed, then noticed Chef's eyes on him. "You've been hit, kid, but it doesn't look too bad." He felt tightness in his throat. In fact, the entry wound didn't look so bad—a small hole, so small in a grown man, it seemed that it should have been harmless. There was so little blood on the chest, almost as if the bullet had entered and cauterized the wound at the same time.

"Hurry up back there! Get in the truck!" Prisoners began to crowd in. Nick faced them, shouting, "We have a wounded man back here! We need a medic now!" Turning back to Chef, he tried to sound calm; he even forced a smile.

"It'll be okay, kid. It's not real bad. We'll get you fixed up in no time."

"Th-that's good," Chef murmured, his words barely audible. "I gotta get b-back ho—home. I gotta—" He coughed, and Nick could see blood pooling in his mouth.

"You will," Nick encouraged, shouting over his shoulder, "We need help back here now!" Then he spoke calmly to Chef once more, "Don't you worry. You'll make it home soon. You have to. You have a fancy restaurant to build and a lot of guys with reservations."

"The—Luchy—Spoo—," Chef's words faded in a gurgling sound. Weakly, he lifted one hand, and Nick noticed the dull metal spoon tucked in the kid's fist. Just then, Chef exhaled a ragged breath and blood spilled from his mouth. His eyes, still on Nick's face, lost sharpness—as if Chef looked at something invisible between himself and Nick. His hand fell.

"It's okay," Nick continued, now unable to disguise the alarm in his voice. "Just a little stitching up and you'll be good as new—better even."

Matthews, who had hovered behind Nick, now knelt next to Chef as well. He placed his fingers against the kid's throat.

"He's gone, Nick."

"No, no he's not! He just needs—he'll be okay if we just get this damn truck rolling!" Again Nick shouted for assistance. He tried to wipe the blood away from Chef's face.

"C'mon, kid, goddamit! Don't you do this, not now, not this close to the end!"

Nick grabbed hold of Chef's shoulders and shook him. "Breathe, damn you! Breathe! Aw shit, you stupid kid, what—are you too fucking stupid to fall off the back of a truck? Jesus Christ, Jake, don't do this!"

Angry words poured from Nick as if a dam had burst, words he was not accustomed to saying and that he didn't even hear himself say. Neither did he realize that he'd cried out his brother's name instead of Chef's. He fought against the men who tried to pull him away from Chef's body and didn't hear Matthews' gentle tone, "Nick. It's too late. There's nothing anybody can do."

Gradually the rage faded and numbness set in. Nick lost his sense of reality as time seemed to slow and race simultaneously. For seemingly interminable minutes he held Chef's body, looking for a spark of light in the kid's eyes. Movement around him slowed and blurred as if everything took place under water. Only an eye blink later, the truck was back at the base, and someone pried the body from Nick's arms.

The numbness and disorientation remained. One minute Nick was aware of lying in his bunk, a horrible emptiness like heavy weight on his chest; the next minute he was conscious of standing outside at a burial site hearing again the mournful strain of "Taps." Yet a moment after that, he found himself back in the barracks, sitting next to a rough-planed table. On the surface lay a jumble of folded papers, two worn pencil nubs, and a spoon. Nick stared at the spoon, so gray and dull that it did not reflect any light. After seconds or minutes or hours—he still didn't recognize time—Nick picked up a pencil, grabbed one of the wrinkled papers, and tried to write.

? April—Don't know what day this is. Chef didn't make it.

He stared at the words, reading them over and over as if he had to convince himself. Written down, the words didn't seem so shocking. They seemed just—there—so matter-of-fact, without question or debate or even feeling. *Chef didn't make it.*

Nick grabbed the paper and crumpled it in his hands. Then he reached for all the notes he'd written in the last few months and crushed them as well. *No more of this,* he raged inwardly, carrying the papers and the spoon to the barracks stove. Prepared to rid himself of all, he paused at the last minute, then threw only one scrap of paper—his last note—onto the glowing coals inside. He watched it blacken then glow and finally flare.

It's over, he thought. *I've had enough.*

The battlefront drew closer. All work details ceased. The men protected themselves as best they could from explosions and fragments when the air base took hits. On the first day of May, the Germans announced that all personnel would evacuate the next day to a place at least two miles distant while they destroyed their own ammo dumps.

"This is it," Murphy voiced everyone's realization. "This is the end of it."

That night, Fritz summoned Nick from the barracks. He claimed a need for a translator, but when Nick stepped outside, Fritz put a hand on his shoulder and directed him toward a truck parked away from the buildings. They climbed into the cab.

"*Wohin gehen wir?*" Nick asked.

"We go nowhere," Fritz answered, then fumbled for words. "It seems—I thought—perhaps we might talk. Not as enemies."

Nick frowned, saying nothing. He simply watched as Fritz pulled a cigarette from a packet of Lucky Strikes and lit it, then held the pack out to Nick, who shook his head. Fritz laid the pack on the seat between them. He puffed, inhaling long, then breathing out, smoke wafting from his nostrils and mouth.

"I am very sorry about your friend," he began. "He should not have died."

Nick felt his jaw tighten. He clenched his fists, waiting for Fritz to say something about Chef being killed by his own forces, not by the Germans. *I swear to God*, he thought, *if he says it, I'll kill him with my bare hands!*

"Another is also dead," Fritz said. "One who perhaps should have died sooner."

Still wordless, Nick anticipated some further remark about President Roosevelt's responsibility, about how his earlier death might have altered the course of the war.

"*Ja, der Führer ist tot*," Fritz pronounced, his tone emotionless. "It is almost certain."

For some reason, the news did not come as a surprise. Nick thought he should have felt relief or a sense of triumph, but he felt nothing—just the same emptiness.

"Too late—" The sound of incoming artillery cut off Nick's words. In seconds, an enormous explosion shook the ground, lighting the area in blinding flashes; further explosions followed as the Germans' ammo dump took a direct hit. Nick and Fritz scrambled from the truck and hunkered low, heading for the nearest foxhole. In the glare of flames and explosions Nick could see others pouring from buildings, racing for protection.

Like scared rabbits, he observed just before he dropped into a trench. He flinched at the tremendous noise: thunderous booms and roaring flames as ammunition detonated, men shouting or screaming, planes buzzing, shells shrieking before meeting and blowing up their targets. The explosions came steadily, so intense that Nick could feel the reverberations deep in his chest, mingling with his heart thrumming against his ribs.

"Looks like we beat you to it!" he shouted at Fritz, though he knew the man could not hear him. When he said the words, something seemed to shake loose in Nick's soul. As the attack continued, the numbness of the last few days began to burn away. Every boom and rumble sparked feelings: a mix of terror and elation, anger and relief.

This is for you, kid, Nick thought then, recognizing his need for Chef's death to have come with earthshaking fury.

Through most of the night, Nick watched the sky continue to flicker and glow with explosions and flames. Eventually the noise leveled as artillery fire ceased and explosions decreased, but the roar and pop of fires continued. Only when predawn light dimmed the glare of flames, did Nick crawl from the foxhole. Other men emerged from various places of safety; they stared in awe at the devastation around them, prisoners and captors alike. Some plopped down on the ground, their arms circling their knees, while others stood, turning this way and that, taking it all in, not knowing quite what to do or where to go.

"It is done. Now we exchange places." Fritz spoke from directly behind Nick, who turned to face him. Fritz held out his rifle, then fumbled inside his coat and retrieved his pistol. He offered this to Nick as well. "Now we are your prisoners."

Nick hesitated, and then took the weapons; he wasn't sure what he should do next.

"I guess—we just wait," he finally said, and the two men sat down against a mound of dirt. Nick laid the rifle across his knees and examined the pistol, its heft creating a pleasant sensation in his palm. He glanced back at Fritz, whose walleyed gaze focused on two distances. The man's face looked craggy, leathery as usual, but his expression was more of exhaustion than defeat. Something else too, Nick realized. Relief? Still studying the weapon in his hand, Nick suddenly asked, "Why me?"

Fritz shook his head, not understanding.

"From the start you singled me out," Nick explained, "but I was never sure about your motive. I never trusted you—still don't entirely—but—why me?"

Fritz chewed on his lip, then slapped at his pockets, looking for something.

"They got left in the truck," Nick reminded him, "if it's cigarettes you're looking for." He waited, then asked again, "Why did you choose me?"

"You reminded me of someone," Fritz finally answered.

"Who?"

"You look a little like my brother. He is missing a long time—since Leningrad. It seemed—" He did not finish his thought.

Nick frowned, studying Fritz's homely face with its crazy eye and deep folds of skin, the brow in permanent scowl, the mouth, even when it smiled, drawn and downward.

"Huh." It was all Nick could say.

A new sound came, the mechanical squeal and rumble of motorized vehicles. Nick stood up, watching, waiting for the vehicles to come into sight. From here and there around the compound he heard cheers. Someone whooped and shouted, "Eggs for breakfast!" Men began to run toward the source of the sound. Still Nick stood and waited until finally he caught sight of the troops. He felt his breath catch.

The Eighth Infantry division arrived, some troops riding on tanks, others walking. Their uniforms disheveled and battle-grimed, the soldiers still looked good to Nick. A lump formed in his throat as he watched their confident stride, their fresh faces grinning as they met the prisoners who ran to greet them. Nick's legs suddenly felt weak, and he sat down again. At the same time Fritz stood; he looked at Nick as if he would say something, then turned away. Clasping his hands at the back of his head, Fritz moved toward the liberating forces, joining a growing number of German soldiers who were then ordered to sit in a cluster on the ground. Still Nick remained, unmoving. He watched as if from outside himself, swallowing hard.

American forces continued to swarm in, met by jubilant prisoners. German civilians also appeared, some of them eager to greet the Americans, others surrendering, somber and resigned. At some point—Nick didn't even notice when—someone had hoisted the American flag on the pole where the swastika banner had flown only yesterday. On his feet again, Nick stared at the flag, the red, white, and blue colors snappy even in the smoke and haze. His eyes stung. Again he tried to swallow the lump in his throat.

We made it, he thought, then amended, *I made it.*

"You okay there, trooper?"

A young captain placed a hand on Nick's shoulder. Nick straightened, then saluted.

"Yes, sir." He thought his voice sounded weak. He cleared his throat and added, "May I say, sir, that you are a sight for sore eyes!"

"You don't look so bad yourself," the captain answered. "Could use a little fattening up, but you seem in better shape than some we've encountered. Unbelievable what humans are capable of." He shook his head and spat on the ground. "Why don't you go on over there"—he pointed his rifle—"and we'll get you guys all sorted out, get some food in your bellies. Here"—he offered to take Fritz's weapons—"I can take care of these. We'll be destroying whatever is left of enemy war equipment—planes, weapons—unless you want a souvenir?" This he added with a conspiratorial wink.

Nick shook his head, handing over the rifle and pistol. He saluted, then called again as the captain turned away.

"Captain?"

"What is it?"

"It's really over then?"

"Just a matter of days—and then the mopping up, of course." The captain tipped his helmet a little farther back on his head, adding, "There's still the Pacific front, of course. But for you this war is over. You're going home, trooper."

Home. For eighteen months, that word and all the memories it brought had kept Nick going. For a year and a half, home had seemed so far away, not only in distance, but also in time. Now here he was, presented the reality he'd so long waited for, survived for, and yet it didn't seem real. Turning to join the other former prisoners, Nick tried to convince himself.

It's over. The war is over. We're going home.

Troop trucks hauled the prisoners from Hagenau south to Hildesheim where the men were deloused and received medical care and fresh clothing. Hungry for so long, they were disappointed with their first post-captivity meals: chicken soup or thin chicken stew, light fare to help their bodies readjust. The disappointment couldn't crush their morale, however; they knew they were on their way home.

Flying out of Germany in C-47s, they landed in Nancy, France, where they received a royal reception, making them feel like heroes rather than hapless prisoners. There at last they enjoyed a full meal, musical entertainment, and the camaraderie of liberated people. There, for the first time since Chef's death, Nick felt the urge to laugh.

On the next leg of the journey homeward, they traveled by railroad freight cars—too much like prisoners, Nick thought—to Epernal, France, where they spent two more days learning to become civilians again, this in spite of rumors that they might all be called upon once more to help fight the Japanese in the Pacific Theater.

Eventually they arrived at Camp Lucky Strike, a military site that looked like an entire city of tents.

Two days later the men boarded a ship, sailing first for England, and then for the United States. During most of the five-day voyage, stormy weather made the ocean wild, and the ship rose and dropped with the waves.

Like a bucking horse in a rodeo, Nick thought as his stomach roiled. Even so, he believed that the journey to home and freedom was worth the difficulties encountered. Looking forward to seeing wives or girlfriends, parents and siblings and children, Nick and his closest companions also realized that in taking leave of each other, they ended a different kind of connection, one that had borne them through a veritable hell on earth. They vowed never to forget their brotherhood, or the brothers who could not make the journey home with them.

When the ship finally sailed into harbor at New York, Nick wondered if, after military discharge, he would ever see his fellow prisoners again, if he would ever learn the fates of those who had disappeared. Watching the water churn as the ship made its way closer to land, he thought again of Chef, so much like a kid brother. He felt in his pocket for Chef's spoon, then took it out and studied it.

Why did I keep this? he wondered, wishing yet again that he could have done more to protect the boy. *Why did I think I needed it? The memories are in me, not in this ridiculous spoon. Poor kid, just wanted to get home.*

Nick, too, wanted nothing more than to go home and renew, or rather to start his peacetime life. He also knew that somewhere in the world, men still fought bloody battles, still tried to survive the tortures of imprisonment, still died trying to reestablish that longed-for peace. Though he dreaded the possibility of being called up again, he decided that if he had to fight the Japanese, he would do it, if only to help get his own kid brother safely home.

"I would try to do it better next time, Chef," he murmured, rubbing the bent spoon's dull surface. Just then he grasped the spoon with both hands and bent it even more.

"Some luck!" he exclaimed, and then threw the spoon overboard, watching its shallow arc and quick descent into the water. It hardly made a splash, whatever ripples it created too tiny and far away to see.

The End

Under the Twisted Cross *is dedicated to the memory of my father,*
Nicholas K. Schuld, who lived it.

ACKNOWLEDGMENTS

As a child and adolescent, I always enjoyed hearing the stories my father would tell about his youth or about his days in the service during World War II. Most enthralling to me were his accounts of the time he was a prisoner of war. The stories he told his children always had a touch of humor; only when I eavesdropped on his stories to adult family and friends, did I hear some of the more serious aspects of his experience.

Many years after these family tales, I found among my father's papers several old documents: penned responses to questionnaires from the Veterans Administration and an Ex-POW organization; a typewritten list of locations and dates my father remembered from the pre-liberation march to the Western Front; a three-page narrative describing activities and incidents that occurred at Stalag IIB; and a copy of the 1943 Military Intelligence report that described the features and conditions of Stalag II B and other POW camps in Germany. These documents held so many gripping details, and I felt my father's story was one worth sharing. Unfortunately, by the time I had come to this conclusion, his memory could not elicit the fine points necessary for an accurate memoir—or he simply chose not to remember particulars. Still, the tidbits he did share inspired me to craft the novel. I only wish he had lived to read it, or to hear it.

I owe thanks to a group of people who advised me during the writing process and who critiqued my work as it developed, specifically to Dave S., Walt I., Mark S., Barbara L., Donna C., Mark T., and other members of our *Writers Exchange;* to my husband Pat and our daughters April, Robin, and Heather for never doubting that a woman could—and should—write a man's prisoner-of-war story; to my mother, who endowed me with a love for words; to my brother Ray and my sister Kathy, who helped me remember narratives we heard as children; and to one very ordinary man: "citizen soldier", ex-POW, husband, father, and grandfather—call him what you will.

I called him Dad.

Notes

"Lili Marlene" (originally "Lili Marleen") is a German love song first recorded by Lale Anderson in 1939. The lyrics were written in 1915 by Hans Leip. It became popular in both Germany and America during World War II.

The "Caisson Song" or "Army Song" as it is sometimes called was written in 1917 by Gruber, and was originally arranged by Sousa; ©Carl Fischer.

"Schnitzelbank" is an old German language folk song, traditionally sung to children to teach them language and rhyme. It was my father's signature entertainment piece.

"Hole in the Bottom of the Sea" is a traditional folk song.

The 1943 "Military Intelligence Report" was compiled in the following document:

Sommers, Stan. *The European Story*. Packet 8. Marshfield, WI, American Ex-Prisoners of War, Inc., 1980.